Discovery

MELISSA TEREZE

ISBN-13: 978-1-915242-20-4

Cover Design: Melissa Tereze
Editor: Charlie Knight

Find out more at: www.melissaterezeauthor.com
Follow me on Twitter: @MelissaTereze
Follow me on Instagram: @melissatereze_author

CONTENT WARNING - DISCUSSION OF COERCIVE CONTROL/EMOTIONAL ABUSE

Also by Melissa Tereze

Another Love Series

The Arrangement (Book One)

The Call (Book Two)

Before You Go (Book Three)

Mrs Middleton Novels

Mrs Middleton

Teach Me (Co-write with Jourdyn Kelly)

Vanessa

The Ashforth Series

Playing For Her Heart (Book One)

Holding Her Heart (Book Two)

Other Novels

The Stepmother

Behind Her Eyes

At First Glance

Always Allie

Breaking Routine

In Her Arms

Forever Yours

The Heat of Summer

Forget Me Not

More Than A Feeling

Where We Belong: Love Returns

Naked

Titles under L.M Croft (Erotica)

Pieces of Me

"Someone's inability to love you is not your inability to be loved."

CHAPTER I

Caroline rarely did anything exciting with her weekends; they usually involved comfy pants and a mountain of work. But not this weekend. *Not* tonight.

She leant towards her bedroom mirror, applying a deep red lipstick and rolling her lips. She looked hot, and she wasn't afraid to admit it. Caroline had spent far too long seeing herself as less than. She'd sat at home with negative thoughts repeatedly playing over in her mind. But now she was ready to move on, or as ready as she could be. After a pep talk from her sister, Joy, and her best friend, Gail, Caroline had psyched herself up... and now she was ready to let her hair down.

This was nothing more than a little fun, but Gail and Joy had promised her that everything would be okay. Caroline had to remember that if she had any chance of stepping foot outside the door tonight. *Don't get this all wrong. Enjoy yourself.*

"You're beautiful. You matter. You deserve happiness."

Caroline smoothed her hands over her new size 14 dress, the soft silky material heaven beneath her palms. She'd lost a few pounds over the last several weeks, but she finally felt comfortable in her own skin again. She'd always had curves—at one time, she'd loved them—and this dress really showed them off.

She slipped her heels on and grabbed her phone from the bed. As she did so, it started to ring in her hand.

"What are you wearing?"

Caroline's brow rose. "That's a little forward of you."

"Ha! There she is. My best friend is back in business." Gail laughed as Caroline turned off her bedroom light and took the stairs. "So, what outfit did you decide on?"

"The green dress."

"Perfect. I bet you look absolutely gorgeous."

Caroline smiled. She loved Gail dearly. She'd always been the one shining light in her life. "I'm trying to remind myself that I do."

"Listen to me, and listen good." Gail paused, making sure she was listening. "You *are* gorgeous. You always have been. And I know this is a huge step for you, it's been so long, but Naomi isn't in your life anymore, Caz. She has no hold over you; you *don't* answer to her. She's *nothing*."

"I know." Deep down, Caroline absolutely knew. Still, old habits were hard to break.

"You walk in that bar tonight, and you knock the socks off Eva."

"I know you mean well, but it's not like there's any point in trying to impress her, Gail. I'm paying her to be there..."

"Correction: *I'm* paying her to be there."

Okay, Gail was right. But if Caroline enjoyed her evening, she may just pay the beautiful, blonde Eva to spend time with her again. She couldn't believe she'd decided to go along with this. Booking an escort wasn't something Caroline had thought she'd ever do. But still, she was excited. For the first time in two years, Caroline would spend the evening with another woman.

It didn't matter why or how. The important fact was that she was doing it at all.

"You still there, Caz?"

"I'm here." Caroline ran a hand through her dark hair, taking her overcoat from the closet under the stairs. "Just...I'm doing the right thing, aren't I?"

"Do you think I'd let you go through something like this if you were going to get hurt? This is just some fun. Relax into it."

"No, I know you wouldn't. But this is just a meaningless meeting, Gail. I'm sure Eva is going to be wonderful company, you said a friend of yours is very fond of her, but this...isn't me."

"And what *is* you? Sitting at home, working yourself into the ground, single for the rest of your life?"

"That's not what I want. But having dinner with Eva isn't going to mean I'm not single. I'm still going to come home tonight alone."

"No, but having dinner with Eva is preparing you to get yourself back out into the world of dating. If you can feel comfortable and confident with a woman like Eva, you can feel comfortable and confident with *anyone*."

Again, Gail was right.

"And tomorrow morning, I'll be over to have brunch with you and dissect how your night went."

Caroline didn't know what she would do without her best friend. Gail had been through so much with her, and instead of pressuring Caroline over the years, she'd sat on the couch drinking wine or eating tubs of ice cream with her. Gail may never understand how much that meant to Caroline, but it did. It meant the world.

"Now, you pretty lady, have a date with Eva. Don't think of her as an escort. Don't worry about the cost or if people are looking. They won't be. And *please*, enjoy yourself."

"I-I will." Caroline swallowed, a sudden dread settling in the pit of her stomach. "If anything goes wrong, I'll call you."

"Correct. And I'll be right over."

"You don't have to do that. Jon and the kids are your priority. You've done more than enough for me. I'll see you tomorrow, okay?"

"If you need me, call me."

Caroline blew out a calming breath, pressing her back against the wall in the hallway. "I will. Goodnight."

Caroline stood at the bar, scanning the room every once in a while. Whenever a pretty woman neared, her heart raced, and her palms grew clammy. It wasn't the ideal way to feel. This experience was supposed to excite her, prepare her for a life without Naomi, but dread continued to plague her. She really needed to get out of her head.

As she scanned the bar again, Caroline promised herself less thinking time. Especially tonight of all nights. Eva would certainly keep her mind occupied; she'd seen her picture online. Gail had insisted she take care of the details, right down to the time and place, so Caroline would go for it and hope for the best. It couldn't be any worse than sitting home alone.

"Caroline?"

A soft voice followed by a gentle hand on her shoulder had Caroline's body thrumming. And then she turned around, her breath catching as Eva stood before her. "H-hi."

Eva wore a little black dress, her long blonde hair straight and falling over one shoulder. But it was her eyes that stole Caroline's breath with every inhale. Cobalt. Intense. Wow...she was striking. God, it was like sunshine in Caroline's usually dreary life.

She'd expected a young woman who oozed confidence, turning heads as she walked into the bar, but Eva didn't draw attention to herself. Really, she didn't need to. This woman was by far the most beautiful woman Caroline had ever encountered. *She's supposed to be beautiful. Don't let yourself get carried away here.*

"Can I get you a drink?" Caroline found her voice, but she couldn't be sure how long that would last. Eva was...a lot to take in right now.

"I'll have a glass of Chardonnay, thank you."

Caroline smiled and turned back to the bar. She ordered two glasses, her eyes closing briefly as Eva came to stand next to her, her eyes burning through Caroline's face. And then Caroline glanced in her direction. "Forgive me, but I've never done this before."

"Had a drink in a bar?" Eva quirked an eyebrow. God, that was sexy.

"No...this." She motioned between them.

Eva smiled and leaned in, her hand placed on Caroline's forearm. "Don't worry. I don't bite."

Heat shot straight through Caroline. It had been far too long since someone said something like that to her. In a seductive tone, Eva's breath washed over her ear. Okay, Caroline had to get a grip on herself. Eva was an escort, not her happy ending.

The bartender placed their drinks down, offering a nod to Caroline as he added it to her tab. She turned and handed Eva's drink to her, with no idea what was supposed to happen next.

"Maybe we should get a table so you can calm down." Eva slid a hand to the small of Caroline's back, heat emanating from her fingertips. "Let's get to know one another."

Okay, Caroline could do that. Talking. Talking was nice. And it was safe. Providing she didn't say anything stupid. "I have a booth over on the back wall. I got here a while ago. Nerves, you know." She smiled weakly, but Eva just beamed that gorgeous smile, her hand still sitting in place against Caroline's body. How was it that a simple touch felt so...electrifying?

They slid into a booth, sitting opposite one another, and Caroline took a moment to breathe. She watched Eva as she took her wine glass between her lips, licking the wine residue as she set it down on the table. "So, Caroline."

"Caz is fine."

"Okay, Caz." Eva nodded. "I like that. It makes you sound fun and adventurous."

"It does?" Caroline couldn't recall the last time someone had suggested she was any of those things. But she had been, once upon a time.

"Mm. Now, tell me..." Eva paused, relaxing back against the leather of the booth, crossing her legs. "What do you do?"

"I'm in education," Caroline said, unaware how deep she should go. The last thing she needed was the staff at school to get wind of this. She'd never live it down.

Eva drummed her fingers on the table. "I thought so. You look like a teacher."

"I'm not sure if that's a compliment or not." Caroline narrowed her eyes, smiling when a smirk played on Eva's mouth.

"It was an observation. That's all. I could probably tell you what half the people in here do during the day."

Caroline scanned the room, women who loved women were enjoying what was likely to be a wild night. "Their girlfriends?"

"Okay, I like you." Eva laughed from deep within her belly. "But, given the fact that we're in a lesbian bar, you're practically stating the obvious."

"Mm. True." Caroline studied Eva. How much could she ask here tonight? "Can I ask what you do? Or is that off the table?"

"I...do this."

"Right. Yeah. I wasn't sure if you had another job." *Don't ask stupid questions.*

"I did. But then I lost it. Hence why I'm here drinking wine with a beautiful woman this evening."

As much as Caroline loved that, Eva was being paid to say those things. She had to remember that above all else. It didn't matter how lovely Eva appeared to be; it was her job to be flirtatious and say what her client wanted to hear.

"I'm sorry to hear that."

Eva shrugged. "Redundancy. It happens to most people at some point."

"I'm sure you have plenty of time to find a career you love. Unless, of course, this is where you see your future."

Eva held up a hand, sipping her wine, "Not at all. I have a daughter to take care of. And I don't want her to wonder where I am at the weekend once she gets older and becomes wise to the things that go on around her."

"She's only a toddler?"

"She's 14," Eva explained. "She's my world."

Caroline smiled when Eva's eyes brightened further. It was clear she loved her daughter very much, and that was already a score in Caroline's book. If nothing else...Eva had a heart. "I'm sure she's proud of you."

"I'd hope she is." Eva twisted her wine glass on the tabletop, eyeing Caroline. "So, Caz. Why me?"

"My friend set it up. Says I need to get out more."

"You have good friends."

"You know what, I really do. And it's something different to what I usually do. It's a nice change." Damn right it was different. Caroline had *the* most uninteresting life behind closed doors.

"Well, I'm glad we met. Your friend certainly knew what you wanted. At least, I think she did."

Caroline winced inwardly. Gail had no filter, and while she loved that about her best friend, it could get them into trouble at times. "What did she say?"

"That I'm to sweep you off your feet for the night...and that you love to dance."

"Oh, I haven't danced in a long time. A glass of wine and some company is perfect, but thank you."

Eva held up her hands. "Hey, I'm just doing as I'm told. But whatever you prefer. I won't tell if you don't."

Caroline grinned. The weight of the uncertainty she'd felt all day was quickly slipping away. Eva was very relaxed, and that was exactly what Caroline needed. "I like you. Gail picked well."

"You really don't want to dance?" Eva leaned in, lowering her voice. "What kind of woman doesn't like to dance?"

A woman who was repeatedly belittled for ten years of her life, Caroline thought. "It's just not really my thing anymore."

Eva eased back in her seat, running a hand through her hair. "Okay, fair enough. I'll just have to convince you before this night is over."

"Oh?" Caroline quirked an eyebrow, a hint of flirtation fighting its way through the doubt and the fear. It had been a long time since she felt a blush creep up her neck, but it was happening now, and she didn't care. "Is that so?"

Eva winked. "I'll have you dancing. Don't you worry about that."

Caroline felt a wave of something unfamiliar wash over her, that heat she felt on her cheeks spreading over her entire body. The toe of Eva's stiletto heel was trailing up the back of her calf, those slender fingers still tapping on the table as she pinned Caroline with her stare. "C-can I get you another drink?" Caroline knocked back her wine, trembling as she slid out of the booth.

Eva placed a hand over her glass. “I’m okay for now. Maybe later.”

“R-right. Yes. Sure.” Caroline kept herself composed, the fear of stumbling her way to the bar a real possibility. Eva was just working. That’s all this was.

Yeah, leave it to you to want to bed the bloody escort, Caz!

CHAPTER 2

What *the hell* was she doing? Eva was working, Caroline had paid for her to be here, but from the moment she'd laid eyes on Caroline, Eva had fallen into another existence. One where Caroline's green eyes infiltrated her world, those long, dark luscious locks flowing so freely down her back. And the dress? God, it made those eyes all the more intense.

This...wasn't good.

Yes, Eva was still a newbie when it came to the world of escorting, but that didn't mean she wasn't aware of the rules. The rules of getting involved, the rules of heartbreak, just...the rules. But Caroline already didn't feel like a client. She felt like someone Eva had stumbled upon in a bar, like an ordinary night. If she hadn't paid to be with Eva tonight, she was absolutely the kind of woman Eva would gravitate towards. But the fact still remained, she *had* paid for Eva. She was working. And Caroline, well...a woman with so much beauty yet pain behind her eyes, wouldn't be interested in Eva and her fourteen-year-old kid.

Caroline was forty-seven. Eva knew that from the details Caroline's friend had provided on booking. It wasn't an issue for her, the age, but this woman had to know exactly what she wanted. She was professional, a teacher, Eva assumed. She would be completely out of her mind to entertain the idea of a real date.

And even if she *did* think about exploring, it would only end one way. Disaster. Eva didn't have time for another disappointment when it came to love. She'd faced plenty of that recently. Her own daughter had asked that she not get involved with anyone unless they meant the world to her, and Eva had to agree. The failed relationships weren't doing either of them any good, but Eva only wanted someone she could love. Someone she could climb into bed beside at night, resting her head on their chest as she slept, them playing with her hair.

This wasn't the life she wanted.

The money was great, but if she had things her way, she wouldn't be escorting. The company was mostly fantastic, but Eva had never imagined herself in this line of work. She'd once had much bigger hopes for the future. But the mortgage on her house needed paying, her daughter needed uniforms and equipment for school—as well as the essentials that came with being a living, breathing thing on this planet—and Eva hadn't known which way to turn. A friend of hers had suggested escorting to help with the bills, but it just wasn't what Eva had wanted.

Okay, she wasn't Eva. She was Hannah. Hannah Adams. But tonight, she had to be Eva. Even though she didn't want to be when she was around Caroline. She couldn't quite explain why Caroline had caught her attention from the get-go, but the beauty of this line of work meant Eva could flirt freely...and Caroline would never assume it meant more.

Caroline came walking towards her, a slight sway to her delicious hips, and held out her hand. "Come on."

"Look at that." Eva grinned, taking Caroline's soft hand. "I didn't even have to try to encourage you. You're a dark horse."

"I love this song. And if the offer of dancing is still on, I'd love to take you up on it."

Could she dance with Caroline while separating her feelings from her job? Eva had never had to do so in the past, but it surely couldn't be that difficult, could it? Besides, she didn't know the first thing about this woman. By the end of the night, that immediate attraction would probably be gone. Fuck, Eva *needed* it to be gone. "That offer will always be there. Let's dance."

Caroline led Eva to the dance floor, the beat flowing through her body as she turned and placed a hand on Eva's waist. *Don't let this go too far.* Eva had never crossed the line with a client, but as she watched Caroline let go, her curvaceous figure a vision in front of her, it only strengthened her claim that Caroline didn't *feel* like a client.

When she eyed Caroline, Eva sensed a nervousness beginning to interfere. Caroline hadn't wanted to dance initially, but Eva was happy she'd changed her mind. This woman knew how to move. Wanting it to continue long into the night, Eva pulled Caroline in by the waist, smiling as their cheeks pressed together.

They looked good together, and that was exactly what Caroline had employed her to do. They were *supposed* to look good together here. They were supposed to blend into the crowd as Eva gave her the girlfriend 'nightlife' experience. And if that was going to happen, she would have to give Caroline a little more.

Just enough to leave her wanting...

Eva's thigh moved between Caroline's legs as their bodies pressed together. A smile spread on Caroline's mouth, and if Eva had heard right, Caroline's breath had just caught as they moulded into one. But this was what Eva craved. Someone who enjoyed being with her and not wondering what she could provide. Yes, Caroline had eyed her on several occasions, but she hadn't done so with the extra payment of sex at the end of the night. It was one of those rules that was broken if the price was right. Not with Eva, but within the industry. Caroline hadn't once given that impression.

She seemed like Eva. *Hannah*. Someone who just wanted to enjoy another woman's company.

Caroline's arm wrapped around Eva's waist, their bodies moving sensually as the beat of the music changed. Eva felt the shift in Caroline as she relaxed more into this, but she quickly realised that slow dancing with this woman wasn't the wisest idea she'd ever had. Eva found herself struggling to pull away. Caroline, her emerald eyes, her soft hands...they did everything without intentionally doing so.

"You move so well," Caroline whispered as she leaned towards Eva's ear. "I'm very impressed."

"And to think you didn't want to dance with me." Eva took her bottom lip between her teeth as she turned her face away from Caroline. God, this woman was gorgeous. "I was initially offended."

Caroline brought Eva's gaze back to her. "And now?"

Aroused! Eva wanted to yell. "Surprised."

"Surprised?"

"Well, you had me convinced that you were a terrible dancer. But you're not. I'm impressed...and your hips are a dream."

Caroline lowered her eyes, a slight smile on her mouth as she blushed. "Thank you."

A swell of attraction held firm in Eva's stomach, her mouth dry as Caroline pressed a hand to her lower back. She didn't want to be Caroline's escort. She didn't want to be *anyone's* escort. But certainly not Caroline's. What she wanted was to ask Caroline on a date, perhaps test the water with a kiss, but it could never possibly work. Eva needed this job; she had bills to pay. And Caroline...well, she wouldn't possibly want to date a woman who allowed others to pay for her. Nor would Eva expect Caroline to. *Nobody* wanted that.

But then Caroline looked at her, a devastating smile spread on her mouth, and Eva felt all control slip through her fingers. She lifted Caroline's chin with the tip of her finger. Eva knew this was going to be a mistake, but she found herself drawn to Caroline. "Did you want to get out of here?"

Caroline visibly swallowed, her bottom lip between her teeth. But then she shook her head. "I can't. I'm sorry. It wouldn't be right."

Eva's brows drew together. "Wouldn't be right?"

"I'm having an amazing night, but I can't pay you...f-for that."

Eva cocked her head, stroking a thumb across Caroline's cheek. Even if she needed the money, she wouldn't take it. No, that wasn't the type of night she wanted to spend with Caroline. "I don't want you to pay me, Caz. I want you to let go and enjoy yourself."

Caroline draped her arms over Eva's shoulders as the music slowed again. "You're my escort. We can't cross that line."

"And if I wasn't your escort?" Why the hell had she asked that question? There was no denying they were drawn to one another, but it didn't matter how Caroline responded to her question. She *was* her escort. Plain and simple.

"God, I'd have left this bar with you an hour ago."

There was a light in Caroline's eyes that Eva was seeing for the first time tonight. A confidence, perhaps. And then it faded no sooner than it had appeared. Caroline had a story to tell, but could Eva—*Hannah*—be the one to listen?

"You're really beautiful. Far too good for me. But I appreciate that you're only doing your job. I know none of this is real... I'd be an idiot to assume it was."

Eva didn't know whether to run away or to grip Caroline's face and kiss her until the bar closed. "I wish I hadn't met you like this. You're not like anyone I've come across in here before."

Caroline's hips continued to move against Eva, that slow sensual beat drowning out everything else around them. "Well, for the first time in over ten years, you've made me feel wanted. So, thank you...for helping me to believe that I can put myself out there again."

"Sweetheart, you should always put yourself out there. You're gorgeous." Eva ran a hand through Caroline's dark hair, thrilled when the softness reached her fingertips. "And this body...it can move."

Caroline looked into Eva's eyes, tears brimming on her lids. She didn't say anything; she just continued to stare as the people around them moved on and off the dance floor.

"Are you okay?" Eva found her voice, concerned by Caroline's reaction to her words. "Have I done something to upset you?"

"H-how much?" Caroline asked, swallowing and looking away as though she didn't want to ask that question. "To spend t-the night with you..."

Eva's heart broke just from the look in Caroline's eyes. She wanted Eva, but not like this. And if Eva was being honest, she didn't want Caroline like this either. "Hey, we don't need to do this. You don't want this, Caz. You don't want to sleep with your escort."

"Right." Caroline untangled herself from Eva, taking a step back. "It's just...those things you were saying." She shook her head, genuine disappointment clouding those intense green eyes. "I should have known it was part of your job. I *do* know it's a part of your job. But nobody has ever looked at me how you do." Caroline suddenly had embarrassment written all over her face. "I'm sorry, I have to go."

Eva's forehead creased as Caroline suddenly rushed away and towards their table. She took her coat and slid it on, turning to leave, but Eva caught her wrist before she could. "Everything I've said to you tonight, I meant it."

"That's sweet, but we both know what this is. And as much as I've enjoyed my evening with you, it's not real. *You're* not real. You're doing your job."

Eva leaned in towards Caroline's ear. "My name is Hannah. If you want to meet me again, tell me the day and time, and I'll be here. As me. Not as your escort."

And just like that, Caroline was gone, the door swinging closed behind her.

But her perfume lingered in the air around Eva. Her eyes burned into her memory.

Escorting...was ruining her potential love life.

Face it. Nobody wants a woman like you.

CHAPTER 3

Caroline sunk down on the couch, dragging her legs up and under a blanket. It was Saturday afternoon, and she'd avoided Gail's calls, embarrassment rolling through her for how she'd handled last night. This was the exact reason why Caroline didn't bother to date...or even go looking. It didn't matter if Eva had been wonderful and accommodating; Caroline had made a complete idiot out of herself the moment she looked at Eva as someone other than an escort.

It seemed they'd just clicked. When Eva spoke about her choice to become an escort, she didn't seem overjoyed by it. But that wasn't Caroline's business to involve herself with, and Eva...when all was said and done...wasn't attracted to Caroline for who she was. It was all a game. A job. Caroline, as miserable as she felt about it, was her client.

The doorbell rang, but Caroline only sunk further down into the couch. It would be Gail, probably with Joy in tow, but she didn't want to get into this right now. It needed to be straight in her head before she even considered telling her sister and best friend about the stupid decision she'd made last night. The decision to ask Eva how much she charged for a night together. God, how humiliating.

Caroline brushed a tear from her jaw, blowing out a calming breath. Would she always humiliate herself? Or would another woman continue to do that for her? The latter wasn't possible, Caroline didn't believe she could give her heart to another person for them to stomp all over it again, but she couldn't be sure that it wouldn't happen in some other way.

"Are you just going to ignore my calls?" Gail appeared in the doorway, glaring at Caroline. "You know I hate using your spare key, but I had no choice."

Caroline clenched her jaw, willing her tears to fade. "I didn't want to see you yet."

"Why? What went wrong?"

Caroline swallowed, pulling back the blanket and offering the other side of the couch to Gail. "Eva was lovely. So, that was something."

"But?"

"I let myself get carried away. But that's your fault for telling her she was to take me dancing!"

"I just told her what I knew you loved." Gail placed a supportive hand on the blanket covering Caroline's knees. Most days, she didn't know what she would do without her best friend. She'd pulled her back from the brink more than once. "Did you enjoy it? Dancing?"

Caroline smiled weakly. As much as she'd loved it, she couldn't get past what had followed. "I haven't been dancing in years. Naomi wouldn't allow it."

"Yeah, well, now you have. And that bitch can't stop you."

Caroline understood where Gail's hatred for her ex-wife came from, but Naomi wasn't a bitch. She just...didn't love Caroline. Never had, apparently. And Caroline wasn't good enough for her, nor was anything she ever did. Then there were the clothes she chose to wear, the hairstyle, the makeup. How she cooked, what she cooked, the time it took. Her career, her friends and family, how much she earned, and whether she could be trusted to not blow it on day-to-day life. Yeah, Naomi really didn't like Caroline very much at all.

"You're thinking about her, aren't you?"

Caroline cleared her throat. "No."

"You were. When will you listen to me? When will you realise that Naomi said the things she did, behaved the way she did, just so she could put you down! Because she wanted to hurt you."

"That's got nothing to do with any of this. Eva was perfect. But then I made a complete tit of myself and asked her..." Caroline paused, bringing her hands up to her face. "Oh, God. I can't even think about it."

"You wanted more," Gail said nonchalantly. "And that's perfectly normal."

"It doesn't make it right, Gail."

"You're only human. And you deserve intimacy as much as the next person. I can't say I would have thought it would be with an escort, but whatever floats your boat, love."

"She told me her real name as I was leaving."

"She did?" Gail quirked an eyebrow, crossing her legs at the ankles as she brought them up to rest on the coffee table. "You're sure?"

"I'm sure." Caroline chose not to reveal her name. Hannah had shared something private with Caroline. It wasn't necessary to reveal her true identity. "She asked if I wanted to leave the club. She was...God, she was just so seductive and—"

"It's her job to be," Gail cut in.

"I know that. But this was different. She asked what I'd do if we met and she wasn't my escort."

"And? What would you do?"

Caroline felt heat rising up her body. For the longest time, Caroline had craved the exact feeling she'd had last night. The want...the passion in another woman's eyes as they looked in Caroline's direction. "Oh, I don't think I should say."

Gail exhaled a long breath, resting her head back on the couch. She turned her head to Caroline, offering the smallest of smiles. "Did I make a huge mistake by booking her for you? Am I going to live to regret this?"

As much as Caroline wanted to call Hannah, to seek her out, she knew it wasn't possible. A date was doable, but a relationship with her would be difficult to maintain. Throw in Caroline's insecurities, and it was a disaster waiting to happen. "No. I won't see her again."

"Not even as an escort?"

Caroline swallowed down the emotion she felt rising. "*Especially* not as an escort."

"It's time for you to get up off the couch," Gail said as she got to her feet. "I'm not sitting around here with you on a Saturday afternoon when we could be out having lunch together."

"I...don't feel like it."

"Tough. Joy has already booked us a table."

Caroline groaned. She knew her sister would come to play a part in this at some point. Still, they were only doing what was best for Caroline. And sitting home alone all weekend wasn't really what she wanted either. "Let me shower. I'll meet you there."

Hannah rushed across the street, checking her watch as she stopped outside a new rustic café that had opened in the city. The reviews had been fantastic, and as she peered through the window, it looked as though lunch was going to be worth it. The place was packed out, not a single table available from what she could see.

Today she was meeting with a client who had become a regular. Juliet was a lawyer, always on the go, but she paid very well, usually handing over a hefty tip on the way out the door. Hannah never knew how long their meetings would last. It could be a couple of hours, it could be thirty minutes. Juliet had rushed off on more than one occasion so far, but Hannah was satisfied based on the repeated bookings that it wasn't anything she was doing wrong.

I can think of somewhere else I'd rather be today...

Hannah hadn't slept very well last night at all. Between her constant worries about her daughter discovering her current job, and Caroline, Hannah had stared at the ceiling for most of the night. She still hoped to hear from Caroline, but realistically, she knew she wouldn't see her ever again. Caroline had a lot to deal with, Hannah knew that just from her demeanour last night, but whatever was going on...she wished Caroline well. It was all she could do.

As she stepped inside the café, Juliet stood from her seat and waved her over. The table was set back against a wall, out of the way of prying eyes, Hannah assumed.

She switched into her escort mindset, shedding her long overcoat as she approached Juliet's table. Her client leant in and kissed her cheek, offering a seat. "Hi, Eva. I'm sorry I called so suddenly, but I found I had a little time to myself this afternoon. Why not enjoy it with you?"

Oh. This was different. Juliet...was different.

"This place looks great. Have you been here before?"

"Once or twice during a working lunch. But today, I'm not working."

Eva quirked an eyebrow. "You're not working? Are you feeling okay?"

Juliet laughed, waving Eva into her seat. "Please, sit down. Let's eat."

She studied Juliet; her dark brown hair pulled up into a French braid. She always had a particular look about her, someone you wouldn't cross at the office, but Juliet was a pussycat, really. Eva had spent enough time with her to know that, and Juliet had been nothing short of respectful with each meeting.

"Now, I know you're already surprised that I'm not working, but I have another proposition for you..."

Eva cocked her head. "Okay."

"I'd like you to come away with me. It'll be a week. I'll pay you very well."

Eva lowered her eyes. She was sure a break away would be perfect, but it simply wasn't possible. She had commitments here, though; she wasn't like a lot of the escorts on the books at the agency. In fact, she was certain she was the only one who had any kids. "I'm sorry, I can't."

"You can't?" Juliet frowned.

"I have responsibilities at home. A daughter."

Juliet seemed surprised by that, her eyebrows almost reaching her hairline. "O-oh. I had no idea."

"I don't usually bring it up unless I have to." That was a lie. She'd spoken freely with Caroline last night about her lack of desire for this job, even mentioning her daughter on one occasion, but she would stick by her opinion of Caroline. That woman was *entirely* different from her other clients. "And I'd love to join you on your trip, but it's not possible for me. I'm sorry."

Juliet held up a hand. "Don't be. I understand."

Okay, that went better than she expected it would. Juliet

didn't look like a woman who took no for an answer, so she was pleasantly surprised.

"Should we order?" Juliet asked, eyeing her phone on the table as it started to ring.

"I...guess so." Eva smiled, cocking her head towards Juliet's phone. "Unless you needed to get that."

"Damn it. I do." Juliet stood from the table, taking her phone call outside. Eva perused the menu, noting one or two things she'd love to try. And then Juliet came sauntering back into the café, a disappointed look in her eyes. "I'm sorry, but you know where this is going."

"You have to leave. Don't worry, I understand."

"But please, stay and enjoy your lunch. You won't get a table for the foreseeable in this place. I'd advise you to eat here while you can." Juliet slipped cash onto the table, resting a side plate over it. "I'll be in touch, okay?"

Eva nodded, offering a smile. "Sure. Don't work too hard."

As Eva watched Juliet leave, the bustle of the café drowning out her own thoughts, she rested back into her seat and exhaled a breath. "Why do people keep running out on me lately?"

While Eva—*Hannah*—would rather spend her Saturday afternoon enjoying lunch, she would have much preferred some company too. And even though Juliet was only a client, they did get on well. At least, she thought so when they spent more than ten minutes with one another. Juliet wasn't looking for anyone serious in her life; company was all she needed. Someone to share a few minutes with in between the never-ending work calls. But as usual, Juliet had been called away.

Hannah set the menu down, smiling as a server came towards her. She placed an order for a sharing platter. It didn't matter that she was eating alone, and this way, she could try smaller portions of several things on the menu. She never could make up her mind when faced with food.

And then she relaxed into her seat, scanning the huge café. Friends shared a bottle of wine with each other, couples tried different foods from one another's plates, and Hannah...well, it just made her miserable. Maybe she could get in touch with a few of the girls she used to meet up with. A couple from school, the ones she used to work with, just anyone, really. At thirty-four, her entire life revolved around her daughter. She wouldn't change that, not in a million years, but adult company when her daughter was at her dad's for the weekend would be wonderful.

Hannah's eyes landed on a particular table. Three women spoke animatedly, laughing with one another as they clinked their wine glasses. She recognised the woman with her back to her instantly. Hannah would know those shapely legs anywhere. She stared harder, willing the woman to turn around, but instead...her friend raised an eyebrow in Hannah's direction.

She smiled and lowered her eyes, forcing herself to sit upright and mind her own business. She knew it was Caroline. She felt her in the room full of people. And if she focused hard enough on the different scents around her, Hannah knew it was Caroline's perfume she could smell. The very same one that had enticed her last night. She'd been stupid to ask Caroline if she wanted to leave the club, but Hannah was certain she wasn't the only one who felt the connection between them. Hannah *never* felt that spark. The rush of blood to the head and...other places. It was rare that she felt butterflies in the company of anyone else. But Caroline had given her all that and more.

Hannah lifted her head ever so slightly, her heart slamming against her ribcage when Caroline turned in her seat and stared directly at her. She wore her hair up today, exposing a beautiful neck. Her casual choice of clothing didn't do anything to put Hannah off, a sheer grey blouse exposing what lay beneath. She considered turning away, but Hannah instead offered a smile, surprised when Caroline got to her feet and made her way over to her table.

"Hi," Caroline said, a slight blush on her cheeks. "Meeting friends?"

"Oh, no. Here alone. Well, I wasn't...but I am now."

Caroline chewed her lip, shoving her hands in the pockets of her form-fitting black jeans. She looked just as good dressed down as she did dressed up. "Did you want to join us?"

"No, thank you. That's a lovely offer, but you know." Hannah lifted a shoulder, picking up the menu again and praying the server didn't bring her food while Caroline was standing close by. "Just a quick lunch, and then I have to get going."

"Right, well...it was nice to see you again." Caroline hesitated as she turned to walk away, her step faltering as she hovered between Hannah's table and her own. And then Caroline turned back. "About last night..."

Hannah held up a hand. She didn't want Caroline to apologise for asking to spend the night with her. Because if Hannah could have things her own way, she would have been waking up with Caroline this morning. But something had held her back. Whether it was the conflicted feelings she had, the thought of Caroline paying her for sex, or something else entirely, Hannah...as Eva...couldn't go through with it. "You really don't have to say anything. We both got a little carried away. I'm sorry if it ruined your experience with me."

"I just wanted to thank you again," Caroline said, shifting slightly nearer and lowering her voice. "You really helped me to get a little confidence back. It means more than you'll ever know."

The crack in Caroline's voice didn't go unnoticed by

Hannah, her heart soaring as Caroline looked at her with genuine admiration in her eyes.

"You're welcome."

Caroline threw a thumb over her shoulder. "I should get back to my table. But if you ever want to join me here, you're more than welcome to. My sister, Joy, owns this place, so we're around a lot."

"It's a great place."

"I'll see you." Caroline turned and moved towards her own table, her shoulders slightly slumped.

But Hannah found herself not wanting to cut a conversation with this woman any time soon. She had a wonderful presence about her. "Hey, Caz."

Caroline turned, wearing a sweet smile.

"You look gorgeous."

CHAPTER 4

Caroline opened the front door, stepping aside to let Gail through. She hadn't expected a midweek catch-up with her best friend, Gail had her own family to take care of, but did she appreciate it? More so than ever before.

"Now, I know you don't drink through the week, but I brought a bottle in case."

Caroline could indulge once in a while. Tonight was the perfect night to do so. She wasn't sure what she wanted to say to Gail; she just knew she couldn't spend time in her own head any longer. It had been four days since she'd bumped into Hannah at Joy's cafe, yet processing her night out with Eva was proving harder than Caroline thought it would. Really, considering her lack of interest in dating over the last couple of years, she shouldn't feel so up in the air with this. Caroline should have been able to move past it all days ago.

She followed Gail through into the back living room, offering a nod when Gail held up the bottle of wine. "Go on. Just a small one." Caroline sunk down into the couch, sighing. "You didn't tell Joy you were coming over, did you?"

Gail returned with two glasses of red wine. "No. I got the

impression on Saturday that you didn't really want to talk much about Friday night."

"Thank you for not pushing it at the weekend. I thought it would all be over by now, but it seems not."

"Have you seen Eva again?"

Caroline cast her gaze to her glass of wine as Gail sat down. "No. But I'm beginning to wish I could."

"You can. What's stopping you?"

"Humiliation. The idea that Eva thinks I want to sleep with her. That's not who I am, Gail. I don't ask women how much a night with them costs. I was overwhelmed, and if nothing else, I'd like to check she's okay."

Gail smiled. "I'm sure she wasn't offended. Eva likely has people asking the same question a lot of the time. While I'd like to think she doesn't actually sleep with clients, I'm sure she's okay. If she wasn't, she wouldn't have spoken to you at the cafe."

"Still," Caroline paused, lifting a shoulder. "I'd like to see her again."

"Okay. Then book her. I'm not going to stop you."

"I...don't have her number. You took care of that, remember?"

Caroline had only seen a picture of Eva before their meeting last week. She hadn't wanted the website details or anything else purely because she didn't want to go looking. Caroline had no plans to become a woman who relied on an escort as time went by. No, she wanted something serious. At least, part of her did. If she was going to step out into the world and make someone happy, she needed the rest of her feelings to match up with that. But right now, they didn't. Not how she wished they would.

"I have the website on my phone still."

Caroline ran a finger around the rim of her wine glass. “Do you think I’m making a mistake?”

“I think you should tread carefully.”

Caroline nodded. She understood what Gail was saying, and she was inclined to agree. Caroline couldn’t get attached or tangled up with this woman. “I will.”

“So, am I giving you Eva’s number?”

“Yes.”

Gail took a pen from the coffee table, jotting down Eva’s number and handing it to Caroline. She stared down at it, chewing the inside of her cheek, her hand trembling ever so slightly. This number would lead her to the woman she’d spent the last four nights thinking about. Caroline wasn’t sure how to feel about that. Delighted...but terrified at the same time.

“Well, there it is. What you do next is your own business. But first, tell me more about this woman.”

There wasn’t much to tell. Not really. Other than the fact that Hannah had lit up Caroline’s *painfully* boring world... “I think if I got to know her, she could be someone special.”

“Oh?” Gail quirked a brow.

“We got along very well. Perhaps she could be a friend.”

“A...friend you want to fuck? I have a feeling that’s not going to work out very well for you, Caz.”

“Look, I know that’s off the table. Eva is an escort, she’s paid to make people feel good, but I don’t know. I saw something more. I felt something more. She says she was genuine, and I believe her. I don’t know why, but I do. I believe that the connection I felt...she felt it too.”

“Then I think you should call her. Book her as your escort and see where things take you. So long as you’re aware of the consequences if you get too close, then I don’t see the problem with booking her again.”

Caroline glanced down at the number in her hand again. "I'll think about it. See how I feel in the morning."

"Good decision. Sleep on it."

Caroline had been sleeping on this for days now. Nothing had changed, and she suspected it wouldn't until she met with Eva—*Hannah*—once again. "Thank you for coming over."

"I'll always be here for you." Gail lay a hand on Caroline's knee. "That's my job. And I'll always stand by you no matter what decisions you make."

Hannah lay beneath the cover, curled up with a romance novel she'd been meaning to start for several weeks. While she loved to live through characters, she'd much prefer to have her own little perfect romance. She'd raised her daughter to be respectful and intelligent, they had a beautiful home... Didn't Hannah deserve someone to share those things with? Couldn't she dream of the perfect life as she sat home alone and her years passed her by? Seems it was all she was capable of these days. Dreaming.

She turned the page, smiling when her favourite character finally went in for the first kiss. There was something about a first kiss, both in books and in real life. The unknown of it all. The taste of another woman's lips. The pleasure, the suppleness, the yearning. Because in those moments before a first kiss, a kiss you prayed for with the woman who meant something to you...that yearning was definitely present. And then, within seconds, that yearning was obliterated...and in its place was a longing for more. Deeper. Harder. More passionate. Just...more.

Hannah's phone vibrated at her side, jolting her from the delightful scene she was reading. It was almost midnight. Who the hell was contacting her via her business number? Whoever it was, they were wasting their time. It was midweek; she didn't work midweek.

Are you available on Friday evening? Caroline.

Hannah's mind spun. She didn't know any other Caroline's, and it surely couldn't be a new one. She read over the message once more, exhaling a breath.

I am. 7 pm?

Hannah didn't want to be purely business to this woman, but if it was all she was entitled to, she would take it. Caroline had not only reminded Hannah of what could be, but she'd also helped her to forget she was an escort several times last Friday.

Can I book you?

Hannah knew Caroline had struggled to ask that. If she closed her eyes, she could see Caroline trembling as she wrote out the message.

Sure. I'd love to see you again. Did you have anything in mind?

Hannah watched as her response sat above a read receipt. This evening, she was happy that Caroline wanted to see her again. After the way they'd left things on Friday night, Hannah had wanted to reach out repeatedly. Caroline had fled, and though they'd bumped into one another the following day, it hadn't quite settled her.

Dinner? I'm not sure what else you enjoy. But I thought maybe something quiet and intimate. Something...ordinary.

Dinner would be great. I prefer quiet and intimate over anything else.

Hannah meant that. While she'd enjoyed dancing with Caroline, those smooth hips beneath her hands, Hannah preferred to be in a quiet setting where she could get to know someone better. Client or not, she always took an interest in people.

I'm not sure if you're familiar with it, but Fernando's in the city is really good. I'd love to meet there if that works for you.

Hannah smiled. Caroline wasn't demanding in the slightest. She loved that. It was refreshing, considering how she was treated by some of her other clients. Caroline wanted Hannah's input. It meant a lot.

Fernando's. 7 pm. I'm looking forward to it.

See you Friday!

Hannah lowered her phone, her lips curling into a smile as she lay quietly, taking stock of what had just happened. Caroline had contacted her direct. Caroline wanted to see her again. God, Caroline was potentially going to make Hannah's entire weekend.

But then Hannah lifted her phone again, bringing up the message thread. Lost in her own thoughts, she'd forgotten to ask Caroline how long the booking would last. Hannah wished it would last all night, but it was her job and if Caroline only wanted to have dinner and call it a night, she would keep her bookings open for another potential client.

How long do you want to book for?

Hannah hated being so formal, so...distant. But work was work. Caroline had made it clear that nothing else was possible between them.

How long are you available for?

Oh, wow. Could this mean that Hannah would have Caroline to herself *all* evening? The possibility alone had her body buzzing.

I don't have any other clients after you...yet.

Three dots.

And then her phone buzzed again.

Can I book the entire evening with you?

Hannah exhaled a long shaky breath. She didn't want to

seem eager, it was ridiculous to pine after a client, but Caroline made Hannah smile more than any other woman had in some time. Considering they'd only spent a few hours together so far, that spoke volumes.

Of course. See you Friday.

Lifting a dress from the rail, Hannah glanced in a mirror as she held it against herself. She'd never gone out of her way to pick up something new for a client, but Hannah had woken up this morning feeling exhilarated by her short conversation with Caroline. That woman was drop-dead gorgeous, and even if she didn't see it herself, Hannah had no issues drumming it into Caroline at every possible opportunity. Christ, she'd even dreamt about Caroline last night.

This...was an unusual feeling.

But it was a feeling Hannah wanted to get used to. While she knew the consequences of seeing a client as something other than business, Hannah was also strong enough to sever that tie if or when the time came. It wasn't as though her relationships had been amazing in the past, so really, she wasn't missing out on anything.

"Nice dress," a voice behind her whispered close to her ear. "How much do you charge them to remove it?"

Hannah barked a laugh as she turned, shoving her best friend back. "You couldn't afford me!"

"As your best friend, I'd hope you'd offer me a discount." Adele placed a hand on her hip, a brow quirked. And then she softened. "I'm glad you called. I've been bored to tears all morning."

"Fancy some lunch when I'm finished here? I'm starving."

"Obviously. It's the main reason I said I'd meet you when you called."

Hannah snorted. "Charming. And there was me thinking you just wanted to see me because you'd missed me so much!"

"I only spoke to you on the phone yesterday. Don't be so dramatic."

Hannah was joking. Adele had bagged herself a new boyfriend, one who was taking every ounce of time they'd usually spend together. But Hannah could live with it. She'd always wanted Adele to find happiness. "How's the love life?"

Adele grinned. "Athletic."

"Oh, I bet it is. Does he have a sister who is available, by any chance? I'm beginning to think I'll never date again."

"Why do you need to date? You have women paying *hundreds* just to look at you!"

As wonderful as that was for Hannah's ego, it wasn't enough. She hated leaving the house each weekend, knowing that nothing would come of her 'date'. There were many women out there quite content with escorting, but Hannah wasn't one of those women. It was a job...for now.

"You really think I'd rather be out escorting when I could be at home curled up in someone's arms?"

Adele cocked her head, regarding Hannah with a gentle smile. "You really are a romantic, aren't you?"

Hannah and Adele were quite opposite in their personalities. While Adele could take or leave a relationship, Hannah dreamt of more. From the outside looking in, people would think they had nothing in common, but they'd been best friends since they were fourteen, and Hannah couldn't imagine anyone else replacing her.

"I just...want more, you know?"

"You'll find someone. One day."

Hannah wanted to believe that, to see the positives of life, but her last relationship had not only done a number on her but on her daughter, too. She was terrified to risk their happy home like that again. "Kirsty broke me in some way. Three years...and then she's gone. Just like that. Maybe I'm not relationship material, and that's why I seem to be doing well with...work."

"Kirsty had no idea what she had when she was with you, Hannah. She always wanted more, and I'll bet you right now that she's sitting somewhere kicking herself. It's only been six months since she left. Give it time, and when you least expect it, the right woman will come along. I *know* they will. You're too much of a babe to be single."

Hannah sighed, eyeing herself in the mirror again. "Maybe. I don't know."

"Anyway, why are you treating yourself to this gorgeous dress? Felt like a splurge?"

"Oh, yeah. Thought I'd update my wardrobe." That was a complete lie, but Hannah wasn't ready to tell Adele about Caroline yet. It was far too soon to have Adele cheering her on from the sidelines with this. Especially when *this* wasn't going anywhere at all. "Got plans with the boyfriend this weekend?"

"Not at the moment. Are you working?"

"I am. Tomorrow, at least. I have a client booked in for the evening, so...that's nice."

Adele winked. "I see."

"Not like that, you dirty dog! It's dinner. Maybe we'll move on to a bar. But that's all. I don't know how many times I have to tell you that I *don't* sleep with them, Del."

"God, not even the *really* gorgeous ones?" Hannah couldn't say she'd *never* sleep with a client, but up to now, she'd avoided doing so. There would have to be one hell of a connection before it even crossed her mind. *Caroline*. Caroline crossed her mind a lot recently. "You do, don't you?"

"No. To date, I haven't slept with a single client of mine. I don't want to go down that path, Del."

Adele stood beside Hannah, watching her through the mirror. "Good for you. Most people probably feel pressured to go back to hotel rooms with their clients, so yeah, fucking good for you."

"If I feel pressured by a client, I cut the meeting short. It's as simple as that. I don't owe anyone anything, especially not my body."

Smiling, Adele kissed Hannah's temple, one arm flung around her shoulder. "Love you, kid."

"Love you, too."

CHAPTER 5

The last two days had dragged on far too slowly for Caroline's liking. Usually, that would work in her favour since it gave her time to stop panicking, but this evening...she felt no panic. No worry. No shame for being here. Tonight, she felt good about her meeting with Eva. As much as she wanted to see her as Hannah, Caroline knew it would only complicate things. So, Eva it was, and Eva it would remain.

She rolled her head on her shoulders, pushing through the door to Fernando's. It was a quaint little Italian on the outskirts of town, only seven or so tables available in the entire place. Caroline had wondered initially if it was too intimate, but she wasn't overthinking it. This was a client/escort relationship, and she wanted to enjoy some fine food.

As she looked up to the small bar area, she caught sight of Eva with her back to the door. The dress she wore plunged to her lower back; part of a tattoo was visible on her right shoulder. The server directed Caroline towards the bar, and as she cleared her throat, Eva turned and beamed a smile.

"Hi."

Her breath stolen, Caroline dragged herself up onto a stool and tried to compose herself. “Hi. Have you been here long?”

“Maybe ten minutes? I didn’t time the journey properly, so I ended up being a tiny bit early. But that’s fine. This place is gorgeous.”

“It really is. I used to walk past it often and wonder what the food was like. Then the thought of coming in alone was dreadful, so I didn’t bother checking it out for a while. Gail, my best friend, put me out of my misery eventually, and now we eat here at least once a month.”

“So, you can recommend some dishes then?” Eva quirked that sexy brow, all sense of time blown away as Caroline stared at her.

“Y-yes. Of course. Anything is good in here.”

“Good to know. So, how was your week?”

Caroline was interrupted by the server behind the bar. She ordered herself a wine and another for Eva. When Eva opened her clutch bag and took cash from it, Caroline frowned. “I’ll get these.”

“No, you won’t.”

Once they were alone again, Caroline leaned in and lowered her voice. “But I’m supposed to pay for this. Not you.”

“And I want to buy you a drink. I’m well within my rights to do that, Caz.”

“R-right.”

Eva placed a hand on Caroline’s forearm, smiling back at her. “Relax. I’m not one of those who expects every last little thing paid for. This is nice. I want to be here. And I want it to feel less like a business transaction for my own sake.”

Oh. She did? “Why?”

“Because I’m tired of being seen as *only* an escort. I know it’s why I’m here, and I know it’s why you contacted me again...but you don't seem as businesslike as some of them. I feel more myself around you."

"Then I'll have a *large* glass of wine," Caroline said, winking. She appreciated what Eva was saying, that she felt safe with Caroline, but she still had to maintain some kind of business relationship here. If she didn't, things would go south quick. So a blasé response was all she could manage.

"Large wine it is."

Caroline sat back and watched Eva talking with the server. This really was the perfect place to spend time together. Caroline loved to go to bars, to dance the night away, but she loved this more. It meant they had one another's full attention. It meant they didn't have to shout over the music or be interrupted by anyone at all. It was just Caroline, and it was just Eva.

"So, your week..."

"Oh, fine. Not much to complain about."

"Sounds far better than mine. I spent most of it looking through job advertisements. When I say there is nothing out there, I really mean it. I just felt miserable by the end of it all."

"You're thinking of leaving escorting?" Caroline spoke low, aware that Eva may not want people to know what was going on here. "I know you said you didn't see your future doing this, but so soon?"

Eva cocked her head. "You seem saddened by that, Caz."

"Well, I suppose part of me is. I enjoy spending time with you. Even if the first time around didn't end very well. But that was entirely on me. I hope you know that."

"Just because I wouldn't be doing this anymore, it doesn't mean we can't see one another."

Caroline focused on the glass of wine that had just been placed in front of her. Eva would still want to see her without payment. But...why? "You'd be far too busy with a new job."

"I could make time."

"Eva, that's really sweet, but—"

"Please, call me Hannah."

Caroline's brows drew together, her skin tingling as Hannah pinned her with her stare. She seemed different tonight. Less... escort-like. "What's going on here?" Caroline asked, clearing her throat. "I don't understand."

"Nothing is going on. As I said, I feel more like myself around you. But if it makes you uncomfortable, we can stick with the arrangement in place."

"It doesn't make me uncomfortable. Actually, it makes me more comfortable. But I don't understand why you'd want to see me outside of your work."

Hannah lifted a shoulder. "I told you on Friday that I meant everything I'd said to you, Caz. While you may not believe that, I can't change it."

Caroline opened her mouth, but the server arrived to take them to their table. Did she want to hear Hannah saying those things to her? Of course she did. She would be completely out of her mind to *not* want it. But was it a good idea to enjoy this woman how Caroline knew she wanted to? No, it wasn't.

As they sat facing one another, Caroline noted the blush that had crept onto Hannah's cheeks. It was satisfying, Caroline hadn't believed she could be in this position again, but it couldn't mean anything. At least, not right now. Hannah was an escort for the foreseeable future, and Caroline couldn't change that.

"Hannah," Caroline spoke low, needing to get this right. "I... know this is probably a terrible thing to say, but if you're expecting us to date, I can't. Not with you."

"I know." Hannah cast her gaze to the menu, a slight shake of her head as she took the corner of her lip between her teeth. "But for a moment or two, it was a nice thought."

Caroline reached a hand across the table, placing it over

Hannah's. The warmth of her skin spread through Caroline like wildfire, and as Hannah looked up into Caroline's eyes, time stood still. "I'm sorry."

"Don't be. I'm aware that I'm not in a position to date. You deserve far better than someone like me. Someone who is paid by a multitude of women."

"My life is all over the place. *You* deserve more than that."

Hannah cocked her head a little. "You've had a rough time, haven't you?"

"Nothing I can't get over."

"Well, when you feel ready, I know you're going to fall head over heels in love with someone who makes you happy. I knew it the moment we met. You just have that something about you."

Caroline was the one to blush this time. Hannah really knew the right thing to say.

"And I'd like to think that maybe down the line, I could take you out on a real date, but you and I both know that this is exactly just this. Company, so neither of us is alone."

Wow. That hurt. But Hannah wasn't wrong. Not really.

Caroline squeezed her hand and pulled away before their conversation could get too deep. "Let's order some food."

Hannah fumbled with the napkin in her lap, sitting as calmly as she could while Caroline was using the bathroom. She hadn't intended to come here this evening and say the things she had to Caroline, but it had fallen so effortlessly from her mouth as she watched Caroline just inches away from her. Hannah didn't want to feel this way, the thought of longing for a woman she couldn't have was only going to break her heart, but Caroline was so easy to talk to. So beautiful to look at. So...

"Are you having dessert?" Caroline touched Hannah's shoulder lightly as she passed her by.

"Oh, I don't think so. I'm not sure it'll fit."

Caroline took her seat again, her eyes soft, her body language far more relaxed than it had been the last time they met. "I feel just right. Do you have any other plans?"

"None. You booked me for the evening, remember?"

Caroline took her glass of wine, covering the smile she was wearing as she sipped. When she licked her lips and found Hannah's gaze again, something flashed in her eyes. "You don't mind that I booked you all evening?"

"Mind? Not at all. I was thrilled when you contacted me. Obviously."

Caroline nodded slowly, that sweet smile still present. Hannah knew Caroline felt good around her; she just hoped this woman could learn to feel good when they weren't spending time with one another. After all, she really had very little in terms of imperfections. Hannah didn't know her, but she knew Caroline was perfect. Bold claim, but one she'd stand by.

"I was wondering if I could take you to a favourite place of mine for a cocktail?" Hannah imagined Caroline would turn her down, but there was no harm in asking. "Unless you had something else planned..."

"I'd love to."

Hannah's heart jumped when Caroline's smile widened. "It's not a rowdy place."

"Even better," Caroline said, calling for their bill from the server. Hannah wanted to offer to pay, to even go halves, but that would once again imply that this wasn't a client/escort meeting. "Let's finish up here and head over there."

"It's just on the next block."

Caroline smiled when the server placed the bill down, slipping her credit card from her purse.

Okay, Hannah couldn't resist. And offering wouldn't do any harm. "Caz, can...I get this?"

"No." Caroline held up a hand, tapping her card against the contactless machine the server held out. "Tonight is on me. The way it was supposed to be."

"Well, thank you." Hannah subconsciously lay a hand over Caroline's, lost in her eyes as they held one another's gaze. "I've really enjoyed tonight."

"And it's not even over yet." Caroline directed a wink at Hannah, sending her heartrate through the roof. "Come on. Let's get out of here." She got to her feet and took her overcoat from the back of her chair, sliding it over those delicious shoulders. But Hannah remained in place, just staring. "Are we leaving or...?"

"Y-yes." Hannah shot to her feet and cleared the desire—*the want*—from her thoughts. "Absolutely. Let's go." Hannah threw down a tip, rushing towards the door and holding it open for Caroline. "After you." As Caroline passed Hannah, she placed her hand to the small of her back. Caroline tensed immediately, swallowing visibly. "You want the escort me, then you get the escort me."

Hannah guided Caroline across the street, stopping suddenly when Caroline turned to her. "It's better than nothing at all."

"You want the escort me, then you get the escort me."

Caroline shuddered as Hannah sauntered back from the bar, cocktails in hand. They'd situated themselves at the back of the bar in a booth, only a handful of tables around them. But Caroline loved this. In the last week, she'd felt more alive than she had in the last fifteen years.

All thanks to Hannah.

"Try this." Hannah bent forward and placed Caroline's cocktail in front of her. As Caroline lifted her head, her eyes immediately landed on Hannah's cleavage.

"Thanks." She offered the best smile she could manage, crossing her legs suddenly. "What's in it?"

"I have no idea. The bartender recommended it." Hannah squeezed around the table, easing down beside Caroline. She could have taken the seat facing her, but no, Hannah's thigh was touching Caroline's. Her smooth, bare, olive thigh. "Taste it, and I'll get you something else if not."

Caroline leaned forward, sipping from the straw. Wow, that was a smooth drink. Certainly perfect for after dinner. "That's good. Really good." Caroline lifted her glass, offering it to Hannah. "Try it."

Hannah sipped it slowly, watching Caroline over the rim of the glass. "My God. That's divine."

Oh, it's not the only divine thing I'm blessed with tonight. Caroline swallowed when Hannah's lips lingered against her glass.

"I'm getting that next time I go to the bar!" As Hannah handed Caroline her drink back, their fingertips brushed. Considering neither of them was in a position to take this further, they seemed to be doing everything in their power to make it all the more difficult. Typical. "Tell me a little more about you."

Caroline exhaled a long breath. Where did she begin? "What would you like to know?"

"I don't know. Past relationships, family, friends..."

"Do...escorts ask that kind of thing all the time?" Caroline lifted a brow, aware that it wasn't the sort of thing escorts really cared about. They wanted payment, not their client's life story.

"This escort does when she's interested in someone."

"Okay, well, I'm two years out of a marriage. Ex-wife was a

CEO of a firm in town. As you know, I'm in education. My sister owns the cafe we bumped into one another at last weekend, and it's just us two. Lost both parents six years apart when we were younger." Caroline turned to Hannah, sitting side on. "I'm sorry to say that I really don't have very much going on in my life. Until recently, anyway."

"Recently?"

"For the first time in over fifteen years, I've had the freedom to enjoy my weekends outside of the house. I may have left my ex-wife two years ago, but if Gail hadn't booked you for me, I'd still be at home...contemplating what the point of life was anymore."

Hannah reached out a hand, lowering it to Caroline's knee. "I'm sorry you've felt that way. But you're picking yourself back up, and you're out here having fun."

"I am. But it's not real, is it? So I don't suppose it really counts. Once you and I go our separate ways, I'll go back to the life I had pre-Eva."

"Do you *want* to go back to that life?"

"Not particularly, no." Caroline knew she wanted to broaden her horizons and get out into the world, but without Hannah, that would never have happened in the first place. To revert back to a few weeks ago...she dreaded the thought. "We're in a place where we can be honest with one another, wouldn't you agree?"

"Absolutely. I want you to know that you can trust me, Caz."

"Booking you was supposed to help me back into the dating scene." Caroline hated admitting that. She was forty-seven; she should be well acquainted with dating by now. But Naomi had put paid to anything Caroline used to be familiar with some time ago. "I...have a feeling it's just going to make things worse for me."

"Worse? What could be worse than sitting home alone night after night?"

Caroline smiled weakly. "Sitting home alone with you on my mind night after night."

"O-oh, I—" Hannah's hand fell from Caroline's knee as she shook her head. "I'm sorry. You've paid for a service, Caz. I'm trying to give you that service."

Caroline propped her head in her hand, resting her elbow on the back of the booth. She studied every inch of Hannah's face, her charming eyes, that uncertain smile. "I wish I was here under different circumstances. It's like I create more problems for myself unintentionally."

"I don't think you're creating problems. I think you're about to step out into an entirely new world from what you're used to, and you're overwhelmed."

"The number one reason I wanted to see you tonight was to apologise, Hannah. For last week."

"There's nothing to apologise for." Hannah's hand landed back on Caroline's bare knee, her thumb slowly soothing in circles. "I really enjoyed last Friday. I was more concerned that I'd done something to hurt you."

"No. Never. But I shouldn't have run away like that. I didn't expect to enjoy myself so much, and I didn't think I had it in me to get so carried away."

"You were letting your hair down, so what?"

Caroline closed her eyes when Hannah continued to stroke her skin. God, it felt amazing. "What I asked you was way out of line. That's not the person I am, and I'm truly sorry."

"Hey." Hannah squeezed Caroline's knee, sending a thrill throughout her entire body. "Stop apologising. Everything is okay."

"Thank you. For being so great. It's made all of this easier for me."

"Well, when a beautiful woman wants to spend time with me, it's hard to be anything else. But I am genuine, Caz. I know you find that hard to believe, I *am* an escort, but my intentions are good, and I'd never lead you on."

"I know." Deep down, Caroline knew Hannah was as genuine as they came. "If I have to pay you to spend time with you, I'll do that. I know this won't last forever, but for the time I have to get to know you, I'd love to do this more often."

"I don't expect any payment from you, Caz. I'm not only here because you booked me. I'm here because I *want* to be."

"Maybe. But one day, you'll realise that this is better how it is."

CHAPTER 6

Caroline pressed a hand to her forehead, willing the ache she felt behind her eyeballs to fade. How was it Wednesday already? She should be thrilled by how quickly the week was passing by, but she'd felt out of sorts lately. Actually, since she'd met Hannah almost two weeks ago. Hannah...was attracted to her? Huh.

She snorted as she brought her coffee cup to her lips, shaking her head. Thankfully the staff room was empty today, offering her five minutes peace after lunch. But those five minutes only meant one thing. Hannah was on her mind.

The school bell sounded, causing Caroline to almost spill hot coffee down the front of her white shirt. Was lunchtime really over already? And when did she become so jumpy?

"Hey, Caz?" Brenda, one of the biology teachers, poked her head around the door. "You still on for Friday with us?"

"So far, yes. I don't imagine anything will change, though." A night out with friends could only distract her from Hannah.

Brenda winked. "Good woman. It'll be a great night. You know what Sharon is like once she gets on that bloody karaoke."

"I'm looking forward to it."

Brenda winked, her heels clicking as they echoed in the hallway. "See you Friday!"

Caroline got to her feet, emptied her coffee down the drain, and placed her cup in the dishwasher. She couldn't recall the last time she'd actually finished a cup at work; something or someone always demanded her attention. And right now, it was her mentor period with the sixth form students. It was rare that anybody showed up to discuss things with her, they liked to think they were fully fledged adults now who could take care of everything on their own, but on the odd occasion, a student did arrive to speak to her. So, Caroline would sit around for the next hour in the sixth form block, doing very little.

"Ms Baker, I hoped I'd find you here." John Rankin, the headteacher, caught her as she was leaving the staff room. "I have one of your form students with first aid."

"One of mine? Which one? What happened?" Panicked, Caroline rushed towards the main foyer with John. "Wait, let me guess...Billy Charlton! He's a bloody nuisance lately. I don't know what's gotten into him."

"No. It's Edie Caffrey."

"Edie?" Caroline frowned. "What happened?"

"Seems Edie got herself into a fight with a number of other students during lunch hour."

No. John surely had it wrong. Edie was bright and quiet. Caroline had never had a run-in with her. Her parents had never been called to the school for even the slightest issue. "Edie? Are you sure?"

"I'm sure."

Caroline scratched the back of her neck, and puffed out a breath. "Right. I'll go and see her."

"She's very upset," John said, adjusting his glasses on his

nose. "But I suppose that's because she's being excluded for three days."

Caroline sighed. Edie being excluded wasn't good. But before she made any assumptions, she would check on her student. "Right, okay. Leave it with me. I'll find out what's happened."

She stepped out into the foyer, pushing through the double doors that would take her towards the reception. She knocked on the door, hearing sniffling as the designated first aider let her into the room. Edie sat on a chair in the corner, her shoulders slumped, her blonde hair wild. Caroline loathed seeing girls fighting. For some reason, they always went straight for the head, taking as much hair as they could in the process.

"Edie?"

Edie looked up at her, her bottom lip trembling. And then she lowered her head again, clearly preparing for the telling-off she assumed she'd receive. But Caroline had never believed that raised voices were the answer when it came to dealing with students. She preferred to speak to them with the same respect she expected them to speak to her.

"Do you want me to call Edie's parents?" Rachel, the first aider asked.

"No, it's okay. I'll deal with this. I think Edie needs a moment or two to calm down."

"Okay, well, I'll leave you to it." Rachel left the room, the door closing softly behind her.

Caroline crossed the room and lifted a chair, placing it in front of Edie. She sat down and gave her student a couple of minutes to compose herself. Armed with a box of tissues nearby, she plucked one from it and handed it over, smiling when Edie looked up at her.

"Mum is going to kill me when she finds out about this."

Edie whimpered and then winced when she blew her nose. "Ow, that hurts."

Caroline lifted Edie's head, frowning when she found scratches all over her face. "Who did this to you?"

"Don't know. All of them." Edie lifted a shoulder, scrunching the tissue up in her hand. "They keep picking on me, and now I've made things worse."

"*Who* keeps picking on you, Edie?"

"The girls in my year. They keep saying horrible stuff about my mum. They don't even know her. And then today they just wouldn't stop saying things in the lunch queue."

"Oh, sweetie." Caroline cocked her head, offering a sympathetic smile. "It must be very hard to hear things that aren't true. And I know it's difficult to rise above it, but you have to try."

"B-but the stuff they say is true. I just don't like how they say it."

"What do they say?" Caroline asked, confused.

"Mum's a lesbian. But they keep shouting a horrible word at me. And I don't want them to call her it. Why does it matter what she is?"

Caroline's heart constricted. No child should have to listen to such things. "It *doesn't* matter what she is. Now, I'm going to call your mum and have her come get you. I'll talk to her, okay?"

"I didn't want to fight, Ms Baker. But I'm fed up with it."

"I know, Edie." Caroline placed a gentle hand on Edie's shoulder, sighing. "We'll sort this all out. Don't worry. Give me a minute, and I'll be back in. You stay here, okay?"

"Kay." Edie huddled into herself, wrapping her school blazer tighter around her trembling body. "Thanks, Miss."

Caroline offered a gentle smile, slipping out the door and heading for reception. The headache she'd been fighting all day had just increased in pressure, but she couldn't help thinking that Edie's retaliation today may work in her favour. She shouldn't be impressed by a child fighting in order to stand up for her mother's sexuality, but she was. Because it meant there was hope for the other kids yet. "Joan, can you call Edie Caffrey's mum for me. She needs collecting. I'll be in my room with her. Send her in when she arrives."

"No problem, Caz. Should I say what this is about?"

"Just tell her there's been an incident at school, but that Edie is okay."

Joan nodded, focusing on the computer screen and bringing up Edie's mum's number. "I'll send her in when she gets here."

Caroline turned and left reception, disappointed by how cruel some children could be. Before this day was over, she would have a list of each child's name, and she would be calling their parents in. This wasn't acceptable, and it had nothing to do with Caroline's own sexuality. Though she knew some would see it that way. 'Kids will be kids' didn't work for her. It never would.

Hannah took a left, parking in the visitor car park at the front of her daughter's school. Her heart had been in her mouth since the school had called her to collect Edie, but she couldn't fathom what had happened. Edie always applied herself and worked as hard as she could, but perhaps the incident wasn't what Hannah was expecting it to be. Maybe Edie had taken a tumble and injured herself.

She rushed into the reception, waiting impatiently while the receptionist was on a call. She could walk the halls looking for Edie, or she could *not* turn into the crazed mother who demanded her daughter back. It wasn't a good look, and it wasn't required.

The receptionist placed the receiver down. “May I help you?”

“I’m here to pick my daughter up. Edie Caffrey.”

“Ah, yes. Ms Baker would like to speak to you. If you head down the corridor here, go through the double doors and up the ramp, you’ll find another corridor. It’s the third room on the left. Would you like me to take you?”

“No, thank you. I’m sure I’ll find it.”

Hannah followed the directions given to her, the school quiet now that lessons had resumed for the day. Why would Edie’s form teacher want to speak to her? What the hell had her daughter done? She found the door she was looking for, peering through the glass in the middle to find Edie with her head down on a desk.

She knocked on the door, not waiting for a response, and opened it. “Edie?”

A sharp intake of breath was heard from the corner of the room, and Hannah frowned as she focused on the woman sitting at the desk. Staring back at her was the very same woman she’d spent every waking moment thinking about. “Caz?”

“Mum?” Edie suddenly broke their stare, her face a complete mess. “Please don’t be angry with me. I didn’t mean it.”

Hannah rushed to her daughter’s side, taking her in her arms. “What happened? Who did this to you?”

“Sophie and all her mates.” Edie sniffled, her gorgeous face full of scratches and marks. “I’d just had enough.”

“Had enough of what, Edie?” Hannah had no idea anything had been going on at school. But now that she did, she wanted to get to the bottom of it. “Has this been going on for a while?”

Edie nodded, lowering her eyes. “They all know you’re gay.”

“So?”

"So they pick on me because of it," Edie spoke barely above a whisper, glancing over at Caroline momentarily. "I had to tell Ms Baker. I'm sorry."

Hannah looked over at Caroline, her face the picture of shock. Yes, she too was shocked to discover that her client was her kid's teacher, but Hannah couldn't focus on that right now. Edie was her priority. Still, her client *was* her kid's teacher. *Fuck!* "Thanks, Caroline. For looking after her."

Caroline smiled weakly, clearing her throat. "No problem."

"Now, I want you to tell Ms Baker the names of these girls. All of them. And don't give me all that 'I don't know who it was' because I'll find out one way or another."

"But it'll just get worse, Mum. I don't want to be a snitch."

Hannah scoffed. "A snitch? Love, they've attacked you. Look at the state of you."

"I started it. The fight."

Caroline got to her feet, rounding her desk and leaning against it. Hannah swallowed as their eyes met, and then they trailed down Caroline's body. Her pantsuit. Navy crushed velvet, tailored, *sexy as hell*. Hannah groaned inwardly. God, this was all totally wrong. She was sheer perfection. And then Caroline spoke. "Edie has been excluded from school for three days."

"What?" Hannah shot to her feet. "You heard her. Those kids are picking on her. And while violence is never the answer," Hannah paused as she eyed her daughter momentarily. "What else is she supposed to do? Just let them name call and say whatever they like?"

"No, of course not." Caroline held up a hand when Hannah opened her mouth to speak. "The other students will be dealt with, too."

"This is complete rubbish. Why should my daughter miss out on important school time because the school doesn't know how to deal with bullying?" Hannah took Edie's bag from the floor, motioning for her daughter to stand. "I thought *you* of all people would understand, Caz."

Caroline pushed off her desk, stepping forward. "Edie, if you could just take a seat for a moment, I'd like to speak to your mum outside."

Hannah rolled her eyes, dropping Edie's rucksack to the floor as she followed Caroline outside. She understood Caroline was only doing her job, but Hannah would always stand by Edie.

"Hannah," Caroline paused as she closed her classroom door. "I understand you're frustrated, I am too, but the head has already made his decision. The students who took part in this will be dealt with. I can promise you that."

Hannah looked through the glass. "Look at her, Caz. She's never hurt a soul in her life."

Caroline offered a gentle smile. "She was defending you. And while I don't condone what she's done, I'd be proud to have a daughter like that."

"Your own kids wouldn't defend you?"

"I don't have any kids." Caroline clasped her hands in front of her, lowering her eyes. And then she swallowed as she found Hannah's eyes again. "Don't you think I'd have told you that when we've been together?"

"I'm sorry, I shouldn't have assumed."

Caroline shook her head. "It's fine. But I had no idea you were Edie's mum. I'm so sorry. If I'd known—"

"If you'd known, what? You wouldn't have asked how much I charge for a fuck?" Hannah winced as those words left her mouth. Caroline didn't deserve that. Not at all. "Oh God, I'm so sorry."

Tears welled in Caroline's eyes, her bottom lip trembling. "No. *I'm* sorry. I just...I won't contact you again. And if I've disrespected you by suggesting what I did that night, please forgive me."

"You didn't. I chose to take up that line of work; it's my own fault. You just did what every other client does. Expects more... knowing I need the money so I won't turn you down." Fucking hell. What was wrong with Hannah today? The things she was saying, the hostility towards Caroline. She needed to leave right now. Yes, Hannah was angry that Edie was being excluded from school, but that wasn't on Caroline. "Okay, I'm just going to leave now. I...I'm sorry. For how I've just spoken to you. You didn't deserve that."

"Hey," Caroline said, placing a hand on Hannah's wrist. "If it means anything to you at all, I don't see you as Eva. I see you as Hannah. And I always will."

Hannah smiled, placing her hand on the door handle. Caroline being honest meant a lot to her. But it wouldn't change anything. This was probably only going to push Caroline away... or scare her off. She opened the classroom door and stepped inside. "Come on, you. Let's get you home."

Edie got to her feet gingerly, tucking her chair under her desk. As she moved towards the door, she looked up at Caroline. "I'm really sorry for disappointing you, Ms Baker."

"Oh, sweetie. You haven't. We all have blips, but you haven't disappointed me. I'll see you next week, okay? Back to normal. Working harder than any of my other students."

Hannah watched their interaction, her heart swelling when Caroline spoke to Edie with respect and honesty. Why hadn't Hannah had a teacher like her back in school? Lord knows she could have done with a supportive teacher like Caroline. But then Hannah's heart softened further when she realised the bond Edie and Caroline had. Her daughter was quiet, always had been, but she seemed different around Caroline. Like, she wanted to show what she was capable of. Not many kids willingly took on board what their teachers thought of them, nor did they seek approval, but Edie definitely had a soft spot for Caroline. She wouldn't usually be so open and honest about her problems.

"Bye, Ms Baker."

Caroline smiled as she winked at Edie, and then she turned her attention to Hannah. "If I have any updates, should I contact you via the number the school has for you?"

Hannah watched Edie skulk off down the corridor, her rucksack hanging off her back. She quickly turned back to Caroline, her voice low as she stepped closer. Caroline's body heat sent Hannah's own temperature raging, that delicious perfume she was becoming too fond of wafting towards her. "Yeah. That's my number. Call me...whenever you want to."

Caroline took her by the wrist. "As Hannah...or Eva?"

"Whatever works for you. But I think you already know the answer," Hannah paused, lifting her free hand and brushing her fingers up the inside of Caroline's wrist. She felt her shudder. "I don't share my personal life with just anyone, Caz. Make of that what you will."

CHAPTER 7

Caroline wasn't sure this was the wisest decision she'd ever made. No, she was certain it was the *worst* decision she'd ever made. But she needed to see Hannah. To tell her that the things she'd said earlier outside her classroom weren't true. Caroline had known this would all turn sour; it was inevitable. But she'd been overwhelmed with everything she'd faced from the night they'd met. How Eva looked at her, how she touched her with the gentlest hand, the things she said to her. Caroline had never felt so confident in the last ten days. Okay, she'd initially been scared half to death when she woke the next morning to the reminder of her actions after their first meeting, but on the whole...she felt amazing. Hannah thought she was attractive—there was life in her yet.

But now, as she stood outside Hannah's home, Caroline felt that familiar dread settle inside her. If the school knew she'd stolen Hannah's address, Caroline wouldn't have a job to go back to tomorrow. But she was putting her trust in a woman she didn't know, praying that Hannah wouldn't put a complaint in at the school. She may have told Caroline to call her whenever she wanted to, but turning up on the doorstep surely wouldn't be met the same way.

Caroline steeled herself, taking the few steps up to the door. She knocked gently, hoping Hannah wouldn't hear and she'd have to turn around and leave. But then the front light turned on, flickering to the side of her head, and the door opened.

"C-Caz, hi."

"I'm so sorry for showing up here. I'm fairly certain what I've done is a sackable offence, but I just needed to see you for a couple of minutes. If this is inappropriate, though, I can leave."

Hannah frowned. "Come in. Is everything okay?"

Caroline stepped into the warmth of Hannah's home, enveloped by the delicious scent of something sweet baking. "I...yes. I think so. I don't know."

"Would you like a cuppa? You look like you need one." Hannah held out an arm, directing Caroline towards the kitchen. When she reached it, Hannah closed the door. "Why have you come here?"

"Because I just had a few things to say to you."

"Is this about Edie?" Hannah sighed, resting back against the counter. "I know I flew off the handle a bit earlier, but I was shocked. I couldn't believe what had happened. Now that we're home and Edie has told me everything, I don't blame her for lamping half of them."

Caroline smiled. "I get it, I really do, but I'm not sure what Edie did was worth getting excluded for."

Hannah shrugged. "So long as the others receive the same, I'm not too concerned anymore. I mean, she's hardly going to start causing trouble in school. You probably don't know she's there half the time."

"Well, you'll be pleased to know that the other students received a longer exclusion period. The school is also putting a team together who will deliver an assembly about LGBTQ+

history and equality. Oh, and Edie can return on Monday rather than Wednesday. I spoke to the head and explained that Edie really wasn't a child who deserved to miss out on important school time...and he agreed. Her record speaks for itself. She really is a wonderful student. She's a pleasure to have in my class."

"Wow, that's...thank you, Caz."

Hannah's gaze pierced Caroline, but she pushed those beautiful blue eyes to the back of her mind.

"I noticed that you two get along quite well."

Caroline motioned towards a seat. "May I?"

Hannah nodded, taking the seat beside Caroline.

"Edie has always been a fantastic student. I've never had any trouble from her. Yes, I was surprised when I was called to see her today, but I understand in many ways why she reacted how she did. And if it's been going on for a while, it was only a matter of time before she blew."

"That fills me with hope. I always knew she was a good kid at school, but it's just me and her here at home, and she spends a lot of time in her room. She's always been quiet like that. And while it means I don't have to worry about her being out with the wrong crowd and causing trouble, I do wish she'd surface more than she does."

"If you're worried about her, I can safely say that she's never given me the impression that anything is wrong."

"No, I don't think there's anything wrong or that something is going on that I should know about. Well, aside from what we learnt today. I just wish she'd come out of her shell more."

Caroline frowned. It had suddenly dawned on her that she was in the home of one of her students. Without a care in the world. "Is she home now?"

"She spends Wednesdays with my mum. It's been that way since she was a toddler."

"Right. Well, I'm not disturbing anything, am I? No plans..."

"If you're asking if I have any clients booked, no. I don't. I only work the weekend when Edie is with her dad."

That wasn't what Caroline was asking at all. "No, that wasn't where I was going with this. It's just that I probably shouldn't be here. You know, with me being Edie's form tutor and all."

"This is my home. Who I have here is nobody's business." A scoff fell from Hannah's lips, and then she got to her feet, flicking the kettle on. "Cuppa?"

"Yes, please." Okay, this was a positive step. Hannah's hostility had gone. Now it was just that beautiful woman standing before Caroline. And besides, today's meeting should never have been about them. Edie was the reason they'd met at all earlier. "You have a really lovely home."

"Thanks. Since I spend most of my time here, I wanted it to feel cosy. You know?"

"I do." When she'd asked Naomi to leave, Caroline had ripped most of the house apart and redecorated. She wanted it to feel like hers and *only* hers. Something with her mark on since she'd not had the opportunity to do so while they were together. Everything had been done on Naomi's say-so. "You know, earlier when you said those things..."

"I was in a terrible mood. Please forgive me."

"I just hope you know I don't think or want any of those things from you. I've had the most wonderful time with you recently, Hannah. I really have."

"But?" Hannah quirked an eyebrow, running a hand through her long blonde hair.

She stared Caroline down with those deep blue eyes, Caroline's throat drying in the process.

"But this has to stop now. You're Edie's mother, and I can't see you again as a client. It wouldn't be right. I'm sorry." Caroline hated this. Why did life have to be so difficult? "I probably shouldn't have contacted you a second time."

"Why?"

"Because I was fooling myself into thinking it was good for me. That *you* were good for me."

"Thanks. I'll try not to be offended by that."

Caroline's heart ached from the look in Hannah's eyes. "It's not you. You're...a dream. It's me. I can't make someone else happy, Hannah. I can't even be happy in myself."

"That's no way to live your life."

"Perhaps not, but it's easier this way. And I know Gail wants the best for me, all my friends do, but they don't understand. Nobody understands. Having said that, you really did make me feel that little bit better about myself. So again, thank you."

"I didn't do or say anything to make you feel better about yourself. I wasn't intentionally doing it because your friend had booked me or because you contacted me. I did it because it's the truth. Anything I said...was the truth."

Caroline felt that familiar blush she often did around Hannah. As much as she loved it, it was kind of pathetic. She was a middle-aged woman. Was she even supposed to blush anymore? "Well, I felt really good about myself. That was all down to you."

"You're gorgeous. There's no denying that."

Caroline hadn't felt gorgeous in a long time. Naomi had stripped everything from her without laying a single finger on her. Could Caroline potentially allow someone to do that to her again? No, not in this lifetime. "So are you. And I hope that one day, you find whatever you're looking for. Whether that is in your career or your love life, I hope you find the perfect person for you."

Hannah offered a small smile, setting a cup of tea down in front of Caroline. "Here. Get this down you."

"Thank you." Caroline's fingers brushed the back of Hannah's hand as she removed it from the cup, a thrill jolting straight through her body. But she had to ignore it. Nothing good could come from feeling this way.

"You know, I'm kinda mad at you for being so against dating." Hannah laughed as she fell down into her seat. "Super mad."

Caroline's forehead creased. "Why?"

"Because for the first time in my life, I felt that genuine connection with you, and you're not bloody available. I've never felt that before. It's always seemed forced. But, if you're happy with the path your life is on, I won't distract you. I'd like to keep in touch though, if you want to?"

"Oh, I didn't say I was happy." Caroline could admit to that. She was fairly certain that anyone who laid eyes on her could see that she wasn't truly happy. "But I left my marriage, and I came away from it feeling...torn apart."

"She broke your heart." Hannah nodded slowly, her eyes focused on her cup of coffee.

Caroline scoffed. That was an understatement. "She broke *me*."

"Do you want to talk about it? Sometimes it can be good for you."

Caroline appreciated that, but there was nothing more to say. "Thank you, but I've dealt with it now." That was a lie. If she'd dealt with it, she would be kissing the woman sitting before her. But she wasn't one for taking risks. "I've come to terms with who I was before Naomi and who I am now as a result of her. I can live with that."

Hannah held up a hand. "Then I will let you be."

"Anyway, I didn't come here to discuss my terrible personal life. I just wanted to make sure we were okay. The thought of hurting you or offending you... I'd be devastated if you thought of me that way."

"Hey," Hannah reached forward, settling her hand over Caroline's. That hand, the gentleness of it, yeah...Hannah felt good. "I know you're different to the others. I knew that from the moment I met you. That's exactly why I told you to call me. It's exactly why I told you who I was the night of your first booking."

"I'm really not your type, trust me."

Hannah squeezed Caroline's hand, and then she lifted it, leaning forward and kissing her skin. The emotion she felt from that simple touch almost floored Caroline, her chest tightening. "I beg to differ, but if you're not interested, you're not interested."

"You don't know the first thing about me," Caroline said, her voice barely above a whisper.

"But I would have loved the opportunity to get to know you."

God, why did Hannah make Caroline want to kiss her every time they were close? Right now, she wasn't sure she could even remain friends with her. It would only lead to a place Caroline wasn't prepared to be—either getting involved in something she shouldn't be or a longing that she couldn't take.

Caroline slid her hand out of Hannah's, smiling weakly. "It's best this way."

Hannah fell back onto the couch, her phone gripped in her hand. She needed some serious thinking space and a swift kick up the arse. How could she for one second contemplate something more with Caroline? Hannah had sworn herself off women after Kirsty, they always let her down at some point, but Caroline Baker...well, she was something else entirely. Hannah wanted to know her, to learn about her, but more than anything...she wanted to hunt down the bitch who'd ruined Caroline and seriously hurt her. Because in Hannah's eyes, Caroline was everything anyone could want in a relationship.

But Caroline was right. Hannah didn't know the first thing about her. That didn't discourage her, though. It only left Hannah wanting to prove she wasn't like Caroline's ex-wife. And truthfully, Hannah had never felt the urge to prove herself to anyone. Especially not another woman.

She lifted her phone, pressed her best friend's number, and brought it to her ear.

"Hello, my little cherub." Adele's gentle voice calmed Hannah instantly.

"Hey, do you have a minute to talk?"

"For you, always."

Hannah smiled, closing her eyes as she brought her hand to her forehead. Adele would know what to do. She always did. "I have a bit of a dilemma..."

"You, a dilemma? Never."

"Ha! You're hilarious."

"No, I'm serious. You never call me because something is wrong. It's usually me calling you."

Hannah sighed. "Yeah, well, the tables have turned, my friend. I kinda did something recently..."

"Did something?" Adele drawled, waiting for more from Hannah.

"So, I had this client two weeks ago. Then again last Friday. She's lovely." How the hell did Hannah fully get into something like this with her best friend? She hadn't quite pieced it all together herself yet. Hannah had been too busy hoping Caroline would give her a chance. "I may have kinda asked her out on a date."

"Like an escort date, right?"

"N-no. With me...not Eva."

Adele barked a laugh. "Well, shit. You got yourself knee-deep into it, didn't you?"

"It doesn't really matter because she's not interested, but I just needed someone to talk to. She's just...I don't even know how to describe it. She has so much beauty, but I see how broken she is, Adele. And I want to show her that there is life still there to be lived."

"As much as I love you and your huge heart, are you sure you want to take on something like that?"

Hannah would sit up all night listening to Caroline if she had to. To help her work through things at her own pace. But the fact still remained...Caroline wasn't interested in Hannah. "I would, for her, but she doesn't want to know."

"Maybe that's for the best, Hannah."

"And then today," Hannah paused, clearing her throat. "I was called into Edie's school. She was in a fight."

"Oh, no. Is she okay? Do we need to visit parents and knock their heads together?"

"She started the fight, Del. Because the kids have been picking on her for having a lesbian mum. Turns out they yell 'dyke' at her whenever they see her. She just...flipped. And I kinda can't be angry with her for that."

"No. I know fighting with other kids isn't the way to handle it, but she's a good kid, Hannah. I love her like my own."

Hannah smiled. Adele was more like a sister than a best friend. "There's something else..."

"Oh, God. What?"

"This client, the one I gave my real identity to. S-she's Edie's form teacher."

The line went silent.

Had Adele hung up?

"Uh, you there?" Hannah frowned. "Del?"

"I-I'm here," She said, her voice wavering. "Did you just say what I think you did? That your client is your kid's teacher?"

"Y-yeah. I only found out today. I had no idea, and neither did she."

Hannah wasn't sure how she felt about it yet. She hadn't for one moment expected to walk into that room to find Caroline waiting for her. It was clear Caroline had chosen to use a different surname for her escort booking, but it didn't change the fact that Hannah had wanted the floor to open up and swallow her whole this afternoon. It was just her luck, though.

"What happens if she books you again?" Adele asked, hesitancy clouding her usual gentle voice. "I mean, you'd turn her down, wouldn't you?"

"Honestly, no. I wouldn't. If it meant I got to spend time with her, I wouldn't dream of turning her down."

"You're out of your mind, Hannah. This is going to end in tears if you don't take yourself out of the situation now." Adele was right, but Hannah needed so much more of Caroline. "Seriously, I need you to be sensible about this one."

"I will."

Adele snorted. "Except, you won't. I know you. This is going to turn into a huge mess, and then you'll be the one who comes out of it broken-hearted."

Hannah's phone vibrated against her ear. She glanced at the screen, finding a number she didn't recognise above a text message. "Look, I should go. I have to call Mum soon to check on Edie. But can we do lunch one day next week?"

Adele sighed. "Fine. If that's what you want. But I'm not done discussing this with you."

"I know, I know. I'll call you when I know what afternoon I can do, okay?"

"Miss you," Adele said. "I'll see you soon."

"You will. Bye, Del."

Hannah ended the call, scrolling straight to her message inbox. She frowned as she opened the message, unaware as to who was contacting her, but then her heart leapt into her throat.

Thank you for hearing me out this evening. I know I shouldn't text, but I'll delete your number now. Both your personal and business. Take care of yourself, Hannah. Caz x

Hannah reread the message several times. Trying to dissect it was pointless. But then she had to wonder why Caroline had her number at all. If she'd shown up here this evening, why had she needed to take Hannah's number from the school system? Hannah smiled. Caroline had taken that number because Hannah told her to. And now, she didn't want Caroline to *not* have her number ever again.

Don't delete them. You never know when you could need it. H x

A bubble appeared, sending Hannah's heart rate soaring.

It's for the best. Bye, Hannah. Caz x

And just like that, the thrill Hannah felt from a simple message from Caroline crumbled into a misery she hoped she wouldn't feel. Caroline had a lot of baggage, but Hannah wanted to unpack every last item. Still, she would let it lie. And if one day in the future she bumped into Caroline, she would hope for a greater outcome.

CHAPTER 8

Caroline was feeling great tonight. She wore a sleek royal blue dress, a pair of heels she didn't imagine wearing ever again, and Gail had been over to keep her company—and sane. Tonight, Caroline was determined to enjoy herself. She was going to hold her head high as she walked into that bar, and she was going to really let her hair down.

Because, as of today, it was officially half-term. No school for a week, no screaming kids, no...nothing. Caroline could get as drunk as she wanted to, and she was going to make sure she made up for every night out she'd missed over the years. Yes, this was her first outing with friends since she divorced Naomi. Two years of drinking wine at home alone ended from this point forward. She was meeting colleagues, and Caroline had never felt more determined to enjoy herself. She had Hannah and the confidence she'd given Caroline to thank for that.

She stepped into the bar, immediately spotting Brenda and Sharon. They waved her over, both grinning from ear-to-ear, a bottle of wine held up in the air. "Over here, Baker!"

Caroline laughed, shaking her head as she shrugged her jacket off and headed in their direction. God, she didn't realise how much she needed this night out. No pressure to be home for a particular time, no arguments because of the fact she'd gone out at all, no asking for money so she could buy herself a couple of drinks. It was quite nice not having anyone to answer to.

But Naomi would always be at the back of her mind. It was hard not to have her there when Caroline knew this was her usual stomping ground. If she didn't think about the potential of bumping into Naomi, Caroline would surely enjoy every moment of tonight with her friends. She'd worked with Brenda and Sharon for fifteen years, and while they hadn't known just how dreadful things at home had been during her marriage, they weren't stupid. They knew *something* had been wrong.

"My God, you're here!" Brenda flung her arms around Caroline, squeezing her tight. "I didn't think you'd show. But I'm so happy you have."

"Me too," Sharon said, offering a wink in Caroline's direction. "Can I get you a drink?"

"No, I'll go to the bar. Does anyone need a top-up while I'm there?"

Brenda grinned. "Unless you're bringing shots back with you, I'm okay for now."

Shots? They actually still did that on a Friday night out in town? Jesus, Caroline really needed to get out more. "You...want shots?"

Sharon squeezed Brenda's shoulder. "Maybe later, eh. Caz has only just walked through the door. I'd like to make sure she can walk back out of it and to the next bar later."

"Right, yes. Good idea."

Caroline threw a thumb over her shoulder. "I'll just be a few minutes."

She made a beeline for the bar, weaving through the throngs of people already in full swing. This bar had always had a nice feel to it, it'd been one of the city's best for at least twenty years, but Caroline hadn't been in here for...seven years. She used to frequent it with Naomi in the earlier days of their marriage, but once things changed...once Naomi changed, Caroline stayed home. Naomi didn't; she met with friends and family whenever she wanted to, but it was always implied that Caroline was to stay home. And if she didn't, there would be a huge fallout at the end of the night. Being at home just seemed easier. It was less aggravation that way.

Caroline approached the bar, slipping in between two couples.

"Oh, MY GOD! Caz?" The bartender rushed from the opposite end of the bar, her eyes wide. "Is that really you?"

Caroline laughed. "It's really me."

Roxanne had worked the bar here for over ten years. She knew everyone, what their choice of drink was, and who they were dating.

"You look fantastic! Did you want your usual?"

Caroline wasn't sure what her usual was anymore. It would be a surprise if nothing else. "Uh, sure."

"And Naomi?" Roxanne peered over Caroline's shoulder. "What's she having tonight?"

Caroline frowned. Did Roxanne think they were back together? "I, um...we're not—"

"I'll have a vodka diet coke, Rox." Naomi's voice sent a shiver down Caroline's spine, her breath hot against her bare shoulder. And then she felt Naomi lean in towards her ear. "Well, well, well. Look what the cat *dragged* in."

Caroline immediately gripped the edge of the bar, exhaling a slow breath as Naomi wrapped an arm around her waist from behind. She hadn't laid eyes on this woman in at least eighteen months, so why did tonight have to be the night they bumped into one another? It didn't matter if Naomi turned around and walked away in the next ten seconds...Caroline's night was ruined regardless.

"What are you doing in here?" Naomi asked, disdain in her voice. "I mean...you could have dressed up a bit."

Here we go...

Caroline closed her eyes, breathing through her emotions... her anger.

"This is why I always told you to stay at home. You have no idea what fashion is, *baby*."

Caroline slipped out from between the bar and her ex-wife, heading straight for the exit. She needed fresh air and time to think. Naomi being here couldn't change anything; she'd progressed too far to revert back now. She stepped past the security guards, inhaling a deep breath as the cool evening air hit her. Everything was going to be perfectly fine. Naomi had no say over her life anymore. She was nothing.

And then Naomi landed in front of Caroline, that evil grin she wore so well spreading on her mouth. This was the entire reason Caroline didn't step foot inside bars anymore. What was the point?

"Where the hell are you? I've been standing here for twenty minutes!"

"I'm leaving the house right this second." The sound of Adele slamming the front door convinced Hannah that she was actually leaving. Finally. "I'll be with you in like...half an hour. Go in and get a table and a drink. I'll be there before you know it."

Hannah shook her head. "I hope you realise that I turned down a client tonight so I could meet you for a girly night out. If you're not here in half an hour, you owe me the two-fifty I've lost out on."

"Yes, Eva." Adele laughed as a car horn sounded in the background. "See, my taxi is here. I'll be there soon."

Hannah hung up, shoving her phone into her clutch bag and rounding the corner onto the main street. When she looked up at the bar, her eyes widened. Caroline was standing outside, another woman with her. Not knowing what to do, Hannah turned back around the corner. She couldn't go into that bar if Caroline was there. Hannah would end up getting drunk and saying things she shouldn't say to her. And tonight, she wasn't an escort. She was just Hannah...plain and simple. To be in the same bar as Caroline was asking for trouble. Heart trouble.

With her back pressed to the wall, she took a few breaths, giving it a minute or two until the coast was clear. Then she would go to the bar next door and call Adele. Her best friend wouldn't care where they spent their night so long as alcohol was involved.

"I'm quite disappointed," An unfamiliar voice said as Hannah heard a sniffle. "A friend said they'd seen you in town a few months ago and that you looked great. That you'd been taking care of yourself. But, well...they clearly have a *very different* definition of great than I do. You've put a lot of weight on, Caroline..."

"What do you want, Naomi?" Caroline's voice held a vulnerability, sending Hannah's stomach sinking. She sounded like a frightened child. "We're divorced. Let me get on with my life."

"Oh, I bet it's a lonely life now, sweetheart. Without me there."

"Actually, it's a pleasant life without you there."

Naomi laughed. "Pleasant is *boring*. But then again, you always preferred that, didn't you?"

Hannah clenched one hand at her side, fighting back the

urge to get involved in their conversation. As much as she hated everything she was hearing, Caroline wouldn't appreciate her stepping in. They didn't know one another well enough for her to do so.

"Well," Naomi said. "It's been a pleasure. But I have to get back inside now. My fiancée is waiting for me."

"Y-you're remarrying?"

"I am. Lucille is amazing. I was sleeping with her before I left you."

Caroline laughed. "I think you'll find that *I* was the one who left *you*."

"Look at that. It's all in your head, as usual. You should really see someone about it. It's not healthy."

"You've met someone else. Let me get on with my life. It's been two years, Naomi."

Hannah heard the sudden calmness in Caroline's voice. She was probably used to trying to diffuse situations like this. Still, it didn't make it right.

"I wish it had been far longer," Naomi said, scoffing. "I wasted so much time with you, Caz. Our life was terrible; you *rarely* made me happy, and the sex?" Naomi paused, a disgusting laugh piercing the air. "I feel sorry for whoever is fucking you now. Disappointing is an understatement."

Hannah's stomach sank at those words. How could *anyone* treat another woman this way? Hannah was shocked, to say the least. But more than anything, she felt sorry for Caroline and the fact she'd ever been subjected to a life with this woman.

"Well, it's not your cross to bear anymore. Who I'm dating isn't your business."

"It should be! Women ought to be warned about getting tangled up with you. You may *think* that you deserve more, that fucking fairytale you lived in your own head, but you really don't. You were a terrible wife, and the sooner you realise you have very little to give in a relationship, the sooner you can be happy alone. You and I both know that you'll never make another woman happy. I was easygoing, and you couldn't even get that right."

"Then I'm not sure what else there is to say."

Hannah couldn't listen to much more of this. If Caroline never spoke to her again, then so be it, but she couldn't stand by and listen to such venom from another woman. Hannah released a breath, praying that she wouldn't have to hear another word. God, her heart ached for Caroline.

"Actually, come with me. I'd like to introduce you to Lucille." The sound of heels on concrete encouraged Hannah to peer around the corner. Caroline and Naomi had gone.

With determination her sole focus, Hannah strode towards the bar, smiling at security as she made her way inside. She scanned the bar, her eyes landing on the back of Caroline as the woman from outside introduced her to a leggy brunette. Caroline stood with her arms wrapped around herself, her legs seemingly a little unsteady. *Be strong, Caz.* Hannah willed Caroline to hear her thoughts. *This woman is nothing!*

Hannah did the only thing she could think of. She walked towards Caroline, placing a hand on the small of her back as she leant in. "Sorry I'm late, gorgeous." Hannah turned her body and stood between Caroline and her ex-wife, her back to Naomi. And then she draped her arms over Caroline's shoulders, leaning in towards her ear. "I'm going to kiss you now. Just go with it, okay?"

Caroline's features softened, those green eyes sparkling as Hannah leaned in and pressed her lips to Caroline's. When that perfume reached Hannah's nose, Caroline's lips so gentle, her knees almost gave out on her. Hannah knew she should pull back, she'd done what she'd intended to do, but she found herself sinking deeper into another world with Caroline Baker.

God, this woman could kiss. It was that dreamy 'first kiss' she'd always craved.

Caroline gripped Hannah's hip, pulling their bodies together, her tongue slipping past Hannah's lips. Heat slid to her core, the entire room of people around them fading away, but then a clearing of the throat brought Hannah and Caroline crashing back down to reality.

Hannah grinned as she spun around, taking Caroline's hand. "Sorry, who are you?"

"The ex-wife," Naomi said, standing heavier on one leg, her fiancée now talking with a group of people.

"Oh, I'm sorry. Caz doesn't mention you. I had no idea..."

"Huh."

"I'm Hannah. Caz's girlfriend." She held out a hand, smirking when Naomi chose not to take it. She turned her attention back to Caroline, aware that the woman beside her was truly stunned. But she would apologise profusely once they were alone. "Babe, why don't you go back to our table, and I'll grab some drinks on the way?"

Caroline nodded, forcing a smile. "Sure. Bye, Naomi."

As Caroline walked away, Hannah cleared her throat. "Hey, Caz?"

Caroline turned, frowning.

"You look fucking *amazing* tonight."

Satisfied that she'd done her job, she watched Caroline blush as she turned and walked away, weaving through the crowd. So long as Caroline didn't make a run for it out the back door, Hannah knew they could figure everything out in a few minutes.

Naomi turned her back, edging towards her group of friends, but Hannah gripped her wrist and stepped up to her side. She leaned in, her voice low. "If I find out you've so much as breathed the same air as Caroline again, you'll be watching your back for a long time. And if I hear the shit you talk once more, things won't be pretty. Leave her *the fuck* alone." Hannah straightened her dress and pulled her shoulders back, offering Naomi a full smile. "Have a wonderful night."

Hannah followed the path Caroline had taken a few minutes ago, catching sight of her as she pushed through the bathroom door. Had she just made a huge mistake in involving herself? Right now, she didn't care. She wanted to be sure Caroline was okay, and then she would let her get on with the rest of her night. She had to be here with friends, surely. Hannah pushed through the door, thankful that the bathroom was empty. "Caz?"

A lock released on one of the stalls, but Caroline didn't appear. So Hannah went to her instead, slipping inside the stall. She was met with the most heartbreaking sight, tears streaming down Caroline's face. "Hey, no. We're not doing that. You're not crying over a woman who is nothing more than a complete bitch."

"Y-you shouldn't have done that," Caroline whispered as she lowered her eyes. "She's not stupid. She knows I wouldn't be in a relationship with someone like you. I'm sure she's having a good laugh right now."

"I don't follow..."

"Oh, come on!" Caroline scoffed. "Look at you. In what world would we be dating? I may be aware of the fact that my ex-wife is a bitch, but even I have to agree with her on some things. And as much as I appreciate you stepping in just then, she knows we're not together. And I'm sure I'll hear all about it the next time we bump into one another."

Hannah swallowed, stepping closer to Caroline as her back pressed against the stall wall. "I don't know what you think you see in yourself, but I'm telling you right now that you are stunning. Remarkable. A woman I could quite easily get lost in over and over again." Hannah lifted a hand, brushing a tear from beneath Caroline's eye with her thumb. "Please, don't cry. She's not worth it."

"I used up all my tears for Naomi a long time ago."

Hannah frowned.

"These?" Caroline smiled weakly. "These were brought on by you."

"O-oh." Hannah stepped back suddenly, her heart sinking as she realised what Caroline was saying. "I'm sorry, I shouldn't have." She held up her hand, disappointed that she'd done what she did. What gave her the right to just step right up and claim Caroline's lips? Who the hell did she think she was, strolling into the bar and saving the day? Pathetic, and all down to the fact that she wanted to kiss Caroline. "God, I made a mess of this here tonight. And I completely get it. You didn't want me to do that, but please, accept my apology. I'd *never* force myself onto anyone. I just...I don't know. I thought I was doing the right thing." Hannah dropped her head on her shoulders, sighing. "I'm sorry, Caz. *So* sorry."

Caroline took Hannah's hand, squeezing it. "It's okay. It was shock more than anything else. And you didn't force anything...I reciprocated."

Yeah, Caroline had. And Hannah still felt the tingle of this woman on her lips. "If it means anything to you, it was amazing."

"You're the first woman to kiss me in..." Caroline brought her fingertips to her lips, closing her eyes. "A long time. Naomi stopped kissing me years before I left."

"You can do so much better than someone like her, Caz. I heard everything she said to you outside, and I need to leave this bar tonight knowing you don't believe a word she said. You're so much more than she will ever be."

Caroline lifted a shoulder. "This is my first night out with friends since the divorce, and she managed to ruin it."

"You go back out there and enjoy yourself. Dance, drink, have fun. And you know, while you do it, give her the middle finger from across the room."

"Oh, I wish I had your confidence." Caroline laughed, and then she cocked her head. "Why couldn't I have met you in a different time?"

"Because we were supposed to meet now." Hannah focused on Caroline's eyes, her tears finally drying. "And as much as I know you want to be alone, I'd really like to take you on that date sometime, Caz."

"I don't *want* to be alone."

"Then say yes. Please. Do what *you* want to do." Hannah wanted nothing more than to see Caz smiling; she just hoped it would be with her. "Forget how we initially met, and please say yes."

Hannah really hoped Caroline could forget how they'd met. Because if she could turn back time, Caroline never would have been a client. She would have been the woman who Hannah spotted across the bar, taken in by her natural beauty and those alluring eyes. Surely, regardless of Hannah's job, they could see where things went between them.

But then Hannah's heart plummeted into her stomach. Caroline would never take this further. One, because she wasn't interested in Hannah, and two, because however you looked at it, Hannah *was* an escort.

Her phone started ringing in her bag, breaking them apart. It would be Adele. She had to be here by now. But Hannah didn't want to spend the evening with Adele. She wanted to sit in a corner, having a quiet drink with Caroline and learning everything there was to know about her.

"At least say you'll think about it?"

Caroline offered one of her gorgeous smiles, bringing her hand to Hannah's cheek. "You're far too good for me. Go and enjoy your night, and please, be safe."

Rather than push this, Hannah would do as Caroline asked. She leaned in and placed a gentle kiss on her cheek, her hand settling against Caroline's chest. "If you ever find it in here to let me in, I'll be waiting for you."

CHAPTER 9

Hannah watched from the corner of the bar as Caroline danced with friends, her impeccable smile so full and wide as she laughed with a blonde woman. They looked as though they'd been friends for a long time, and judging by how they all presented themselves, Hannah would say they were colleagues of Caroline's. It made her smile to see Caroline enjoying herself...Hannah just wished she could have been dancing with her, too.

But it wasn't to be. And Hannah would never do anything to make Caroline feel uncomfortable. She'd already caused tears earlier, something she never wanted to see again.

Adele nudged her as she returned from the bar, sliding a tray of shots and two whiskeys onto the tall table Hannah stood beside.

"Are you still watching her?"

Hannah turned around. Adele was right. She'd watched Caroline for the last two hours. "I need to get a grip on myself. She's not even interested. I mean, I kissed her and made her cry. If that's not self-explanatory, I don't know what is."

"I think she's a fool considering how gorgeous you are, but

perhaps she realises the trouble you'd be getting into with one another if she took things further."

"I hate that she was a client."

Adele handed a shot over, motioning for Hannah to join her as she knocked it back. They both winced, coughed, then laughed. "Phew. Now I remember why I hate these things."

"I'm going to need *a lot* of them if we're staying in this bar all night." Hannah didn't usually drink excessively; she wanted to show Edie that there was more to life than her mum having a hang-over because it was the socially acceptable thing to do. But since Edie wasn't usually around on Saturday and Sunday, Hannah was letting her hair down this evening. "What do you think of Caz?"

Adele rolled her eyes. "I think that she seems happy with her friends, and I'm not prepared to stand here all night talking about her."

Hannah nodded, glancing over her shoulder momentarily. Caroline was watching her over the rim of her wine glass. God, she wanted to disappear with her right this second. "Right, yeah. I'm sorry."

"Hey, I'm not having a go. I just don't think this is a good idea."

Then why did being with Caroline feel like the perfect idea to Hannah? If it was so terrible and such a huge mistake, why did it feel incredibly satisfying when they were in one another's company?

And then Adele's eyes widened. "Oh, shit. She's coming over."

Hannah winced. "Probably to ask me to stop creeping her out and watching her." As she turned, Caroline stopped dead in front of her. "Hi, is everything okay?"

"We...wondered if you and your friend would like to join us?" Caroline threw a thumb over her shoulder, and as Hannah looked past Caroline, her friends were grinning and waving. "I'm sure you're probably headed off elsewhere soon, but maybe we could all have one drink together?"

Hannah eyed Adele. "What do you think?"

"We'd *love* to," Adele said enthusiastically, winking as she took the tray of shots and whiskey from the table. "Hannah doesn't speak about you much, so it'll be nice to get to know you."

Caroline frowned. "I don't—"

"That was me being sarcastic. This one here does *nothing* but talk about you. So thank you...for saving me from it." Adele stepped past Caroline, leaving Hannah alone with her.

"I'm sorry about her. She's talking shit." Hannah would have to lie her way through this conversation. Caroline had made it clear that they would never date. It was time to accept that. "But we'd love to have a drink with you if you're sure it's okay."

"You...talk about me to your friend?"

"What? No. She just likes to fool around, you know?"

"That's, um...yeah. I know." Caroline offered a single nod, seemingly disappointed. "Anyway, my colleagues caught you kissing me earlier, and now they want to meet you."

She couldn't lie to Caroline. Hannah could lie to herself all day long but not to Caroline.

"I-I mean, I *was* always talking about you, but I'm trying to stop." Why did Hannah suddenly feel flustered? She was usually confident around women. Perhaps it was the hot and cold Caroline kept blowing. Hannah couldn't keep up. "Look, what am I to be when I walk over there with you?"

"I, uh...yourself?"

"No, I mean, do they think we're together? Is that what you need me to do? Because I will...for you."

"I can't ask you to do that. I haven't even booked you tonight."

It seemed Hannah's plan to deter Naomi was beginning to backfire on her. Hannah hadn't thought about the implications of Caroline's friends seeing her little show, and now Hannah was guessing Caroline wanted her to fake some kind of relationship for the rest of the evening. While Hannah would love *nothing more* than to be on Caroline's arm tonight, she knew it didn't mean anything. Honestly...this was becoming a struggle.

A woman she'd met only two weeks ago...had her world up in the air.

"Caz?"

Caroline sighed, scanning every inch of Hannah's face. "You want more, and I can't give that to you. Expecting you to pretend for me is something I'd never want you to do. I don't want you to walk away from here tonight feeling hurt that I'd done that to you."

Hannah took Caroline's hand at her side, stroking her thumb across her knuckles. "I'd *only* do it for you."

Caroline smiled weakly. "How much, and can I pay you via bank transfer? I don't have that kind of cash on me."

"I don't want you to pay me." Hannah frowned, dropping Caroline's hand. She never wanted Caroline to pay her a penny ever again. "But if that's all I am to you...your escort...then tonight is the first and last time I do this. And then we'll go our separate ways because you're right, it'd be for the best."

"Oh, God no. That's not all you are to me, Hannah. Never."

"Kinda hard for me to see it any other way, Caz. You've just asked me how much I want you to pay me. Have I ever given you the impression that I *only* want to be your escort? When I kissed you tonight, was that how it felt to you?"

"N-no."

"Then how do you want to do this? They're your friends,

your colleagues. You're the one who has to deal with them at work, not me."

Caroline held up her hands as she took a step back. "I'm sorry. Just friends. They can make their own assumptions."

"Fine." Hannah took her bag from the table, puffing out her cheeks. "Just friends."

Caroline stepped out of the bathroom, eyeing Hannah as she stood so confidently talking to Brenda and Sharon. Caroline would give anything to feel an ounce of it, but she had no idea where to begin. Could she ever return to the old Caz? The woman who used to live her life however she pleased, wore what she wanted, and stumbled home all hours of the night without a care in the world? Honestly, the thought of it filled her with dread. Whenever the idea floated through her mind, she felt humiliation building. Humiliation was her default setting, after all.

"Caz?" Brenda waved a hand in front of her. "You with us?"

"Sorry, yes." Caroline laughed, shaking her head.

"We're dancing. And you're coming with us." Brenda dragged Caroline towards the dance floor, spinning her around as her heels hit the large illuminated square to the side of the bar. "Your friend is nice." Brenda shifted closer. "But you and I both know that she's not just your friend, Caz."

"She is."

"Oh, so you kiss all of your friends in bars?" Brenda quirked an eyebrow, stopping as she placed her hands on her hips. "I don't know how my Phil will feel about that."

"Don't worry, Brenda. I'm not going to have my wicked way with you."

"Ha! Imagine!"

Caroline didn't want to imagine. Brenda had been her colleague since the day she started at St. Peter's High School. Colleagues was exactly how it would remain. "Hannah is a friend. There was the potential for a date, but I'm not really in the position for dating."

"And why is that exactly?"

Caroline frowned. "You know why."

"Oh, honey. It's been two years. Live a little. Let go and have fun. It may not go anywhere with Hannah, but you're entitled to a little fun until you find the one for you."

"That's the problem, though. I fear it *will* go somewhere with her."

"Do you have any idea how she looks at you?" Brenda asked, spinning Caroline again and then stepping closer. "Tell me right now what you want to do..."

"I..." Caroline paused, frowning. What did she want to do? Deep down, she knew, but on the surface, everything felt uncertain. "I don't know."

"That's a lie." Brenda looked at her pointedly. "Did she ask you out on a date?"

"Y-yes."

Brenda nodded. "Right. Well, you're going to accept that invitation. That woman is absolutely gorgeous, and I know she wants to see you again. Anyone in this bar tonight can see it."

"She won't want me," Caroline murmured.

"What was that?"

Caroline cleared her throat. "I said she's too young for me."

"Oh, nonsense. All that age stuff is irrelevant. If she makes you happy—she certainly makes you smile—then what does it matter?"

Caroline had a lot to consider. That was all she knew right now.

And then a gentle hand on her shoulder had her spinning

around. Hannah was standing in front of her looking as delectable as ever.

"I'm...headed off."

Why did the idea of that sadden Caroline so much? She was the one who had pushed Hannah away at every given opportunity. "Oh, going somewhere else?"

"Just home." Hannah diverted her eyes to Brenda. "It was lovely meeting you. Take care."

And then Hannah spun on her heel, leaving the dance floor without another word.

Caroline hated watching her go. But she was the one who had cut contact with Hannah. Even though she knew getting tangled up with an escort was a mistake, her heart said differently. Because whatever Caroline did, she still thought about Hannah. About the potentials. The smile she brought to her face. The happiness she felt in her company. And then Hannah had strode in here tonight and been completely selfless in diffusing the Naomi situation. She didn't have to do that, to get one over on Caroline's ex-wife, but she had. Because she cared. Because she wanted Caroline to feel good. To feel...wanted.

Then there was the kiss. Jesus, she'd never been kissed like that in her life.

"You could always go after her since you look so sad watching her leave."

Caroline side-glanced at Brenda. Could she do that? Really?

"Go," Brenda whispered in her ear. "Grab your things and follow her outside."

Caroline shook her head.

"If you don't, you may never get the opportunity again, Caz. Do something for yourself for a change. I know you want to, and I know Hannah wants you to."

How could Brenda possibly know something like that? Unless... "Has she said something to you?"

Brenda lifted a shoulder, and then she guided Caroline back to their table. "She spoke very highly of you. That's all I'm saying. Now, are you going after her or what?"

Caroline inhaled a deep breath, eyeing the door. Hannah was outside using her phone; if she didn't leave now, she probably wouldn't catch her. "Can I? Should I?"

Brenda thrust her coat and bag at her, shooing her away and towards the door. "Call me through the week. I want to know *all* about it."

Caroline turned and strode out of the bar, landing behind Hannah on the pavement. She stared at her back, how her dress clung to every curve, and then she cleared her throat.

Hannah glanced over her shoulder, frowning. "Did you need something?"

"I...I'm sorry. About everything."

Hannah met Caroline's eyes as she turned slowly. If Caroline concentrated hard enough, she would say Hannah had tears in her eyes. "You know what, it's absolutely fine. I got myself into this mess by taking on a job at the agency. I saw a beautiful woman, and for the first time, I struggled to separate the job from my personal life. I won't make that mistake again because, quite frankly, I wouldn't wish how I feel on anyone. But you've done nothing wrong. I started all of this when I crossed the line the night we met."

The truth was, Caroline was struggling to separate Hannah's job from her personal life, too.

"Hannah, I was wondering if maybe we could go somewhere else. Just...you and I?"

Hannah gripped her clutch bag against her, shivering as a light drizzle started to fall. "I really don't have the energy for any more bars tonight. And I think it's probably a waste of time. But thank you for trying."

Caroline stepped towards Hannah, placing a hand on her

forearm. She had no idea what she was doing, but she knew she wanted to see more of this woman. The rain became heavier, pelting them both as Hannah lifted her bag above her head. "Come on, there's a shelter at the side of the bar. They rushed towards it, laughing as they found cover. "That came out of nowhere."

Hannah turned to Caroline. "Kinda like you."

"I'm sorry. I'm a mess. And I find it hard to believe that someone like you would have an ounce of interest in me. But I do want to see more of you. I-if that offer still stands."

Hannah seemed to consider Caroline's words for a moment or two, yet Caroline understood the hesitation. She'd done very little to convince Hannah that she was worth a shot. Caroline hated feeling so unsure about herself, but she had to remember Hannah's heart was on the line here, too. It wasn't all about her.

"I'm not sure you know what you want, Caz."

"I do. I'm...trying. I'm just not very good at this."

With her eyes narrowed, Hannah chewed the inside of her cheek.

Caroline moved in, her eyes sparkling against the street-light. "But I know I can do better, *be* better. So, that offer?"

Hannah grinned as she pressed her body to Caroline's, one hand settling on her hip. Their lips brushed, heat slid to Caroline's core, all sense of control evaporating as Hannah wrapped an arm around Caroline, her hand resting firmly on her backside.

"The offer definitely still stands." Hannah spoke low, seductively. "I'm waiting for a cab right now."

"Any chance I could share it with you?"

"Depends if I'm dropping you off...or coming in with you?"

Caroline took her bottom lip between her teeth, their foreheads touching. She wanted so much to throw her rulebook out the window, to say 'fuck it' and live her life, but it was hard to do. Then Hannah pressed her against the wall of the shelter, her lips brushing Caroline's ear.

"I'd really love to get to know you better, Caz."

"N-now? T-tonight?" Oh, God. The thought of Hannah touching her had Caroline's body fired up and trembling.

"Let me take you home and show you just how much I want to see you again..."

Caroline exhaled a shaky breath, her eyes closing when Hannah trailed her lips down her neck. It was now or never... and Caroline, however uncertain she may feel, really wanted to jump in at the deep end. "Okay."

Hannah squeezed her backside, her breath hot and heavy against her neck. "I want to make you feel good, Caz. I have no ulterior motive here."

Caroline had no choice but to take Hannah at her word.

This could turn out to be the biggest mistake of her life...or it could blossom into something she'd missed for so long.

CHAPTER 10

Caroline took the stairs slowly, her legs turning to jelly as she reached the landing. Her bedroom door was ahead of her—open with the corner of the bed visible—just the sound of Hannah's calm breathing keeping her grounded. She turned to face Hannah, swallowing as those tender blue eyes stared back at her. Caroline had no idea what had led her to bring Hannah home with her this evening, but here they were.

Staring at one another.

Neither sure of what the other expected.

"Are you okay?" Hannah reached out a hand, lacing her fingers with Caroline's. "We don't have to do this if you don't want to, Caz."

God, when Hannah said things like that, it only made Caroline want her more. She tugged Hannah closer, their bodies colliding. "Truthfully, I don't know what I want. But I know with certainty that I'm happy you're here."

Hannah beamed a smile, lifting a hand and cupping Caroline's cheek. Her touch was light, not intrusive at all, the perfect pressure applied by her palm.

If nothing else, Hannah made Caroline feel safe.

"You have the softest hands," Caroline whispered, her eyes closing as she leaned into Hannah's touch.

And then Hannah kissed her unexpectedly, those lips so full and filled with a hope Caroline hadn't expected to feel again in her lifetime. She opened her eyes, gripping Hannah's upper arm, pressing their foreheads together. Nothing about this woman was troubling. Well, nothing except for her job.

Caroline couldn't think about that tonight, though. If she did, she wouldn't go through with anything she hoped for this evening. Yes, Hannah was an escort, but tonight she was here as herself.

But how will you feel tomorrow when she meets a client?

Caroline lowered her chin to her chest, blowing out a breath as she willed her thoughts to shift to the back of her mind. She wanted this, no...she *needed* this with Hannah.

She guided Hannah towards the bedroom, Caroline's back connecting with the doorframe as she stopped and took in the woman she was about to spend the night with. Caroline wasn't sure how impressed Hannah would be, it'd been so long since she'd had sex, but thinking about it was only making Caroline more anxious. And she didn't need that tonight. She'd spent too many years of her life feeling anxious. Or like she wasn't enough. A failure.

But Hannah never made her feel like that.

"Come with me," Hannah spoke so low that Caroline wondered if she'd actually said anything at all.

And then she found herself being pulled into her bedroom and sat down on the edge of the bed. The sad thing about all of this was that it felt totally foreign to her. Being with another woman, having someone look at her like they wanted her, arousal. It had all become foreign, but Caroline had once been a fun-loving, carefree woman who enjoyed life to the fullest.

How the hell had she ended up here? Sitting on the edge of her bed, frightened to breathe.

Hannah took a seat beside Caroline, brushing Caroline's hair from her face. When those blue eyes softened further, Caroline held her breath. "Caz."

"Y-yeah?"

"You...don't want this. Not really."

Wait, what? Was Hannah backing out? Caroline lowered her gaze between them, to the hands holding her own. Of course Hannah was backing out. Why would she want to sleep with Caroline? Boring, lifeless Caroline. "I...it's okay." Caroline slipped her hands out from under Hannah's, smiling weakly. "Really, it's okay. I understand."

"Understand what?" Hannah looked back at Caroline, confused.

Caroline got to her feet, pulling her shoulders back as she wiped a tear from her jaw. She turned back to Hannah, putting on her best smile. "Can I call you a cab?"

"Caz, wait." Hannah joined her in the middle of the room, so close that Caroline could feel her body heat. Right now, that wasn't good. Because all she really wanted to do was feel Hannah against her. But then Caroline knew deep down that she wasn't ready for this. It may have been two years since her divorce, but she wasn't ready to be with another woman yet. "I want to, believe me I do...but not like this. Not so quickly. You deserve better than that."

Caroline relaxed at those words, but only ever so slightly. Hannah was being sweet and respectful, but there had to be a deeper reason as to why Hannah had suddenly decided she didn't want this. Back at the club when they'd been waiting for a cab, she seemed more than ready. "Like I said, it's okay. You don't have to explain anything to me, Hannah."

"I do. Because I don't want you to think I'm having second

thoughts. I mean, I am," Hannah explained, taking Caroline's hand again. "But not because I don't want you. I *really* do. I just...I'd rather do this properly. Not on a whim because of what happened back at the club earlier. I may not know you very well, but you mean more to me than that."

Caroline could cry, but she refrained from doing so. Hannah likely already saw her as weak; to add fuel to *that* fire would be a mistake. "I appreciate that."

"And I don't want you to call me a cab. I want to stay a while. To just be with you. Can I do that?"

"I...yes." Caroline's brow furrowed. Hannah wanted to spend time with her? And without being paid? This felt entirely strange to Caroline. "If that's what you really want."

Hannah smiled, pressing her body to Caroline's. That heat roared through her again, her hands tingling as Hannah moved into a slow, lingering kiss. "It's really what I want. Kissing you... is something beautiful." Caroline trembled at that. Hannah... God, she was divine in every sense of the word. Hannah touched her forehead to Caroline's, stroking a thumb across her cheek. "Okay?"

"O-okay."

"Come on." Hannah guided Caroline towards her bed, slipping her heels off before she made herself comfortable. As she lay down, Caroline stared down at her. "What? I said no sex, not no bed."

Caroline barked a laugh, shaking her head as she slid her own heels off. "Fair enough." Caroline followed Hannah in her position, lying beside her as the room fell silent. While this hadn't been the plan on the way here, Caroline couldn't complain. Hannah was incredibly sweet in wanting to stay a while longer.

"How are you feeling about what happened at the club?"

Caroline turned her head slightly. "About the kiss or Naomi?"

"Both. I guess." Hannah turned on her side, propping her head up in her hand.

"Bumping into Naomi was always going to happen at some point. We live in the same city and enjoy the same bars. I think it was the initial shock of seeing her for the first time in so long. But really, she's not my concern. She hasn't been since we divorced."

"I heard the pain in your voice when she was saying those things to you. Nobody deserves that. I'd say you're better off without her."

Oh, Caroline *was* better off without Naomi. If only she'd recognised what was happening sooner, she wouldn't have put herself through so much of the pain her ex-wife had caused her. "Naomi will never change. I think I realised that quite some time ago. I don't know why I was shocked by the things she said. Perhaps I just thought when the day came to see one another, it could have been different. That she'd see we were happier apart. But well, Naomi only cares about herself, and I know that."

"Well, the things she said were *entirely* inaccurate...just so you know."

"Thank you," Caroline whispered, facing Hannah. "For having my back when it happened. You didn't have to do that for me."

"I did. You may think that the kiss only happened because of the situation you were in, but I don't regret it. I regret how it made you feel afterwards, but I enjoyed it far more than I should have."

"Yeah?" Caroline grinned, thrilled by the thought of someone as young and beautiful as Hannah enjoying being with her. "There really was no hint of Eva in it?"

"None whatsoever. There hasn't been at any point tonight."

"Wow." Caroline was speechless. Not only had Hannah been incredibly honest this evening, she'd done something extremely kind for her. Nobody else would have gotten involved in the Naomi debacle, but Hannah had, and it meant a great deal to Caroline. "I find the perfect woman, and she's off limits."

"I...am?"

Caroline gave Hannah a knowing look. "You know you are, Hannah."

"Because of my job," Hannah said, taking Caroline's hand that sat in the space between them. "I wish things were different. I want you to know that." She lifted Caroline's hand, kissing her skin. "But only you know what's right for you. While I'd love to know you on a much deeper level, this is your life, Caz. If I'm lucky enough to be a part of it in any way, I'll take what I can get."

God, that was painful. Hannah was here, she was saying all the right things, but Caroline couldn't move past the idea that this would be a monumental mistake down the line. While they were alone, like this, life felt significantly better for Caroline. But tomorrow was likely to be an entirely different story.

"I'm sorry."

Hannah shifted closer to Caroline, taking her in her arms. "Don't be sorry. *Never* be sorry for wanting the best for you." And then silence enveloped them once again, just the sensation of Hannah's breath against Caroline's hair soothing her. "I couldn't go through with tonight because it would only end up causing one or both of us pain. But if I'm ever lucky enough to find a job that means we can be together, you better believe I'm taking you on a date."

Caroline swallowed, placing her hand on Hannah's hip as she snuggled closer. "Hannah?"

"Yes?"

Caroline pulled back, staring at Hannah. As conflicted as she felt most of the time, she wasn't sure this could be it for them. Caroline needed more. She needed to see where it went. Because as she lay here this evening, it was clear that Hannah meant something to her. "Do you think this could work?"

Hannah's eyes lit up as she brought a hand to Caroline's cheek. "I'd love to at least try..."

Caroline shifted, resting up on her elbow as she lowered Hannah down to the mattress. Every time she looked at Caroline, her heart stuttered. Every time she was close, Caroline felt as though she couldn't breathe. Instead of thinking too much, Caroline leaned down and brushed her lips against Hannah's. The way in which her body lit up, how her lips tingled at the very sensation of this woman against her...Caroline surely had to give it a chance. Hannah, if she didn't think about her job, was one of the most compassionate women Caroline had ever met.

Hannah lowered a hand to the hem of Caroline's dress, snaking her fingers just beneath the material. Caroline could only moan into her mouth, fighting back the urge to follow what her body craved. If she knew one thing, it was that Hannah was right to stop them from going further this evening. Slow and steady. Who knew where it could lead.

"Hannah?"

"Mm?" Hannah slowly traced her fingertips across Caroline's bare thigh, helping Caroline to lose her train of thought in the process.

"*Fuck*, I want you."

Hannah smiled against Caroline's lips, inching her fingers higher. "All in good time. No need to rush this."

But God, Caroline really wanted to rush in this very

moment. She wanted to be pinned to the bed by Hannah and reminded of the beauty of being with another woman.

"And besides," Hannah whispered as she placed wet kisses along Caroline's jawline, moving closer to her ear, "teasing is all part of the fun."

Caroline practically melted into the bed at those words. Hannah was sexy, that was a given just looking at her, but how her voice dropped...the way her hand felt so delightful against her skin. And those lips, those lips could bring Caroline to the edge in no time at all. "You're bad."

"Oh, Caz. You've no idea."

Hannah woke fully clothed, her hair stuck to the side of her face. A small smile settled on her mouth as she inhaled against the pillow; it smelled like Caroline. She rolled onto her back, side-glancing in Caroline's direction. She slept peacefully, her face free from any of the pain Hannah often witnessed in her company. Last night...God, it should have been different. Hannah should have done exactly what they'd come back to do. Even if she knew it was wrong, she desperately craved Caroline.

But when all was said and done, Hannah just wanted Caroline to see her worth. To know that she could be happy. Because as much as Hannah had delighted in seeing Caroline in a different light once they got comfortable and lay together last night, she had no idea how she would be feeling this morning. It could go either way, and Hannah had to prepare herself for further resistance from Caroline. She really didn't want to see this end, even if nothing had really started. She hoped—prayed—that Caroline may come around to the idea of something more one day. But not just sex. Never just sex.

She watched Caroline for a moment, that long dark hair

splayed across the pillow, her perfectly sculpted eyebrows, the single freckle to the right of her nose. This woman had everything going for her, sheer beauty, so why had Naomi stripped everything from her? Naomi was an attractive woman, they likely looked amazing together, but Hannah couldn't fathom why she would be so cruel, so demeaning, so...truly terrible to the woman she was supposed to love and care for. A woman who likely brightened Naomi's world from the moment Caroline opened her eyes every morning.

But Hannah knew better than to let her naïveté get the better of her. Women, when threatened, could be ruthless. Naomi was clearly one of those women. But Hannah wasn't concerned by the threat she'd handed out last night; Naomi was in a relationship and seemingly happy. Hannah's only hope was that Naomi's new girlfriend didn't fall into the same trap Caroline had. Nobody deserved to go through what the woman beside her had.

Hannah's phone buzzed on the floor at the side of the bed. She shifted as carefully as she could, reaching for it and squinting as the bright screen woke her up once and for all. Great...just what she needed. A booking with a client. It may have only been Juliet, but it was a client, nonetheless.

A mixture of dread and panic set in, but Hannah couldn't show Caroline that she was worried. Yes, she wished Caroline could be okay with Hannah and her job, but it wasn't the case. Even if Caroline had hinted at the potential last night. Hannah knew she wouldn't have a chance with this woman whether she knew about Hannah's plans for the day or not.

Caroline was undoubtedly going to run a mile in the not-too-distant future, and Hannah couldn't blame her.

So Hannah did what was best. She locked her phone, lifted up on her elbow, and pressed a kiss to Caroline's temple. As her lips lingered, she whispered, "you're so beautiful," and then

Hannah slid from the bed, grabbed her heels, and crept out of Caroline's bedroom.

With tears in her eyes, Hannah took a few shaky steps down the stairs, stopped by the clearing of a throat behind her. She exhaled a calming breath, preparing herself for the look of disappointment in Caroline's eyes.

"Were you just going to sneak out and hope you didn't bump into me again?"

Hannah turned; Caroline was leaning against the doorframe. "No, of course not. I mean, I was sneaking out so I didn't wake you, but I *definitely* want to bump into you again."

"You're leaving..."

Hannah lowered her eyes, rolling her lips as she tried to figure out how best to get through the next few minutes. This conversation was one she never wanted to have. It didn't feel right. "I...have to work."

Caroline ran a hand through her hair, a sarcastic laugh working its way from her mouth. "R-right. Of course."

"I don't want to. But I have no choice. It's my only source of income."

"I was so desperate to get closer to you that I completely disregarded the following morning. And I know it doesn't mean anything, it *can't* mean anything, but falling asleep with you last night was surprisingly comforting for me."

Hannah took the few stairs separating them, dropping her heels to the floor. "Hey, I'd rather be here with you. I need you to believe me when I say that. But...this is just work. It means nothing to me. They're just clients, Caz."

Caroline nodded, taking a step back. "Like me. Last night was just the job for you, wasn't it?" Hannah opened her mouth to speak, but Caroline cut her off, holding up a hand. "I get it."

"You know what we had last night was nothing like I have with my clients. You're *not* a client. That's not fair."

"Yeah, well, life isn't fair, Eva."

Hannah's heart tore as Caroline glared at her, those usually beautiful green eyes cold...haunting. She understood that Caroline must be feeling conflicted, last night was unexpected—this morning could have been far worse if they'd slept together—but Hannah didn't deserve this attitude. She needed money if she was going to survive and keep the home Edie had grown up in. Honestly, she was struggling to find the words she needed to convince Caroline that what they had was entirely different from that of her clients.

Caroline turned around, placed her hand on the door, and closed it. Hannah heard a sniffle, followed by a sob, but the fact still remained that she needed the money. She'd already turned down two clients last night so she could spend time with Adele; she couldn't afford to miss out on today too.

"Caz?" Hannah pressed her forehead to the bedroom door, her hand hovering over the handle, but she wasn't sure Caroline wanted to see her face ever again. "Caz, please?"

"Go home," Caroline whimpered.

But that didn't work for Hannah. She couldn't leave Caroline while she was upset. No way. Not after the meaningful night they'd had. She turned the handle, devastated when Caroline sat on the edge of the bed in a baggy T-shirt, looking back at her. "I can't leave you like this."

"Do you stay with all your clients when they're having a moment?" Caroline scoffed, wiping a tear from her jawline. "I should have known. If I hadn't convinced myself last night to bring you here, that everything you said...meant more, then we wouldn't be having this conversation right now. I wouldn't have to think about who you're going to be with when you walk out my door."

Hannah crouched down in front of Caroline, dipping her head to meet Caroline's eyes. "Hey. It *did* mean more. You just...

God, you've no idea how good it felt just being with you last night, Caz. If I didn't have to go to work, I wouldn't be leaving right now. And deep down, you know that."

Caroline feathered her fingertips across Hannah's cheek, smiling with tears in her eyes. "I never got the chance to touch you," she whispered into the silence of the room. "I never had the opportunity to lie with you and look at you and kiss you for longer than we did."

Hannah wanted there to be more opportunities for that to happen. She *needed* it to happen.

"You made me feel so very special last night. Nobody has ever taken so much care. Nobody has ever made me feel how you did." Caroline leaned forward, whimpering as she kissed Hannah softly and then pulled back. "But you have a job to do, and I...well, I can't continue this with you."

"Caz."

"I've spent my life being second best. I had a marriage from hell while my wife was out there sleeping with whoever she pleased. I can't go through that again. Not with you. I'm sorry."

"I-I'm not sleeping with them," Hannah said, frowning. "Please give me a chance, Caz."

Caroline dropped her hand and got to her feet, stepping away from Hannah. "You should go. My sister will probably be here soon, and I don't really want to have to explain all of this to her."

"Fuck," Hannah muttered as she stood up, her entire body heavy. "I mean, that's it? You're not willing to give me the benefit of the doubt?"

"I've been there and done that. And now look at the state of me." Caroline turned her back, staring out of her bedroom window. "I had my chance to find a happy ending a long time ago, Hannah. It ended in tears. I think I'm finally done once and for all."

"Can I come by this evening, and we'll talk?"

Caroline shook her head. "I won't be available. And I'm sure you'll be wined and dined tonight by one of your clients, so have a wonderful night."

"I'll cancel."

"No, you won't. We both know that you won't."

Hannah stared at Caroline's back. If she wanted to be happy, she would have to quit the agency. But in doing so, it would leave Hannah with nothing. She couldn't do it until she found something else to keep her going. But...would Caroline be willing to wait?

"Please leave, Hannah."

Hannah simply nodded; her phone gripped against her chest. "Right. Well, take care of yourself, Caz."

"Yeah, you too."

Hannah turned and stumbled from Caroline's bedroom, grabbing her heels from the landing as she rushed down the stairs. As she'd delighted in Caroline moaning beneath her last night from a single kiss, she hadn't expected this. And of course Caroline would never be expected to just deal with her being an escort, but Hannah had truly believed they could figure it out at a later date. After all, she did bring Hannah back here last night, knowing exactly who she was.

With decisions to make at the back of her mind, and Juliet waiting on a response from Hannah, she sloped out of Caroline's door and exhaled a shaky breath. Her life was falling apart.

And all because of a job she never wanted but never would have met Caroline without.

CHAPTER 11

Caroline fell down into a seat in Joy's office, delighting in the aroma of strong coffee as it wafted towards her. Joy knew something was going on, she'd been looking at Caroline funny since the moment she stepped through the doors to the café, but Caroline wasn't sure she had the strength to discuss it today. From the moment Hannah had left this morning, Caroline had felt dreadful.

It wasn't a hangover, she hadn't drunk as much as she'd anticipated last night, but everything felt hopeless when she considered the possibility of pursuing something with Hannah. She couldn't be the other woman, even if Hannah's job was purely business. Caroline meant it when she told Hannah she'd always been second best because it was true. To prevent that from being the case ever again, Caroline was fully prepared to shut down when it came to love. She couldn't stand the thought of being walked all over again, and if she gave Hannah the benefit of the doubt, Caroline suspected it would happen sooner rather than later.

"Okay, what's going on?" Joy closed her office door, pulling her long dark hair up into a ponytail. She was three years younger than Caroline, but they'd always been ridiculously close. Factor in the likeness of one another, and many people had mistaken them for twins. "You seem jumpy and...hesitant."

"I'm fine. Just a late night."

Joy looked pointedly at Caroline. "Caz, I know when you're lying."

"I...bumped into Naomi last night at Rox's bar."

Joy almost choked on her coffee as she sipped it. "You're joking!"

"No. I'm not. And she was as charming as ever," She didn't know whether to be relieved by Hannah's actions last night when it came to Naomi or whether to be horrified that her escort had heard everything her ex-wife said. It was humiliating enough without other people overhearing. "She still hates me...just so we're clear."

"I think it's time I had a word with Rox. We go way back."

"Have a word?"

Joy nodded. "Why should Naomi have free run of the city, playing the sweet and innocent card in all the regular haunts, while you feel uncomfortable around her? Rox will kick her out if she knows what's gone on in the past."

Caroline held up a hand. While she appreciated Joy's concern and her help, it wasn't necessary. "Please, leave it. After last night and this morning, I don't think I'll step foot in another bar again. I really have zero inclination to socialise anymore."

"Talk to me, Caz. Please..."

Caroline lowered her eyes, chewing the inside of her cheek as she thought about Hannah. That woman had the hands of a goddess, the lips of an angel, and a voice that could arouse Caroline in seconds. But it wasn't to be, and Caroline only had herself to blame. If she hadn't let go of control last night, if she hadn't given in to what she craved, she wouldn't be hiding in Joy's office on a Saturday lunch time. God only knew the state Caroline would be in now if she'd actually slept with Hannah.

"Caz?"

"M-my escort from the other week," Caroline paused, shaking her head. "She overheard Naomi last night outside the bar. She kind of came to my rescue, walking in the bar and kissing me, just so she could get one over on Naomi."

"Okay, I like this woman already." Joy grinned. "Do you think it worked? Does Naomi think you're a couple?"

"I don't know. Probably not. You've seen Eva, she's gorgeous. Naomi wouldn't believe we were together, I don't think."

"Uh, you're gorgeous, too."

"Not Eva gorgeous, though. But that's not what the issue is, not really."

Joy frowned, crossing her legs as she sat back in her seat, her elbow perched on her desk. "Okay, talk to me. I'm not letting you leave until you do."

"Can this...not get back to Gail first? I love her, but I don't want her to push this. You know what she's like."

"Sisters," Joy said, holding out her pinkie.

Caroline smiled, reaching out and linking her own little finger. "Sisters." And then she exhaled a shaky breath, running her palms down her thighs. "Eva came home with me last night."

"Oh, for a nightcap?" Joy raised an eyebrow.

"N-no. She stayed the night."

Joy gasped, clapping when what Caroline was saying finally sunk in. But Caroline didn't feel an ounce of the happiness Joy seemed to feel. "Please tell me you woke up naked with her this morning."

"No. But it almost happened."

"Caz, this is amazing. You're finally realising your worth and putting yourself first. This is huge."

"Hardly. I brought my escort home with me, Joy. What's normal about that?"

Joy laughed, shaking her head. "It doesn't matter *how* you went about it. It's the fact that it happened at all. I knew booking Eva would be good for you. I'm glad Gail twisted my arm about it."

"You...didn't agree at first?"

"Why would I want my sister to book an escort?"

Caroline smiled weakly. "Honestly, I don't know. And I'm beginning to wonder why you went along with it. It's only complicated my life, and I really don't need that right now."

"How on earth has it complicated your life, Caz? You had some fun last night; I'd say you're doing pretty damn well for yourself this weekend. It doesn't matter that you didn't sleep with her. You let go and had a good time."

"With Ha...Eva, it's not like that."

"Then what's it like?" Joy smirked. "I suppose most escorts are good at making people swoon. You're paying them a pretty penny, after all."

"There...was no payment."

"But—" Joy's forehead creased, that smirk she was once sporting turning to a look of concern. "Oh, no. You didn't fall for her, did you? Come on, Caz. People pay her for a shag!"

"Will you keep your voice down!"

Joy held up a hand, scoffing. "I know Naomi ruined your life, and I know you want to get the old you back, but this is *not* the way to go about it."

"Her name is Hannah. She's thirty-four and has a fourteen-year-old daughter. She's honest, she's intelligent, and she's only escorting because she was made redundant from her old job."

"Oh, well, that makes this all okay then."

"She asked me out on a date, and I turned her down. Then last night happened with Naomi, and I just let things get carried away."

"Your escort asked you out on a date?" Joy looked as dumbfounded as Caroline had initially felt about it all. But if an escort wanted to date her, someone who came across all kinds of different people, that had to be an ego boost, didn't it?

"She did." Caroline swallowed down the emotion rising in her throat. "Last night was everything, Joy. She didn't come home with me as an escort. She was there, fully, as Hannah. Every minute we spent together was more mind-blowing than the last, and I don't know how to get her out of my head. And she *really* knows how to kiss."

"If she's so perfect, as *you* claim, why are you trying to get her out of your head?"

"Because the fact that she's an escort still remains. I can't date someone like that, Joy. As much as I wanted to arrange to see her again as she left this morning, I can't put myself through it. Because it would all turn to shit one day, you and I both know that."

"I see your issue. You certainly do pick them, Caz."

Caroline bit back a sob, the thought of Hannah with another woman kicking her in the stomach whenever it floated through her mind. "She left this morning because she had a client. I should have known it would happen, it was inevitable, but I let myself get carried away last night and chose not to think about the following day. I just...defence mode kicked in."

"Oh, dear."

"But that's my own fault for taking her home. And I think I upset her with some of the things I said."

"Well, it makes a change from other people upsetting you, sis." Joy got to her feet, pulling Caroline up with her. "Come here." With their arms wrapped around one another, Caroline felt the weight of this morning crash down on her entirely. She sobbed into Joy's shoulder, tightening her arms around her sister's waist. "Everything is going to be okay."

"I'm not so sure about that," Caroline whispered. "I desperately want to see her, but I know it's a bad idea. I can't change what she does, but I also can't let it go and be with her."

"I know." Joy pulled back, running her thumbs under Caroline's eyes. "Come on. Let's go outside and have some lunch. We'll figure this all out."

Caroline blew out a breath, squeezing her eyes shut and willing her tears to subside. She'd spent far too long crying during lunch with Joy in the past. It was time to put herself first and get on with her life.

"You're not hungry?" Juliet looked up from her plate of food, frowning in Hannah's direction. "Is there something wrong with it?"

"N-no. I'm just not feeling great today. I'm sorry."

From leaving Caroline's this morning, Hannah's day hadn't improved. She'd contemplated cancelling with Juliet, she needed to get her head straight, but it all still came down to the fact that Hannah needed the money. She'd spent an hour before she left home looking through websites with advertising jobs, but still, nothing worth applying for came calling. Maybe Hannah needed to bite the bullet and just apply for anything at all, but she didn't want to work a job that she hated. Okay, she didn't enjoy escorting, not really, but did she hate it? Not quite. It was hard to hate something that sometimes brought in two to three thousand a month.

Still, that money wasn't going to keep her warm at night.

Hannah knew that. And if she had any hopes of being in a committed and loving relationship, she had to find something else. She could have all the money in the world, but without someone to share her life with, she'd be miserable.

"And on the one day when I had plans for you and I..."

"Plans?" Hannah frowned.

"I thought maybe we could finish up here and then go back to my apartment," Juliet said, smiling so fully that it almost blinded Hannah. "I know it's not what we usually do, but who says we can't have a little fun every now and then, Eva?"

Hannah's heart sunk. Juliet was a wonderful client, but part of the reason for that was the idea of not having sex with her. "You've only booked me for two hours." She turned her watch towards her. "And we're already almost an hour in."

"I know, but I'm sure you can fit me in for a while longer." Juliet winked, her eyes cast back to her food.

As Hannah opened her mouth to respond, she looked towards the bar, surprised to find Caroline coming from a door to the left. She walked out with a woman who looked a lot like her, her eyes red and swollen. Caroline dabbed at her cheeks with a tissue, her shoulders slumped, and her legs seemingly struggling to move of their own accord.

Oh, no. Hannah's heart constricted when Caroline looked up and locked eyes with her. And then her own eyes filled with tears when Caroline switched between Hannah and Juliet, a weak smile forming on her mouth. Caroline looked devastated, and Hannah...well, she felt like the world had just caved in on her.

"So, what do you say?" Juliet interrupted Hannah's stare.

"About what?"

"Coming back to my place with me," Juliet said. "I promise we won't be interrupted. I've already diverted my work calls for the next few hours. I thought you deserved more than me running out on you every time we meet. You're going to get a complex soon."

"Honestly, it's fine. I understand you're busy."

"Well, my old personal assistant decided to leave me in the lurch around seven months ago. She was good at her job, and I've had several new assistants since then, but...it's easier to work alone. So, I'm running the lot single-handedly."

"Sorry to hear that." Hannah pushed her food around her plate, eventually dropping her fork to it. "Look, would you be really offended if I declined your offer to come back to your place?"

Juliet frowned when Hannah's voice cracked.

"It's just...I can't give you any more time today."

"Hey," Juliet whispered, reaching a hand across the table and settling it gently on Hannah's wrist. "Please don't be upset. It's not a big deal."

Hannah offered a faint smile. Juliet really was lovely. "I know, but you paid for a service, and to be honest, it's shockingly poor today." Hannah would admit to being in her own head from the moment she arrived at Juliet's table, but she had too much whirring around her mind. Leaving Caroline this morning, God...she'd never seen a look of disappointment and heartbreak like it in all her years. "I'll have the agency refund you."

"No, you won't." Juliet squeezed her wrist gently. "You seem to have a lot on your mind, and as much as I hoped I'd get a few more hours with you today, I understand that you're only human. We all have bad days."

Hannah nodded. What she would give to discuss everything going on for her right now. "I know. It's just..." She stopped herself. Juliet wasn't her friend or therapist. She was a client. Just as Caroline had been. "Never mind. I'm sure I'll be fine next time."

"What is it?" Juliet's soft brown eyes stared back at Hannah, melting her heart. "You've listened to me complain about work for long enough; let me return the favour."

"No, I couldn't." Hannah lowered her eyes, pushing her plate away. She really couldn't stomach the delicious food this afternoon. "Let's just enjoy the rest of our time together here, and next time, I'll make myself available for whatever you want."

Hannah *never* wanted to make herself available for sex. It wasn't who she was...or who she thought she'd become. But here she was, offering her body to keep up with her mortgage payments.

"You don't like this job, do you?" Juliet cleared her throat. "Escorting."

"Honestly? No."

"Then why do you do it?"

Hannah puffed out her cheeks, relaxing back in her seat as she took her cup of coffee from beside her lunch plate. "It was the only thing I felt was available when I needed something financially stable. And in time, I hope to get out of it."

"What was it that you used to do? Or have you always done this?"

"No. I was a personal assistant. I lost my job four months ago when the company went bust. I was one of the lucky ones who managed to keep my job until the very end. They let a lot of people go much earlier than me. You're probably familiar with them. Jenkins law firm?"

"I am. I actually took on a few of their staff. The PA who ghosted me was from Jenkins."

"Oh. Who?"

Juliet wiped the side of her mouth with a napkin as she finished her lunch. "Kirsty Hardacre..."

Hannah laughed. Was the world just trying to piss her off lately? "Ah. My ex."

The thought of Kirsty made Hannah's stomach turn. She'd given her all in that relationship, too much some may say, only for Kirsty to drop *and* ghost her after a three-year relationship. Hannah had no idea Kirsty had worked for Juliet Saunders, so that said a lot about their relationship. Kirsty had told Hannah she was working a general admin job in an office in the city. She never *once* brought up Saunders Law.

"She's good at keeping quiet, I'll give her that."

"Your...ex. Care to say *why* she's an ex?"

"Not really." Hannah smiled over the rim of her coffee cup. "But I'm sorry she left you in the lurch." Seemed Kirsty was good at doing that to people. Whether it was personal or business didn't appear to matter to her. "I'm sure you'll find someone who can replace her one day soon."

"You...wouldn't be interested, would you?" Juliet narrowed her eyes, and then she cocked her head when Hannah stared at her, open-mouthed. "Eva?"

"W-why would you offer the job to me?"

Juliet shrugged. As she did so, Hannah looked over her shoulder to see Caroline staring back at her. "Because I get the impression that you're desperate to move onto something else, career-wise. If it's not something you're interested in, that's absolutely fine."

Hannah glanced in Caroline's direction again, swallowing. If she took on the position Juliet was offering, perhaps things would work out with Caroline. Surely it had to be worth a shot. "I-I'd love to take the position."

"It'll be on a trial basis, of course. But I'm not concerned or worried that you won't be up to the job. How long did you work at Jenkins?"

"Ten years."

"Then George Jenkins must have known you were good." Juliet smiled. "Look, give me a couple of weeks to get a contract together, and my life, and then I'll be in touch. How does that sound?"

Hannah felt a sudden weight slip from her entire body, an excitement building in the pit of her stomach as she spied Caroline once more. But Caroline turned away, leaning forward towards the woman she was with. And then the other woman turned around, looking Hannah up and down. Well, this was going to be fun.

"It sounds perfect."

Juliet beamed a smile, holding out her hand. Hannah took it and shook. "Welcome to my team..."

"Oh. Hannah."

Juliet cocked her head, her smile softening. "I didn't pin you for a Hannah."

"No?"

"No. But I like it. It suits you. Much better than Eva does."

Hannah barked a laugh. "I'm not sure I'll ever be an Eva. But then again, I never *wanted* to be an Eva."

"What will you do until I contact you? Keep escorting?"

Hannah recounted what she had in her bank account at the moment. She had enough to see her over for the next two months' worth of mortgage payments. "You know what? I don't think I will."

"Well, the job is definitely yours, okay? Trial basis, like I said."

"Of course. I wouldn't expect anything more at the minute. But Juliet, thank you. It really means the world to me."

"Small glass of champagne to celebrate?" Juliet quirked an eyebrow.

"Absolutely."

Caroline dropped her handbag beside the coat stand, kicking off her shoes and pressing her back to the wall in the hallway. Today had only gone from bad to worse for her, and seeing Hannah with another woman...drinking champagne, had well and truly thrown her. Her head tossed back as she laughed, the other woman with her hand on Hannah's, the sheer joy as her client had Hannah's undivided attention. In all honesty, Caroline wanted to run from the cafe before she threw up in public.

Joy had offered to come home with her, suggesting they call Gail on the way, but Caroline needed to be alone. So she could fester in this house that had brought her nothing but bad luck... and bad memories. She didn't want to group Hannah in with the bad memories, but just the reminder of last night—Hannah's hands almost touching her in places she'd forgotten existed—Caroline regretted the time they'd spent with one another. It didn't matter how much she'd enjoyed last night; Hannah was with another woman. Client or not.

God, the thought of it made Caroline's stomach turn for the millionth time today. What the hell had she been thinking, getting involved with this woman? Someone who was too young, too free, and honestly...too good for Caroline. Someone who, when all was said and done, had no qualms with being with *her*...and then another the following day. Because even though Hannah had told her she didn't sleep with her clients, Caroline knew it happened from time to time. *Everyone* knew it happened. And judging by the way Hannah was with the brunette at the cafe today, Caroline found it highly unlikely that they would be sitting somewhere discussing the weather. She saw exactly how Hannah's client was looking at her. Hunger, *desire*. She probably felt the exact same way Caroline had when Hannah lured her in.

But then Caroline realised she was being unfair to Hannah. She had willingly gone to that first meeting with her—thrown herself at Hannah—then booked her again. As much as it pained Caroline to say it…Hannah was only doing what she was paid to do. To make Caroline feel good, to give her an experience to remember, to help her forget. Hadn't that been the whole point of Gail booking Eva that night? To remind Caroline what it was like to have attention from another woman? Hannah, or Eva, had done exactly that. She wasn't in the wrong. No, this was all on Caroline.

The doorbell rang, dragging Caroline from all thoughts of Hannah. She steeled herself as she moved towards the front door, tugging it open to be met with two smiling faces. Joy and Gail always had her back.

Still, she wanted to be alone.

She glared at Joy. "I thought I told you I didn't want you to come over?"

"And I thought when we were kids that we always promised to stick by one another."

Okay, when Joy said things like that, it was hard to be angry with her. "Fine. Come in."

Joy and Gail made their way inside, chatting amongst themselves as Caroline remained at the door, enjoying the fresh air against her skin. Maybe they wouldn't stay too long. Or maybe, knowing Caroline's luck, they'd be here for the night. She really didn't have the energy to go over something that would have the same outcome.

"You running away, Caz?" Gail poked her head around the door, grinning.

"No. I'll be in now. Give me a sec."

Gail nodded, closing the door and giving Caroline a moment to herself. She had no idea what she was doing, but the thought of going inside and spending the evening with Joy and

Gail filled her with dread. She felt almost suffocated by their presence.

And then someone stopped at the end of her garden path, a huge bunch of orange roses hiding the face. But Caroline knew who it was. She would recognise *those* hands anywhere.

"I think you got me mixed up with one of your other clients," Caroline said, her voice low. "But whoever they are for should really count themselves lucky."

Hannah lowered the roses, placing a hand on the gate. And then she opened it, stepping towards Caroline. "I wanted to give these to you. An apology. For what, I'm not quite sure, but I feel as though I've hurt you, and I never wanted to do that."

Caroline frowned. She couldn't recall the last time someone had brought her flowers. "Thank you."

"And I know that you probably won't invite me in, I wouldn't expect you to, but I really would love to see you again, Caz."

Caroline's bottom lip trembled as she stroked the rose petals. She wished things could be different, but they weren't. Just seeing Hannah with her client today had devastated Caroline. Even though she knew it was going to happen, it didn't hurt any less. She couldn't put herself through that every time Hannah left. "I'm sorry, I can't take them."

"Please, don't give them back to me. I've never bought a woman flowers, so please...accept them."

Caroline nodded slowly. "They really are beautiful."

"Orange roses signify pride," Hannah said, shoving her hands in her pockets. "And I know we don't really know one another, but I *am* proud of you. For doing something for yourself last night. For letting go and living your life. For refusing to leave when you knew Naomi was at the club. And perhaps you wish you'd never met me or invited me back here, but I just wanted you to know that I'm proud of you, okay?"

Caroline couldn't remain on the doorstep much longer. Hannah was saying all the right things, but Caroline's heart had different ideas. It couldn't take another emotional beating, and Caroline couldn't blame it. "That means a lot. Thank you."

"So, I'll go. I'm sure you're busy. But you know, if you ever want to catch up, have a drink or whatever, I'd really love to hear from you. I had some things I needed to say. To discuss."

Caroline frowned. "Things? About what?"

Hannah's eyes shifted to the right of Caroline, and she shook her head. "Maybe some other time, yeah? You have people over."

Joy suddenly appeared behind Caroline, placing a gentle hand on her shoulder. "Dinner is getting cold."

Caroline smiled inwardly. They weren't having dinner, so that was Joy's way of getting her out of this conversation. The problem was, she didn't want to let Hannah go just yet. "I'll be in now."

"Mmhmm. I'm sure you will."

Hannah lifted a hand. "Hi. I'm Hannah. Nice to meet you."

"Sure. Yeah." Joy said, her tone despondent. "Caz kinda has plans."

Hannah backed up down the path, throwing a thumb over her shoulder. "Sorry, I didn't know. I was just dropping something by."

"Right." Joy kept a hand on Caroline's shoulder, the animosity in the air quite startling this evening. "Well, we should get inside. Plans, like I said."

Hannah nodded as she lowered her eyes, her back connecting with the garden gate. "I'll see you around, Caz. Bye."

Hannah almost fell out of the garden, rushing down the street and climbing into a car. Caroline watched her drive away, sadness swirling around in her belly, but Joy was only doing what was best for her.

"Sorry, but I could see how undecided you were." Joy guided Caroline inside, closing the door. "And while the flowers she brought you are absolutely gorgeous, you need some time to yourself without her around."

"I know."

"Come on. I'll put the kettle on." She took the roses from Caroline, offering a sympathetic smile. "They really are gorgeous."

"S-she said she was proud of me." Caroline frowned, staring at the bright orange petals. "For last night. For enjoying myself. How can someone who doesn't know me be proud of me?"

"Huh. Maybe I have this all wrong," Joy said, glancing up at Caroline. "Maybe she really is into you."

"I don't know how or why. But it doesn't matter. Letting it go is for the best."

Joy sighed, pushing the living room door open. "Yeah. If you say so..."

CHAPTER 12

Caroline took her work bag from the boot of her car, locking it as she traipsed towards the school reception. She'd come in early this morning, a staff meeting forcing her from her bed a little earlier than she would have liked, but it was Monday, and she was prepared to make this week count. Gail had set her up on some dating app that required you to swipe a particular way based on whether you wanted to see the person with the profile, but she'd only had a flick through it last night. Nobody had really caught her eye, but it didn't matter because Gail had also set her up on a blind date with someone she knew from work. Caroline wasn't fond of the idea, but she was done with moping around at home. It hadn't changed a single thing, and neither she nor Hannah had contacted one another since Hannah had shown up at her door with roses.

That alone told Caroline that it wasn't meant to be.

For three weeks, she had gone over the pros and cons of dating an escort. And honestly, her list of cons was much larger than her list of pros. But she'd somehow managed to find the strength to *not* see her time with Hannah as a regret as she initially had. Instead, she'd sent off a thank you into the night sky for bringing someone so caring into her life, if only for the shortest time. Caroline could continue to be angry with herself for taking Hannah home with her, or she could be proud of herself for taking that step with a beautiful woman and enjoying every second of it. She'd chosen the latter. Beating herself up never worked in the past.

As Caroline reached the main entrance, she found a familiar student sitting on a bench, her earphones in. She checked her watch. Edie was definitely far too early for classes.

"Edie?" She waved a hand in front of Hannah's daughter.

Edie smiled as she removed her earphones. "Hi, Ms Baker. Did you have a nice weekend?"

"I did." Caroline took a seat beside Edie, lowering her work bag to the floor. "You're a little early for school. Is everything okay?"

"Oh, yeah. Mum had to work, so she dropped me early. I'm just waiting for the computer room key so I can do some work."

"Your mum had to work? This early in the morning?" Who the hell was booking Hannah at this time, and since when did she extend her working hours to through the week?

"She's got a new job. Today is her first day. I'm really excited for her. It's for a big law company in the city centre."

"Oh! That's fantastic." It really was. It meant Hannah wouldn't have to escort anymore. Caroline knew how much she disliked doing so. "Tell her congratulations from me, okay?"

"I will." Edie swung her legs on the bench, not quite tall enough to reach the floor yet. "Hey, Miss? How do you and my mum know each other?"

"We...don't," Caroline said awkwardly.

"Oh. It seemed you did when she came to pick me up the other week. Sorry."

"I mean, we know each other. But we're not friends. We just

say hello in passing." God, when had Caroline started to think it was acceptable to lie to her students?

"That's a shame. I thought it would have been kinda cool if my mum knew my teacher." Edie laughed, putting one earphone back in. "I got a new playlist. It's really great."

"Well, you enjoy your playlist. I have a meeting to get to." Caroline offered Edie a gentle smile, pushing the fact that Hannah had a new job from her mind. "See you, Edie."

"Bye, Miss." Edie popped her other earphone in, back into a world of her own as Caroline got to her feet.

She wanted to ask more questions, to know exactly what Hannah had been doing for the last few weeks, but Edie wasn't the person to ask...even if really, she was the ideal person to ask.

Caroline pushed through the double doors, heading for the staff room. She would come to terms with the fact that Hannah was now in a steady job. After all, wasn't that what she'd wished for when they first met? Still, she felt a loss sitting low in her stomach as she took the long corridor towards fresh coffee and chatter. Hannah knew the one obstacle holding Caroline back was her work. That was no longer an issue. If she'd wanted to see Caroline again, she would have been in touch.

You barely know a thing about her!

And it was true. Caroline was pining for a woman she didn't know. She was praying for something that could be a disaster, regardless of Hannah's job. And the fact that she was Edie's teacher still weighed at the back of her mind. It wasn't forbidden, not at all, but Edie had enough going on without Caroline steamrolling into her life. The other kids would have a field day if they found out her teacher was dating her mother. And as fond as she was of Edie and Hannah, Caroline wasn't sure she could put Edie through the potential hurt down the line if Hannah and Caroline didn't work out.

"Caz!" Brenda rushed up behind Caroline, falling into step with her as she too hauled a heavy bag on her shoulder. "So, we missed you for the last two weeks..."

"Missed me? I've been right here."

Brenda gave her a knowing look. "Friday nights? You've let us down now for the last two weeks. What's going on? Does that gorgeous *friend* of yours have you tied up for the weekend?"

Oh, Caroline wished... "No. Nothing quite as exciting as that. That didn't work out, as I imagined would be the case."

"Okay, so why didn't you show last Friday?"

Honestly? Caroline had been worried she'd bump into Hannah. Or worse...Naomi. Rather than put herself through the potential pain of seeing either, she'd retreated to the bedroom with a book, not surfacing until Saturday when Joy called about lunch. "I wasn't feeling up to it."

"Right. I see."

"But I had a great night with you and Sharon the other week. I'm simply not one for doing it weekly, you know."

"Okay, so this Friday then? Since you've had a few weeks off from us."

Damn it. Why did Brenda have to put her on the spot like that? Caroline never could say no when faced with something head-on. But this time, she felt different. She'd taken time to work on herself, and she guessed improving on that was about to begin now. "I can't. I already have plans."

"Oh, who with?" Brenda quirked an eyebrow.

"A book."

Brenda groaned, stopping Caroline as they reached the staff room door. "Please tell me you're not turning into one of those people?"

"What people?"

"Lonely. Happy with your own company. Unsociable."

Caroline was actually fine with all of that. It sounded wonderful in her head. “I have a busy week coming up. Friday is the one night I enjoy having to myself. But the week after, I will definitely join you and Sharon at the bar.”

“Promise me?”

Caroline offered a single nod. “I promise.”

“Okay, well, that satisfies me.” Brenda grinned, stepping into the staff room. “Now come on. I’ll make us a cuppa while John bores us all to tears.”

Okay, this was more like it.

Hannah was on her lunch break, walking around the city while she pondered how delicious her lunch was going to be. If she could find an empty bench, she wouldn’t have to think about it much longer. Juliet had told her to take an hour today, giving Hannah the opportunity to process the impressive new job she had. Juliet really was wonderful, a brilliant boss and perhaps a friend. Hannah couldn’t thank her enough for giving her an opportunity to get out of escorting.

But this worked for her. And the pride Edie had in her eyes this morning as she dropped her daughter at the school gates was enough to make Hannah’s heart burst from her chest. Edie was her number one supporter; her admiration would always light up Hannah’s world.

Then there was Caroline.

For the last couple of weeks, Hannah had been to the local bar and Joy’s café. But Caroline hadn’t been around whenever Hannah was. She’d even sat in the bar the Friday before last for the entire night, hoping to bump into her. She had Caroline’s number from a previous conversation, but Hannah wasn’t sure it was wise to contact Caroline. Her sister had made it painfully clear that she wasn't fond of her, even staring at her from behind the bar in the cafe for the last two Saturdays, and really...Hannah didn't want to insert herself into Caroline's life anymore if it wasn't what she wanted.

It didn't matter what Hannah, herself, wanted. Caroline was the most important person in all of this.

She spied a bench, rushing towards it and sitting down. The sun shone against her face as she tilted her head back and smiled, only a light breeze whipping around her as she unwrapped her chicken salad sandwich. Edie had taken the same thing for lunch, both of them preparing it last night when her daughter arrived home from spending the weekend with her dad. She didn't like the idea of Edie sitting around at school earlier than she needed to be there, but Hannah wanted to be sure she arrived at Juliet's office early this morning. It wouldn't be required any other day, she didn't think, but this morning had been important for her. It meant the end of working weekends...being in the company of someone she wouldn't usually choose to spend her time with. Minus her stint with Caroline, of course. That woman could demand her attention time and time again.

Hannah bit into her sandwich, frowning when she focused on the woman walking towards her. Her heart fluttered in her chest...*Caroline.* She spoke animatedly on the phone, laughing as she strode along the pavement, the sun kissing her beautiful skin. Hannah wanted to look away, to run and hide, but she found herself staring at Caroline in her navy blue sleeveless dress, those shapely arms and legs naturally tanned and muscular. Her nude heels, that long dark hair flowing freely... God, this woman was a picture of perfection.

And then Caroline stopped dead as their eyes met, her lips parted slightly. She lowered her phone from her ear, offering the smallest of smiles. "H-hi."

"Hi, Caz." Hannah placed her sandwich back in her lunchbox, rubbing any crumbs from her hands.

"I, um...h-how are you?" Caroline asked, hesitantly taking another step towards Hannah. "You look well."

"So do you," Hannah said, her voice husky as she trailed her eyes up and down Caroline's figure. She'd always loved curvy women; Caroline was no exception to that. "You're not working today?"

"Yes. I've been in this morning." Caroline explained, lowering her eyes to her phone. "I have an appointment with the doctor, and then I'm..." Caroline frowned, exhaling a breath. "Then I have a date."

Ouch. That stung. But Hannah's job was done here. Caroline had hired her to help with dating, and here she was...going on a date.

"I bumped into Edie this morning. She says you have a new job."

Hannah felt that pride escalate again. "I do. I'm working for Juliet Saunders. Personal Assistant."

"Ah. That's who you were with at Joy's cafe. I thought I recognised her. Well, congratulations. That's quite impressive."

Everyone knew who Juliet Saunders was. She was one of the most brutal lawyers in the north. And Hannah knew Caroline had seen them together at the café the day she'd left to be with her client. Back then, the idea of being with someone else after she'd spent the most wonderful night with Caroline hadn't felt great, but the opportunity she'd gained out of it had brushed that aside. If she hadn't gone to that booking, she wouldn't have a new job.

Hannah lifted a shoulder. "She gave me the opportunity to get out of escorting. I'd have been a fool to turn down her offer."

"And does she still get the benefits she once had with you?"

Caroline winced as those words left her mouth. She lifted a hand. "I'm so sorry. I didn't mean..."

"Yes, she used to be my client. But she's not anymore. She is my *boss*." Hannah sunk back into the bench, disappointed that Caroline thought of her that way. "So, no. She's not fucking me in her office when she feels like it."

"God, Hannah...I didn't mean it like that." Caroline stepped closer, but Hannah held up her hands, scoffing. "I'm sorry."

"It really doesn't matter what you think of me, Caz. I'm kinda over it all now."

Caroline frowned. "Over it?"

"Wanting to pursue you. Wanting to know you and be with you." Hannah might have been slightly exaggerating, but she wouldn't give this woman—or *any* woman, for that matter—the satisfaction of hurting her. "I showed up with flowers, hoped you'd call, but it's been three weeks, and I got nothing from you. Still, I understand. I'm not the kind of woman you'd consider yourself with, and that's okay. Your sister is frightening enough to encourage me to back off."

"My sister? Has she said something to you?"

"She didn't need to. I've stopped booking a table at the café because she stands around watching me. As much as I don't find people intimidating, it would be nice to enjoy lunch without feeling uncomfortable."

"I-I had no idea," Caroline said, taking a seat on the bench beside Hannah. "She can be...overprotective at times."

"Well, she has nothing to worry about. I'm throwing in the towel, but I guess you already hoped I had."

"Actually," Caroline paused, running her palms down her thighs. "I wanted to call. There were a couple of times when I considered it, but I didn't know how to reach you."

"You had my number."

"I didn't. When I told you I'd delete them, I foolishly did so."

Hannah's brows rose with surprise. "You're certainly very honest."

Caroline smiled weakly. "Respectful."

Hannah checked her watch, disappointed that she didn't have as long left on her lunch break as she thought she did. She finished her sandwich, neither of them willing to break the silence that had settled between them. But then Hannah looked in Caroline's direction, finding tears in those pretty green eyes. "Oh, please don't be upset. I think we can both agree that this was just a big mess from the beginning."

"If that's how you see it, fair enough." A tear slid down Caroline's cheek as she got to her feet. "Take care, Hannah. I'm really happy you took the job. I hope it all works out for you." Caroline slowly walked away, her head down as Hannah watched her shoulders shake ever so slightly.

"Hey, Caz?"

Caroline turned, wiping tears from her jawline. "Yeah?"

"Good luck with your date. Show them the real you, and they'll love everything they see."

With the tiniest smile on her mouth, Caroline simply nodded and walked away. Hannah never wanted to make Caroline cry, she never wanted to hurt her in any way at all, but this had been doomed from the moment they'd met. And now that Caroline had a date, Hannah could live with the knowledge that she'd likely meet a woman who could complete Caroline and give her everything she wanted. Hannah may believe that she could be that person deep down, but Caroline was moving forward with her life, and that had to be good enough for her.

It was all she ever wanted for that broken woman she'd met.

A happy ending.

CHAPTER 13

Sometimes Caroline wanted to improve her social and love life, sometimes she wanted to be the woman she once was, but today was not one of those times. That date she was supposed to have on Monday...well, it didn't happen. She hadn't stood her up—that wasn't the kind of woman Caroline was—but she had sent a message explaining that she'd been held up at work and wouldn't make it to the restaurant. Gail hadn't contacted her to ask why it never went ahead, and Caroline was hoping she wouldn't do so in the near future.

Seeing Hannah on Monday had thrown her completely. While Caroline hadn't quite known how she'd react to seeing Hannah again, she imagined it may have ended better than it had. It hadn't been her intention to offend Hannah when they spoke about Juliet. God, it really hadn't. But Caroline had done so, and now she had to live with that. Hannah, beautiful and intelligent Hannah, deserved better than that.

Swallowing down her emotion, Caroline shot to her feet when the doorbell rang. She'd invited Brenda over. It appeared she needed someone to speak to now that Hannah had a new job. Gail would only tell Caroline to go for it. Joy would try to deter her. So Brenda was perfect for this. She had no reason to sway Caroline at all.

She approached the door and cleared her throat. How would Brenda react to the news that Caroline had been paying for an escort? She opened the door, knowing she was about to find out. "Hi. Come in."

"How was the date?" Brenda strode through the door, turning as she reached the living room.

"It...didn't go ahead."

Brenda's brows drew together. "Oh. Is everything okay?"

"Of course. I wondered if I could run something by you. I know I was vague on the phone earlier, but I didn't want to get into it too much."

Brenda shed her coat, hanging it up in the hallway. As she smiled, Caroline exhaled a breath. Thank God she had someone to talk to. "Come on. You look like you really need a friend tonight."

Caroline wouldn't argue with that. She absolutely needed a friend.

"So, what's going on?"

"Come into the kitchen. I'll put the kettle on." Caroline busied herself, trying to shake the anxiety from her. Brenda wasn't a judgemental person. Caroline had never once been given the impression that she would be disappointed. "So, you met Hannah last month..."

"Ah. Your friend...that's not really your friend." Brenda winked, leaning against the counter as Caroline prepared two cups of tea. "How is she?"

"She's good, I think. At least, she appeared to be when I bumped into her on Monday. But we're not friends. We're not...anything."

"Caz, sweetie, I know you feel as though you're not in a

place where you can find a relationship, but you don't have to lie to me. I want you to be happy."

"No, it's true. We're not anything right now. And I'm not sure we ever will be." Caroline placed two cups on the dining table, pulling out a seat for Brenda. They sat facing one another, but Caroline felt distant from everyone and everything lately. "It's complicated."

"But does it really need to be?"

"It's been complicated from the start, but now...no, it doesn't need to be." Caroline dragged a hand through her hair, sighing. "I think I've missed my chance, though. Which isn't really surprising given the fact I don't know how to even behave around women anymore, but I would have liked to have made amends."

"You've fallen out." Brenda nodded, lifting her cup of tea.

"Can I be completely honest with you...no judgement?"

Brenda cocked her head. "Caz, we've been friends for a long time. You know you can talk to me about anything. We may not have known how dreadful life was for you during your marriage, but I want you to know we would have been there for you then, too."

Caroline bypassed the comment Brenda was making regarding Naomi. She was the least of her worries right now. "Hannah is...*was*...an escort. That's how we met."

"Oh." Brenda's brows shot up, but a slight smirk was present on her lips.

"I know, I know. It was a ridiculous thing to do. Gail pushed me into it, and while it was really lovely getting to know Hannah, I couldn't take it any further."

"So, you didn't go home with her that night after the bar?"

"Oh, I did. She stayed over, but nothing really happened. Then the following morning, she had to leave because a client had booked her..."

"Ah. I see your issue."

"It was always going to be difficult, but since that night, she's all I think about. I cannot get her off my mind. Still." Caroline clasped her hands under her chin.

"Still what? You clearly want to see Hannah again, Caz. And from what I remember, you couldn't keep your eyes off one another at the bar. If she makes you feel that way after everything you've been through, why not give it a chance? And I know. Believe me, I know how difficult it must seem when you think about her being an escort, but that's just a job...and quite frankly, life is too bloody short to worry about that stuff."

"That's the thing. She's not an escort anymore. She's working for one of the best law firms around now."

Brenda frowned as she lowered her cup. "Then why are we having this conversation?"

"I don't know. So you can tell me what I should do?"

"Oh, Caz. Only you know what you want to do. You've spent so long being guided by...her, but now you're free to live your life on your terms. Do that, sweetie. And I'll support you all the way."

"There's another thing," Caroline said, gripping her cup tight. "Hannah's daughter is a pupil at the school."

"So?"

"So, if this all goes wrong, I'd hate for it to affect Edie."

"Edie Caffrey? Your star pupil?"

Caroline smiled. Edie always brightened her day the moment she walked into the classroom. She was often the first to line up outside her form class, the first to put up her hand to answer a question, and the first to help another student. Hannah should be happy with the knowledge that her daughter was one of the kindest, most compassionate children at the school. "Yes. Edie Caffrey."

"Well, this is like a match made in heaven if you ask me."

"It...is?"

"The mother loves you, the kid loves you...you just have to love yourself enough to make the right decision. I can see how torn you are, Caz. But this is your chance to be happy. She's the first woman since Naomi, right?"

"Right."

"And why is she the right one for you? Why, two years on, have you put yourself on the line for her?"

"Because the connection is...it's consuming. I feel like an entirely different person when I'm with her. She doesn't pressure, she doesn't demand, she's just there...making me smile. And she has a great personality. Considering she was once paid to look good with other women, she's quiet and unassuming. I really like that about her."

"Caz," Brenda paused, reaching across the table and taking Caroline's hand. "Please, for the love of God, try again with her."

"I blew it on Monday. I said something awful to her, but I didn't mean it how it came out. Her new boss is an old client. I made a comment about still getting the benefits she once did, and she assumed I meant they were sleeping together. When really, I purely meant that she was lucky enough to still be seeing and spending time with Hannah. Probably having working lunches with one another. Something I wish I had with her. Not this fucking woman she's working for."

"Jealousy. I've never seen that from you before. But it means you care."

"Oh, I *am* jealous. But what's the point in feeling that way? Hannah has known about this job since we stopped seeing one another, and she chose not to tell me. I only found out because Edie was at school early on Monday, and she told me."

"I don't follow."

"Hannah knew I couldn't see her while she was still escorting. Not only because it wouldn't feel right to me, but I wasn't sure being her child's teacher *and* her client was a good idea."

"O...kay."

"Well, this job surely didn't just land in her lap last Sunday evening. She must have known about it. If she wanted to see me again, she would have called me. I don't know. Maybe I'm just overthinking it all."

"Maybe you are, but I can understand what you're saying." Brenda regarded Caroline with a sympathetic smile. "You've had no contact at all?"

"Not since she turned up here the afternoon after we'd spent the night together." Caroline hadn't known what to do in that moment. Women didn't bring her flowers, and they certainly didn't tell Caroline they were proud of her. "She brought me a beautiful arrangement of orange roses."

Brenda slid her phone from her pocket, narrowing her eyes as she typed on the screen. "Hmm. Orange roses signify pride."

"I know. She told me she was proud of me." Caroline's voice broke as she spoke those words. She still couldn't believe just how perfect Hannah was. "When we saw one another today, she said she hoped I'd call her. And I know I should have, but I couldn't when I knew it wouldn't change anything. It's been a few days since I found out she has a new job, and now that I know, it only makes me want her so much more."

"Then you know what you have to do."

Caroline swallowed. "W-what?"

"Make amends, Caz."

"Okay, so about the trip I have to make next month. I know you'll probably struggle with childcare, but if you're able to make it, I could really use you with me."

Hannah sipped her wine, pushing her plate away. She could get used to working dinners with Juliet. It was a far cry from her last job. It seemed much more pleasant when you didn't feel as though you had to perform as the perfect dinner guest. "I'll call my mum. She'll take Edie for me."

"I wasn't sure if it was possible. When I asked you to come away with me last time, you couldn't make it."

Hannah nodded. "Yeah, but this is a completely different job to my last one. I'm your assistant, Juliet. Not your escort. If we have to leave the city for a case, then I'll be there. I promise."

"Perfect." Juliet pushed her own plate away, relaxing back into her seat. "So, how are you finding your first week?"

"I love it. It's nice to get back into doing something I enjoy."

"I have to say, I'm impressed by your work. I'm not sure your trial period will last very long at all."

This week had been strange for Hannah in some ways. While she'd relished getting back into a professional setting and a routine, seeing Caroline on Monday had shifted something inside her. "I'm happy to hear that. I'd love to stay at the office if you think it's something that could work."

"You know what you're doing. I don't have to hold your hand. That, for me, is the most important thing." Juliet eyed Hannah across the table, sipping her wine. "But I do have to ask something."

"Ask away!"

"As this week has gone on, you've been...distracted. Not with your work, that's impeccable, but you seem to be in your head a lot. Quiet."

Hannah chewed her lip as she cast her gaze on the table. She knew she'd felt off, but she didn't think it was obvious to the people around her. It was Wednesday evening, Caroline continued to infiltrate her every thought, but Hannah didn't know what to do for the best. Caroline was probably laughing and joking right now with the woman she'd gone on a date with on Monday. "I'm sorry. That's my personal life getting in the way. It won't happen again."

"As I said, I'm not concerned about your work. But I am entitled to be concerned about you. So, I'm here if you need to talk."

"It's an ex-client."

"Giving you grief?" Juliet quirked a brow, the lawyer in her flashing in her eyes. "Is there anything I can do?"

"No. She's not giving me grief. Not at all. We kind of *almost* crossed the line while I was her escort, and we both wanted more."

"Then what's the problem?"

"I didn't have this job at the time. It was actually you who booked me the following day. It didn't go down very well when I woke up beside her and had to leave because of work."

"Ah. I see. She wants the good parts but not the rest?"

Hannah frowned. What did Juliet mean? "I don't—"

"You slept with her, and while she probably thought she could have her cake and eat it...the realisation of what you do set in."

"No, it wasn't like that. We didn't sleep together. She's been through a lot in the past, and she felt safe with me. I felt safe with her, too. I wouldn't expect anyone to stay with me while I'm being paid by other women, but it almost happened...until it didn't."

"And now?"

"Well, I'm sitting here with you. And as lovely as this has been, I know where I'd rather be."

"You miss her..."

Hannah twisted her wine glass on the table, swallowing down the emotion lodged in her throat. This was a business dinner. She shouldn't be confiding in Juliet. "Let's talk about something else. This isn't the relationship we have. You're my boss."

Juliet sat forward, staring directly into Hannah's eyes. "Do you miss her, Hannah?"

"So much." Hannah's bottom lip trembled, tears stinging her eyes. "Far too much."

"Then as your boss, I'm telling you to fix it with her."

"And not as my boss?"

Juliet sunk back in her seat, sighing. "I'm jealous that she has the potential to see you naked."

"O-oh." Hannah swallowed, and then she cleared her throat. She'd never been attracted to Juliet. Yes, she was beautiful, but she'd never felt that way towards her.

"Oh, come on. You're absolutely gorgeous, Hannah. Forgive me for finding you attractive. Why do you think I invited you back to my apartment the last time I booked you?"

Hannah smiled weakly. "To chat?"

Juliet laughed from deep within her belly, settling Hannah a little. "No. I had no plans to chat. But I'd much prefer you as my employee than anything else. I think you're going to be invaluable to me."

"Thank you. I appreciate that. I still can't believe you gave me a job."

"When we were sitting together that day, I saw in your eyes that you didn't want to be there. And I know it was nothing to do with me, so I wasn't offended. Then you said you'd worked in law before, and I knew it was meant to be. I think this is going to be a very good working relationship, Hannah. I'm looking forward to it."

Hannah lifted her wine glass, clinking it to Juliet's. "Me too."

"So, this client turned almost potential girlfriend. What are you going to do?"

"I think I'll sleep on it and maybe contact her at the weekend. I'm not really in a position to see her before then anyway with work and having my daughter home. Once she's gone to her dad's at the weekend, I'll call Caz. She may not have my number, but I have hers. And I know where she lives if all else fails."

Juliet groaned. "God, why isn't there a woman out there desperately wanting to seek me out?"

"There is. You just have to wait for her."

Juliet bulged her eyes as she puffed out her cheeks. "Well, I fear I'll be waiting a very long time."

"No, I don't think so. And now that you have me as your wingwoman, I'll help you find someone."

"I'd like to think it's possible, but my hours demand far too much of my attention. *I* wouldn't date me, so that says a lot."

"Give it time. You never know when the woman of your dreams will fall into your lap."

"Never mind me. My love life is hopeless. We need to figure out how to get you back in with this woman you're infatuated with."

"Oh, it's not infatuation. I'm not sure what it is, but it's far more than that."

Juliet's brows rose. "Really?"

"Yeah. But it's going to be a slow process if it ever happens. There's a lot to work through."

Juliet tipped her wine glass towards Hannah. "I admire that. Not many people would willingly take on a woman with a lot of baggage. But you...you're a rarity."

"I just believe that everyone deserves a chance to be happy. We could be gone tomorrow. We deserve love while we can grab it."

"Cheers to that!"

CHAPTER 14

The silence of the room didn't do much to settle Caroline's thoughts. She had been pacing for the last twenty minutes, Hannah the only thing on her mind as the week wore on. Right now, she was at a point of craving Hannah. Her voice, her gentle smile, her incredible hands. She hated feeling like this, out of control, but Caroline could barely refrain from calling her. That was clear this afternoon when she stole Hannah's number from the system at school *again*. She'd thought about showing up at Hannah's home, but she couldn't deal with rejection face-to-face, and she also didn't want to disturb Edie if she was home.

Caroline pressed her back against the kitchen counter, staring at her phone in her hand. She had a message on the screen from the woman she'd cancelled her date with on Monday, but Caroline didn't want to open it. That date would have been dreadful in every way because it wasn't with Hannah.

She swiped it from the screen, deleting it. Caroline couldn't deal with Grace tonight. It was Hannah her focus needed to be on. Because she had to get this right. Caroline was going to call

Hannah. To tell her how she was feeling and what she wanted. And if it meant there was any hope of something more with her, Caroline would do everything she could to show Hannah she was genuinely interested. Monday lunchtime had been a disaster, but Caroline felt as though she was in a better place as the end of the school week came around. And with Brenda's support, it had only reminded her that she *could* do whatever she pleased.

With a shaking hand, Caroline exhaled a deep breath and punched in Hannah's number. It started to ring, sending Caroline's heart rate through the roof.

"Hello?"

Caroline cleared her throat. "Hi, it's Caz."

"H-hi." Hannah sounded confused, but Caroline could hardly blame her. She'd wasted enough of this woman's time in the past. Hannah probably expected the very same thing tonight. "Is...everything okay?"

"I wanted to apologise for Monday. I shouldn't have walked away how I did."

"Caz, it's fine."

"No, it's not," Caroline paused. "And I just needed to say a few things to you." She lifted and then relaxed her shoulders, trying but failing to release the tension. "I want to try again with you. And maybe I'll mess it all up along the way, but I feel I owe it to myself to try, Hannah. I've spent the entire week thinking about you, and quite frankly, I'm tired of wondering what could possibly be between us. I understand that I say one thing then another, but I need to see where this goes."

"Caz..."

"In the short time since we met, you've made me feel like an entirely different person. For a start, I smile more. That's usually when I'm thinking about you, but does it really matter why? Considering I rarely felt happy, I'm taking whatever I can get. And I'm hoping it's going to include you. You just...I...I'd really love to see you again, Hannah."

Hannah didn't speak. She didn't make a sound.

"I understand that you're probably torn, I don't blame you for that, but if you'd just consider it, I'll wait to hear from you. It would mean a lot if you gave me another chance. I know you asked that of me the other week and I wouldn't entertain the idea, but I'm hoping if you can forgive me, we can try again." Caroline was on a roll for the first time since she met Naomi. She may as well continue. "I want to explore. W-with you. I want to discover the life I've been missing, the fun I could have been having, and I only want to do it with you, Hannah. You're the only woman to turn my head in as long as I can remember... so please, if you decide you want to see me again, call me."

"Caz, now isn't really a good time."

Caroline frowned. That was all Hannah had to say? Yeah, she *had* blown it.

"Did you want to order in? Maybe have a glass of wine?" Another woman spoke in the background, sending Caroline's heart directly into her stomach.

"Sorry, I'll be right there. Just a minute." She heard the muffled response as Hannah covered the phone with her hand. "One sec."

And then Caroline clenched her fist and brought it to her mouth, praying her tears remained at bay.

"Caz, can we do this another time? I'm a little busy at the minute."

Caroline shook her head, her bottom lip trembling. She wouldn't cry on the phone. No way. "That won't be necessary. I'm sorry for disturbing your evening. H-have a lovely weekend. Bye, Hannah." She cut the call, calmly placing her phone down on the counter.

And then the tears flowed so freely that Caroline didn't

bother to try and stop them. Taking a chance had felt good for once, and now it was obliterated. Hannah...had met someone else. While Caroline loved knowing Hannah was thriving in her personal life and her career, it only reminded her of everything she craved. She had the job she'd always wanted; she'd worked hard to get to where she was, but Caroline's love life continued to elude her.

Leaving her phone in the kitchen, she reached for a glass and a bottle of wine and moved sluggishly into the living room. It looked like she did have plans with that book after all.

Hannah gathered the paperwork she'd been wading through for the last two hours, slipping her heels on where they sat under her desk. Juliet had asked her to work late, she had a big court case coming up, and the overtime pay had more than convinced Hannah to do so. It seemed like a good idea since Edie was with her dad, but then she'd received a call from Caroline, and suddenly, Hannah didn't want to be working late on a Friday anymore.

She put the papers back into the files they belonged in, crossing the room and slipping them into Juliet's filing cabinet. With a heavy heart, her emotions all over the place, Hannah sighed and turned towards the door. Juliet was watching her from the doorway, a sympathetic smile on her mouth. "You're sure she sounded upset?"

Hannah nodded. "She was definitely upset."

"Then perhaps you should head over there and make things right with her. From what you've said, it's clear you're very fond of her, Hannah."

Could Hannah show up at Caroline's? Would it be worth it

in the long run? She didn't know, but it was always worth a try. "And if her sister is there like last time?"

Juliet pushed off the frame, grinning. "You work for me now. And we don't take shit from anyone. Siblings of potential love interests included."

Hannah would love to have that confidence Juliet possessed. It was frightening at times, but Hannah had spent the entire week in awe of her boss and how she carried herself. Hannah had always felt confident, but Juliet's confidence was something else. "Maybe I should just send you over there."

"I don't think that would go down very well," Juliet said, collecting her coat from the hanger in the corner of her office. "But if you need any tips on the way over, call me."

"I think if I'm going to do this, I have to do it all myself. Caroline has been through a lot, and she deserves the chance to sit down and discuss whatever the hell is going on between us. Or not, at the moment."

"I'm sure she'll be happy to see you, Hannah. Just be yourself and be honest. There's no more you can do than that."

Hannah blew out a breath, offering Juliet a nod. "Right. It's now or never." As she approached the door, she turned back. "Thanks for not telling me to sort this out outside of work."

"Oh, I expect you to sort your personal issues out when you're not working, but you stayed back to help me out this evening so I can let it go this once. Now, get out of here before I find something else for us to work on."

"See you Monday."

Juliet nodded. "Nine. Not a moment later. And Hannah?"

"Yeah?"

"If it all goes wrong, I'll be at the bar on the corner of Raven Street. You're more than welcome to join me."

"Thanks. But don't expect to see me. I'm not leaving until she speaks to me. Until we've figured everything out."

Juliet laughed, following Hannah out the door and turning out the light. "I wish all women were like you. Have a wonderful night with your girlfriend."

Oh, if only Caroline was her girlfriend. But Hannah hoped she would be someday. "Goodnight, Juliet. See you Monday."

Hannah placed a hand on Caroline's garden gate, staring up at the huge Victorian house as it towered over her. She hadn't realised how big it was on the previous occasions that she'd visited, but Hannah remembered it being warm and inviting. It may look intimidating, but the woman who owned it was a sweetheart. One who had enough baggage to last a lifetime. But the baggage wasn't Hannah's concern, and it never would be. The issue she faced was trying to explain to Caroline that her call earlier wasn't anything untoward. Even if it had been, Hannah wouldn't exactly be in the wrong, but she'd heard the sniffle as Caroline ended the call, and the thought of Caroline being alone and upset weighed Hannah down.

If she could have been here an hour ago, she would have, but Hannah had a serious, well-paid job now. That should excite both her and Caroline, but in this moment, Hannah had no idea what to expect when she knocked on Caroline's front door. The only thing she knew with certainty was that she was tired of not seeing more of Caroline. When they'd bumped into one another on Monday, Hannah hoped for something... anything, but Caroline had thrown her just by walking down the street.

She opened the garden gate, strode towards the porch, and knocked loudly.

After a couple of moments, the lock clicked, and the door opened. Caroline stared back at her; those gentle eyes tired. She offered a small smile in Caroline's direction, lowering her eyes when Caroline continued to stare. Honestly, Hannah wasn't sure she was welcome here.

She took the final step, stopping in front of Caroline. So close that she could smell her soft scent, but emotionally a million miles away. Caroline looked gorgeous in her figure-hugging dress, barefoot, with her dark hair swept to one side. God, Hannah had been a fool to not contact her sooner. She'd missed those emerald eyes. "I never saw you coming. I never imagined you, and I *never* expected you. But here you are, constantly in my head, always on my mind, and I don't ever want to go back to a life where you don't exist, Caz. Never." Hannah inched forward, taking one of Caroline's soft hands. "I have no idea where we go from here or if you'll even want me down the line, but I need to be here. With you."

Caroline visibly trembled, those green eyes hesitant as she frowned.

"Whatever you think was happening when you called me... you're wrong. I was working late. Juliet feels awful for interrupting your call, but I swear nothing was going on."

"You don't have to explain yourself to me, Hannah. What you do is your own business." Caroline spoke, her voice hoarse.

"No. You're not listening to me, Caz. *Nothing* is going on with her."

"But if it was, what gives me the right to have something to say about it?"

Hannah exhaled slowly. "Those things you said to me on the phone...did you mean them?"

Caroline nodded, lacing her fingers with Hannah's. "I did. I suspected it would probably backfire on me, I've never done that before, but I've spent the entire week desperately wishing to see you."

Hannah's heart fluttered. It was a waste of time trying to

hide the grin spreading on her mouth. Caroline made her feel good; Why not let it run its course? "Yeah?"

"I feel like a different woman when I'm with you. And that probably sounds ridiculous, but it's *huge* for me, Hannah. When I'm alone with you," Caroline paused, blushing. "I don't know how to explain it."

"Try." Hannah guided Caroline backwards, finally stepping foot inside her house. She kicked the door shut, then found Caroline's eyes again. Beautiful. "Go on...try."

"Y-you look at me like I'm worth something. You make me feel as though my life could be incredibly fulfilling again. And maybe I'm reading it all wrong, but it's how I feel. How I've *wanted* to feel for so long."

"You're not reading anything wrong, Caz."

Caroline frowned as what Hannah was saying finally started to sink in. "N-no?"

"When I came here with those flowers," Hannah paused, running a hand through her hair. "I'd just been offered the job. I came to tell you I'd accepted it on the spot because I was watching you across the room as Juliet suggested it. It could have been the most terrible position, and I still would have taken it."

"Why?"

Hannah lifted a hand, feathering a thumb across Caroline's cheek. "Because I'd woken up beside you that morning. I'd watched you sleeping, wishing I never had to leave to do the job I was doing. And while I didn't enjoy escorting, I have to love it in some way. Because if I hadn't been an escort, I never would have met you."

Caroline smiled, pulling Hannah into the living room. Her eyes had brightened, she didn't appear so hesitant, and Hannah's heart continued to soar at the thought of being something more with Caroline.

"Hannah, I don't know what the hell I'm doing."

"Then let's figure it out together." She lifted Caroline's hand and kissed her knuckles. "Let's enjoy this and get to know one another."

Caroline dragged a hand through her hair, puffing out her cheeks. "I'm not just any ordinary relationship material. I don't want you to feel stuck when days are a little hard for me. When I'm unsure or my past creeps in. But I also want to get my life back on track."

Hannah cupped Caroline's face, smiling when Caroline leant into her touch. "If you want me, I'm here."

Caroline's eyes fluttered closed. "God, I do..."

"You said you wanted to explore," Hannah paused, studying Caroline's eyes. "But you *do* want a serious relationship, don't you? This isn't just you having no-strings fun?"

"No. Never."

"Then you should probably direct me to the wine glasses so we can get comfortable for the night." Hannah pulled a bottle of red wine from her satchel.

"Y-you're staying?" Hannah noted the suppressed excitement in Caroline's eyes.

"Do you want me to?"

"I'd love you to..." Caroline's voice dropped a little lower, something changing in her eyes.

Hannah could hazard a guess as to what that look was, but she would wait for Caroline to come to her in her own time. She leaned in, pressing her lips to Caroline's. "I'm not going anywhere."

CHAPTER 15

Silence had never been Caroline's favourite part of the evening. Not when she was with Naomi, and not since she'd been alone. But tonight, as Hannah held her on the couch, silence was her best friend. It just felt right. It felt normal to not fill the air with meaningless words. They were both comfortable.

She placed a hand on Hannah's stomach, not impressed that she had multiple layers on. But she had to admit, Hannah looked sexy in a business suit. Hannah looked sexy period. "How was your first week at your new job?"

"Amazing. Hard work, obviously, but it's nice to be back doing something I enjoy."

Caroline tilted her head where it rested against Hannah's chest. "I'm proud of you."

"Yeah?"

"Of course. I know you wanted something stable and suitable."

Hannah lowered her lips to Caroline's forehead, kissing her. "I couldn't lose you. And I know you may not be entirely sure about that, but I mean it. I needed a job change so I could be with you."

"Hannah, I'd never want or *expect* you to take a job because of me."

"I know. I did it for us. Because I want there to be an us, Caz. I *need* there to be an us." Hannah lifted a hand, stroking her fingers through Caroline's hair. "And if it would be okay with you, I'd like *us* to go to bed soon."

"To...bed." Caroline tried to hide the anxiety she knew was present in her voice, but Hannah would understand. That was the beauty of this woman. She understood.

Without another word, Hannah sat up and urged Caroline back on the couch. She braced her hands against the arm of the couch, lowering herself to Caroline. "Don't worry. We don't have to do anything you're not ready for. But I'd at least like to be comfortable while I kiss you for as long as I possibly can." And then Hannah drew Caroline into one hell of a kiss, slipping her tongue into Caroline's mouth. Her thigh rested between Caroline's legs, perfectly placed in all honesty. "Can I do that? Kiss you for hours on end?"

"Y-yes." Caroline couldn't help how her body moved against Hannah's thigh, and as she pulled back, Hannah smirked. "Sorry."

"Don't apologise. *Never* apologise to me. If you need a little more, you take what you want." Hannah nipped at Caroline's bottom lip, their foreheads touching. "Are you wet for me, Caz?"

Caroline swallowed, her world spinning as Hannah spoke those words. If she hadn't been, she certainly was now. "Yes."

Hannah shifted from the couch slowly, taking Caroline's hand and guiding her to her feet. "I think it's time for that bed I mentioned, don't you?"

As Caroline stared into Hannah's eyes, she felt courage building inside her. Courage she should never have to muster up. Many years ago, Caroline would have torn Hannah's clothes from her body long before now...but this wasn't many years ago, and Caroline was an entirely different person now.

Still, there was no denying just how much she wanted this woman. God, she wanted her like she needed air to breathe. "Yes. I think it is time..."

Hannah powered the TV off, turning back to Caroline and squeezing her hand. She cocked her head towards the door, grinning when Caroline blushed. "I'm in for a treat, aren't I?"

Caroline reddened further, shaking her head as she wore a shy smile. "I wouldn't get too excited."

But Hannah only dragged her up the stairs, kicking the bedroom door shut once they were safely inside. She sat Caroline down on the edge of the bed, kissing her knuckles. Hannah crouched down in front of her, her blonde hair swept to one side, smiling. "Do you have any idea how you make me feel?"

Caroline exhaled a shaky breath, unsure as to whether Hannah actually wanted her to answer.

"You know, when I met you, I saw so much pain and uncertainty behind your eyes. I saw a woman who didn't know how to enjoy life anymore. But more than anything, I saw the sheer beauty inside you. Because you do, Caz, you have so much beauty and so much love to offer. And seeing you like this, unsure of yourself, it breaks my heart."

"I-I... It's been so long since I had sex," Caroline murmured, knowing full well how sad that sounded.

Hannah nodded slowly, sitting back on her knees, her hands placed on Caroline's thighs. "Well, thank God for toys, hey." Hannah lifted a shoulder. "We don't need other people to complete us."

"N-no," Caroline paused. "I couldn't even touch myself. It's only recently that I've been able to look back at myself in the mirror without being disappointed."

Hannah placed her hands against the bed, getting to her feet. And then she stood between Caroline's legs, tilting her chin as she leaned down into a kiss. But it wasn't just any kiss. No, this kiss was all-consuming, turning Caroline's world upside down, her entire body throbbing with an intensity that had the potential to make her pass out. This kiss...God, it was a kiss that told Caroline everything she needed to know. Hannah was here, she wasn't going to be scared off by anything, and she cared a great deal.

When Hannah pulled back, leaving Caroline breathless in the process, she guided her further back onto the bed, crawling towards her. "You deserve to be happy, Caz. You deserve to feel good about yourself and enjoy an amazing sex life. And being here, knowing you trust me, means the world."

Caroline shook with anticipation...and nerves. Could they turn out the light? Would Hannah be disappointed when she removed her dress? Probably. Naomi always had been. "H-Hannah," Caroline pressed a hand to her shoulder, sitting up on one elbow. "Are you sure you want me? That you want to be here tonight?"

Hannah smiled as she leaned forward, nipping at Caroline's bottom lip. It only left a throbbing between Caroline's thighs. Hannah's eyes had suddenly darkened, a devilish look in them. "No, not only tonight. Any night I'm lucky enough to get with you."

She kissed Caroline slowly, sensually, easing her back down on the mattress. Caroline instinctively placed her arms over her stomach, hiding whatever she could. She carried a few extra pounds, most women did, but she didn't want Hannah to see her that way.

Sensing that Caroline was drowning in her thoughts, Hannah pulled back. "Do you have any candles?"

Caroline nodded. "Yes, why?"

"Just...trust me." Hannah climbed from the bed, slipping her heels off and placing them out of the way. "Can I use the decorative ones that are placed around here?"

Caroline nodded again, watching the confidence that oozed from Hannah. Honestly, she was jealous.

Hannah's eyes landed on the lighter on top of Caroline's dressing table, lighting one candle, then another...and another. Hannah crossed the room, turning out the light. And then she shrugged, lighting another on the nightstand, and a final one on the chest of drawers.

"Perfect."

Okay, it was perfect. The lighting, the ambience in the room, it had just calmed Caroline's nerves dramatically. "I think you could be."

"Oh, not me. I'm far from perfect." Hannah offered a sexy smirk as she sat on the edge of the bed, relaxing Caroline further. She wasn't here to *only* have sex—that much was clear by the time she took with Caroline. "We all have our imperfections, but sometimes, they make us who we are." Hannah got comfortable, lying beside Caroline, her hand propping her head up. "But so far, I love *everything* I see with you."

"I'm afraid I'm going to disappoint you." Caroline had never been so forthcoming with her feelings before; talking freely had been knocked right out of her some time ago. Not physically, but talking about how you felt was frowned upon at one time in this house. "But if I'm fucking it all up, you'll tell me, won't you?"

"I'm not sure you've ever fucked anything up in your life, Caz." Hannah lifted a hand, stroking a single fingertip from her wrist up to her shoulder. "You take good care of yourself, don't you? I don't think I've ever felt skin so soft."

"I have very little else to do with my time, so yes...I focus on improving what I can." Why was she saying this stuff? That vulnerability was creeping in, and though she'd worked on it for a long time, it had no plans to back away.

Hannah lowered her lips to Caroline's, smiling against her mouth. "I don't see a need for any improvements. I wish you could see that too."

"You're very sweet...but full of shit." Caroline laughed as she wrapped a hand around the back of Hannah's neck. Kissing this woman may be the greatest thing to happen in her lifetime. She never wanted to stop. "I really don't want to disappoint you," she whispered against Hannah's lips.

"Hey," Hannah replaced her mouth with her thumb, feathering it across Caroline's bottom lip. "You're so beautiful. You won't disappoint me. But the more I lie here kissing you, the more I want to touch you." Hannah dropped her hand, running it up and down Caroline's thigh. Her body quivered, arousal pooling between her legs. "*May* I touch you?"

"Y-yes." Caroline's breath caught when she stared back at Hannah, desire flashing in her eyes. This woman, without a doubt, wanted her. And as much as Caroline couldn't fathom why, she wasn't worrying about it tonight. Hannah's hands, her breath, her lips...all felt too good against her skin. "Hannah," she whispered as she took in a sharp breath. Hannah paused, watching her expectantly. "Thank you."

"No, thank *you*. For trusting me. For letting me be here with you tonight." Hannah got to her knees at the foot of the bed, her hands disappearing beneath Caroline's dress. "I don't pretend to understand how hard things have been for you, but I hope one day you'll let me in." A thrill rushed through Caroline when she felt her underwear being slid down her thighs, over her knees, and thrown to the floor. "But tonight, I want you to just lie back and enjoy every moment of this. I know *I* certainly will."

"Oh, God." Caroline's chest heaved as Hannah pushed her

dress up higher, lowering her head and kissing her way up and down Caroline's legs. This woman knew exactly what she was doing.

Thankful that her choice of dress provided easy access tonight, Caroline smiled when Hannah lifted a hand, tugging the front of her dress down to expose a strapless lace bra. "Okay, that's hot." Hannah's eyes lit up when she spied the front clasp on Caroline's bra. "Almost as if you dressed entirely for me tonight."

Caroline took her bottom lip between her teeth, fighting back the grin she felt working its way to her mouth. Hannah knew all the right things to say, exactly when she needed her to say them. "I can't say I haven't thought about you..."

"I hoped you had," Hannah said, popping the clasp on Caroline's bra, a delighted glint in her eye when Caroline's breasts spilled out. "Fuck."

"W-what?" Caroline frowned.

"God, you're so gorgeous." Hannah palmed Caroline's thighs, urging her to bend her knees. When she did so and her legs fell open, Hannah slipped between them, lowering herself onto Caroline. "You really are, Caz. Absolutely beautiful."

"Y-you really mean that?" Caroline asked, her voice cracking.

"I don't say anything I don't mean. I'd never lie to you." Hannah kissed her way along Caroline's collarbone, moving higher, nipping at her earlobe. "Trust me when I tell you that I can't wait to kiss every last inch of your skin."

Caroline buried her head into a pillow, squeezing her eyes shut as tears threatened. She wasn't going to be one of those women who cried during sex. She didn't need Hannah to run after this.

Hannah took a nipple into her mouth, rolling her tongue over it slowly, teasingly. Caroline held her breath when Hannah repeated the movement, pinching her other nipple at the same time as she sucked harder. "O-oh." Caroline dug her fingers into the bedspread, her hips arching ever so slightly. She couldn't remember a time when her body felt so free and uninhibited.

"Mmhmm." Hannah grinned against her, taking a long slow lick up her nipple. "See how good it feels when you let go?"

"Y-yes." Arousal flooded Caroline's body, her hips rolling, desperate for more friction.

Two years of being unable to imagine touching herself, so many negative thoughts whirring around her mind, never feeling good enough. Hannah had the power to obliterate it all in mere seconds, and Caroline suspected she would never be the same again. And in every way imaginable, that was the outcome she hoped for. Because she was tired of second-guessing every decision she made, she was tired of staring at herself in the mirror and feeling that heavy disgust she had for herself, and she was tired of feeling worthless. Caroline had always strived to be happy, to love with all of her heart, but fifteen years with Naomi, ten of those married, and she didn't know who she was anymore. She craved to find that woman she'd buried deep down, craved a love that was so all-encompassing that she couldn't breathe. She needed more. So much more than she'd been given over the years.

As she forced herself out of her thoughts, Caroline shuddered. Hannah was trailing her warm tongue along her hip, moving lower with each press of her mouth to Caroline's skin. God, she wanted to sob with sheer joy; she wanted to scream with the pleasure she felt building in the pit of her stomach. And then Hannah lowered a hand to her soaked sex, gathering her wetness on her fingertips. Caroline arched from the bed, biting down on her bottom lip as Hannah's tongue slowly but expertly circled her clit.

Oh, Lord. This was what happiness felt like. This...Hannah... was a revelation.

Caroline relaxed her body, sinking so deep into the mattress that she wasn't sure she'd ever surface again, and kicked all thoughts of Naomi from her mind. That woman didn't deserve Caroline's headspace anymore, but Hannah? God, she deserved the world.

Hannah eased two fingers inside her, her thumb pressing against Caroline's clit as they lifted their heads, their eyes pinning one another. "You feel so good," Hannah whispered, pressing her lips to Caroline's stomach. "Fuck, I don't ever want this night to end."

Caroline's bottom lip trembled as she lowered her head back down to her pillow. She felt the same way, but the truth was, this night *would* end. Except tonight, things were different. Hannah wasn't here on the basis of being paid, and she wasn't here because she felt obligated in any way. No, Hannah had come here herself and told Caroline everything she'd wished to hear for this entire miserable week.

She wanted love, she wanted incredible sex, she wanted to feel as though she mattered to another person. And as Caroline lay here, pleasure igniting every dark corner, she felt those things with Hannah.

Hannah increased the pressure against Caroline's clit, curling her fingers inside. Caroline's entire body tensed, her toes curling as she dug her feet into the bed. The woman between her thighs was the greatest gift she ever could have received. She was giving every ounce of attention she possessed to Caroline, and that meant the world.

Caroline's thighs shook when Hannah sunk deeper, harder. "O-oh, God."

"Let go, Caz."

She couldn't. When this ended, life would return to how it

was before Hannah climbed the stairs with her. Or...would it? It didn't feel that way. No, it felt as though Hannah was here for the long haul.

"There's so much I want to do to you, I want to fuck you all night long, but let go, baby. Feel good."

Every emotion she possessed crashed through Caroline, her body shaking and convulsing as she came undone. She could barely remember a time when she knew what an orgasm felt like, and even when she had enjoyed one, it had *never* felt like this. So intense, so full of care and thought, so...

Tears spilled from her eyes as Hannah coaxed everything she possibly could from Caroline. She felt Hannah smile against her thigh, her hot breath only encouraging her body to continue trembling. She brought the heels of her hands to her face, pressing them to her eyes as sobs wracked her entirely.

Hannah climbed up her, rolling off Caroline and settling beside her. And then her arms enveloped Caroline, Hannah's hands in her hair as she held Caroline against her. Nothing was said, the silence of the room startling compared to only a few moments ago. But Caroline knew exactly what Hannah wanted to say because her gentle touch was incredibly beautiful. This woman... Caroline had no way of describing Hannah, this moment, anything. Overwhelmed by how her night was ending meant that Caroline couldn't possibly process it tonight.

She turned her face into Hannah's chest, disappointed that Hannah was still fully clothed. But if it was at all possible, if Hannah wanted to see Caroline again, she would absolutely return the favour. "Hannah..."

"Shush." Hannah tightened her arms around Caroline's body, pressing a kiss to her hair. "Close your eyes and just relax."

Caroline did exactly that, her body truly spent. If she was ever going to make something more of this, she'd have to get her stamina back up and running. She'd been lacking for far too long.

"Don't leave, okay?" Caroline snuggled against Hannah, her breathing soft.

"I'm not going anywhere." Hannah stroked a hand up and down Caroline's back. "Are you feeling okay?"

"Amazing."

Hannah sighed contently. "Good."

CHAPTER 16

W*hy does it feel so damn good with her?*

Hannah lay still, Caroline's gentle breath tickling her shoulder. She'd woken up twenty minutes ago in the same position they'd fallen asleep in. Caroline was spooning her, one soft hand placed on her stomach while Caroline's other arm was wedged under Hannah's pillow. Over the years, she'd hated being spooned. It was never as comfortable as people made it out to be. Someone usually ended up with a dead arm, cold feet against her were also a no, and she generally preferred to separate in the night for a little space.

But not with Caroline.

No, this woman felt incredible wrapped around her. Their legs were tangled beneath the cover, Caroline's naked body was warm and soft, and as Hannah imagined the things Caroline was capable of, heat spread throughout her. It didn't matter that they'd fallen asleep in one another's arms without Hannah feeling Caroline all over her. It didn't matter that Caroline had felt emotional as she toppled over the edge. The only thing that mattered was that Hannah was still here this morning, and she had no plans to leave yet.

Not like last time.

But she would admit to feeling slightly fearful when it came to moving from her position. The last thing she wanted was for Caroline to wake up and get the wrong end of the stick. She'd considered slipping out quietly and starting breakfast, but Hannah was yet to actually do that.

Caroline stirred behind her, that hand on her stomach slipping lower as she stretched. Hannah could only hold her breath, regulate her heart rate, and think of anything other than sex this morning.

Why? Because Hannah would never expect that so soon from Caroline. She may have given Caroline the most intense orgasm of her life last night, but Hannah had done so with the intention of showing Caroline just how much she *could* enjoy sex again. How she could *not* allow her thoughts to take over the good stuff. That's exactly what Hannah hoped for last night. For Caroline...to let go.

Hannah lifted her head and checked the alarm clock. Not only did Caroline feel safe and warm, she loved to sleep in too. She was definitely onto a winner. Hannah spent enough time waking up early through the week. She had absolutely no issue with spending a little longer in bed at the weekend.

"Making a run for it?" Caroline murmured, her fingertips stroking Hannah's lower stomach.

Fuck. Me. That felt good. Too good. "N-no. But unless you plan to move that hand lower, you should really stop doing that."

Caroline shifted a little, smiling against Hannah's shoulder. "I didn't have the pleasure of touching you last night..."

"Mm. But *I* had the pleasure of touching *you*." Hannah moaned lightly, those fingers magical against her skin. "Caz."

"Yes?" Caroline dipped her hand between Hannah's legs, placing soft kisses on her skin.

"Oh, God." Hannah pushed her backside into Caroline's lap, gripping her pillow. "Shit."

"Just so you know," Caroline whispered, stroking her fingertips up and down Hannah's lips. God, she was more than wet for this woman. "I could *definitely* get used to this."

"M-me too." Hannah clenched her jaw, and her nostrils flared when Caroline spread her legs, Hannah's body resting back against her. "Caz, you'd better do something soon."

Caroline sat up on her elbow, kissing down Hannah's bare arm. But Hannah lifted it and tangled her fingers in Caroline's hair, directing her towards one of her taut nipples. Caroline took it into her mouth, those delectable full lips sucking slowly.

"Y-yes." Hannah's lips parted when Caroline gathered her wetness, stroking her clit so delicately. "Oh, my..."

"Last night meant so much to me, Hannah."

The way Caroline spoke her name as her fingers were close to her entrance had Hannah trembling. God, she really didn't want to come so soon, but she definitely couldn't hold back. Caroline felt too good.

"And I'd really love to keep doing this with you. If it wasn't too disappointing for you..."

Hannah lowered her hand to Caroline's, encouraging Caroline to push her fingers inside. If she wanted an idea of how much Hannah had enjoyed last night, surely her arousal told her. "I woke up wet for you, Caz. I'm not sure you ever have to worry about disappointment."

"I never thought I'd make it to this point with you," Caroline spoke low. "And I know this is just the beginning, but I never thought we'd be here."

Hannah looked back over her shoulder, Caroline's green eyes pinning her. "Well, we are. We're here, and I really love that."

Caroline lowered her eyes, but a smile remained. Hannah

really didn't want her to hesitate this morning, not now that Caroline was deep inside her, but she had to prepare herself for the possibility. Caroline wasn't as sexually free as Hannah. Not yet.

"Talk to me," Hannah said, enjoying how full she felt with Caroline inside her. "I don't want you to think you have to—"

"No." Caroline spoke suddenly, shifting out from behind Hannah. She braced herself above Hannah, smiling down into a kiss. "No talking. Just...let me enjoy you. I don't know if I'll ever have this chance again." Caroline's mouth fell open against Hannah's as she pushed deeper. "God, you're so wet."

"For you, Caz." Hannah rocked her hips in rhythm with Caroline's thrusts, the edge nearing. "Fuck, I've been wet just thinking about you before today."

"Yeah?" The shy smile Caroline wore as she pulled back and looked into her eyes practically melted Hannah.

"Oh, far more than you'd believe." One day, this woman *would* feel sexy again. One day, Caroline wouldn't hesitate, and she wouldn't second guess her worth. Because Hannah was going to show her just how sexy she was. "You know when I bumped into you in town? Before your date..."

"You looked so good that day. In your business suit. You really looked the part."

"You looked good too. So much so that part of me wanted to slip my hand up your dress and feel you."

That snippet must have awoken something inside Caroline. Because as Hannah initially felt wary about saying it, Caroline was sinking harder into her, their breath mingling into one. Caroline touched her forehead to Hannah's, grinning. "You really know how to make me feel special...and wanted."

"I've wanted you since the night you booked me, Caz. Don't ever think I won't want you."

"I know you do," Caroline whispered against Hannah's lips.

"If you didn't, I wouldn't be here now...having the pleasure of fucking you."

Caroline's voice as she spoke those words sounded incredibly good. It sent a shiver down Hannah's spine. But then Caroline pressed the heel of her hand to Hannah's clit, curling her fingers inside her. "Oh, Caz..."

"Spend the day with me." Caroline didn't falter, those slender fingers working Hannah up to her first orgasm of the day. "And tonight. I don't want to let you go."

Hannah released around Caroline's fingers, arching up into her as she came undone. "Y-yes. Shit, don't stop." Hannah wanted to wrap herself up in this woman for the rest of eternity. And as Caroline stared down at her, a swell of something she hadn't expected settled deep in her stomach. Hannah...was going to fall for this woman. There were no two ways about it. "O-oh." Hannah shuddered as Caroline slowly slid out of her, watching every reaction that danced across her face. "God, Caz."

Caroline settled against Hannah, brushing Hannah's hair from her face. "Thank you for still being here this morning."

Hannah wrapped her arms around Caroline, drawing her into a kiss. "I can't think of a single place I'd rather be than here."

Caroline pulled a throw down from the back of the couch, draping it over them. Hannah had gone home for an hour to collect some fresh clothes, but no sooner had she left, and Hannah was back again. Caroline couldn't help but love it. Considering she'd been terrified as she climbed the stairs last night, Hannah had only made her feel more and more at ease. But Caroline should have known Hannah would do that; she was beginning to understand exactly who Hannah was. And it was nothing like the woman she'd initially met.

"Don't you usually have plans on a Saturday?" Hannah rested a hand on Caroline's knee, squeezing it gently. "With your sister?"

"Oh, I cancelled."

"You didn't have to do that."

Caroline smiled. "I did. Because I'd rather be here with you. I've spent the last two years meeting Joy and Gail every Saturday. It was about time I got to stay home and relax."

"They worry about you, don't they?"

"They do. And while I appreciated that in the beginning, it's not what I need anymore. I'm in a much better place than I was when my divorce went through."

"While I can understand that it must get to be a bit annoying having them around all the time, it's nice that you've got people who are there for you."

"I know. I'm grateful for them, believe me I am...but I do like my own space after I've been working all week."

"You don't mind that I stayed?"

Caroline rested her hand over Hannah's, and then she laced their fingers. "Not at all. And I asked you to stay."

"Yeah, you did." Hannah blushed, chewing the corner of her lip. "This morning was nice."

"It was. It was very nice." After Caroline had woken up and got herself fully acquainted with Hannah's body, Hannah had taken the time to double-check that she, herself, hadn't missed anything last night. It was midday before they'd left the bedroom. "I can't tell you the last time I had such a wonderful morning."

Hannah leaned in, kissing Caroline's cheek. "Plenty more where that came from."

Caroline's insides trembled. The more she was around

Hannah, the less she ever wanted to be without her. While she wanted to love everything they seemed to be sharing, Caroline knew she had to be very careful going into this. If Hannah broke her heart down the line, Caroline wasn't sure she'd survive it. It was still beaten and bruised from being kicked repeatedly by Naomi and that mouth of hers over the years.

But then Caroline had to consider whether it would ever fully heal.

Naomi had broken her in so many ways.

"You're thinking," Hannah whispered as she drew back from their kiss. "Do you want to talk about it?"

"No. I'm fine."

Hannah cocked her head, regarding Caroline with a knowing look. "While I want to believe that, I understand that last night...today...is probably difficult for you."

"But I don't want it to be that way. Not with you."

"I came into this knowing it wouldn't always be easy, Caz. So long as we communicate, there's no reason why this can't be something really special."

God, Caroline wanted it to be something special. It already was in some ways, truth be told. Still, the worry and the insecurities crept up on her when she least expected it. But she shouldn't sit here worried today. Because Hannah was here. What more could she possibly want?

"If things get to be too much, I'll tell you. Okay?"

"Okay." Hannah smiled into another kiss, cradling Caroline's jaw in her hand. When she pulled back, taking her own bottom lip between her teeth, Hannah lowered her eyes to Caroline's lips. "So good."

"Mm?" Caroline's eyelids fluttered closed, her fingertips pressed to her lips.

"Kissing you. It's so good."

CHAPTER 17

Hannah folded the laundry into piles on the dining table, grinning to herself as she reminisced about the last couple of weeks. Caroline was out tonight with friends for a late dinner, and since it was only midweek, they rarely saw one another anyway. Edie was only gone at the weekend, it was an arrangement she'd worked out with Dylan a few years ago, but it had always worked for them. Until now, when Hannah had a girlfriend.

She wouldn't disturb Edie's routine. Caroline was perfectly happy with spending weekends together, so that was that. And in all honesty, Hannah barely had the strength to give all her attention to Caroline throughout the week. Juliet had her run off her feet from the moment she started at her firm. But Hannah still loved the job; she wouldn't change anything she had right now.

"Mum?" Edie came into the kitchen, dragging her feet. "Can we get takeout tonight?"

"Depends what takeout you want, kiddo."

Edie stood beside Hannah, taking a pile of laundry and

helping to fold it. “Dunno. Maybe from that Indian restaurant we like?”

“Yeah, okay.” Hannah grinned. “And then maybe a film before you go to bed? Or we could watch one in bed?”

“Do you think Ms Baker likes Indian food?”

Hannah stopped mid-fold. “I...have no idea, Edie. Why?”

“She was really kind to me today at school. I stayed back in my maths class because I was struggling with some equations, and Ms Baker used her lunch hour to stay and figure it out with me.”

God, this woman was going to be the death of Hannah one of these days. Truly, she was the biggest sweetheart. “And you want to take Indian food to her?”

“No. But I have some pocket money put away, and I thought I could get her a gift card. Then she can have a nice meal with her husband and kids. Because she deserves it for being a really kind teacher.”

Hannah smiled, lowering her eyes. Would it ever be possible to tell Edie what Caroline meant to her? Would it shatter her perfect image of Ms Baker? Hannah felt torn. “If that’s what you want to do, I’m sure she’d really like that.”

“You think?” Edie looked up at Hannah, brow creased. “It wouldn’t be weird?”

“You could always invite her over here to have Indian food with us.”

“Uh, no. That would *definitely* be weird, Mum. She’s my teacher.”

Hannah lifted a shoulder. “We know one another. It wouldn’t be that weird.”

“How *do* you know her? I asked Ms Baker the other week, and she said you weren’t friends.”

Hannah puffed out a breath. “We’ve known one another for a few months. We have the same friends.”

Okay, she didn't like this. Lying to her daughter had never been something Hannah imagined herself doing, but she couldn't come right out with the truth. She at least needed to discuss it with Caroline first. "So we're kinda friends, but not good friends."

At least that part was true. Because they weren't friends in the ordinary sense. No, they were lovers. And sweet Jesus could Caroline make love. Those gentle hands, once they gained a little confidence, really knew what Hannah's body craved. And when Caroline had gone down on her last weekend, Hannah hadn't known it was possible to feel so euphoric. Caroline was a wonderful lover...

"Mum?"

"Sorry, what?" Hannah snapped out of her aroused thoughts, holding a blush at bay. She really had to refrain from doing that when her daughter was around.

"I said will you call her and ask her?"

"You want to invite her over tonight?" Hannah frowned. "It's a little late to ask someone over for dinner now, Edie. She probably has plans."

"Yeah." Edie smiled weakly. "Never mind. It was a stupid idea anyway."

Hannah's heart broke a little seeing her daughter miserable. Caroline really had left an impression on her. That could go one of two ways when the truth came out. Edie could be thrilled that her mum had found someone like Caroline, or she could be mortified and never speak to either of them again.

"Tell you what, I'll give her a call. But you have to be prepared for the possibility of her already having plans. And if she does have plans, it's not the end of the world...we can pick another day, okay?"

Edie's eyes lit up. "Will you really?"

"Call her? Sure..." Okay, this may be a waste of time, but

she'd score points with Edie if nothing else. Caroline did have plans; Hannah knew it. "You go and change out of your uniform, and I'll give her a call."

Edie threw her arms around Hannah, squeezing her. "Thanks, Mum. Love you."

Hannah pressed a kiss to the top of Edie's head, smiling as her hair tickled her nose. "Love you, too."

Edie rushed out of the kitchen, suddenly turning back as she reached the door. She approached the dining table and lifted a pile of laundry, barely able to see above it. "I'll take these up for you, Mum. Save you a trip."

Hannah watched Edie go, shaking her head as she smiled. She really had raised her daughter better than she ever thought she would. Hannah hadn't felt prepared when she found out she was pregnant at twenty, but her mum had been right. She *was* a natural.

Hannah took her phone from the counter, surprised to find a message waiting for her. It had been sent over an hour ago, but it was the fact it had been sent at all. She grinned as she read the words.

Missing you. Caz x

Hannah's heart fluttered, leaving her slightly breathless. She couldn't recall the last time anyone had missed her but hearing it from Caz instantly brightened her evening.

Hannah pressed the call icon above Caroline's message, chewing her lip as she waited for the call to connect.

"Hi." Caroline spoke low, her voice instantly arousing. "Did you get my message?"

"I did," Hannah said, taking her call towards the back door and away from listening ears. "I'm missing you, too."

"Yeah?" She felt Caroline smiling down the phone. "How was your day?"

"Busy...again. But I'm still loving it. Juliet is ruthless, but I kinda like that about her. I know where I stand then. You know?"

"Mm. Just don't let her work you into the ground. I want a functioning girlfriend at the weekend."

Hannah smirked as she rested against the wall by the utility room. "So, I know you have plans already, and that's absolutely fine, but Edie asked me to call you."

"Why?" Concern instantly grew in Caroline's voice. "Is she okay? Did something happen at school again?"

"No, she's fine. I mean, I think my kid loves you, but I can see why. She told me you stayed during lunch with her today to help her out."

"Oh, yeah. It was nothing. She needed a hand with some maths work."

"Look, don't feel as though you have to...but she's asked me to call to invite you over for takeout. She thinks we're sort of friends."

"I'd love to. Just tell me when and I'll be there."

Hannah cleared her throat. "She wanted you to come over tonight, but I told her you'd probably have plans already. I knew you did, but I couldn't exactly explain how I knew. So, maybe next week? I make a rule of not having takeout too often, so I don't want to encourage her by inviting you tomorrow. And then she's at Dylan's Friday and Saturday, so..."

"I could do tonight. If you wanted me to."

"Caz, you're going out to dinner with friends. I wouldn't expect you to change your plans for me. Edie knows it likely wouldn't be possible, so we'll rearrange. It's no big deal."

"Honestly? I'd rather be with you," Caroline explained. "And I know we can't exactly *be* with one another tonight, but I'd still love to be there with you."

Hannah grinned, every inch of her skin tingling with the thought of seeing Caroline. "You would?"

"Absolutely. Should I go home and change, or did you want me to come straight over? I was just picking up some shopping on the way home from work."

"Whatever you want to do. Just let me know if you want me to wait for you before we order."

"Oh, order for me. I don't mind. I'm sure I'll like whatever you pick."

Hannah reached for the takeout menu, perusing the options. "How about if I just order a banquet? Indian..."

"Mmhmm. You can absolutely count me in."

"Okay, well, I'll see you when you get here. No rush." Hannah's belly swirled. It didn't matter that they had to hold back while Edie was home during the week. If she could be in the same room as Caroline, that was just as good. "Hey, I'm looking forward to seeing you."

"Me too. I'll be there in half an hour."

Hannah lowered the phone from her ear, staring down at it as Caroline ended the call. This unexpected midweek get-together was just what Hannah needed. She hadn't seen Caroline since she left her place on Sunday afternoon, needing to get home in time for Edie to be dropped off by Dylan. Honestly, she could hardly wait.

"Did you call Ms Baker?" Edie startled Hannah.

"Y-yeah. Uh, she's free. She'll be here soon."

Edie's eyes widened. "Oh, my God. Really?"

Hannah's forehead creased. Why was Edie suddenly not so keen on the idea? "You didn't want her to be available?"

"I don't know now. She's my teacher, and she's coming to my house."

"She's my friend. That's no different to Adele being here. Just think of it that way."

"K-kay." Edie wrung her hands, taking her school blazer

from the back of the dining room chair. "I'll just do some homework till dinner gets here then."

"Okay. I'll call you down when Caz gets here."

Edie nodded, slowly turning around and walking away. As much as Hannah was looking forward to seeing Caroline, she needed Edie not to feel awkward. There was absolutely nothing wrong with her teacher being here. So long as Edie didn't find out they were sleeping together, this would all be fine.

Yep. You keep telling yourself that.

Caroline sat across the coffee table from Hannah and Edie, surprisingly comfortable given the situation. When she'd agreed to come for dinner, Caroline had Hannah purely in mind and the thought of seeing her, but as she approached Hannah's home, it didn't feel as good as it had on the short drive over. It wasn't the fact that she was in her student's home; plenty of teachers were friends with kids' parents—some parents even taught their own children. It was the fact that she felt she was here based on a lie. And if Edie discovered that, Caroline would be devastated.

They would have to come clean one day, but when exactly was the right time to do it? Sooner rather than later? Caroline had no idea. She'd never been in this position before.

"Do you like Indian food, Ms Baker?"

Caroline smiled as she tore into her naan bread, scooping up her korma with it. "I do. And I haven't had it for a while, so it's wonderful."

Edie smiled. "It was my idea."

"Good choice," Caroline said, winking. "Thank you for inviting me over."

Edie smiled as she lowered her eyes to her plate, lifting a shoulder. "Mum said you are friends so it would be okay."

"Perfectly okay."

"Would you like a drink? A glass of water or a can of pop?"

Caroline smiled as Edie scrambled to her feet. "I'd love a glass of water, thank you."

When Edie left the room, Caroline's eyes found Hannah's. She really had missed her this week. And then Hannah leaned forward, her smile bright. "You doing okay? I know this isn't ideal, but I didn't want to miss out on the chance to see you."

"That's exactly why I'm here," Caroline whispered. "I thought I'd be fine not seeing you through the week, but it's been really miserable without you."

"You can come over whenever you like. More so now that Edie seems okay with you being here."

"I don't know. I hate lying to her. She thinks we're just friends, and while I'm okay with that for now, what happens when she finds out? When she knows we've lied to her..."

The sound of glasses clanging had Hannah smiling. They had another second alone before Edie returned. "We'll figure it out together, okay? I'd never tell her without your input first."

"Okay."

"Here you go, Ms Baker." As Edie entered the room again, they tore apart. Hannah almost knocked over the bowl of mango chutney, catching it before it hit the cream carpet. "And one for you, Mum."

"My God, you're like creeping Jesus!" Hannah splayed a hand across her chest. "Sit down before you give me a heart attack."

Edie returned to her cushion on the floor, staring at Caroline. Had she overhead them from the kitchen? Surely not. "So, how has school been since the incident?"

Edie lifted a shoulder. "Fine. I just stay out of their way."

"Good idea."

"But I think they might stop now." Edie spooned rice into her mouth. Swallowing before she continued the conversation. "Thank you for getting them excluded, too."

"You shouldn't have to listen to the things they were saying. We're all different, and it's nobody's business to say hateful things to *anyone*."

"Are you a lesbian too, Ms Baker?"

Caroline almost choked on the piece of chicken she'd just shoved into her mouth. Edie was never this vocal in class. Perhaps being on her own territory wasn't the best idea for Caroline. "I...uh..." She eyed Hannah, but her girlfriend just sat with her mouth agape.

"It's okay if you are."

"Well, I mean...my personal life is exactly that. *Personal*."

"That's cool." Edie went back to eating her dinner, silence falling over the three of them.

"H-how was work?" Caroline swallowed as she gave Hannah a knowing look. If she didn't say something soon, Caroline was certain the walls would close in on her. "Any cases of interest?"

"A few, yeah. It's amazing the things you're faced with in a criminal lawyer's office."

"I'll bet." Caroline nodded, satisfied that she'd eaten more than enough this evening. Which was just as well, really, because Caroline was beginning to feel a little anxious about being here. "Well, that was delicious."

"It's our favourite restaurant. You could come over again next time we order in."

"Oh, I'm sure you two would prefer a girly night without me around."

Edie grinned. "That's the best idea. You should come over and have a girly night with us. Shouldn't she, Mum?" Edie turned to face Hannah, catching her off guard. "Wouldn't that be great?"

"I'm not sure a girly night is really Caz's thing, love."

"Oh."

"Maybe you could have your mum call me the next time you're planning to have one of these nights. If I'm available, I'll come over and have dinner again."

Edie nodded, a slight smile on her mouth. And then she eyed the clock, frowning. "Okay, well, I have to get ready for bed now."

Caroline switched her gaze between Edie and Hannah. It was only seven in the evening. "Already?"

Edie rushed to her feet, kissing Hannah on the cheek. "You didn't tell me the time," she whispered.

"Sorry, love. I didn't realise what time it was. But go on up. I'm not going to bed yet, so you'll be fine."

Caroline watched their interaction, confused as to why Edie was suddenly a little frantic. But she wouldn't question it. Edie seemed preoccupied enough without Caroline preventing her from getting to bed. And then Edie rounded the coffee table, reaching down and hugging Caroline. "Bye, Ms Baker. Thanks for coming."

"I'll see you soon, Edie. Goodnight." Edie took her glass of water from the table and ran up the stairs, her bedroom door slamming shut. Caroline waited a couple of seconds, and then she focused on Hannah. "What was that about?"

"Edie worries about getting into bed at a particular time. She gives herself an extra hour on weekends, but Monday to Thursday, she's in bed at seven."

"O...kay."

"It started a couple of years ago. She has to go to sleep as soon as she can because she worries that she'll be the only person still awake in the house as it gets later. I don't know why it happened or when she'll grow out of it, but she's been known to walk out the room while Adele is over without saying goodnight. It's just...habit? I don't know."

"Does she do the same thing when she's at her dad's?"

"For a while, she wouldn't go there. Because she thought something bad was going to happen to me."

"That sounds awful," Caroline said, offering a sympathetic smile. "But I hope things get better for her."

"She's definitely improved. I just have to reassure her now and then. But she'll sleep perfectly fine tonight because you're here, so she knows I'm not sleeping. She used to creep around the house to make sure I was still up."

Hannah got to her feet, stacking the plates on the table. As she shoved the wrappers from their takeout into a bag, their eyes met. Caroline instantly felt that shudder ripple through her. Arousal, excitement, everything Hannah made her feel... only tenfold.

"Did you want a hand before I head off?" Caroline asked, also getting to her feet. "I'll wash. You dry."

"Sure. Thanks."

Caroline followed Hannah out into the kitchen, immediately filling the sink with hot soapy water. But Hannah stepped up behind her, placing her hand on the small of Caroline's back.

"What's the rush?"

Caroline swallowed when Hannah's breath washed over her ear. "No rush. I just wanted to help you before I left."

"Stay a while. Catch up."

"I shouldn't." Caroline turned, pinned to the edge of the counter as Hannah pressed her body against Caroline. "Hannah, we can't. What if Edie comes down?"

"She won't. Trust me."

Caroline switched her gaze from Hannah's eyes to her lips, overwhelming arousal flooding her body. She couldn't deny how much she wanted to kiss her, but the fear of Edie catching them was currently winning out. "Hannah..."

Hannah gently gripped Caroline's jaw, smiling as she inched closer. "Do you have any idea how much I've missed you?"

"God," Caroline whispered, her hand fisting in Hannah's T-shirt. She pressed their foreheads together, delighting in the feel and warmth of Hannah against her. "You're so bad."

"Oh, babe...you've no idea." Hannah slid her fingers under Caroline's blouse, grazing them against her skin. "But don't worry, I'll show you one day."

"S-show me?" Caroline's breath caught when Hannah popped the button on her pants. "H-Hannah, shit."

Without another word, Hannah slid her hand into Caroline's pants, cupping her through her underwear. "When I say I've missed you, I mean that I've *really* missed you, Caz."

"Oh, God," Caroline whispered into the silence of the kitchen, her knees trembling when Hannah pushed her underwear between her lips. "O-oh."

"You wanted to explore, so let's begin right now." Hannah nipped at Caroline's bottom lip, smirking. "Because if I've realised anything this week, it's how much I want to make you feel good."

"Hannah."

Hannah withdrew her hand, only to slip it past the waistband of Caroline's underwear. When her fingertips touched her clit, the lightest pressure applied, Caroline gripped the edge of the counter. God, this woman had the ability to ignite Caroline's soul, and right now, she wouldn't want to be anywhere else. As wrong as it felt to be here doing this, Caroline couldn't stop the orgasm she felt building. And how Hannah touched her, how she had that dirty look in her eyes...she'd never had this before. Caroline had never been with a woman who was so sexually free, raw, animalistic. Honestly, it was hot. Almost too hot.

Caroline's head fell back on her shoulders, Hannah's lips working the skin visible on her chest. This woman...fuck, Caroline couldn't describe how she made her feel. Elated. Aroused. *Euphoric.* "Y-yes." She whimpered when Hannah's hand moved lower, two fingers filling her. "Oh, fuck."

"Mm. Did I ever tell you how fucking delicious it sounds when you moan, Ms Baker?"

Jesus. Christ. Caroline gripped the counter tighter. She knew Hannah would be good in bed, great even, but Caroline had a sneaky suspicion that life was about to become mind-blowing for her. Honestly, she could hardly wait. "C-close," Caroline spoke in a throaty moan, Hannah's fingers working so perfectly inside her. And then Hannah dropped to her knees, tugging Caroline's pants and underwear down her thighs, separating her folds and diving right in. "S-shit." Caroline's chest heaved, her hand instinctively gripping the back of Hannah's head.

"Mm," Hannah murmured against her, lapping up everything Caroline had to offer. At forty-seven, she thought her days of unexpected sex were over, but with Hannah Adams? *Never.* It simply wasn't possible. "Fuck, you taste like heaven."

Caroline's thighs shook, Hannah's fingers and tongue working her up to the most incredible orgasm of her life. And then her entire body trembled as she released against Hannah's tongue, short sharp gasps filtering quietly through the air.

Hannah dragged her nails down the back of Caroline's thigh, teasing her clit with the tip of her tongue as her fingers slowed inside her. "See. That wasn't so hard, was it?"

Caroline caught her breath as she stared down at Hannah. Her girlfriend looked back at her with hooded eyes, a devilish grin on that incredibly talented mouth. "You...are something else."

CHAPTER 18

Hannah relaxed back on the couch, watching as Edie and Caroline sat on the floor at the coffee table. Their last get-together had clearly been enjoyable for her daughter, and for the last three nights, she'd begged Hannah to call Caroline to come over again. Caroline had initially questioned whether it was a good idea, but ultimately wanting to spend time with one another had prevailed. And thank God for that.

"You know, Caz isn't here to work, love. The evening is her time off."

Edie lowered her pen to her workbook. "Sorry, Ms Baker."

"It's fine. I'm just watching you work. I don't mind." Caroline eyed Hannah, offering her a full smile when Edie went back to her workbook. "Are you still going away next week with Juliet? I know you hadn't decided..."

"I am. My mum is going to take Edie for a few nights and then drop her at Dylan's on Friday. I'll be back late Saturday night."

"I can't wait. I love staying at Nanna Ivy's."

"Then remind me not to give you any homework that weekend. We wouldn't want to spoil the fun." Caroline focused back on Edie, quietly speaking to her as she pointed out an error on the page.

Hannah could only stare, her gaze surely burning through Caroline. This was all she'd ever wanted. Someone who accepted them as a package and to not have Edie thought of as a hindrance. "You out with the girls next week? You missed dinner last time."

"Not that I know of. I'll probably catch up on work at home."

"Sounds incredibly exciting," Hannah said, catching Caroline's eyes again.

"Well, my usual plans are out the window, so what more can I do? I'm being abandoned."

Hannah's chest swelled at that. Caroline really did enjoy being here with Hannah and Edie. She couldn't say she'd expected things to feel so perfect so soon. As slow as she knew they should go with all of this, it was hard to hold back sometimes. In this moment, Hannah could picture Edie finishing her homework while Caroline was holding Hannah on the couch after dinner. They'd be their own little happy family. God, that thought had Hannah's stomach somersaulting.

Hannah swallowed, her hands tingling as she sat them in her lap. "Maybe we could arrange something for the week after?"

Caroline beamed a smile, shifting back and getting to her feet. "I'd like that." As she moved towards the door, she cleared her throat. "I'll just be a minute. Need to use the bathroom."

Hannah smiled as she watched Caroline walk away, and then she turned her attention to Edie. "You doing okay down there, kiddo?"

Edie, dragged from her own world, looked up at Hannah. "I like Ms Baker being here."

"Yeah? Why so?"

This would be an interesting conversation. Edie had taken more of a shine to Caroline as the last week had progressed. All she did was talk about her.

"She's really nice. And she's nice to you, too." Edie looked to the door and back to Hannah. "Mum, *is* Ms Baker a lesbian?"

Whoa. Not my story to tell. "Why are you so interested in her sexuality, love?"

Edie lifted a shoulder, casting her gaze back on her homework. She was doodling now. "Because I wish she was."

"You...wish your teacher was a lesbian?"

"I wish she was here with us all the time." Edie crawled across the floor and sat beside Hannah. "I think you like her."

"Of course I like her. She's my friend."

Edie rolled her eyes. "No, Mum. Not like that."

She wanted everyone to be honest here, but Caroline wasn't at that place yet. "Edie, sweetheart—"

"Okay, are we watching this film or not?" Caroline landed back in the living room suddenly. "I believe there's popcorn in the kitchen with my name on it."

Edie shot to her feet. "Yes! I'll get it. And the other snacks. You can sit next to Mum, Ms Baker."

Caroline switched her gaze from a retreating Edie to Hannah and frowned. "What's that all about?"

"I'll tell you later when she's gone to bed." Hannah wanted to reach out and take Caroline's hand, but she refrained from doing so. Caroline would see red and panic. "Have a seat. Wherever you like. Take no notice of Edie."

Caroline shifted uncomfortably, taking one side of Hannah and leaving the other for Edie. "She's been different tonight. Is she okay?"

"She's fine. Actually, I get more out of her when you're here than when it's just the two of us. Maybe I should have you over more often."

Caroline smiled, stroking a fingertip across the back of Hannah's hand where it sat at her side. "I've enjoyed this lately. Thank you for having me over."

Hannah lowered her voice, nudging Caroline's shoulder. "You're welcome here every night, babe."

"Hannah," Caroline paused, eyeing the kitchen door. When she turned back to Hannah, she laced their fingers together. "Is it just me...or are things getting a little serious?"

Hannah couldn't say things were serious, but they were definitely progressing faster than she imagined. "I...think we're letting things go at whatever pace they go at."

"Right." Hannah watched a number of emotions cross Caroline's face, but fear was the one that remained. "It's just that I'm a little concerned by how enjoyable this is, and Edie seems to like having me around."

"You're concerned by those things?" Hannah frowned, squeezing Caroline's hand. "Why would that concern you?"

"Because if this doesn't work out—"

"Mum, do you want your Pringles now or halfway through?" Edie shocked Hannah from her conversation, their hands breaking away from one another's.

"I, uh...later is fine." Hannah blew out a breath. "Now sit down before you only get through half of the film. It's already five-thirty."

"Okay. I'm ready." Edie flopped down, the snacks laid out on the table, and grabbed a huge throw from the back of the couch. She spread it over the three of them, and as it landed over Caroline's lap, Hannah felt her tense. "Press play, Mum."

Caroline stifled a yawn as the credits rolled, aware that she should probably call it a night. They both had to work tomorrow, and Edie was sitting curled up against Hannah, her eyes barely open.

"Well, I enjoyed that for the tenth time," Hannah said, laughing as she reached forward for the controller. Her free hand beneath the blanket fell to Caroline's knee, remaining in place as Hannah sat back. "Edie, it's almost seven."

As with the last time, Edie shot up and turned to them both. "Night, Mum. Love you." She leaned down and hugged Hannah, lingering and squeezing tighter. Then she pulled back and stepped towards Caroline. "Night, Ms Baker." Edie's arms landed around her neck, a feeling of belonging anchoring in her chest.

"G-goodnight, Edie."

"You're not leaving yet, are you?" Edie stood upright, chewing her bottom lip.

Caroline saw that worry in her eyes and shook her head. "Not until you're fast asleep, no."

"Kay. Thanks." Edie took her glass of water from the coffee table and left the living room. Stomping...then the door slamming shut.

"Thank you for saying that," Hannah whispered, her head resting on Caroline's shoulder. "And thank you for being so great with her. Hard to believe you don't have kids of your own."

Caroline rolled her lips inward. "I was supposed to. Naomi decided I wasn't cut out to be a mother."

Hannah lifted her head, her brows drawn together. "What?"

"Naomi. When we met, she wanted kids. But things changed, and she told me it was best if we didn't bring children into the world. That I didn't have the time or focus for a family because I was too dedicated to my career."

"So she never really wanted kids?"

"I think she did. I even considered going to the clinic alone and going through the process, then surprising her. But at that point, she already hated me. I couldn't raise a child with her knowing she'd likely hate them too."

Hannah's bottom lip quivered as she turned on the couch and faced Caroline. "I'm so sorry she took that away from you."

"I have the kids at school. I've been blessed with the opportunity to watch so many of them grow and come into their own...and I can live with that."

"It doesn't change the fact that you should have raised your own family, though, Caz. It doesn't change the fact that she ruined every last thing for you." Caroline hadn't had the in-depth conversation about her past with Hannah yet, but in time it would come. Still, it spoke volumes that Hannah could hazard a guess as to the life she'd had with her ex-wife.

"I was a coward who didn't walk away. It wasn't her fault."

Hannah took Caroline's hands. "I know that's how you feel, but she was your wife...she was supposed to love you and protect you. She was supposed to share a life with you *and* your hopes and dreams."

"I didn't make her happy," Caroline said, shifting away from Hannah ever so slightly. "But it really doesn't matter anymore. My time has been and gone. There's no use talking about something that can never be."

"I know it's not my business. I just...wish things could have been different for you. I'm entitled to that, aren't I?"

Caroline softened, cupping Hannah's cheek. "You are. And I appreciate it."

"Will you stay longer? I don't want to let you go yet."

Those were the things Caroline could get used to hearing. The words she'd longed for over so many miserable years. If Hannah wanted her to stay longer, then she would. "Okay."

"I really don't want to go away for work next week."

Hannah lay her head back on Caroline's shoulder, sighing. "Spending a night with you midweek has been lovely."

"That's the life of working for one of the best lawyers. But I'm proud of you. I hope you know that."

"It was touch and go for a minute, wasn't it? Almost not having the chance to be here with you like this."

Caroline didn't want to think about how things started for them. It wasn't going to play a part in the future, so it really wasn't an issue they needed to concern themselves with. "Things turned out the way they were supposed to. Now, tell me more about Edie and her change in mood tonight."

"Okay, but don't freak out."

Caroline frowned. Freak out? God, she hated that. Naomi always used to say it. "Why would I freak out?"

"Edie said something to me before. When you went to the bathroom."

"Okay." Caroline got comfortable, bracing herself for what was to come. "And what was it she said?"

"She asked again if you were a lesbian. And said that she likes you being here. And...that I like you."

"So, she's suspicious?" Caroline ran a hand down her thigh. "Okay, so..."

"I wouldn't say she's suspicious, Caz. She just notices that her mum is happy for once. And while I understand it's not what you want at the moment, I can't help but feel warmed by the conversation I had with her." Hannah sighed, shaking her head. "What I'm trying to say is, when the time comes, I don't think we have anything to worry about."

"Easy for you to say. She's not your student."

Hannah smiled, stroking a thumb across the back of Caroline's hand. "Don't think too much into it. Edie would be discreet if we asked that of her. And she wouldn't expect any kind of special treatment. Not that you'd give her it."

"Hannah."

"Yeah?" Those blue eyes shone as Hannah's gaze bored into Caroline.

"Can we give it some more time? We need to be absolutely certain here. I won't hurt Edie because we couldn't be adults and make the right decision. She means too much to me."

"Sure." Hannah slid her hand away from Caroline's, turning back to the TV. "I just feel really good about this, and I'm sorry you don't feel the same way. But only you know what you see in your future."

Caroline hadn't meant to upset Hannah, but it appeared to be exactly what she'd done. "Part of me sees you in my future, Hannah."

Hannah nodded slowly, chewing the inside of her cheek. "But part of you doesn't."

"I'm trying." Caroline placed a hand on the back of Hannah's neck, stroking her fingertips against her shoulder. "I really am."

Hannah suddenly brushed a hand across her cheek as a tear fell. Caroline tried to lean in, but Hannah shifted away. "Please, don't."

"Hannah..."

"You're trying, and I get that, but if you have to try...then I'm not sure I'm the right person for you. This should be effortless. It should be exciting. Trying shouldn't really come into it."

Caroline understood why Hannah felt that way, but she'd come out of a relationship that had destroyed the very person she was. In the months after leaving Naomi, Caroline wasn't sure how she could function alone. In the two years that had passed, she'd not only blocked out the idea of finding love, but she'd locked her heart away too. While she wanted Hannah to be the one who made her happy, Caroline hadn't expected this whirlwind romance. Because that's how it felt to her. Unexpected, uncertain, but yes…exciting. Whatever the outcome of it, she could safely say that Hannah had excited her.

"I think maybe we need a deeper conversation here," Caroline said, sitting forward. "Not tonight, I'm not sure you have much attention left for me given how I've upset you, but it is needed. At some point."

"When I fall, I fall hard. At least, that's how it's been in the past. I've always fallen for the wrong people, but you…I felt differently about you the moment we met. I'm sorry. I'll give you the space you need."

"You say that like it's a bad thing, but I felt that connection with you the moment we met, too. So please, don't think that I'm trying to push you away. Life with and after Naomi was incredibly hard for me, so I'm processing. Can you allow me that?"

Hannah lifted Caroline's hand and kissed her knuckles. "You mean a lot to me. I can allow you whatever you need from me, Caz. If that's more or less, say the word. I don't want to do anything to jeopardise this with you."

Caroline chanced leaning in again, smiling into a kiss when Hannah didn't back away. "You mean a lot to me, too. This isn't about you, you're perfect, but I want to get it right. For me. For us."

"Come here." Hannah opened her arms to Caroline, laying them down lengthways on the couch. "I like having you in my life. We can take this at your pace."

CHAPTER 19

Caroline turned her watch towards herself, groaning when she realised she still had an hour before her train reached the station. She'd decided to be bold, to travel down to London and surprise Hannah now that her court case was almost over, but the journey could have been better. She'd already get in later than expected because of a delay on the line an hour into the journey. And now she sat here wondering if she'd done the wrong thing. Hannah was away with her boss. Her successful lawyer boss. A woman who, by the sounds of it, didn't take kindly to Hannah being interrupted at work.

But Hannah wasn't working this evening, and she was only travelling home tomorrow, so Caroline needn't worry. Juliet surely couldn't command Hannah's time at night, too. Could she?

She can try, but Hannah's all mine once I get to that hotel.

Caroline grinned, watching the world go by outside the carriage window. Rolling hills, clear blue sky. She couldn't recall the last time she'd done something so spontaneous. Naomi would have scoffed at Caroline's arrival if she'd done something like this for her. But Hannah wouldn't do that. No, Hannah would have that adorable grin and that sexy gaze waiting for her. It was her default setting when Caroline was around.

Her phone buzzed on the table.

We won! Hannah x

Caroline smiled, instantly pressing reply. Hannah had been nervous as the week progressed, her first court case approaching since she'd started working for Juliet. But Hannah was gifted in many ways, her career included, so Caroline hadn't worried for one moment. All Hannah could do was the very best. And as Caroline had explained to Hannah, it was Juliet's reputation on the line. Not Hannah's.

That's amazing! I'm so happy for you. Caz x

Juliet has already called the hotel and ordered champagne. What a change to my old job! Hannah x

Caroline felt a slight pang of jealousy hit her in the stomach. Juliet got to wine and dine Hannah last night. There was *no way* she was getting her tonight too!

Do you two have plans then? Caz x

God, no. I'm too tired to go out to any bars. And I didn't exactly bring any outfits for a night out. We'll have dinner, and then I'm calling it a night. Hannah x

What's the hotel like? Caz x

Caroline didn't particularly care what it was like. But she did need to know Hannah's room number. She could ask, but it would ruin the surprise. Well, providing Hannah was surprised by Caroline's arrival.

Juliet upgraded my suite too. She already had a fancy one, you know what she's like. So I'm in the prestige suite now. Check me out! Hannah x

Very swanky. Well, have fun. Don't get too drunk while I'm not there to look after you. Caz x

I wish you were here. My suite is going to be far too big for me alone. Who will keep me warm? I'm sad. Hannah x

Oh, I'll keep you warm. Caroline grinned, shaking her head slightly.

You'll be home before you know it. Text me when you're back at your room. Caz x

I will. Missing you. Hannah x

Missing you, too. Caz x

Caroline locked her phone and lowered it back down to the table. The prestige suite. Sounded wonderful. Caroline could hardly wait to see it for herself.

Now if the train could move a little faster...

Hannah lowered her satchel to the floor, eyeing the huge bed as she closed her suite door behind her. Juliet had come back to her room with her, but Hannah wasn't quite sure why. They'd had a light dinner, and now Hannah was ready to shower and climb into bed. It wasn't late, but Hannah wanted to sleep so she could be fresh for seeing Caroline tomorrow. "You really didn't have to upgrade me. The one I was in was absolutely fine."

Juliet looked out at the River Thames, glancing over her shoulder briefly. "I've told you, you work for me now. We don't stay in the small, cramped rooms."

Okay, but her other room had hardly been small and cramped. She hadn't even been treated to hotels like this when she was escorting. Not that she'd seen the inside of any hotel rooms with clients. But she often met clients at the hotels they were staying at and had dinner there.

"Well, thank you. It's lovely."

"Heard from your lover this evening?" Juliet turned, folding her arms across her chest. The way Juliet referred to Caroline as her 'lover' seemed a little odd, but Juliet was a woman who did and said what she pleased. Hannah was beginning to get used to it. "How does she feel about you being away with someone who used to pay you for company?"

"She...doesn't feel anything about it." At least, Hannah assumed that. Caroline hadn't made any kind of comment about Hannah and Juliet being away together. But this was business. Nothing more. "Should she?"

"Did you tell her what I said to you when we had dinner all those weeks ago?"

"Oh, about how you're jealous of her?" Hannah laughed, throwing herself down on the bed. She sat up on her elbows, watching Juliet as she moved around the suite. "No, I didn't. Why would I?"

"I just thought it may have come up in conversation."

Hannah arched a brow when Juliet poured another glass of champagne and handed one over. "Trust me, I've been far too busy to be having pointless conversations with Caz. *Far* too busy."

Juliet lifted a hand, stopping at the foot of the bed. "Okay. The less I know, the better."

But Hannah wanted to know more. Juliet had always been so closed off while she was her client. She sat up, kicking off her heels and folding her legs under herself. If they were going to get on well at work, Hannah wanted to know how Juliet felt. She wouldn't have *anyone* interfering with her relationship. Not even the woman who had thrown her a lifeline with this job. "You really were interested in me?"

"Mmhmm. Perhaps I should have said something before this thing started with your girlfriend." Juliet remained at the foot of the bed, her hip jutted as she sipped her champagne. "How foolish of me."

"Why didn't you?"

"Would the answer change anything for you?" Juliet

lowered herself to the edge of the bed, turning to face Hannah. "Would it mean anything to you?"

Hannah cleared her throat. "No."

"Then I don't know why you're asking the question."

"Intrigue, I suppose. You never once gave me a hint of how you felt, but now that I'm involved, you have no issues saying it..."

"I didn't want you to think I wanted to sleep with you just because you were an escort. I was biding my time, getting to know you...but then it was too late."

Hannah narrowed her eyes, not quite believing what Juliet was saying. "Did you offer me this job for that reason?"

"God, no. And I'd also never do anything to jeopardise what you have. I offered you this job because I could see how much you loathed the one you had. When you mentioned your previous employment, I knew I wouldn't have to worry about you. And I was right. You're a natural at this."

"Juliet, if this is going to cause issues between us, I need you to tell me now. I...can't lose Caz. I won't do *anything* that could put me in a position to lose her. She means too much to me."

"That's not me, Hannah. You're involved. I'd never do anything to ruin your relationship. You have my word."

A light knock on the door had Hannah groaning. "What have you ordered now? I don't even know if I can finish this glass of champagne."

"I...haven't ordered anything. I only came back here to finish the champagne with you and maybe have a look at the suite." Juliet watched the door with a confused look on her face. "I really don't know who it is."

Hannah frowned, approaching the door. When she opened it, the biggest smile spread on her mouth. "Caz! What are you doing here?"

Caz didn't respond. She stepped forward, gripping the

lapels of Hannah's suit jacket, and pushed her to the wall just inside the suite. Her lips claimed Hannah's with an unexpected but very welcome urgency, a low throaty moan escaping Caroline as she pulled back. She touched her forehead to Hannah's, smiling as her thumb brushed Hannah's bottom lip. "God, I missed you."

Hannah knew how that felt. They hadn't seen one another since last Sunday morning. It was now Friday night.

But then Juliet cleared her throat, shocking Caroline. She took a few steps back, eyeing Juliet as she appeared from behind the wall.

"Hi." She held out a hand. "Hannah's boss, Juliet. Lovely to meet you."

Caroline managed a smile, but there was something there in her eyes that Hannah hadn't seen before. Was that...jealousy? Caroline stepped forward and took Juliet's hand. "Caroline. Hannah's partner."

"Oh, I know who you are. I've heard all about you."

Caroline's shoulders seemed to relax ever so slightly at that. While Hannah loved the fact that Caroline had shown up, she was really hoping she hadn't done so with the intention of catching Hannah doing something she shouldn't be.

"I'm going to leave. You two have plans," Juliet said, stepping around Caroline. "Great work again, Hannah. If I don't see you both in the morning at breakfast, I'll see *you* on Monday at the office."

"Y-yeah. See you soon." Hannah's brow creased as she watched Juliet leave, the door closing softly behind her. And then she turned her attention back to Caroline. "I...didn't think you were coming here."

"I wanted to surprise you." Caz leaned in again, dropping her overnight bag to the floor. Hannah accepted the kiss, but something didn't feel right. "But...you don't seem to be taking this surprise very well."

"You brought a bag and everything."

Caroline separated from Hannah, frowning. "I did. But I feel as though you want me to pick it up and leave your room if I'm being honest."

"Why *are* you here, Caz?"

"Because I missed you. Because I thought it might be a lovely idea to come here on a whim and spend the night with you. Because..." Caroline paused, watching Hannah where she rested against the wall. "Because I wanted to be with you. Is... that not okay?"

"Right."

"Yeah, this hasn't quite gone to plan." Caroline lifted her overnight bag again. "I thought you would have been happy to see me."

Hannah placed her hand on Caroline's wrist. "Put the bag down, babe."

Caroline dropped her bag onto a nearby chair. As she stepped away from Hannah, moving towards the window, she wrapped her arms around herself. "I didn't think it would be a problem."

"It's *not* a problem," Hannah said, approaching Caroline. She placed a hand on the small of Caroline's back, kissing her shoulder. "I didn't expect you. But I'm happy you're here."

Caroline turned to face Hannah. "Why did you ask me why I was here? I saw that look in your eyes. Questioning."

"D-did you come here to catch me?"

"To catch you?" Caroline continued to stare through Hannah, slight frown lines between her brows. "Catch you where?"

Hannah swallowed, aware that putting this idea in Caroline's head could backfire on her. "Here. With Juliet."

Caroline's brows shot up, genuine surprise now in her eyes. "You think I wanted to catch you cheating?"

Hannah slowly lifted a shoulder, casting her gaze on the space between them. She really didn't want that to be the reason, but she couldn't recall the last time anyone she cared about 'surprised' her. "I don't know."

"I...no. That's not why I'm here. Do you really think that of me? That I'd show up somewhere hoping to catch you in bed with another woman?"

"It's not just any other woman, though, is it, Caz? It's an ex-client. And I know she's my boss, but that thought must still be there."

Caroline nodded, lowering the arms she'd had wrapped around her. "I see. You think I don't trust you. I had no idea you felt this way."

"I saw that jealousy in your eyes when you realised Juliet was here." Hannah couldn't lie to Caroline. It was clear as day. Juliet likely noticed it, too.

"Of course I was jealous. She's spent the last three days with you and was in your suite when I arrived. But I didn't think for one second that you'd be sleeping with her. God, Hannah. You really believe that?"

"I'm sorry."

"I just wanted to be here with you. It's been a miserable week without you, so I thought I'd jump on a train and be with you. Simple as that."

Hannah felt dreadful. Mostly because if the shoe were on the other foot, she'd be jealous to find Caroline in a room with someone else. It wouldn't mean she didn't trust Caroline, not at all. "I feel like an idiot now."

Caroline's shoulders sagged as she puffed out her cheeks. "I don't ever want you to feel that way, Hannah. Like I don't trust you. I travelled here to be with you, not to catch you out."

"I'm sorry."

"After the things I said to you on Sunday..." Caroline took a hesitant step forward. "I know I hurt you when I said I was trying, and...well, I wanted to show you that I *do* want to be with you. That even though I'm a mess sometimes and fully believe you'll see sense one day in the future, I want to be with you in the here and now. That it's not just part of me that wants to be with you, as I foolishly said, but *all* of me. And it always has been deep down. I just...I try to protect myself."

"I know you do. That's why I didn't take it to heart too much. Caz, I know life has been hard for you in the past, that it's taken a lot for you to trust me and let me in...but I want this to work for us. If it's what you want, I really want it to work."

"It *does* work. It works more with you than it ever did with Naomi. God, it *really* works, Hannah. I suppose I just...try not to get my hopes up. It's a downfall, I'm aware of that, but you've been patient with me, and I wanted to surprise you."

"You really missed me so much that you wanted to surprise me?" Hannah's voice unexpectedly broke, the idea that Caroline missed her quite overwhelming. Hannah knew she could love Caroline with everything she possessed, but when Caroline's true self unexpectedly broke through the self-doubt, yeah...it *was* overwhelming. She took Caroline's hands, bringing them to her lips. "I'm so happy you're here."

"Are you sure about that?" Caroline smiled, cocking her head.

"I am. I think it was something Juliet said that sort of put the idea in my head as to why you were here."

Caroline tensed. "What did she say?"

"Nothing that matters right this second."

"No. I want to know. Whatever she said, I need to know."

"Before I came to your place that night. The night when we basically got together. Well, we'd gone out to dinner earlier in the week while we were working, and Juliet made a comment about how she was jealous you'd potentially get to see me naked one day."

Caroline rolled her lips inward, nodding slowly.

"And then tonight, she asked if I'd told you about that conversation. She mentioned how you felt about it. What she'd said."

"Well, I knew nothing about it. But even if I did, why would I worry? I'm the one you spend your evenings with. I'm the one who gets you outside of work...not her."

"I know, babe. I think it just stuck with me. Then you showed up, and I wondered if you were feeling something about us working together. But I know you trust me. I really do."

Caroline snaked an arm around Hannah's waist, taking her bottom lip between her teeth. "So, the hot lawyer is jealous of me?"

Hannah pressed a hand to Caroline's chest. "Excuse me? Hot lawyer!"

"Oh, come on. Anyone with a pulse probably thinks she's hot. The issue I have with that is that she knows it. It's not my idea of the perfect woman."

"It's not mine either."

Caroline pressed her body to Hannah's. "What *is* your idea of the perfect woman?"

"You. Always." Hannah held Caroline close, kissing her way along her jawline. When she reached Caroline's ear, she whispered, "Would you like to get naked, gorgeous? This room is going to waste if we don't make full use of it."

"Mm. I thought you'd never ask."

CHAPTER 20

Okay, this was the life.

Hannah stood at Caroline's kitchen sink, rinsing their dinner plates while Caroline sat on the counter. Life had been fairly straightforward lately; Caroline was definitely coming out of her shell more. That much was clear when she landed in the kitchen before dinner wearing Hannah's clothes. But she loved that. It meant Caroline felt comfortable. They had a long way to go in terms of meeting one another's friends and family, but Hannah was happy to take it all in Caroline's stride. Rushing things may only set their relationship back, and Hannah wasn't prepared to risk that.

Caroline meant far too much to her.

But Hannah did want to mention Edie. Her daughter was becoming more and more suspicious of her mum's newfound happiness, and there were only so many times Hannah could blame it on the joy work brought her. Nobody was *that* enthusiastic.

"You have something on your mind," Caroline spoke suddenly.

"Well..." Hannah paused, slotting the final plate into the

dishwasher and turning the tap off. "When you're sitting there in my clothes, *a lot* runs through my mind."

"I'm wearing sweatpants and a T-shirt. Hardly anything special."

"Special to me." Hannah dried her hands on a tea towel as she came to stand between Caroline's legs. "And *so* beautiful." She drew Caroline into a kiss, smiling when Caroline deepened it immediately. Few things in life pleased her as much as Caroline's lips did. She'd quickly figured that out.

Caroline moaned, grinning against Hannah's mouth before pulling back. She brushed Hannah's hair from her face, studying her.

"I had something I wanted to talk to you about," Hannah said, palming Caroline's thighs slowly.

Concern flashed in Caroline's eyes as she reached for her glass of water and sipped. "Oh. Is everything okay?"

Hannah cocked her head, smiling. There was something incredibly beautiful about Caroline showing her vulnerability.

"Is it the clothes? Or was it dinner?" Caroline shot from the counter.

"It wasn't the clothes or dinner," Hannah said softly, catching Caroline by the wrist.

Caroline frowned. "Then what is it? What did I do?"

"You didn't do anything." Hannah took Caroline's hand, their bodies pressed together. "Hey, relax."

Caroline's cheeks flushed, her eyes cast between them. It didn't happen often, but Caroline did appear wary at times. As though she didn't want to rock the boat in any way at all.

"Look at me." Hannah lifted Caroline's chin with two fingers, hoping her own eyes reassured Caroline. She hated the thought of her girlfriend imagining Naomi when they were together. Hannah knew she could be wrong, but Caroline's body language told her everything she needed to know. She *had* been imagining Naomi then. “You’re perfect, okay? Dinner was amazing. *You’re* amazing.”

Caroline scoffed. “I’m pathetic.”

“Hey! Don’t talk about my girlfriend like that.”

A gentle smile settled on Caroline’s mouth, her shoulders relaxing. “I had a moment. Sorry.”

“I just wanted to talk to you about us. Nothing to worry about.” Hannah added quickly. “But maybe we should do it another time.”

“No. Let’s do it now. Whatever it is, I want to get it out of the way.”

Hannah nodded, resting back against the opposite counter. “How do you feel about me telling Edie we’re together?”

Caroline toyed with the hem of the T-shirt she wore, chewing her lip. “Is that a good idea?”

“I don’t know. That’s why I wanted to run it by you first.”

Hannah would never go behind Caroline’s back about something so big. What she thought mattered the most. After all, Caroline was Edie’s teacher, and if she had any doubts, Hannah would let it lie until Caroline felt more comfortable.

“Honestly, I don’t know,” Caroline said, lifting herself back up onto the counter. “I’m not worried about me. I’m worried that the kids at school will find out and make life difficult for Edie. She’s had a bad enough time as it is.”

Hannah’s heart melted. “You really care about her, don’t you?”

“I care about all my students,” Caroline paused. “But yes, I’ve been fond of Edie since she started at St Peter’s. She’s bright, she’s driven, and she’s very caring. I just...worry.”

“Worry?”

“That she’ll find out about us, I’ll mess everything up, and then she’ll hate me for hurting you.” Caroline’s eyes held a genuine fear, but Hannah knew nothing like that would ever happen. Edie didn't have it in her to hate anyone. "Because you and Edie are what matters to me most right now. I can deal with the secrecy if it means we're doing the right thing."

"I don't see that happening." Hannah held out a hand, grinning when Caroline tugged her back between her legs. When she showed even just a hint of confidence, Hannah swooned for this woman all over again. And she knew deep down that Caroline Baker was potentially the sexiest woman Hannah had ever laid eyes on. She just needed to search for it a little. "We've been dating for eight weeks now, and I see...I *feel* nothing but great things."

Caroline leaned down, kissing Hannah gently. And then she pulled back, pressing her forehead to Hannah's. "If you think telling Edie is the right thing to do, then okay. Tell her."

Hannah frowned. "Of course it's the right thing to do. We're together, Caz. I'm happy, and I hope you feel the same way."

"I...do."

Hannah took a step back. "But?"

"But I feel as though you'll be missing out on so much by being tied to me. I'm boring, Hannah. I always will be."

Shocked, Hannah's brows rose. Caroline *was not* boring.

"And I know you're only going to tell me that I'm wrong, that you're happy with how we are, but I find it hard to believe that I spark *anything* exciting inside you, Hannah."

Hannah couldn't bear hearing Caroline say these things. God, this woman was everything to her. "How long have you been feeling like this?"

"Most of the time." Caroline smiled weakly. "I've loved *every* second we've spent together, I hope there can be so many more, but I'm not stupid...and I don't want you to bring Edie into this unless you're *absolutely* sure about me."

"I am sure, Caz. Why don't you believe that?"

Caroline's intense green eyes stared back at Hannah, a

sadness that she never wanted to see sitting in them. "Because things like this don't happen to me. A gorgeous woman and a lovely kid in tow? It doesn't happen to people like me. I know what I want, but I'm not sure you do. I'm forty-seven, Hannah. Why would you possibly want to settle down...settle *for*...me?"

Hannah's heart tightened. Why *wouldn't* she want to settle down with Caroline?

"All I'm saying is that I need you to be sure before you tell Edie anything. Don't tell her about me if there's *any* doubt in your mind." Caroline slid off the counter, squeezing Hannah's hand as she stepped away. "I know you'll do the right thing. Edie is your world; you'd never intentionally hurt her."

Caroline left the kitchen, but Hannah found herself rooted to the spot, unable to follow her. That woman was quickly becoming everything in Hannah's eyes, but would telling Caroline that scare her off? Would Caroline even believe her? Hannah knew it could be a risk worth taking, and as she stood here, she knew it was certainly something she had to consider.

Caroline sat lengthways on the couch, chewing her lip as she recalled the conversation she'd had in the kitchen with Hannah. She hadn't meant to sound so...ridiculous, but her time spent with Hannah lately felt a little overwhelming. Caroline wasn't the kind of woman who fell for the first person she came across, but with Hannah, oh...with Hannah, she was well on her way there. And that's where the fear came from. Falling in love for it to not be returned. Getting so deep into something Caroline knew she'd never come back from. Because this? What she felt with Hannah... It was far more intense than Caroline thought it ever could be.

This...was life-changing territory.

But the atmosphere between them as they sat on separate couches felt a little murky. She didn't want to go through that uncomfortable silence phase with Hannah; she'd spent long enough doing that with Naomi. No, what she wanted was to explain herself in a way that Hannah would understand. She would love nothing more than to have the perfect life with this woman, but Caroline and perfect had *never* gone hand-in-hand. If she hadn't been through such a dreadful marriage, Caroline would have been head over heels in love by now. She would have been planning a future with Hannah and Edie. But the scars of the past would never truly heal. They may fade on occasion, they may lay dormant during those perfect moments she shared with Hannah, but they'd always be there...somewhere.

"I don't know what she did to you, Caz. I don't know why *anyone* would want to hurt you, but I'm not her. I never will be," Hannah paused as Caroline turned to her. Had Hannah been watching the cogs turning in her head? Probably. "I know being in a relationship must be incredibly difficult for you, to throw the past away and just live for you, but you deserve to be happy. I-I want to be the person you feel happy with, but will you ever allow me that chance?"

Caroline offered a faint smile. She hadn't meant to upset Hannah earlier, but the hour-long silence was beginning to make sense.

"I'd *never* force this with you. I'd never do anything you don't want me to do. I thought by asking you your opinion on telling Edie, it would have been good for us. That maybe we could have come to some kind of agreement. But all I ended up with was you telling me how I should feel about you while offering me an out at the same time. A-and now I don't know what to think."

"Hannah..."

"There are so many feelings I have for you. God, the more

I'm with you, the harder I find it to let you go. But I get the impression that you're trying to push me away. And if you are, if you don't want to be with me, I'd rather you came out and said it. If this is the point where I have to let you go because I don't make you happy, then please...be straight with me."

Caroline sat forward when she noticed a tear slowly slip down Hannah's cheek. She wanted to reach out and catch it, but Hannah held up a hand.

"I know you've been hurt, Caz. But so have I. All I've *ever* wanted is someone who takes me and Edie as we are. All I've ever *dreamed* about is waking up with someone who wants me in their life. I thought you were that person," Hannah paused, running her hands down her thighs as she exhaled a shaky breath. "But whenever I bring up Edie...telling her about us... you shut me down. I-is that a red flag? Should I be concerned?"

Caroline hadn't expected Hannah to say any of this. She also hadn't intended to come across that way. But Hannah wasn't finished.

"Nobody knows about us. You don't invite me over when Gail or Joy are here, and you won't meet anyone in my life." Hannah frowned and then laughed as she nodded. "Ah. I see what's going on here."

"W-what?"

"You have no intentions of this getting serious."

"Whoa, no. You're wrong." Caroline scrambled to her feet, the heartache in Hannah's eyes sending Caroline to her knees in front of her. "Completely wrong."

Hannah looked down at her, reaching out and cupping her cheek. "You're going to make someone *very* happy one day, Caz. If you can just accept your worth, if you can open your heart enough to let people in, I know you'll find the person for you. And when you do...God, when you do, you'll realise just how special you are. How beautiful you are inside and out. The past won't matter because all you will feel is the love. And I wish you could feel that with me, it's all I've wanted since you opened a part of yourself up for me, but we're on different paths. I see that now."

The weight of those words stunned Caroline.

Hannah had said *someone*.

Not *her*. Not *them*.

Just...*someone*.

"I should get my things together and head off." Hannah leaned down, pressing her lips to Caroline's forehead. But she lingered, sniffling as though she was saying goodbye. "Keep the clothes. They look good on you."

"Hannah, please don't go..."

"When Kirsty left me, I told myself I'd never be in that position again. I spent three years loving her in every way I possibly could. I thought I knew what I wanted when I was with her. I swore I'd never entertain something serious again. But then I walked through that door and saw you waiting at the bar, and it was as though everything aligned once and for all. The night I met you, I knew you were going to be it for me. Completely. Wholeheartedly. I just knew it. And then there was the part of me that I'd buried away once I knew I was attached to you. The part that didn't want to put Edie through anymore letdowns or bad mistakes because of me. So telling her about us was a huge deal for me."

"I never intended for our evening to turn out like this, Hannah. But I'm scared. I'm terrified of giving myself to you completely, only to lose you in the end."

"Why are you so convinced you're going to lose me?"

Caroline swallowed. If she had any hopes of Hannah staying, it was time to put her heart on the line.

"Caz?"

"I'm falling in love with you, Hannah."

The slightest twitch at the corner of Hannah's mouth was visible, but Caroline needed more of a response. Hannah just wiped fresh tears from her cheeks, though.

"I want nothing more than to come home to you and Edie, sitting down to dinner together, doing all the things a family would do, but I'm so scared to let down every last wall I've built...and just enjoy this."

Hannah lifted both hands, cupping Caroline's face. "Let us in, Caz. Live for yourself and be happy."

"What if I fail?"

Hannah shook her head, smiling. "That's not possible."

"How can you be so sure?"

"Because it's not possible to fail at something that feels so beautiful. And because I'm falling in love with you too. Every last thing about you, Caz."

Caroline's heart fluttered, every vein throbbing throughout her body. "Y-you are?"

"Honestly," Hannah whispered against Caroline's lips. "I think I'm already there."

Caroline really needed to *not* get carried away right now. Hannah was giving her something she'd always wanted, but could it be absolutely true? God, she hoped so.

And then those blue eyes shone with a love that left Caroline breathless. "H-Hannah?"

"Yes?"

"We should tell Edie."

CHAPTER 21

T*wo weeks later...*

Caroline lowered herself to the couch, picking up her coffee and wrapping her hands around it. They'd discussed telling Edie about them, and two weeks on, neither had made the next move. So this evening, while Edie was at her dad's, Caroline wanted to be open and honest with Hannah. She wanted no secrets, nothing surprising to creep up on them when they least expected it, and then they could make a final decision on when they would tell Edie. It was becoming increasingly clear to Caroline that she couldn't wait much longer. Avoiding one another throughout the week was torture.

"Hannah?"

Hannah poked her head around the door. "Yeah?"

"Come and sit with me for a few minutes. We'll clear away dinner together in a while."

Hannah's brows drew together, that familiar unease present as she slowly made her way towards the couch. "What's up?"

"I want to tell you about my past," Caroline said, studying Hannah's face. She didn't need it to become an issue, so if they could get it all out in the open, that was step one completed. "If you wouldn't mind listening..."

"Honestly, I was hoping you'd feel comfortable enough to tell me one day." Hannah took Caroline's hand, shifting closer. "So, yes. Of course I'll listen."

Caroline smiled, staring down at her coffee. While she wanted to be open, she didn't want to come across as weak. Because before Naomi, she wasn't weak. She was strong and full of life. "Just...promise me you won't run."

"I'm not going anywhere, Caz. Well, only to bed with you, but I don't think that's what you're getting at right now."

Caroline couldn't help the grin she wore. Hannah always said things that would ease Caroline's racing mind. Inappropriate or not, Caroline loved that about her girlfriend. "I'm sure we can figure that part out later."

Hannah made herself comfortable, lifting Caroline's legs over her thighs, her undivided attention now firmly on Caroline. "Talk to me, Caz. I don't ever want you to feel as though you can't."

"I think you're the only one I feel completely comfortable talking with. Even if it doesn't always feel that way. Which I'm sorry about."

Hannah lifted a shoulder, toying with Caroline's fingers. "I knew you'd come to me when you were ready to. It's why I've never pushed to know anything other than what you tell me."

"I...met Naomi seventeen years ago. It was during a night out. We connected right away, but something always felt a little off about her. She was overly confident, some may say conceited, but I liked that confidence in a woman. I guess I chose to see what I wanted to see, and even though friends told me to be careful...to take it slowly, Naomi just had this pull. Looking back, I knew it was just a case of me wanting to find love. To settle down. I'd just turned thirty, and all my friends were happy, engaged, some even pregnant with their second child. But I was...stuck. I had my job, but it wasn't enough."

Hannah nodded. "I get that."

"At first, I thought it was all rainbows and sunshine. Yes, Naomi liked to do her own thing, she lived life on her terms, but I didn't mind that. When she told me she was going out with friends, but I wasn't invited, I wasn't particularly bothered. I'd been working all week, so a night in was what I preferred a lot of the time. Again, my friends told me to watch my back. Some people had seen her out in town with other women, but Naomi always reassured me if I questioned it. It got to the point where I stopped questioning it because she made me feel awful whenever I did. That I was insecure and needy. She threatened to leave if I questioned her trust again."

"Mm. I know how that feels. But our gut is always right, isn't it?"

"Usually, yes." Caroline smiled weakly. "Once we got married, five years later, everything changed. She went out of her way to say nasty things, and most mornings, I didn't know what kind of Naomi I was going to get. On the rare occasion she was nice to me, it made me wonder why. You know, had she done something she shouldn't have and felt guilty about it?" Hannah nodded, squeezing Caroline's hand. "But I didn't have the energy in me to fight about it. So, I'd just go along with whatever mood she was in. There were times when we went five days without a single conversation. She'd fly off the handle about something, but I'd find myself apologising. And then she'd give me the silent treatment, slamming doors and whatnot. God, I'd sit in the living room alone, wondering what the hell I'd done. And when I couldn't think of anything, I thought I was losing my mind. Because, for the way she treated me, I must have done something wrong."

"Was it ever physical?" Hannah asked, her voice shaking.

"No. But sometimes, I wonder if that would have been easier. Because at least then, I'd have known where I stood. If she'd ever lay a hand on me, I'd have walked away. That moment...I'd have packed my things and left. But the mind games...I never knew if I was coming or going. And the way she used to look at me," Caroline paused, a shiver travelling through her. "She used to look at me with so much disgust that I wondered if she wished I wasn't breathing. And if I asked her why she was in a bad mood, she'd tell me I'd caused her mood. Dinner had been terrible, or the house was a mess, or the dishes hadn't been put away. She used to tell me that she worked her arse off and the least I could do was keep our home in shape. But I worked just as hard, Hannah. Some days I didn't get home until after five in the evening."

"Hey, you don't have to tell me how hard you work. I know just how much you do..."

"I'll always remember one night. Naomi had come home one day and said that we'd been invited to a charity event through her firm. For the next few days, she was so excited...and she included me in all of her plans. She took me out, bought me a gorgeous ball gown, and I'd booked my hair and nails. It was the first time in months that she'd shown me any interest whatsoever, so you can imagine how delighted I was to be invited to something so swanky."

"Bet you looked amazing in that ball gown." Hannah grinned, lifting Caroline's hand and kissing her knuckles.

"I wouldn't know because it never happened." Caroline noted the confusion in Hannah's eyes, her only saving grace being the fact that Hannah was the complete opposite of Naomi. People could argue that they didn't know one another well enough for Caroline to claim that just yet, but Caroline had always had doubts in some way about her ex-wife. She'd always been different from the outset. But Hannah... She was genuine from day one. "I came home that afternoon, hair and nails done. My gown had been hanging up for three weeks. I couldn't wait to let my hair down and enjoy myself. It wasn't often that I had the chance to mingle with Naomi and her 'rich friends'."

Hannah swallowed, sadness anchored in her eyes. "What happened?"

"Naomi was already home. She strode through the kitchen and told me that our plans were off. I assumed she wasn't going either, but then she explained that the one ticket she had for me...was being given to her new assistant at the company. Bryce. American. Very pretty."

"She just gave her wife's ticket to another woman?"

"Mm. Bryce seemed very fond of Naomi when we bumped into her a few weeks later in town. Very touchy, you know?"

"Do you think something was going on between them?"

Caroline hated to admit it, but she knew it had been. "Something was going on with someone. Naomi hadn't touched me in about six months at this point. Considering she was very sexual in the years before, she had to be getting her kicks elsewhere. They always say if your partner shows no interest, something is probably happening, right?"

Hannah smiled weakly. "Generally, yes."

"So, I went up to the bathroom, took off the professional makeup I'd just had done, and had a soak in the bath. She didn't even say goodbye to me that night. And I knew in that moment that I couldn't stay for much longer. It was making me miserable. She was ruining my life." Caroline scoffed. "She stripped me of who I was. That confidence I'd had when we met didn't exist anymore. I knew I was unhappy, but when I put it to her, she'd tell me she loved me and wanted a future with me. That she married me for a reason"

"So she could repeatedly hurt you?"

"I'm just not sure she ever really loved me. And that's okay, but I wish she'd been honest from the start. She proposed to me. She asked to move in with me."

"What made you end your marriage?"

Caroline couldn't say it was one thing in particular. Other than the fact that she'd woken up one day and realised what was happening. "It was everything rolled into one. I'd spent the week alone after she'd flown out to Greece with her friends and their partners. She called midweek and asked what plans I had for the weekend. I told her I'd arranged to meet friends from work. That didn't go down very well. She wanted to know which friends, and when I told her, she said I wasn't to go. That Sharon had always been flirty with me and that Naomi wasn't home to keep an eye on things. Sharon has a husband and three kids. She's the straightest woman I know."

"I know I've had the unfortunate pleasure of meeting Naomi, but she's far more vile than I first thought she was."

"It wasn't always that way. But once she started to stop me from accessing my own wage each month, insisting that she take care of our finances via the joint account, I knew it was only going to be downhill. Still, I wanted to try. Because I was a fucking idiot."

"No, babe. You're not an idiot. You married a woman you loved and expected the same in return. That's not idiocy; that's generally the way a relationship works. I'm sorry she treated you that way."

Caroline felt a weight lift from her chest. Hannah appreciated her honesty instead of her clamming up. "So, the other week when I had that moment in the kitchen, it was just... sometimes little things take me back."

"You mentioned the clothes you were wearing," Hannah offered, squeezing Caroline's hand. "My clothes."

"They smelled like you. I couldn't resist."

"But it was the clothes that took you back and started that moment you had."

"It was ridiculous, really. I thought I may have crossed the line."

Hannah shifted closer to Caroline, holding her jaw tenderly as she leaned in and kissed Caroline. "There is no line for you and I. Be yourself...because I love it all."

"I really hope you mean that." Caroline trembled inside. The idea of Hannah walking away was quite frightening. This was one of the reasons why she hadn't dated since her divorce. The pain of losing someone who means a lot to you. Okay, Naomi had come to mean practically nothing as time went on, but it was the knowledge that Caroline could get her heart broken all over again that had her in a constant state of fear. "Because I'm not sure I could imagine my life without you and Edie in it."

A tear slid from Hannah's eye as she closed them. "God."

"W-what?"

"You didn't just say me. You included Edie, too. You've no idea what that means, Caz."

"It means I want you both in my life."

"I feel like we could be really happy. And I know you have your doubts, your reasons for feeling the way you do, but...do you feel it too? At all?"

Caroline smiled, taking Hannah in her arms. "I feel it. And tomorrow, we tell Edie about us. That's that. I don't want to hide any longer."

Hannah exhaled a long slow breath as she relaxed against Caroline. "Tomorrow."

CHAPTER 22

Hannah woke to Caroline wrapped around her, that soft hair wild...and so fucking beautiful. They'd come back to Hannah's last night, ready to tell Edie about them today once she arrived home from Dylan's. Hannah wasn't worried. Caroline had told her a few weeks ago that she was falling in love with her, so it was hard to feel worry about anything at all, and this morning, after a night of mind-blowing sex, Hannah was on cloud nine.

She looked down. Caroline's arm was bent and resting on her chest, those naked shoulders begging to be kissed, touched...lavished by Hannah's tongue. Caroline had an extraordinary body. Every curve, soft and delicious beneath her palms. But it was the way in which Caroline's body responded beneath Hannah that really thrilled her. Hannah had never come across a woman who got lost in her entirely. Really, it was something to hold onto forever.

Hannah gently trailed her fingertips up and down the back of Caroline's arm, feeling her smile against her, the smallest moan rumbling in her throat. "If you keep doing that, we won't leave this bed."

"Now that's something I could consider for our Sunday morning."

Caroline tilted her head up, smiling as Hannah lowered her lips to hers. "Morning," Caroline mumbled. "You have the comfiest bed in the world."

"Oh? Been in that many beds that you'd know?"

Caroline blushed, lowering her head. "Don't be silly."

"Oh, no. That won't work for me. Speak, woman. I want answers." Hannah sunk further down the bed, meeting Caroline's eyes. "You were a minx once upon a time, weren't you?"

Caroline smirked. "Maybe."

"Oh, I like this. No, I love this. I knew you had it in you."

Caroline shook her head. "No, that's not me anymore, Hannah. I'm an entirely different person now."

"But I always knew that deep down you had it in you. You just have to remember who you were, Caz." Heat rushed through Hannah's body at the thought of Caroline letting go a little.

"Be careful what you wish for, Hannah."

Hannah frowned. "I don't..."

"I met Naomi the night I was out with my girlfriend at the time. We ended up taking her back with us to the hotel we'd booked for the night."

"No!" Hannah's mouth fell open. "Y-you—"

"Had a threesome, yes. And then I fell in love with Naomi. The girlfriend I was with at the time wasn't really anything serious, but Naomi...I was captivated by her."

Hannah shuddered. "Right."

"At least I thought I was. It was the thrill, you know? The excitement that came with some extremely hot sex. Back then, sex was absolutely my thing. I didn't give a shit what I got up to." Caroline laughed as she rolled onto her back. "I mean, I was always safe. But sex was incredible before I met Naomi."

"And now?"

"Oh, with you, it's... I'm not sure I can describe it. Being with you is probably the greatest achievement of my life. And I really mean that."

Hannah's heart swelled in her chest. The pride she had for this woman up there with one of her greatest achievements too. "Well, that's what matters. But you know, feel free to boss me around the bedroom anytime you like." Hannah shifted closer, sucking gently on Caroline's neck. "Mm, knowing what I now know is making me kinda hot for you more than I already was."

Caroline giggled when Hannah's hand slowly lowered down her stomach.

"Maybe I need to buy you some sexy lingerie to get things going," Hannah growled, her lips enveloping one of Caroline's pebbled nipples. "Fuck, you'd look amazing."

"Mum?"

The sound of the front door slamming shut and heavy footsteps up the stairs had Hannah's heart slamming against her ribcage as they separated and covered themselves quickly. Caroline tensed beside her, squeezing her hand beneath the cover.

Hannah was about to shout out, but Edie knocked on her bedroom door, and then the door flew open suddenly.

"I'm going to be a big sister!" Edie grinned proudly as she stood in the doorway, her eyes straying towards Caroline. "Mornin', Ms Baker."

Hannah glanced at Caroline. Thank God they were both covered up. Caroline just stared...right through Edie.

But Edie didn't appear to care that her teacher was in bed with her mum. "Yvonne is having a baby, Mum. I always wanted a sister or brother."

"That's wonderful, love. Tell her congratulations from me, okay?"

"I will. She's getting me a picture printed out when they go today for a scan thingy." Edie stepped further into the room, perching herself on the edge of Hannah's bed.

"Why, uh...why are you home early?"

"Because Yvonne has an appointment with the doctor. Dad has to take her because she keeps vomiting and doesn't want to drive." Edie lifted a shoulder, resting her ankle on her knee. "I haven't had breakfast yet."

"Well, I'll be down in ten minutes to make you some."

"Kay." Edie shrugged. "Ms Baker, are you staying for breakfast?"

"I..." Caroline cleared her throat when Hannah ran her thumb across her knuckles. "Yes, I'll be here for breakfast."

"Great." Edie got to her feet, shrugging her coat off as she approached the door. "I'll put the kettle on for you both. Tea or coffee, Ms Baker?"

Caroline puffed out her cheeks. "Coffee would be lovely, but Edie?"

"Yeah?"

"You don't need to call me Ms Baker when I'm here. Caz will be fine."

Edie grinned, her gaze switching between Hannah and Caroline. "Really happy for you, Mum."

And then Edie was gone, a whirlwind passing through momentarily. Caroline released a long slow breath, sinking down the bed until her head was under the covers.

"Well, that went well..."

"Your daughter has just caught me in bed with you. Her teacher." Caroline groaned as she rolled onto her side, taking the cover with her and cocooning herself.

Hannah, very naked, shot from the bed and closed the bedroom door, flicking the lock on the back as she turned back to face the bed. "Caz, this is the best outcome we could have hoped for. I mean, Edie didn't even bat an eyelid."

Caroline flung back the covers, blowing her hair from her face. "I'm. Mortified."

"Could have been worse, babe. She could have walked in while my head was between your legs."

Caroline shot bolt upright, a look of complete horror on her gorgeous face. "Oh, my God. I'd have died. On the spot, Hannah...I'd have died."

"It would have been a good way to go, though, right?" Hannah winked, and then she flung herself forward onto the bed, landing in front of Caroline. "Come on. Stop worrying. Edie bloody loves you."

"This can work, right?" Caroline swallowed, a slight frown line present between her brows. "How Edie was then... It wasn't just shock?"

"No. She's happy. I know she is. If she'd been upset, she would have turned around and walked out." Hannah grinned, her body thrumming with the excitement of what this meant for them. Edie knew...and she didn't hate it. "Please stay for breakfast. I know you probably want to run out the door so you can process this, but stay for breakfast at least."

"I'll be here. Don't worry."

With a steady hand placed on the wall beside her, Caroline took the stairs slowly, shaking all panic she could from her body. Edie...had caught her in bed with Hannah. It would have been humiliating whether she was Edie's teacher or not, but knowing the relationship they had with one another outside of this house...yeah, it was damn right humiliating.

But now, she had to put on a brave face and answer any

questions Edie had for them. Perhaps she wouldn't have a single one. Or maybe Caroline would still be here at three this afternoon answering Edie. Who knew?

She heard giggling and the sound of cutlery, but it didn't help to settle Caroline. Because the unknown was there waiting for her. Potentially ready to ruin all of this.

"Ms Baker!" Edie pulled out a chair for Caroline, her smile wide. "I've set the table; you can sit here."

Caroline eyed Hannah as she stood behind Edie, unable to suppress her own smile. "Perfect." Then she turned her attention back to Edie. "But Edie, it's Caz, remember."

"Sorry. I forgot."

Caroline took a few steps closer, leaning towards Edie. "That's okay. It'll take a little while to get used to."

"I'll try to remember."

Caroline squeezed Edie's shoulder and smiled. "I know. Now, what's for breakfast? Can I help?"

As much as Caroline wanted to get the discussion out the way, it seemed sensible to wait until they were all sitting around the table together.

"No, it's done. We made pancakes while you were still upstairs."

Still upstairs. That sent both a shiver and a thrill through Caroline. "Well, thank you."

Caroline took a seat, a cup of coffee already waiting in front of her. She gripped it, bringing it to her lips, and waited until someone decided to speak. She, herself, had no idea where to begin.

"Poached or fried eggs, Caz?" Hannah's voice floated towards Caroline, reminding her that everything was okay. "Or I can do boiled, whichever."

"Try mum's poached eggs," Edie whispered. "They're really good."

"Poached it is."

"Edie, Caz may not want or like poached eggs, love."

Caroline held up a hand. "Poached would be great. But don't go to any trouble for me if nobody else is having any."

"Edie will only have poached. Not sure who she thinks has raised her. Fancy pants!"

"So, Edie...you're going to be a big sister." Caroline had noted the excitement in Edie's eyes as she burst through the door. She had no idea the kind of relationship Hannah and Edie's dad had, but it was nice to see her included in what could only be an exciting time for her dad and his partner.

"Yeah. I hope it's a girl. But if not, I don't mind."

"I think you'll be a fantastic sister whichever way."

"I asked mum for a brother or sister for Christmas once. Then she had to tell me it wasn't possible. But it was the top of my Christmas list."

"Ah. Santa may be impressive with gifts, but he's not *that* good."

Caroline watched Hannah, a faraway look in her eyes as she stared out of the kitchen window. "Need a hand, Hannah?"

Hannah snapped out of her thoughts, turning her attention to the eggs. "No, babe. It's okay. Won't be long now."

Edie giggled, grinning to herself when she sat down facing Caroline. As adorable as it was to see Edie laughing at a simple term of endearment, Caroline needed to speak up. She couldn't wait much longer. "Edie, how do you feel about me being here this morning?"

Edie shrugged, sipping from her glass of fresh orange. "Fine."

"Is there anything you wanted to ask or wanted to know?" Caroline hated being so formal, but she had to remember that the child sitting across the table from her was her student.

"Will...you always be here?" Edie looked up slowly, hesitant in her questioning.

"Well, no. Not for the time being. I'll have to go home and get ready for work."

Work.

"Would you be upset if I didn't tell people you and my mum are seeing one another? The kids and stuff..."

"Not at all. I understand that school isn't the place to discuss that stuff. And really, nobody needs to know."

"Will you get in trouble if people do know?" Edie swallowed, lowering her eyes. "We don't want to get you into trouble."

We? Oh, bless her. "No, I wouldn't get into trouble. Nobody is doing anything wrong here. But when we're at school, I'm Ms Baker first and foremost."

"Kay."

"Eggs are ready! Who wants to eat?" Hannah arrived at the table with a stack of pancakes and eggs on a separate plate. "Bacon is coming now."

"Bacon, too? I could get used to this." Caroline winked in Edie's direction, garnering a smile from her student. It meant a lot to know that Edie supported them in this, but Caroline shouldn't be surprised. Edie was a shining example of what she hoped for with her kids at school. At home, she was only sweeter. More vocal.

"Caz?"

Caroline swallowed as her eyes drifted to Edie. She hadn't called her Ms Baker. "Yes, Edie?"

"Thanks for making Mum happy."

"Thank you both for inviting me into your home the way you have."

CHAPTER 23

"Please, *always* remind me how much I hate food shopping!" Caroline dropped three bags onto the worktop, smiling as she spun around to find Hannah watching her. If she hadn't noticed the car outside, Caroline would have been shocked as she walked through the door. She hadn't known Hannah would be here already. "It's your turn next time."

A week on from Edie walking in on them, and Hannah was spending the weekend at Caroline's. Being with one another at any given opportunity had just become normal, natural. Edie had left for her dad's this morning, her weekend bag in tow as she went to school beforehand, and hugged them both as Caroline had stayed over. For the last three mornings, Caroline had woken up at Hannah's.

Yes, she considered things moving too fast, but Hannah and Edie made her happy. Why deprive herself of that feeling? Why, after the dreadful few years she'd had alone, would she want to spend minimal time with the people who meant so much to her?

"Never mind the shopping. I have the entire weekend with

you!" Hannah wrapped her arms around Caroline's waist, moving into a lingering kiss. "God, you taste so good."

Caroline smiled against Hannah's lips. "What are you after?"

"You." Hannah grinned, holding Caroline at arm's length by the waist. "You seem different today. What's going on?"

"Nothing. I've just had a good week at work, and I've come home to you. What could possibly be better than that?"

"Sweet-talker."

Caroline had slipped her spare key into Hannah's hand two evenings ago, not expecting her to use it any time soon. But walking through the door to the smell of home-cooked food, the dining table set, Caroline couldn't help but be thrilled by it. "I didn't expect you to be here."

"I said I was spending the weekend with you." Hannah frowned, turning her attention back to the stove. "Didn't I?"

"Yes. You did. I just assumed you'd call me once you were home and let me know what time you'd be coming over."

Hannah's hand stilled mid-stir. "Shit. I'm sorry. I didn't think you'd mind if I let myself in."

"No, it's not that. Not at all."

"Sorry, babe. I should have called." Hannah lowered the sauce on the stove to a simmer, turning back to Caroline. "I just thought with you giving me your spare key, you know..."

"I want you here. Stop worrying." Wow, this made a change from Hannah reassuring Caroline. "I didn't expect you to be here, that's all. But am I happy you are? God, yes."

"I was only working a half day, so I thought if I came over early and started dinner, it was one less thing for you to worry about when you got in from work."

Caroline swooned all over again for Hannah. This...was her dream. She took Hannah in her arms, swaying them to the music that played low through the radio. "You're too good to me."

"You've been working all week. I've only been in three days. It's the least I can do."

"Well, thank you. I appreciate it."

"Edie texted before. Dylan and Yvonne had a little gift waiting for her when she got there. With the baby scan. She's so happy."

"Yes. She was very excited in form class this morning. She was telling her friends all about the baby."

"I'm happy for her. She's always wanted to be a big sister. It's not something I could ever give her, and I'm glad Dylan and I are on such good terms. It makes all of this so much easier. And Yvonne is lovely. She's always treated Edie like her own."

Could Caroline one day do the same? It was early days, but she felt protective towards Edie. She wouldn't ever expect either of them to see her as anything more, but it was a lovely thought. "I'm glad she has that with them. You...didn't want any more kids?"

Hannah cleared her throat and stepped away, focusing on dinner. "Need to get dinner finished. It'll be about ten minutes if you need to do anything beforehand."

Caroline's brows drew together. "Hannah?"

"Mm?" Hannah glanced over her shoulder briefly, not finding Caroline's eyes. "Do you want me to hang fire on dinner?"

"No. I want you to look at me."

Hannah turned, puffing out her cheeks.

"Are you okay? Have I said something I shouldn't have?"

"N-no. It's just...I'd rather not talk about it right now."

Caroline nodded slowly, still frowning. "Okay. But if you *did* want to talk, I'm here for you. I'm sorry if I said something to upset you." Caroline reached out a hand, taking Hannah's. "When you're ready, okay?"

Hannah smiled weakly. "There's not much to say. I just... can't have any more kids. Can we leave it at that? Please?"

Caroline lowered her head, squeezing Hannah's hand. "Of course. I'm so sorry."

"No, *I'm* sorry. I should have told you before now." Hannah moved towards the dining table, fiddling with the cutlery that already sat perfectly in place. "It's the kind of thing partners should know in the beginning. So, yeah. I'm sorry."

"I don't—"

"You should really change and stuff. Dinner is ready now. I'll plate up while you do what you need to do. Glass of wine?"

Caroline chose not to question Hannah further. It was clearly hurting her to speak about it. "A glass of wine would be lovely. I'll have whatever you decide to open."

"Perfect!"

Hannah cleared the table while Caroline sat back and finished her wine. Dinner had been quiet, uncertain, but she couldn't let this get to her. Yes, she should have told Caroline about her fertility issues long before now, probably the day she turned up here and told Caroline she wanted to be with her, but she couldn't change that now. All she could do was hope that Caroline would still be here in six months time. In a year. Hopefully the next ten of them.

She'd done her grieving after her traumatic birth with Edie. When the doctor had told her about the uterine scarring, the secondary infertility, Hannah had lain in bed and processed it all. Edie had been a miracle, really, considering Hannah had always been far more attracted to women. Dylan and her pregnancy had been the result of a drunken night. But thank God for Dylan. She couldn't have picked a better dad for Edie. She was Dylan's entire world. Hannah just hoped that was still the case when Yvonne's baby came along. But she shouldn't worry, not really. She meant it earlier when she told Caroline that Yvonne thought of Edie as her own.

"Can I help you clear away? Since it *is* my kitchen..."

Hannah forced a smile as she turned to Caroline. "Stay there. Enjoy your wine. I'm just pottering about."

"I see that. But why?"

Hannah laughed. "Because dinner needs clearing."

Caroline narrowed her eyes over the rim of her glass. "Mm. If that's what you want to believe, okay."

"Caz."

"Something changed earlier," Caroline said, getting to her feet. She stood behind Hannah, pressing the most gentle kiss to her shoulder. "I don't know what, but I'd really love to have a nice weekend alone with you. If what I said before was out of line—"

"Babe, it's not you. You asked a perfectly acceptable question. It's just..." Hannah relaxed against Caroline when she wrapped her arms around Hannah's waist from behind. "It's ruined everything in the past."

"What has?"

"The fact that I can't have kids."

Caroline turned Hannah in her arms, cocking her head slightly. "Please talk to me."

"Do you think it's a coincidence that my girlfriend of three years left me nine days after I told her I couldn't have kids?"

Caroline frowned. "It...could be. But I don't know. It's something you'd have to discuss with her."

"She ghosted me. Packed her stuff and left. Just...gone, just like that."

"I'm sorry she did that to you. I'm assuming if it lasted three years, it was serious?"

"It *was* serious. Nine months before, she asked me to marry her." Hannah didn't want any of this information to scare Caroline off, but they were definitely in a position where being honest was for the best. "We got talking one night. Kirsty told me how much she wanted kids. I was thrilled. Because I assumed she would be able to carry."

"And she couldn't."

"No. It seems neither of us was in a position to have a child. It was a miscommunication, I guess. She couldn't believe she'd met someone who also couldn't carry."

"I'm sorry." Caroline brushed Hannah's hair from her face, cupping her cheek. "I hate that she ghosted you. I really do."

"I guess it worked out for the best in the end. I wouldn't be here with you if Kirsty and I were still together."

Caroline beamed a smile, those green eyes soft and inviting. "I guess you're right."

"It's just...is it going to be an issue for us? That I can't have kids?"

Caroline appeared taken aback by that question. She opened her mouth to speak but fell short of any words. "I-I..."

"You can be honest with me, Caz. If you still dream of kids, I need you to be honest with me."

"I have *you*. That's all I need. I would love for you to consider me your family. Perhaps Edie too, down the line. Though I *completely* understand that I'm probably expecting too much when I say that. She has her parents and her stepparent. I wouldn't dream of coming in and rocking the boat. But she means a lot to me, Hannah." Caroline took a step back and held up her hands. "I'm not making any sense, and I don't want to put any pressure on this. What I'm saying is...I need *you*. I'm *happy* with you. I'm not going to get months, potentially years, into this and want more."

Hannah settled entirely at those words. Anyone else, and she may not believe everything they were saying, but Caroline was honest. She had no other setting. "If you're sure?"

"One hundred percent sure. I'm happy with my life now that you and Edie are in it. This works. It means so much to me."

"You said...Edie down the line."

Hannah noted the blush on Caroline's cheeks as she lowered her gaze. "Never mind."

"Tell me." Hannah reached out a hand and gripped Caroline's. "Please."

"I just meant that down the line, if it was okay with you, I'd treat Edie like my own. If things between us really took off, then I'd protect her as though she was my own."

Hannah bit back a sob, shaking her head as she pulled Caroline against her. This woman was everything Hannah had wished for in life. Kirsty made her happy to a point, but Caroline? There was no comparison. It simply wasn't possible.

"Hannah, you don't have to accept that from me. I just wanted you to know that I wouldn't see her as *just* your child. I'd love her and take care of her. Be whatever she needs me to be. But...only if it was what *you* wanted. What her dad wanted. I have no right to walk in here and do any of those things, but—"

Hannah held onto Caroline as though she would lose her at any moment. "I *would* want you to do that. I really would."

With her arms securely wrapped around Hannah, silence fell over them. Hannah knew Caroline was processing because she was doing the very same thing herself. But this was perfect. It was comfortable. It was safe. Caroline had always felt safe, and Hannah was glad her girlfriend was beginning to see herself as more than before. Because as the weeks progressed,

Caroline didn't appear worried by every little thing. She didn't question every step she took. No, Caroline was moving forward, and it was the most beautiful sight.

"Hey," Hannah whispered as she pulled back. She studied Caroline's eyes, the slight gold flecks, and smiled. "I love you."

Caroline's bottom lip quivered, her eyes brimming with tears.

"I do, Caz. I'll never hurt you. You mean the world to me. To Edie, too. So, when I tell you that I love you, I mean it with my whole heart."

Caroline cupped Hannah's cheek, stroking a thumb across her skin. "I love you, too."

"Let's leave the clearing up for now." Hannah guided Caroline out of the kitchen and into the living room. She could think of far better things to do than clean right now, and holding Caroline was top of that list. "Thank you for not running away."

"The way I feel about you...I'd be a fool to consider it for a single second."

"Hey," Caroline stroked Hannah's shoulder as she lay between her legs. "Did you want to go up to bed? You're falling asleep."

Hannah palmed Caroline's thighs, shaking her head. "No. I'm fine. I'm comfortable."

"Okay, if you're sure."

"I am. I could lie here all night. All I need is a blanket, and I'm never moving again."

Caroline loved that. How Hannah felt so protected by her. Because it was true. Caroline would protect Hannah and Edie until her dying breath. Coming into this, Caroline hadn't imagined feeling so strongly about another woman, but she couldn't help the feelings that seemed to be growing more intense every day. Hannah made her happy, Edie made her smile at the most unexpected moments, and Caroline couldn't imagine giving that up for anything in the world.

"Can I ask you something?"

Hannah tilted her head back on Caroline's shoulder. "Sure."

"What happened between you and Dylan? Why didn't it work out?"

"Oh, we were never together. Dylan was my best friend from the age of ten. I always hung around with the boys. The girls were too bitchy for me once we went to high school. But Dylan always had my back. We went to a party one night with a group of friends, and both got stupidly drunk. One thing led to another, and we slept together."

"Oh." Caroline was quite surprised by that. She didn't know why, but she was.

"Obviously, we both thought nothing of it. Why would we? We were invincible back then." Hannah rolled her eyes, dragging her nails gently up and down Caroline's thigh. "And then the periods stopped. And then I realised we weren't invincible. And then Edie was growing inside me."

"And look at the beautiful girl she is."

Hannah sniffled. "You have to stop saying things like that, Caz. It makes me want to drop to one knee and ask you to marry me."

Caroline chuckled. "Trust me, you wouldn't want me to be your wife! But back to your wonderful kid. She hasn't said anything we should worry about, has she?"

"Do you really think Edie has anything on her mind when you're here? She bloody worships you, Caz. If I didn't love you, I'd be concerned that you were going to run off with her."

"She's great. But then again, she has an amazing mum, so I shouldn't be surprised."

Hannah turned in Caroline's lap, gazing up at her. "You really mean that?"

"Of course I do."

"I've always tried to put her first and give her everything she needed. Not to make her spoilt, but because it's just the two of us. I know she has Dylan, and he really is amazing, but all her friends have both parents at home, and she doesn't. I didn't want her to feel as though we didn't love her when she was younger. And I know she'd never think that, but I was the one who foolishly slept with Dylan when I could barely look after myself."

"You wouldn't change the past, though. I know you wouldn't."

"Not for anything. I missed out on the holidays with the girls, nights out with work, but I wouldn't change anything because Edie has been my everything from the moment I realised I was pregnant. It wasn't even a question as to whether I'd keep her. Dylan's eyes lit up, and we decided to do it together while being apart."

"I admire you both."

"He's always on the phone with me, asking if I've met anyone. When Kirsty left, he was fuming—seething—because she'd moved in here with me, and Edie wasn't expecting her to disappear. She was quite upset by it all."

"I hope you know I'd never do that to you." Caroline pressed a kiss to Hannah's forehead. "And I know everyone probably says that, but like I said before...you and Edie are more than enough for me. I can't wait to see where this goes, and I can't wait to see Edie grow into an impeccable young woman. Though, if I'm being honest, she's already there."

"She really does love having you at ours. When you're in the shower and she's having breakfast, she asks if she can make your morning cuppa. And if she can set the table for you. She never did that for Kirsty."

"She does?" Caroline's heart fluttered at those words. "Really?"

"Oh, yeah. It's true. I'm surprised she's not waiting outside the bathroom door for you with your brew."

"You two are too much! But I really love it. All of this. All of you."

Hannah leaned up, cradling Caroline's chin in her fingers. She drew her closer, ghosting her tongue across Caroline's bottom lip, and smiled into a kiss. "We love you. All of you."

CHAPTER 24

"Mum?" Edie came rushing through the door, slamming it behind her. "Is Caz coming over tonight? I *really* want her to come over!"

Caz smiled as she shook her head, stirring her coffee. Edie expected Hannah, not Caroline. But that made sense given the fact that Caroline was at Hannah's and not her own place. Seemed to be a common occurrence these days.

"Mum?!" Edie slung her rucksack off, stopping dead in the kitchen doorway. "H-hi, Caz."

"Hi, Edie. You're home earlier than expected."

"My uh...my homework club finished earlier because I was the only one there."

Yes. That sounded about right. Edie was one of the few students who applied themselves every minute of the school day. "How was it?"

"Fine." Edie chewed her lip, slipping into a seat at the dining table. "I didn't know you were here."

"I gathered that."

"Are you, um—"

"Coming over this evening?" Caroline finished for Edie. "I think so."

"How come you're here already and Mum isn't?"

"Because I decided to treat you and your mum tonight. She's been caught up at work, but I spoke to her an hour ago, and she told me steak is your favourite dinner."

"Oh, my gosh! It is. I love it."

"Then why don't you run upstairs and change, and I'll wait here for you. Then we'll drive together to the steakhouse I've booked a table at. Your mum is meeting us there since it's already in town."

Edie's brow furrowed. "You're taking us for dinner? But why?"

"Does there have to be a reason?"

Edie lifted a shoulder, tugging the cuff of her school jumper. "Nobody usually takes us out for dinner. But I did take Mum once with the pocket money I'd saved."

"I'm sure she really loved that." Edie was the sweetest child Caroline had ever had the pleasure of knowing. And that knowledge that she was going to be a part of her life was huge for her. Caroline couldn't quite believe how her luck had changed this year. "So, should we get ready to head out?"

"Yeah." Edie shot to her feet and rushed out the room. Her usual stampede up the stairs ended with a thud. It was music to Caroline's ears. It was normal, the usual these days.

She took her phone from the counter, followed by a sip of her coffee before she texted Hannah.

Edie is home. She's changing and then I'll drive into town. Caz x

More movement upstairs had Caroline smiling again, the weight of her day the furthest thing from her mind. Tonight she was practically having a family meal. Wow. That...was a lot.

Perfect. I'm leaving the office in ten minutes so we'll

probably get there at the same time. Make sure Edie behaves for you. Hannah x

Edie? Behave? That child didn't have a disobedient bone in her body.

I'm sure she will. See you soon. Caz x

Caroline yawned as she placed her cup in the dishwasher, staring out of the kitchen window for a moment or two. The dark nights were rolling in, autumn approaching, and she couldn't wait. It meant longer evenings with snuggles on the couch. It meant crisp leaves and hot chocolates. It meant...a lot of love.

Caroline's phone buzzed in her hand. She looked down and almost lost her breath.

I love you. Hannah x

She never thought she'd have this. Someone texting to tell Caroline they loved her. Someone who took a moment out of their day to say those three important words. And most of all, someone who meant it.

I love you, too. Caz x

"Ready!" Edie yelled as she came barrelling through the house once again. "We won't be late, will we?"

"No." Caroline stopped Edie, placing her hands on her shoulders. "So please, take a breath before you break a bone, and your mother kills me."

"She wouldn't. She loves you." Edie grinned. "She does, you know. I heard her telling Adele on the phone last night."

Caroline narrowed her eyes. "Do you always eavesdrop, Edie Caffrey? I'm beginning to learn some things about you. Having said that, I know. I love your mum, too. A lot."

Edie's eyes lit up. "You do?"

"Of course I do."

Edie leaned in and hugged Caroline so tight and so hard that she almost knocked her off her feet. "Thank you for making her happy. I always want her to be happy. She's the best mum in the world."

Caroline pulled back, curbing her emotions. "Oh, I think it works both ways, Edie. She's a great mum because she has a great daughter. And you're a wonderful daughter because she's the best mum."

Edie hugged Caroline again, nuzzling her face into her. "I really like it when you're here."

"I really like being here. Now, should we go and meet your mum and have some very impressive steak?"

Edie nodded, and she pulled out of Caroline's embrace. "Yeah. Let's go!"

Hannah stood as Caroline and Edie walked through the door of the restaurant, waving them over. She'd managed to get here on time for their reservation, Juliet being the understanding boss that she was. As Edie held onto Caroline's arm, her cheek pressed to it, Hannah could only grin while fighting back tears. Edie had *never* taken to anyone quite how she'd taken to Caroline.

"Now that my girls are here, let's eat."

Edie sat down and picked up a menu while Caroline rounded the table and offered Hannah a soft kiss. "Hi.

"Hi, babe." Hannah squeezed Caroline's hand, smiling against her lips when she went in for another kiss. "Traffic okay?"

"Wasn't so bad. Edie kept me company, so that was nice."

Hannah eyed Edie, poking the menu she hid behind. "Excuse me?"

"Yeah?" Edie popped her head up, frowning.

"You didn't even hug me when you arrived." Hannah knew

Edie was busy picking out the best steak she could find, but Hannah still expected her daughter to greet her.

"Sorry. Just hungry." Edie lowered her menu and got up to hug Hannah. When she nuzzled her face into her neck, Edie whispered, "It's very expensive in here. Will you order whatever I'm allowed to have, please?"

Hannah smiled, turning her head. "Don't worry about the price. Pick whatever you'd like. This is a treat."

"But I don't want Caz to pay so much money. It's so expensive."

Hannah looked up at Caroline, smiling when she regarded her with a questioning look.

"Everything okay?"

"Yeah. Edie just needed an extra-long hug." Hannah squeezed her daughter's waist, encouraging her to sit back down. "Go and choose your food before I waste away."

"Can I go to the toilet first?" Edie asked, shifting from left to right in front of Hannah.

"Of course you can. You don't need to ask."

Edie sloped off through the other tables, and Hannah watched her go. Caroline placed a hand on Hannah's thigh, lowering her menu. "Is everything okay with Edie?"

"Yes. She's worried about the price of the food." Hannah cleared her throat. She understood that Edie was anxious, but tonight she could have anything she liked. Even if Caroline hadn't offered to pay, Hannah was bringing in a great wage now.

"Oh. No need to be. My treat, I told you that."

Hannah smiled as she took Caroline's hand. This woman wanted to see both Hannah and Edie smiling. Hannah couldn't ask for anything more. "I know that. We just didn't really eat out very much in the past. Had to tighten my belt, you know."

"I get that. But I wanted to spend the evening with you

both, and this is where I want to do that. Edie can have whatever she wants on the menu. Please make sure she knows that, Hannah."

"I will, babe. Don't worry." Hannah lifted Caroline's hand and kissed her knuckles. "Thank you. This is really lovely."

Caroline nudged Hannah with her shoulder. "Anything for you two."

Edie came back to the table, sitting down as inconspicuously as she could, but Hannah felt that nervousness across the table.

And then Caroline took charge.

"So, what's your favourite steak, Edie?"

"Um, what was that one I had last time when Nanna Ivy took us for food?" Edie turned her attention to Hannah. "The small one with the really nice sauce on the side."

"The fillet, love."

Edie lowered her eyes to the menu. When they widened, she looked back up at Hannah. "I don't think I feel like that one today." Hannah caught the worried look in Edie's eyes, breaking her heart as she did so.

"You don't feel like the fillet?" Caroline asked, feigning shock. "Oh, I'm not sure we can be friends if you don't feel like the fillet, Edie. That's my favourite!"

Edie's eyes brightened. "It is?"

"Oh, yeah. *Always* the fillet. But only if you have the chunky chips on the side. And onion rings too." Caroline leaned in towards Edie. "The onion rings in here are *so* good. Should I order some for us to share?"

Hannah squeezed Caroline's hand, emotion lodged in her throat. Seeing Caroline reassure Edie had her bursting with love. That seemed to be the norm these days.

"And vegetables. You know what, let's just order all kinds of different things. Maybe you'll find some new food that you like too then."

"O-okay." Edie nodded, her grin not fading. "Yeah. Can we, Mum?"

Hannah held up a hand. "Hey, I'm just going to eat whatever you two are eating. Caz knows this place well, so I think we should trust her."

"We should. We definitely trust you, Caz."

Caroline exhaled a deep breath, calling for the server. "Well, thank goodness for that!"

"Dinner was lovely," Hannah said as she leaned in and kissed Caroline below the ear.

Caroline closed her eyes, enjoying Hannah's lips on her skin. It was becoming far more common than Caroline expected it would. Mostly because she couldn't believe she'd made it to this point in her life.

"I think Edie is tired." With her head resting on Caroline's shoulder as they strolled through the city, Hannah yawned. "She gets quiet when she's tired."

"I don't think she's the only tired one." Caroline pressed her lips to Hannah's hairline, an arm wrapped around her waist. "Looks like a quiet night for us all."

"I love that. A quiet night. Especially with you."

"Me, too." Caroline enjoyed the silence, watching Edie as she walked ahead a few steps, her shoulders hunched. "Is she okay?"

"She's fine. Don't worry about her." Hannah lifted her head and wrapped her own arm around Caroline's waist. Those arms protected Caroline no matter the situation. "I think she's a little bit overwhelmed with this evening."

"I'm sorry."

Hannah smiled as she turned her head, those blue eyes holding so much love for Caroline. "Don't ever apologise for taking us out for dinner, babe. Edie wasn't expecting it, that's all."

"I'm just trying to get this right. I've never been in a relationship with someone like you or someone who has a child."

"Someone like me?"

Caroline squeezed Hannah's hip. "Someone I love so much that I don't want to lose. Someone who not only takes care of me but allows me to take care of them in return. Just...you. I never thought I'd fall in love with anyone again, but certainly not you."

"You're a part of this family now, Caz."

"I-I know."

Hannah leaned in to kiss Caroline, but Edie suddenly turned around, stopping dead in front of them. "I have to tell you something. I...did something."

Caroline and Hannah froze, the fear in Edie's eyes clear as day.

"What did you do, Edie?" Hannah slid her arm from around Caroline's waist and took a step closer to her daughter. "Whatever it is, it's okay. We can figure it out together."

"W-when I asked you that night if Caz could come over for dinner..."

Hannah frowned as she eyed Caroline, then she turned her attention back to Edie. "You mean months ago when we had the Indian banquet together?"

Edie lowered her eyes. "Y-yeah."

"What about it?"

Caroline had to smile at the reminder of that night. It was basically the night when everything got very serious. They were already dating, but having dinner with Hannah and Edie had only shown Caroline what she could have if she got out of her own head for long enough.

"I saw your phone that night. The message from Caz. I didn't go snooping. I was in the kitchen when it came through, and I saw it on the screen."

"O...kay."

Caroline was just as confused as Hannah sounded.

"Caz said she missed you. And I knew you liked her because since you met, you were always way happier. So, I asked you if she could come for dinner."

"You...tried to set us up together?" Hannah grinned as she switched between Edie and Caz. But Caz could only raise her eyebrows with surprise. "Is that why you did it, love?"

"Yes. I'm sorry." Edie scratched at her forearm. "It's just that I really love Caz and she said she missed you. I didn't want her to miss you because you were stuck at home with me. I wanted you to be together. All of us to be together."

"Oh, Edie." Hannah pulled her daughter into a hug. Caroline watched their interaction, a tear slipping down her face. "We were already together then. But we'd only just met, and we didn't want to tell you until we knew for sure."

Caroline sniffled, turning her back on Hannah and Edie. God, she needed to get it together. She was standing in the middle of the city, crying.

"Babe?" Hannah suddenly placed a hand on Caroline's shoulder, startling her. "Are you okay?"

"Yes. Of course." Caroline wiped her cheeks, exhaling a deep breath as she turned around. "I just wasn't expecting any of that."

With tears in her own eyes, Hannah sniffled. "I know. I didn't either."

"Caz, I'm really sorry," Edie said as she clasped her hands in front of her.

"Come here." Caroline embraced Edie, closing her eyes as she allowed the love she felt to overtake her. Edie had brought them together; Caroline couldn't help but adore that. "You have nothing to be sorry for." She kissed the top of Edie's head, smiling back at Hannah. "You gave us the kick up the backside that we needed."

"You're not angry?"

Caroline laughed. "You and I have been through this before, Edie. I don't recall a time when I've ever been angry with you."

"Can we all go home now?"

Home. Caroline's body fizzed at that.

"Yes, we can." With Hannah on one side of her, Edie on the other, they moulded into one perfect family as they strolled along the stretch of road that would take them to their cars.

"Can I go back with Caz, Mum?"

Hannah placed her head on Caroline's shoulder and sighed. "Yes. You can."

CHAPTER 25

With a bunch of flowers cradled in her arms, Hannah pushed her hip against the front door, almost falling through it. Caroline was due here in the next thirty minutes... and Hannah was far from prepared. She wanted to go all out this weekend to make Caroline feel special. Hannah strived to make Caroline feel that way daily, but this weekend was going to be incredible. Edie hadn't been well for the first three days of this week, the common cold thriving in their household, so Hannah really hadn't had much of a chance to see Caroline. They'd spent Sunday with one another, but once Caroline had left for work on Monday morning, Hannah had suggested she avoid the house for a few days. She didn't want her to catch whatever Edie was spreading around the place.

Thankfully, Hannah hadn't caught it.

With a feeling of euphoria pumping through her veins, she hummed along to a song she'd been listening to in the car and slammed the front door shut. She wanted to at least start dinner. That way, when Caroline arrived, her girlfriend could relax for the rest of the night. "Oh, you're so in for a good night." Hannah grinned to herself, pushing the back living room door open with her foot.

But as she did so, she almost dropped the flowers in her arms. The dining table had been set, candles lit, and wine breathing on the table. But it wasn't Caroline standing before her. No, it was Kirsty.

"Thank God! I thought you weren't going to show up!"

Hannah's lips parted, her gaze cast on the beautiful table. Rose petals lay scattered between the cutlery, a huge arrangement set down in one of Hannah's vases. "W-what's this?"

"I know I fucked up, babe. I know you're probably not at all happy to see me. But...I'm sorry. I'll explain everything."

Hannah turned and walked towards the kitchen, lowering Caroline's flowers to the counter. She slung her bag onto the small kitchen table, clenching her hands into fists at her sides. What...the hell?

"Hannah, would you at least hear me out? Please?"

"I have nothing to say to you. I owe you absolutely nothing. Quite frankly, I've no idea why you're in my house." Hannah held out a hand. "And I'll have my keys back, too."

Kirsty lowered her chin to her chest, sniffling. But Hannah wasn't interested in any of this. Kirsty being here...meant nothing to her. And if she didn't get rid of her soon, her weekend would well and truly be ruined.

"Don't start with the tears."

A sob escaped Kirsty's mouth, but Hannah only rolled her eyes.

"Hannah, please. I've been having a really tough time."

"That's not my problem. I came home to find you gone. I don't know what you could possibly have to say to me that would make any of this okay."

"I lost my head. Mum is sick, and I got the call from her when you were out. Terminal. Brain tumour. She just called me and told me down the phone. Like it was nothing. And then she expected me to just get on with things and pretend it wasn't happening."

"I'm sorry to hear that," Hannah said, genuinely saddened by that news.

"I packed my stuff, bought a bottle of vodka on the way to the station, and then sat on that train like some alcoholic. I knew I was going to lose it, and I couldn't have you with me for it. I knew exactly what I was turning into the moment I got that call. I just...it was for the best."

Kirsty had always struggled to deal with the things life threw at her. Hannah had known that from the moment they met. But these...excuses? Well, they weren't good enough. "I would have been there for you."

"I know that. I really do. But I was disgusting. Mum even told me to get it together within a week of being home." Kirsty stepped forward, taking Hannah's hand. "I know I hurt you, but please...give me a chance. I wanted to call. To show up here. But I had to get my life together again before I even considered being in the same home as you and Edie. How I was, I'd never allow Edie to see me like that."

Hannah had to smile at that. Even though Kirsty had disappeared, she had loved her. Before all of this, they'd had a happy life. Quiet and content. They'd been good together. "You really upset Edie when you left."

"Is she with Dylan tonight?"

Hannah nodded. "As always. It's Friday."

"As much as I can't wait to see her, I did purposely plan this for tonight. I needed to be alone with you before I saw her."

Hannah frowned, pulling her hand out of Kirsty's. "No, Kirsty. I'm not doing this. You left me, and whatever the reason for it, you still left. You didn't even call me. I wondered where the hell you'd gone, and I didn't know how to find you. You deleted your social media, and I'd never gone home with you. I couldn't seek you out. But then I realised that was probably your plan all along. Because if I'd meant so much to you, I'd have been with you all those times when you visited your parents."

"No, not at all. It was never like that. I love you, Hannah. I left *because* I love you."

Hannah studied every inch of Kirsty's face, concern for her ex-girlfriend at the forefront of her mind. "Kirsty, are you okay?"

"I am now that I'm here."

"No, I mean...are you okay?"

Kirsty lowered herself into a chair at the table, puffing out her cheeks. "It's been really hard—I have no issues admitting that. But it also gave me a chance to be with Mum and do anything she needed. Even if I went to my old bedroom every night and drank myself stupid, I was with her every day."

"Kirsty," Hannah paused, blowing out a breath. "I understand that you've had a difficult time, and I'm so sorry you've gone through all of that, but I don't understand why you're here and sitting in my kitchen."

"I...asked you to marry me." Kirsty lifted her gaze slowly, finding Hannah's eyes.

"Yeah, you did."

"And that still stands." Kirsty's eyes showed no signs of hesitation. The way she was looking at Hannah, she meant every word. "I want to be your wife. I'd sat at home wondering if I could go through with a wedding if Mum wasn't around, but I know what she'd want. She'd want me to be happy. And you and Edie make me so happy. S-since she's stable at the minute, maybe she could even make it to the wedding if we start planning it now."

Hannah felt her world caving in at those words. How could

Kirsty be sitting here saying these things...when Caroline was due any moment.

Fuck. Caroline!

"I...need you to leave, Kirsty."

Kirsty looked around the kitchen, eyeing the oven. This woman had actually shown up and helped herself to Hannah's kitchen. Something definitely wasn't right. Kirsty...needed help.

"But dinner is in the oven."

God. How was Hannah supposed to let her down gently? How could she be the bitch she knew she'd have to be to make Kirsty understand? Her poor mother had a brain tumour, and Hannah was about to kick her out. "We're...not having dinner together. Not now, and not in the future."

"But why?" Kirsty's bottom lip trembled as she shook her head. "Before I left, we were in love. You can't have just fallen out of love with me."

Hannah took a step forward, holding Kirsty's hands in her own. She offered her a weak smile. "We were. You're right. But you left with no regard for how I'd feel. I know you've explained why you left, but it's not good enough for me. Your reasons... aren't really acceptable reasons. If you'd left me a note or called when you'd got there, I would have understood. But I had to lie in bed with my daughter at night and try to explain why you'd gone. She questioned whether it was her fault. She asked if you hated us. I'm not going through that again, Kirsty. I'm happy now."

Kirsty wiped a tear from her jaw. "How can you be happy alone? You hate being alone."

Hannah exhaled a breath, squeezing Kirsty's hand. "I'm not alone. I've met someone, and I'm happy. Edie is happy. If you really cared about us, you'd understand that and walk away. Just like you did not too long ago."

Kirsty grimaced, and then her features turned to disgust.

"You've met someone? So, you've cheated on me. That's what you're saying?"

"Cheated on you?" Hannah barked a laugh as she allowed those words, that accusation, to sink in. "No, Kirsty. You left me. We're not together anymore. And whatever you're going through, it doesn't give you the right to treat me how you did. I deserve better than that. That may be hard to hear, and you may think I'd just wait around for you, but why would I do that? I didn't think you were coming back." Hannah stepped away, lowering Kirsty's hand. "And even if you had come back, I'd have still had this same conversation with you whether I was involved or not. You can't treat people like that and expect them to sit at home pining after you. Life doesn't work that way."

"Well, thanks!"

Hannah wasn't doing this any longer. Kirsty really did need to go. Even if Caroline wasn't due here, Hannah was still done with this entire conversation. "Get yourself together. You've got ten minutes, and then you need to be gone."

"Yes, I'm just walking through the door now. I'll see what Hannah wants to do, but don't expect us. I think we're having a weekend in together."

"Caz. Come on."

Caroline groaned. She loved Brenda and Sharon dearly, but the thought of putting on a pair of heels again tonight had dread sinking deep into her stomach. She just wanted to see Hannah and lock the door. It surely couldn't be hard for people to understand. "Hannah's had a busy week at work. But let me ask and see what's what."

Caroline turned the key in the lock, smiling when the scent of Hannah's home enveloped her. She'd missed coming over through the week. It was just a shame Edie was at her dad's and wouldn't be joining them tonight.

"Fine. Okay. Well, we'll be at the usual bars if you can drag yourselves out the house for friends."

"Don't guilt me into it. It simply won't happen, Brenda." Caroline lifted a brow as she spoke those words. Six months ago, she wouldn't have dreamt of saying something like that, but Hannah made her feel brave and comfortable in her own skin. Something nobody had made Caroline feel in a long time. "I'll let you know. But now I have to go because Hannah will be waiting for me."

"See you soon, Caz. Have a lovely weekend."

Ah. Bliss. Brenda had taken the hint. "Yeah. See you soon."

As Caroline ended the call and locked her phone, she pulled the bolt across the back of Hannah's door. They had no plans to leave this place tonight, none whatsoever.

"Hannah, you here?" Caroline placed her set of keys into the bowl by the landline handset, dropping her handbag to the floor. She'd gone home from work and showered, and as she'd stood in her bedroom, staring into the mirror, Caroline had decided to wear the new lingerie she'd picked up through the week. No time like the present, right? This was their weekend. Their chance to have fun. And Caroline wanted to make the most of it. She may be slightly terrified, but Hannah would settle her. She couldn't recall the last time she'd worn sexy lingerie. "Hannah?"

Caroline's forehead creased when she heard talking in the kitchen. Following the voices, she cleared her throat and moved towards the doorway.

"Babe, hi. I thought I heard you coming in." Hannah gave Caroline a look. One that said 'go along with me here'.

"I told you I'd be home not long after you." Caroline eyed

the dark-haired woman standing in front of Hannah. She had no idea who she was. "This a friend?"

Hannah smiled at Caroline when Kirsty turned to face her. "This is Kirsty."

Kirsty? Oh, Kirsty!

"Can...we help you?"

"I was making dinner for Hannah. Until she ruined the night by telling me she's involved. I'm assuming it's you she's sleeping with now?"

"Oh, I wouldn't quite call it *sleeping with*. We're together. Practically living with one another." Caroline turned to Hannah. "I waved Edie off when Dylan picked her up. He got out of the car to say hi to me, which I thought was nice of him."

"I told him who you were. That you're Edie's teacher. He was impressed." Hannah cocked her head towards Kirsty, giving Caroline a knowing look. "So, Kirsty was just leaving."

"Well, it was lovely to meet you. But I'm just home from work and need a long soak. So..."

Kirsty scoffed. "So...what?"

"So it's time for you to leave," Caroline said, stepping closer to Kirsty and turning off the oven. "Hannah and I have plans. Plans that don't include you."

Kirsty laughed. "You don't even know her! She's going to be my wife."

"No, Kirsty. I'm not." Hannah sighed, dragging a hand through her hair. "I understand this is a hard time for you, but we're not together. We're not getting married. And we're not having dinner with one another. Caz is right. We have plans."

"Would you like a lift to the station?" Caroline asked, aware that the atmosphere had changed. Kirsty looked as though she was ready to blow at any moment. Caroline really didn't need that. Nor did Hannah. "The bus station? Train?"

Kirsty turned and stood toe to toe with Caroline. She tilted her chin, grinning. "No. But you can get in your car and fuck off. I was here long before you." Kirsty's eyes trailed down Caroline's body, and then she scoffed. "You're a bit *old* for her!"

"Kirsty, that's enough!" Hannah stepped between Caroline and Kirsty. "You can't just come here and behave like this. Have some respect, for the love of God!"

Caroline cleared her throat and prepared a cup of coffee from the machine. While it brewed, silence hanging over the three of them, she turned back to Kirsty. "I've had enough drama to last me a lifetime. It's time for *you* to leave."

"And I've already told *you* to fuck off!" Kirsty spat.

"Yeah, this isn't working for me." Caz held up a hand, wanting to remove herself from the situation she seemed to have walked into. She focused on Hannah. "Would you mind if I didn't stay for the rest of this conversation?"

"Kirsty is leaving now. You change and I'll be right up, okay?"

Caroline smiled weakly, offering a slight nod. While she wanted to watch Kirsty walk out the door, she couldn't help but feel that by being here, she was only aggravating the situation. "You know where I am if you need me." Hannah nodded, but Caroline saw through the neutral facial expression she tried to wear. The situation wasn't ideal, but if Caroline had to stay for Hannah, she would. "I...can stay, if that's what you want?"

"No, it's okay." Hannah turned her face towards Caroline's ear, her voice low as she said, "I think if this remains a two on one situation, it's only going to make things worse. I'll speak to her, humour her, and get rid of her, okay?"

Caroline eyed Kirsty, but she didn't appear to care that Caroline was in the room at all. She just stood there, her arms folded, glaring.

Caroline lifted her coffee from the machine, laughing.

"While I get that it must be hard seeing Hannah moving on, it's *not* my problem. So...do the right thing and leave, please."

And then she calmly turned her back and walked away, hoping that was the end of this ridiculous situation. Hannah had better things to do than entertain an ex who had ghosted her, and that was exactly why Caroline wasn't worried about the ex being around.

CHAPTER 26

Hannah stared, dumbfounded, as Caroline walked away. When she woke up this morning, she hadn't for one second imagined Kirsty turning up. Especially not letting herself into Hannah's home so brazenly. But now that she had, Hannah needed to nip this in the bud and get rid of her ex-girlfriend.

"She's a bit feisty, isn't she?" Kirsty scoffed, turning back to the oven and twisting the temperature dial. "Like I said, dinner won't be long."

"N-no, Kirsty." Hannah took a step closer to her ex, placing a tentative hand on her wrist. "You're not listening. You have to leave."

"Why?"

Hannah rolled her head on her shoulders, sighing. "Because we're not together anymore. We never will be. Please accept that and leave. I've been working all day, and I just want to wind down for the night."

Kirsty leaned in towards Hannah's ear. "Why don't you ask that one to leave, and we'll get comfortable together?"

"Tell you what," Hannah said, offering the best smile she

could manage. Kirsty wasn't listening, and as Hannah stood here, she realised Kirsty had no plans to do so. "Why don't you head off to wherever you're staying, I'll speak to Caz, and in a couple of days, we'll meet up. Catch up, you know?"

Kirsty narrowed her eyes. "You won't do that."

"I will. You have my word. It's just been a long day, and I don't really want to do this now. You coming back is a bit of a shock to me."

"A good shock, though, right?" Kirsty grinned, moving in to kiss Hannah, but Hannah pulled away. "Not a good shock."

"Just...a shock." Hannah shrugged, stepping around the dining table to create a space between them. Kirsty was behaving erratically, and Hannah wasn't here for it. "Can I call you next week?"

"I...guess."

"Okay, cool." Kirsty had agreed, and that was all Hannah needed to hear. "Well, I'll tidy up and whatever. Don't worry about it."

"Can I come and see Edie next week?"

"If she's not busy." Edie was rarely busy with anything other than schoolwork, but if Hannah had to make the both of them busy, she could arrange that. "Leave me your number and I'll call you."

"You have my number."

"I...don't. When you left, I deleted it."

Kirsty lowered her chin to her chest, dropping a tea towel she was holding to the floor. "H-Hannah...do you still love me?"

Could Hannah be honest without Kirsty losing her shit? She guessed she was about to find out.

"No," she said quietly. Caroline was upstairs, and she was right. She'd been through enough drama. Hannah didn't want raised voices and arguments inside the home that was supposed to be a safe space for Caroline. "And I think that deep down, you already know that."

Kirsty smiled weakly as she found Hannah's eyes. "But...we can all hope, can't we?"

"While I agree with that sometimes, now isn't one of those times. I'm happy with Caz, Kirsty. I know you're having a dreadful time, and I'm really sorry about that, but we're not in the same place we once were. I can't lie to you to make you feel better, I really can't."

"So, that's it? No chance of me being forgiven?" Kirsty slumped back against the kitchen counter, her voice trembling.

"I do forgive you. You've come here and explained, and I get it." Hannah didn't, not really, but she was at a point of just wanting Kirsty out the house. Sooner rather than later. "But forgiving you and being in love with you are two *very* different things."

Kirsty pushed off the counter, taking her jacket from the back of a dining chair. She sniffled, kept her head down, and moved towards the door. "I hope you know what you're doing. We could have been really good together. We *were* really good together."

Hannah smiled weakly. "And then you left me."

Kirsty spun around. "I'd never leave you again."

"No, Kirsty. This is it. We're done. And now I'm asking you one final time to leave."

"And if I don't?"

"I'll call the police." Hannah said, not even flinching when Kirsty's eyes flashed cold. "Don't make me. Walk away."

Kirsty scoffed, rushing out of the kitchen and slamming the front door shut. But Hannah? She simply lowered herself into a chair and exhaled a long, slow breath. This had been a wild evening, and it was only just beginning.

Caroline flinched as the front door closed with an almighty thud. She peeked out of the side of the blinds in Hannah's bedroom, watching Kirsty run away down the street. Caroline didn't know how the conversation had exactly gone, but judging by her first meeting with Kirsty, she needed help.

Aware that their night together had been ruined, Caroline untucked her blouse from her high-waisted skirt and kicked off her heels. She would change into something comfortable and hope Hannah was in the mood to at least spend some time together tonight.

Caroline turned away from the window and unbuttoned her blouse. As she looked up, Hannah was standing in the doorway.

"Hi."

Caroline managed a very slight smile, shedding her blouse. "Hi. Everything okay?"

"For now, yes. I think so. I *hope* so." Hannah pushed off the doorframe and stalked towards Caroline. "You look really good tonight."

"Yeah, I was trying to be more myself. Old me, at least. But I'll change and...I don't know. Maybe we could still have dinner together and play it by ear."

"Please don't change."

"Hannah...as much as I'd love to just carry on like nothing has happened, it has. Your ex has just been standing in your kitchen making you dinner. I've had a really long day at work, and while I'd like to say this isn't an issue, it is."

Hannah swallowed, tears sitting on her eyelids. "Are you going to leave?"

"No." Caroline took Hannah's hand, encouraging her to move a little closer. Caroline felt the hesitation, the fear, but Hannah shouldn't worry. It was going to take more than an ex-girlfriend to get rid of her. Six months ago, that may not have been the case, but Caroline was well on her way to discovering who she truly was. And it was all down to this very woman standing before her. "I'm not going to leave. I'm not going to get angry. I do, however, think you need to deal with this."

"I'm a little bit worried about her," Hannah admitted as she guided Caroline to the bed. They sat down, Caroline offering a nod for Hannah to continue. "She seemed completely different from the Kirsty I know. She said her mum has a terminal brain tumour."

"I'm sorry to hear that."

"Me, too. But I can't let that be a reason to keep her in my life. She's not right. Something isn't right. But I don't know what I'm supposed to do about it."

"Could you reach out to her family or friends?"

Hannah laughed. "No. I was never a part of that side of her life."

"You were together for three years, but you don't know her family and friends?" Caroline lifted a brow, quite surprised by that. "Did that not strike you as odd?"

"Not really. We had friends together, people we met over the years, but Kirsty rarely went home to visit her parents. When she did, it seemed to be when I wasn't available to go with her. Either I had to work, or Edie was home with me. I didn't really think anything of it until she left, and I had no way of knowing where she was."

"So you have nobody you can contact?"

"Nope. Afraid not. But she seemed to take the hint as she was leaving. At first, I was trying to humour her just to get her out of the house, but I don't know. I think she realised that we wouldn't be getting back together."

"And are you okay? It had to be a shock when she arrived."

Hannah cleared her throat, squeezing Caroline's hand. "She

was already here when I got home from work. Making dinner. I didn't let her in."

"S-she has a key?"

"*Had*. She had a key. She's left it in the kitchen, don't worry."

While Caroline wanted to figure this out with Hannah, she couldn't get her head around the fact that Kirsty had let herself into someone else's house. Hannah was right. Kirsty needed help and support. "Okay, so what's next?"

"I think I'm going to leave it alone and pray she doesn't show up here again. I don't have her number anymore, so I can't really chase her down anyway. Not that I'd want to. I may not have been so brave in asking her to leave repeatedly had you not been up here. She looked as though she was going to flip her shit at any moment once you came upstairs."

"So she feels threatened..."

"I'm not sure threatened is what she's feeling. Helpless, alone, I don't know. But again, I can't be the person who sees her through whatever she has going on. If she can understand that she can't just leave people and then walk back into their lives, things may pick up for her soon."

"I hope you're right."

Hannah got to her feet, standing between Caroline's legs. She grinned as she stared down at Caroline's cleavage, that penetrating gaze doing *everything* to fire Caroline up. "I may not be, but all I'm interested in right now is my girlfriend in sexy lace lingerie."

Caroline blushed. She knew she looked nice, but the look Hannah was giving her meant anything other than nice. "Does it look okay?"

"Okay?" Hannah barked a laugh, throwing her head back. But then she focused back on Caroline and took her bottom lip between her teeth. "Oh, you look far better than okay, Caz. Right now, I want to remove this with my teeth."

That was exactly the reaction Caroline hoped to get when she was half-naked in front of Hannah. It stopped her from questioning herself. Her body. How she appeared to those around her.

"I wouldn't be opposed to that," Caroline whispered, reaching up and slowly unbuttoning Hannah's shirt. When she exposed her stomach, Caroline pressed wet kisses to her skin.

Hannah fisted her hand in Caroline's hair, pressing her lips down harder. "You know," she said breathlessly. "There was something incredibly sexy about you taking control downstairs before. How you didn't back down."

Caroline smiled against Hannah's stomach, popping the button on her pants and lowering the zipper. "Yeah?" She lowered her mouth to the waistband of Hannah's underwear, overcome with arousal when Hannah tightened her fist in Caroline's hair. "You like that?"

"Which? The thought of you controlling me or your mouth so close to where I need it?"

Caroline stared up at Hannah with hooded eyes. "Both, I guess."

"Oh, I really like it." The way in which those words slid from Hannah's mouth, a moan, had Caroline slowly lowering her pants down her thighs. "And I really like where this is going, too."

"Mm. Me, too."

Hannah raked her nails through Caroline's hair as she leaned down and drew her into a kiss. Those lips, the promise they represented, Caroline was entirely in love with this woman.

As Hannah stepped out of her pants, kicking them across the room, she placed one knee, then the other, on the bed.

Straddling Caroline, she rolled her body, moaning when she deepened the kiss. "Caz?"

"Yes?" She responded breathlessly.

"I'm so wet for you."

Oh, God. When Hannah spoke those five simple words, the ground could open up and take Caroline...and she'd be unaware. When Hannah straddled her, grinding in her lap, nothing else mattered.

Caroline lowered her hand, pressing Hannah's underwear between her lips. "Mmhmm. Yes, you are."

"Oh, fuck." Hannah lowered her head to Caroline's shoulder, moving back and forth against her fingers. "Please, babe."

Caroline pushed the material to one side, gathering Hannah's arousal on the tips of her fingers. "Hannah," she whispered, placing a kiss on Hannah's shoulder. "I need you out of these right now."

Hannah shot from the bed, her underwear gone before Caroline had time to blink. She reached behind herself, unclasping her bra, her eyes not leaving Caroline's. "Where do you want me?"

"Fuck. I don't know." Caroline got to her feet, stalked towards Hannah, and wrapped a hand around the back of her neck. "But I do know I want to be inside you."

Hannah took Caroline's hand, placing it between her legs. "Take control, babe. Take *me*."

Caroline shivered at those words, goosebumps spreading across her skin. She watched Hannah, her eyes so focused, so... blue. But it was when she smoothed two fingers between Hannah's swollen lips that a thrill rushed through her. She'd spent many nights with Hannah now, but nothing could ever prepare Caroline for touching her. Every day was a new experience.

She guided Hannah back, pressing her to the wall, and sunk

to her knees. Tasting Hannah, feeling that aching clit on the tip of her tongue...fuck, Caroline's mouth watered at the thought. She spread Hannah's lips, Caroline's bottom lip between her teeth, as she teased Hannah with her thumb. "You're so beautiful."

Hannah's legs trembled. "C-Caz, please."

Caroline shifted closer, wrapped her lips around Hannah's clit, and sucked gently. She knew what Hannah needed and when. She knew every last reaction Hannah would have. "Mm. So good."

Hannah held the back of Caroline's head, slowly rolling her hips. Knowing this woman wanted Caroline, knowing she made Hannah this wet, Caroline often found herself unable to comprehend it. But she was sure now that Hannah really did see a future with her. She knew without a doubt that they made one another happy. She knew...this was it for her.

Caroline slipped one finger inside Hannah, enjoying the reaction Hannah had. Then she slid another inside, Hannah's walls clutching her.

"*Y-yes*. Fuck, right there."

Caroline sucked harder on Hannah's clit, almost pulling out only to sink deeper, harder. "Oh, God." Caroline whimpered when she rested back and watched Hannah. She lifted one of Hannah's legs over her shoulder, enamoured by the woman rocking against her fingers, playing with her nipples. "I could watch you like this all night."

Hannah pressed her head to the door, pinching her nipple harder. She was lost in the moment, lost in the feeling of Caroline filling her, lost in their love. "Caz, I'm so close."

Caroline lashed her tongue against Hannah's clit, chancing a third finger inside.

"Fuck, yes. Oh, God." Hannah responded by rocking harder, her bottom lip between her teeth. "Fuck me hard."

Caroline would have shied away at those words just a few months ago, but with Hannah, and now? Never. She wanted to give this woman her every desire. Caroline fucked Hannah hard and fast, grinning against her soaked clit as she tightened. "Mm. That's it." Caroline curled her fingers, coaxing Hannah's orgasm towards the edge.

Hannah lowered a hand, spread her lips further, and rode harder. "Yes. Take me, Caz." Hannah thrust her hips, moaning when she released around Caroline's fingers. "Fuck, don't stop."

Caroline watched with delight as Hannah swallowed her fingers entirely, wetness slipping down the palm of her hand. There was something incredibly satisfying about another woman feeling this way about her. Happy, fulfilled. "Oh, Hannah." Caroline sat back on her knees, her fingers slowly pushing in and out. She never wanted to stop touching Hannah; she never wanted to feel anything other than this euphoria. She never wanted anyone else. "God, you're so sexy."

Hannah shuddered, forcing Caroline's fingers from her, and pressed her palms flat to the door. Her chest heaved, her breathing ragged, but the smile on her face told Caroline everything she needed to know.

"Caz," Hannah whispered, her eyes closed. "Y-you."

Caz got to her feet, stroking a hand between Hannah's thighs as she offered a lingering kiss. "I'm what?"

"God, I don't even know what I was going to say."

"That's okay. You can show me instead."

Hannah's eyes opened, a devilish grin on her mouth. "Oh, I'd love nothing more."

But Caroline could only study Hannah for a moment or two. There was something extremely beautiful after Hannah had orgasmed. "I love you."

Hannah cocked her head, her breathing beginning to slow. "I love you too, babe."

CHAPTER 27

Hannah slumped in her seat at her desk, tiredness not shifting this morning as she sipped her third coffee. Kirsty had swam around in her mind all weekend, that unusual look she'd had in her eyes prickling Hannah's skin with goosebumps. Something wasn't right. No, something was *very* wrong. But Hannah stood by what she'd told Caroline on Friday. It wasn't on Hannah to look after Kirsty. And if Hannah wanted an easy life, she had to stand firmly by that.

"You look how I feel," Juliet said as she came sauntering into her office. "Late weekend?"

"Long weekend, more like."

"Caz seems to be keeping you very busy, Hannah."

"It wasn't Caz. Well, it was for a little while." Hannah paused, her skin flushing from the simple reminder of Caroline on Friday night. Saturday morning and afternoon too. Phew, she hadn't known her girlfriend had it in her. Okay, she had, but she hadn't expected it so...freely. The confidence in her eyes as she sunk to her knees had sent Hannah entirely wild with want.

"Can you not replay your nights of hot passion in your head while you're at the office?"

"Sorry."

"I'm happy one of us is having fun, don't apologise." Juliet took a seat behind her own desk, eyeing Hannah from across the room. "So, what's going on? You seem worried about something."

"It's Kirsty. She's back."

"Kirsty Hardacre? My old PA, Kirsty?"

Hannah nodded, her eyelids heavy. "She came to my place on Friday."

"And how did Caz take that? Not very well, I'd imagine."

Caroline wasn't the issue. Not at all. It was the situation they could potentially find themselves in because of Kirsty. "Caz was great. She's far calmer than I am. If it had been her ex making her dinner, I'd have had something to say about it."

Juliet placed her palms to her desk, sitting forward. "Hold on. She was cooking dinner for you? How exactly did you get to that point with her?"

"Juliet, she was already *in* my house when I got home from work."

"That's...not normal behaviour, Hannah. She's been gone for what? Nine months or so now?"

"Yeah. She still had a key. I never thought about that when she left, and I certainly never expected her to let herself into my house and start cooking dinner."

Juliet slid her glasses on as she frowned. "How did she seem to you?"

"Unwell." Hannah didn't want to assume anything, but the Kirsty she knew was *not* the same Kirsty she'd had an encounter with just a few days ago. Juliet would back her on that, given the fact she used to be her boss. "She's been at home with her mum. Terminal."

"Oh, God. Really?"

"Yeah. Brain tumour. And while I can understand that she's

probably really out of sorts, I don't like how she just showed up. I also don't like how she spoke to Caz. She was very hostile. Actually, she was a complete bitch to her."

"Do you want me to contact her?"

Hannah dragged a hand through her hair and crossed her legs. This didn't need to become a thing for any of them. "No, it's okay. I don't want to antagonise her. If you call, she may think that's exactly what I'm doing. She doesn't even know I effectively have her job. If I pay no attention, I'm sure she'll realise that there is no us anymore."

Juliet laughed and shook her head as she powered up her computer. "She actually thinks there's a chance?"

"Seems it, yes."

"I know we've only spoken briefly about the fact you two were ever together, but how serious was it?"

Hannah swallowed. She wasn't in the habit of spending three years with someone for the sake of it. "Very serious. We were engaged."

"Oh, wow." Juliet's eyes widened with that knowledge.

"I'm going to assume she never mentioned me then." Hannah wasn't bothered by that now, but if she'd known back then, she would have questioned why Kirsty kept her a secret at work. Juliet was openly lesbian, so it couldn't be that Kirsty felt she had to hide who she was. "Shows what she thought of me, doesn't it?"

"She...didn't really talk about her personal life. Kirsty was very quiet when she was here. While you and I go out to lunch or working dinners, she avoided that. I don't know why, but I just put it down to her being a little introverted."

Huh. She'd never been introverted with Hannah. "Maybe. I don't know."

"I wouldn't think too much into it, Hannah. You're happy with Caz."

"Oh, God. I know. I'm not even contemplating that." It was becoming increasingly clear that Caroline may just be the love of Hannah's life. There wasn't a single thing that sprung to mind in terms of red flags. Nothing. "Caz is the one for me."

"Good. But I *would* suggest you keep your wits about you if you're certain Kirsty isn't in the right frame of mind. It's not your job to deal with her—remember that."

"I know. It's Caz I worry about."

Juliet got to her feet and moved towards the coffee machine in the corner of her office. She took two cups, aware that Hannah needed a lot to make it through the morning alone, and prepared coffee for them both. "Why are you worried about her? I may not know her very well, but she seems like she can handle herself."

"She can." Hannah wasn't one to discuss other people, but Caroline had been through a lot. "But she doesn't need it."

"Do any of us?" Juliet eyed Hannah, a brow quirked.

"No. It's just...Caz is divorced. She had a dreadful marriage. I don't want her to think that I'm going to bring problems into her life now she's finally back on her feet and putting herself first."

"Dreadful marriage," Juliet said, expecting more.

"It's not my place to say. But it was bad. Toxic. You know?"

Juliet nodded slowly. "I see. Well, I think you two are perfect for one another. I'm glad you found her."

"She kinda found me. But I'm so thankful that she did. My life has really changed in the last few months. Between meeting Caz and getting this job, I didn't know it was possible to just be so content."

"What can I say? The women in your life are very fond of you, Hannah."

Hannah grinned, her mind beginning to calm now that she'd offloaded on someone. Juliet didn't mind. She had no issue telling Hannah she wasn't interested when that was the case. "I'm very fond of them, too."

Juliet crossed the room and placed a fresh coffee on Hannah's desk. She smiled down at Hannah, shaking her head. "You really do have it all, don't you? I'm jealous."

"I've told you. Your time *will* come."

"Hi, babe." Hannah pressed herself to Caroline, kissing the back of her neck. "How was work today?"

"Oh, fine. I told Edie I'd pick her up tonight from Beth's if Beth's mum is unable to drop her off. Left her at the gate after school." Caroline turned around, smiling when those arms of Hannah's sat securely around her waist. "How was work?"

"Okay. It was a long day, but I'm home now, and you're here, so that's all I care about."

Caroline was happy about that. She'd known Hannah was in her own head all weekend, processing the fact that Kirsty was back in town. Caroline had thought about it herself for all of ten minutes, but she'd decided she wasn't going to allow it to affect her. What she had here with Hannah and Edie was what counted. Exes could stay in the past. "Since Edie is having dinner at Beth's, I thought maybe we could just order in and get into something comfortable. Have a lazy night."

Hannah yawned, resting her head on Caroline's shoulder. "I'd love that. I don't think I have the energy to even shower. But give me ten minutes, and I'll sort myself out."

"Let me make you a cuppa while you get your heels off and sit down for a minute." Caroline noted the tiredness in Hannah's gorgeous blue eyes as she stepped away, trying but failing to stifle a yawn. "Go. Sit down before I carry you into the living room myself."

Hannah cocked her head as she reached out and took Caroline's hand. The softness had Caroline wanting to follow Hannah, wrap them up in a blanket, and never leave the house again. "Do you have any idea how proud I am to call you mine?"

"I swear if you make me cry—"

Hannah squeezed Caroline's hand. "Only happy tears in this relationship, babe."

"You're supposed to be going to sit down but here you are, just making me want to kiss you." Caroline pulled Hannah back in by the waist, capturing her mouth. When Hannah melted into her, Caroline could only smile against those gorgeous lips. Soft and inviting. Filled with hope. "Now, please, go and rest. I know you haven't been sleeping."

"W-what? I...have."

Caroline gave Hannah a knowing look. There was no use in Hannah lying. She'd done nothing but toss and turn all weekend. "Don't lie to me. I see right through it."

Hannah lowered her eyes, toying with Caroline's fingers.

"Tell me what's on your mind. Please."

"Just this whole Kirsty thing. I don't want her to become an issue for us."

Caroline cupped Hannah's cheek. She had a feeling Hannah had been worrying about it but hadn't Friday night given Hannah all the answers she needed as to how Caroline felt? "She won't become an issue. I had no idea it was playing on your mind so much. I knew you'd thought about it. I'm sorry I didn't see it sooner."

"What we have here, Caz, it's...perfect to me. Edie and I are so stupidly in love with you, and I don't want that to *ever* not be the case."

"Come with me." Caroline guided Hannah out of the kitchen and into the living room. They sunk down into the couch together, Caroline holding Hannah when she curled around her. “If you think I’m willing to allow someone to come between us, you’re *very* wrong. This means so much to me too, and I don’t care who Kirsty is...she’s not going to interfere. Unless you still feel something for her, then I have no reason to be worried, Hannah.”

“I don’t feel anything for her, Caz. And I hope you know that.” Hannah splayed a hand across Caroline’s chest, leaning up and kissing her slowly. “She means nothing to me. I just... don’t want her to keep coming back here. I don’t know how unstable she is.”

“Everything is going to be fine, okay?” Caroline pressed her lips to Hannah’s forehead, tightening her arm around her. “Stop worrying about something that isn’t for us to deal with. We have one another, and we’re going to be okay.”

“You think?” Hannah asked, her voice breaking.

“No, I know it. Because this...it’s all I’ve ever wanted. You make me so happy, Hannah. I may not look like much when it comes to confrontation, and I may have been weak some time ago, but not anymore. And that’s because *you* have reminded me of who I am deep down. You have given me back the confidence I’d lost the moment I met Naomi. In my book, that says everything. It tells me that we’re meant to be.”

“We are. Without a doubt. And I *am* proud of you, Caz. So proud.”

Caroline smiled into another kiss, lingering...never wanting to let Hannah go. “I love you.”

“Not as much as I love you.”

CHAPTER 28

Caroline took her satchel from the side of her desk, turning out the light in her classroom. She couldn't wait to get out of here today, mostly because she was spending the evening with Hannah and Edie. Edie had left it up to Caroline to choose their midweek takeout...and the pressure was real. It was only dinner, but Caroline wanted to get it right.

Deep down, though, Caroline knew she couldn't get it wrong. Edie was polite and would be happy with anything she selected.

"Hey, Caz!"

Caroline turned at the sound of Brenda's voice. She smiled, stopping in the corridor. "Hi. Everything okay?"

"Yeah. I was wondering if you and Hannah wanted to come over tonight for a glass of wine? Sharon is getting to mine around seven. Nothing exciting, just a catch-up."

"Tonight is no good for us, sorry."

Brenda narrowed her eyes as she approached. "You...never seem to be available anymore. Should we be worried?"

Huh? Worried. Why would her friends possibly need to be worried? "I'm not following your line of thinking here."

"You meet Hannah, and suddenly, you can't make it out with friends. Is she another Naomi?" Brenda linked her arm through Caroline's, leaning towards her ear. "I know you wouldn't find yourself in that position again, but if you're concerned that she's not giving you time to yourself...you can tell me."

Caroline, shocked and surprised, practically looked through Brenda. "Hannah is not another Naomi. Not even close. The reason we can't make it is because Edie is home tonight, and she's asked if we can order takeout. I promised her a fancy banquet."

"O-oh. I'm sorry."

"It's okay. I appreciate you looking out for me, but Hannah is a good one. The best."

"I know she'd never hurt you, but we were so oblivious last time that I never want you to find yourself in that position again. We weren't good friends to you."

Caroline smiled. "You were. The fact I chose to hide the grim life I had was on me. Not you or anybody else."

"Okay. Well maybe another time, then?"

"Absolutely. I'll mention it to Hannah. Midweek isn't really good for us because Hannah is run off her feet at work, but maybe a weekend in the future?"

"A weekend. Got it. Perfect." Brenda squeezed Caroline's arm, taking a step back. "I've got a meeting with a parent, so I'd better get back to my classroom. I'll see you soon, okay?"

"See you soon." Caroline strode away, thrilled by the cosy night in she had planned.

She rushed out of the main entrance before anyone else could stop her from reaching her car, almost running through the main gates and to the overspill car park. Hannah had kept her busy this morning, meaning she had just about made it to her first lesson. That, in turn, meant her usual parking spot had been taken.

As Caroline turned the corner to cross the busy street filled with students leaving for the day, she stopped abruptly. Was that...Edie? With... Oh, no.

"Edie!"

Edie spun around, a slight fear in her eyes. "Ms Baker, um...I don't want Kirsty to pick me up."

Caroline took a step closer, reaching out a hand to Edie. When Edie remained where she was, Caroline noted the hand wrapped around her wrist. Kirsty's hand. Around Edie's wrist! Oh, this wasn't happening. "Come on. You're coming with me today."

"Am I?" Edie's eyes lit up. Caroline could appreciate that later when Kirsty wasn't trying to abduct her girlfriend's daughter. "Kirsty said Mum asked her to collect me. But I usually get the bus."

"Hannah did ask me to get Edie today!" Kirsty spat, glaring at Caroline. "And I have stuff to do, so we need to leave now."

"Let go of her." Caroline kept her voice calm and low, stepping between Edie and Kirsty. "Before you do something stupid," Caroline paused, her nostrils flared, "take your fucking hands off my student."

"She might be your student, but she's practically my daughter."

"Do you have parental rights? A contact order?"

"What?"

"No, you do not. Now take your hands off Edie, and then we can call Hannah and put this all to rest. If she has told you to collect her, then no harm has been done, but as her teacher, I have a responsibility to protect Edie. From you and whoever else I have to contend with."

Kirsty scoffed, letting go of Edie's hand. "You're a bitch."

Caroline turned to Edie and crouched until she was at her level. "Can you do me a favour and wait inside at reception for me? I'll be ten minutes, and then we can get you home."

"Did you decide what we're having tonight?"

Caroline grinned, squeezing Edie's shoulder gently. "I did, but it's a surprise. Now go on. Scoot."

She watched Edie cross the road, her anger just about ready to blow at any moment. When she turned back to Kirsty, it was clear from her facial expression that Hannah's ex really didn't believe she'd done anything wrong. She appeared surprised. Kirsty...was unstable.

Tread carefully, Caz.

"Look, if you really want to spend a few hours with Edie, I'm fine with that. But you can't just show up out of the blue."

"You're *fine* with it? Who the fuck asked you for your opinion?"

Stay calm.

"Like I said, as her teacher, I have a responsibility, Kirsty. That's all."

"You're not fucking Hannah anymore?"

Huh. Maybe Caroline could use this to her advantage. She wasn't sure what else to do. If Kirsty knew she was about to call the police, she would flee. That was the last thing they needed. "No, I'm not."

"Then move out of my fucking way and let me take my kid for something to eat."

Caroline took her phone from her pocket and waved it at Kirsty. "I'll just call Hannah and let her know so she doesn't turn up here to collect Edie herself. She can have an hour or two to herself then."

Kirsty's eyes lit up as she nodded. "Sure. Yeah. She needs a break. I can help with that."

Caroline turned her back, dialling 999 immediately. She

took a couple of steps away, smiling as she looked over her shoulder at Kirsty.

"Emergency. Which service?"

"Police, please." Caroline strolled further away from Kirsty, but not far enough for her to be suspicious.

"Police emergency."

"Hi, yes. I'd like to report an attempted abduction. St Peter's High. Thorncross Street."

"Okay, I have a unit on its way to you, but I'm going to need some other information."

"Of course, yes."

"Can I take your name?" The call handler asked, clicking away on the keyboard.

"Caroline Baker."

"And can I ask what's happened, Caroline?"

"I was leaving the premises. I'm a teacher at St Peter's. A student I know was being led away by her mother's ex-partner. My main concern is that the ex-partner in question is spiralling. She's been around to their house recently after leaving for quite some time. She's not stable—I'm certain of that. She's also here with me now and unaware that I'm on the phone to you, so..."

"I see. Is she likely to run?"

"I believe so. She thinks I'm calling the student's mother to tell her everything is okay. I'm worried that this is going to get worse if she isn't hospitalised. Given the fact that we have no way of contacting her family, I think it's best for the police to handle it."

"Can I take her or what?" Kirsty asked, clearly aggravated judging by the tone of her voice. "Give me the phone!"

Caroline turned and held up a hand. "Just give me a few minutes. Hannah is working and doesn't have the luxury of just answering calls from me."

"Okay, I can hear that the assailant is agitated. The unit is a minute out and coming without sirens. Please keep a distance if you're worried they may lash out."

"I'm okay. And the child has gone back into the school. They're safe."

"You're a fucking liar. You haven't called Hannah!" Kirsty lunged towards Caroline, her fist connecting hard with Caroline's breastbone. "Who the fuck are you calling?"

As Caroline considered her next move, trying to hide the fact that Kirsty had likely broken something, a police car pulled up behind Kirsty, and two officers shot out of it.

"I'll fucking kill you!" Kirsty lunged at Caroline again, forcing her back against a garden wall. Her lower back connected with the jagged stone, and a searing pain coursed through her.

This wasn't how she'd planned her day. And while she wanted to fall to her knees, she couldn't. She had to take care of Edie first and foremost. She could hurt later. And boy would she hurt.

The officers restrained Kirsty, pushing her front to the car she'd been standing at since Caroline left the school premises. She didn't know if it belonged to Kirsty, but she didn't care.

Once she was safely in handcuffs, one officer directed her into the back of the police car while the other came to Caroline. "Are you okay?"

Caroline held up a hand, wincing. "I'm fine. I need to get back inside to my student."

"Along with the attempted abduction, she will be further charged with assault."

"Look, I just want someone to help her. I'm not interested in pressing charges for assault." Caroline rubbed her palm against her sternum, puffing out her cheeks.

"Do you need medical attention?" the officer, a woman with kind eyes, asked.

"Really, I'm fine."

"Then I need to take some details. Another officer will come by to take your statement. I'll need your address, along with some other information..." She removed her notepad, and then looked back up at Caroline.

"Is that really necessary?"

"It is, yes."

God, why did Caroline have to get herself into this position?

Caroline sat in the reception area, wringing her hands, as Edie sat playing on her phone. The school had called Hannah once Caroline had come back inside, and now she wanted to get home and have a hot bath. She needed a moment to herself, to gather her thoughts, and then she would be good to go again.

But now she just had to explain the fact that Hannah's ex-girlfriend had been arrested. Edie seemed oblivious to everything, which in Caroline's book could only be a good thing. She never wanted Edie to witness violence, especially not violence directed at Caroline.

"What's going on?" Hannah came flying through the double doors, straight towards Caroline and Edie.

"Hi, Mum." Edie smiled. "What are you doing here? Ms Baker said she was bringing me home."

"Don't worry, Edie. You just sit there while I speak to your mum." Caroline got to her feet and guided Hannah away by the elbow. Once they were alone inside an empty side room, she sighed. "Kirsty was here. She tried to take Edie with her."

"What?" Hannah frowned, sheer disbelief in her eyes. "Kirsty?"

Caroline ran a hand through her hair, trying not to grimace

as her body ached. "Yes. I was leaving school and caught her outside. Edie had no idea what was going on."

"Hang on, you're not making any sense. Kirsty...tried to abduct Edie?"

"It...seems so, yes."

"Seems so? She either did or she didn't, Caz." Hannah scoffed, then threw up her hands. "What the hell is going on? Kirsty may be a bit out of sorts at the minute, but she'd never do anything to hurt Edie."

Taken aback by Hannah's reaction, Caroline took a step, then another away. "I was just trying to help. She was about to put your daughter in the back of her car!"

"Caz," Hannah said, reaching out a hand.

"No. Please don't. Whether we're together or not, I have a duty of care for every student in this building. If I see something suspicious, I have to act on it."

"And I'm glad you did."

"Tell that to your attitude." Caroline straightened her blazer out and opened the door to the office. "Hey, Edie." She waved a hand in front of Edie, smiling when she removed her earphones. "Your mum is going to take you home, okay?"

"With you?"

"No, sweetheart. Not with me. But I'll see you real soon, okay?"

Edie lowered her eyes, nodding slowly. "Kay. Bye, Ms Baker."

"Bye, Edie." Caroline turned to Hannah. "The police will be coming to see you. They need a statement from Edie. I should head home in case they turn up at mine."

"The...police?"

"Yes. I had to call them. That may not have been what you wanted, but as I said, I have a duty. I'll see you soon, okay?"

Caroline stepped away, but Hannah stopped her. "Hannah, please. I really need to leave now."

Hannah backed away and held up a hand. "Okay. I'm sorry."

"Take care of Edie. I'm certain she's fine and doesn't know what's happened, but just...keep an eye on her."

Caroline took her bag from the side of the chair she'd been sitting on when Hannah arrived and left the building. She didn't look back, she didn't reconsider, she just kept walking. As the adrenaline began to wear off, the pain tripled.

"Yes, okay. Thanks."

Hannah stared at her phone when the screen dimmed, her head spinning. She'd been home for two hours, and she could barely understand what had happened. Edie had been quiet, but she would have to speak up eventually because that had been a call from a police officer telling Hannah they would be with her soon.

"Edie?" Hannah called her daughter from the bottom of the stairs. "Could you come down?"

Edie's bedroom door opened, and heavy footsteps followed. "What for? Has Caz called? Is she coming over?"

"No, love. I texted her, but I've not heard back yet." Hannah noted the sadness in her daughter's eyes as she landed in the hallway and walked away. "Is everything okay? Did you want to talk about what happened?"

Edie sniffled. "Mum, I'm sorry. If I'd just gone with Kirsty, you and Caz wouldn't have broken up."

What? Broken up? This was news to Hannah. News she really hoped was entirely off the mark. "Why would you think that?"

"Because she's angry with me now." Edie wiped a hand

across one cheek, and then the other. "Why did you ask Kirsty to pick me up from school?"

"I didn't. Caz did the right thing." She was sure of that even if Hannah still wasn't quite sure what had happened. "Was Kirsty mean to you? D-did she hurt you?"

"No. But she wouldn't let go of me." Edie flopped down on the couch, pulling at the cuff of her hoodie. "Mum, if something was wrong...like, between you and Caz, would you tell me? I-if you didn't love each other anymore because of Kirsty."

"Of course I would. But Caz and I are fine." Hannah hoped so, anyway. It was difficult to know how Caroline was feeling because she wasn't accepting Hannah's calls. Still, Hannah understood. The last thing Caroline would have wanted was to call the police today. Hannah sat beside her daughter, squeezing her knee. "And would you tell me if something was wrong? If you knew more than you wanted to say, would you tell me?"

"Yeah. It's just... Is Caz at the hospital?"

"Why would Caz be at the hospital?" Caroline, as far as Hannah knew, had gone home to wait for the police. The reason she hadn't heard from her—Hannah assumed—was because of that. But then Hannah recalled the way she'd spoken to Caroline. She could have handled it all far better than she had. "Edie?"

"Kirsty punched her."

Hannah's chest tightened at those words. "What do you mean?"

"She punched Caz. Then she shoved her. Caz nearly went over the wall into Mrs Trenton's garden."

"R-right." Hannah turned her face away from Edie, closing her eyes. "I just need to call Nanna, okay?"

"Why?"

Hannah took a calming breath. "Because I know you were

supposed to be staying here tonight, but I think you may have to stay with her. I need to speak to Caz."

"I don't think she likes me anymore. I am sorry. But Kirsty left, and you always tell me not to go with people I don't know. And really, I don't know Kirsty now. She scared me today."

Hannah tried to exhale the most calming breath she could manage, but this evening, she was furious. At Kirsty. At the position she found herself in. At the sheer thought of someone laying a finger not only on Edie but on Caz, too.

And then there was the idea that Caz was home alone...and hurt. God, she needed to be with her.

"You did the right thing. And you've done nothing wrong either with Kirsty or Caz. I know we should have been having a girls' night in, but you know you need to be alone when you're upset?" Edie nodded. "That's what Caz has to do, too. That's all."

"She's upset with me?"

"No. She's just upset. Maybe a little bit hurt, too. But don't worry; I'll go and see her. And if she needs to be looked after, we can do that together, right?"

"Yeah. I can help you look after her." Edie got to her feet. "Should I make something to eat?"

"No, no. Nanna can feed you tonight. Once the police have been by, I'll drop you off."

Edie tentatively lowered herself back to the couch. "Okay. I'll wait here for the police."

"When they get here, I want you to be honest with them. Tell them everything you saw. It doesn't matter if you don't want to upset anyone. I need you to be honest."

"I will."

Hannah got to her feet and sighed. "I'm sorry Kirsty came to the school, Edie."

"I hate her."

Hannah's brows rose.

"I do. She hurt Caz, and I hate her."

Hannah stared down at Edie, feeling the very same thing. It was going to take time for their anger to subside, Hannah's more so since she wanted to find Kirsty and hurt her, but they would be okay. They had to be. This budding relationship meant too much to Hannah to even consider the possibility of losing it.

Go to Caz and make things right.

CHAPTER 29

Hannah stood at Caroline's garden gate, looking up at her dimly lit home. She loved being here with Caz, it was a sanctuary for them, but the day's events—especially now that she'd heard Edie relay everything in her police statement—left her feeling dreadful.

Caroline still hadn't contacted Hannah. But Hannah couldn't blame her. Hannah's ex had assaulted her, and Hannah had doubted the initial information Caroline had given her about it. Why the hell had she done that? Because she wanted to believe Kirsty could redeem herself in some way? Because she wasn't sure someone she'd shared three years of her life with was capable of that? Hannah knew people, when challenged, were capable of anything.

And now she had to repair the damage she'd caused.

She considered knocking, but if Caroline was resting, she didn't want her to have to get up and answer the door. So Hannah looked down at the keys in her hand, pushing through the gate.

Hannah opened the front door, nothing but silence greeting

her. She would check downstairs, hoping that Caroline wasn't in a bad way. "Caz?"

Nothing.

Hannah went through to the living room, smiling weakly at the sight before her. Caroline sat propped upright on the couch, frozen in place. "Babe, why didn't you answer my messages?"

"I've been with the police. Sorry."

Hannah crossed the room and got to her knees in front of Caroline. "I'm so sorry. I had no idea what actually happened."

Caroline frowned. "I don't know what you're talking about."

"She hurt you. I know she did. Edie saw it all." Hannah placed a gentle hand to Caroline's knee, palming it slowly. "Tell me what you need. Let me help."

"I'm okay. I'll be fine in a few days," Caroline said, her voice void of that happiness Hannah usually heard. She'd become so used to it recently that she'd taken it for granted. "You go home to Edie. I've taken the rest of the week off work to recover."

"It's bad, isn't it?"

"I've had back issues over the years. Being shoved full force into a wall hasn't helped."

Hannah sat back on her knees, sighing. "She's been arrested. She's not had a very good time since she went home. And this isn't the first time she's been arrested recently. But she's in the right place to get any help she needs now. They're going to do an in-depth assessment on why she's behaving this way."

"Good. That's good."

"So, should I get some things together and we'll get you back to mine? Just let me know what you need, and I'll get it."

Caroline smiled weakly. "No. I'll be okay."

"I'm not leaving you here like this. You can't move, Caz."

"I've taken some stronger medication. It'll ease off soon. It's just a spasm."

"Okay, well, I'll put the kettle on until it eases off, and then we're going to mine. I'm not leaving you here."

"Why are you so worried?" Caroline asked, looking at Hannah as she stood up. "You didn't believe a word I said to you at the school, so why do you care?"

Ouch. Caroline had never spoken to Hannah like that before. But she supposed it went both ways, and Caroline was only offering the same attitude Hannah had given earlier.

"Of course I care."

"Now that the police have confirmed it." Caroline nodded slowly, grimacing. "You couldn't take my word for it. But I should have known you wouldn't. She shared your bed with you for three years."

"Caz, come on. Let's not fall out." The last thing Hannah wanted was to lose this woman. Their time together—minus Kirsty—had been perfect recently. "I'm sorry. I didn't know what the hell was going on. And then you said Kirsty had tried to abduct Edie, and I lost my mind. I didn't understand how it could possibly be true."

"You know, I'd have done anything to protect Edie today. I'd have taken one hell of a beating for her if I'd had to," Caroline whispered, her eyes closing. "To hear you say that Kirsty wouldn't do something like that after I'd just been assaulted by her..."

Hannah's stomach lurched at those words. At the pain in Caroline's voice. But Caroline was right, and Hannah had to accept that. She *had* foolishly believed that Kirsty couldn't be capable of something so terrible. Hannah got to her knees again, taking Caroline's hands. "If I could take back the way I've handled this, I would. I'm so sorry, Caz."

"I don't know why I was so surprised." Caroline focused ahead of her, refusing to make eye contact with Hannah. That only pained Hannah further. "This...me...I'm not capable of keeping Edie safe, Hannah. Today I got lucky, but what happens next time?"

"Not capable of keeping her safe?" Hannah dipped her head, finding those eyes she desperately craved. Only they were dimmed, and miserable. Because of Hannah. "Babe, if it hadn't been for you, Edie *wouldn't* be safe."

Caroline scoffed lightly. "You really thought I was lying to you today, didn't you?"

"No." Hannah lifted Caroline's hand and held it against her own cheek. She needed to feel that connection, that softness, Caroline's warmth. "Caz, I'm so sorry about today. I should have listened instead of panicking. I should have sat down in that office with you and waited for you to explain. Please give me another chance. Let me help you and take care of you. J-just...let me love you, please?"

Caroline sniffled as Hannah spoke those words. This couldn't be it for them, Hannah refused to allow it.

"Tell me how I can fix this. Please, babe. I love you so much. I can't lose you."

"You can go home and be with Edie. Make sure she's okay. And leave me to get over this alone. I really don't need any help. I've managed before."

"I don't want you to manage. I don't want you to struggle to get into bed or get dressed. I want to be here for you. Edie is with my mum, so I don't need to get back. And even if I needed to get back for her, you'd be coming with me."

Hannah got to her feet, turned, and walked away. Caroline needed to cool off for a moment or two, and Hannah had another call to make.

She took her phone from the back pocket of her jeans and brought up Juliet's number.

"Hannah, hi."

"Hey. So, the whole Kirsty thing came to a head, and I need

to take the rest of the week off. I can work from home, no problem, but I won't be able to get into the office."

"What do you mean it came to a head? Are you okay?"

"I am, yes. But Caz isn't. Kirsty turned up at the school today and tried to take Edie. I'm fucking livid, but she's been arrested. Not before she assaulted Caz, though."

"She assaulted her? Christ, what's going on with her?!"

"She's really changed, Juliet. It turns out, she's on bail for assault. You and I both know that's not the Kirsty Hardacre we had in our lives. But since she went home, she's had some kind of anger management issues going on. Fights in bars, flipping her shit if someone looks at her the wrong way... I think with everything happening with her mum, she just...broke. I don't know. And I don't particularly care. My focus is on Caroline and Edie."

"Is Edie okay?"

Hannah smiled. "Edie is fine. She thinks she's broken me and Caz up, but I've reassured her. It's just...Caz is in quite a lot of pain at the minute, and she can't really get around the house properly. It's her back."

"Don't worry about it," Juliet said. "Take care of her and I'll see you back here on Monday if things are better. If they're not, work from home next week. That's fine with me."

"Thank you for understanding. I really appreciate it." Hannah felt a wave of relief wash over her knowing she wouldn't have to leave Caz. It made her life easier, and it meant she wouldn't be sitting at her desk worrying.

"Oh, and Hannah?"

"Yeah?"

Juliet cleared her throat. "If Caz needs representation, it's on me. Pro bono."

"Oh, wow. That's...uh." Hannah paused, frowning. She

hadn't expected such a huge offer from Juliet. "Yeah, thanks. That really means a lot, Juliet. I'll let her know."

"Call me if you need anything. I'm only on the end of the phone. Bye, Hannah. Take care."

Hannah locked her phone and shoved it in her pocket, making two cups of tea while she was in the kitchen. She wasn't sure Caroline had eaten or wanted to, but she would tackle that next.

"Babe?" She slipped out of the kitchen and back into the living room. "I've put the kettle on. Do you want something to eat too?"

"No. I don't feel like anything at the minute."

"You said you've had back problems before. Has anything helped ease it in the past?"

"Usually a hot bath. That's about all, really."

"Hot bath. Got it. I'm on it." Hannah turned and rushed up the stairs, getting to work on Caroline's bath. If that's what she needed, then that was what she'd get. "Anything in particular you want in it?" she yelled down the stairs.

"Just a load of Epsom Salts, please."

"Okay. I'll be back down in a minute to get you."

Caroline let out a groan when she relaxed into the steaming hot water, closing her eyes as she rested her head back. Just a little while in here, and she should loosen up a little. Probably not as much as she'd like to, but anything was better than nothing.

The most humiliating thing in all of this, though, was the fact that Hannah had to help her into the bath. She just couldn't do it alone.

Even if she'd initially been angry with Hannah after how she'd spoken to her back at work, Caroline was grateful Hannah was here. She didn't want to fight, but she also didn't appreciate being spoken to out of turn when she'd done nothing wrong.

Caroline scoffed. Gone were *those* days.

"Caz?" Hannah knocked gently on the bathroom door, opening it slowly. "I've brought you some warm towels."

When Hannah did things like that, it softened Caroline. "Thank you. Come in."

Hannah skulked around the door, smiling weakly. "Is the water hot enough?"

"It's perfect. Thanks."

Placing the towels down, Hannah got to her knees at the side of the bath and brushed stray hair from Caroline's face. "Babe, what happened today? I heard Edie's account, but you sent her back into school, didn't you?"

"I did. I didn't want her to hear or see anything, but clearly, that didn't work."

"She's really upset about it all. Thinks she's broken us up."

Caroline lifted a hand from the water slowly, taking Hannah's. "Everything is going to be fine."

"Promise?"

"I don't need to promise. You know I love you." Caroline moaned lightly as the water soothed her, and then she sighed. "I tried to play stupid at first, so Kirsty didn't make a run for it. She thought I was calling you about taking Edie, and then she realised I was on the phone to the police."

Hannah's eyes drifted to Caroline's chest. She reached out, stroking her skin so carefully. "Is that when she punched you?"

"Yeah. Knocked me for six at first," Caroline explained, looking down where the bruise had formed on her chest. "She's got a good aim, I'll give her that."

"I'm so sorry she hurt you."

"It's not your fault. But I couldn't let her take Edie. And Edie told me herself that she didn't want to go with her. I'm glad the police arrived when they did. The mood she was in, I could have been in a far worse condition."

"You protected my daughter today. I can never truly thank you for that. And it wasn't on you to do so, but it just shows how much you care for Edie."

"Except it is on me. When you can't be there, and Dylan can't be there, then it *does* fall to me. Teacher or not, it falls to me because she's my responsibility too. Because she's your daughter, and I love you both."

Hannah chewed the corner of her lip, and then rested her forehead on her arm against the bath. Caroline heard Hannah sniffle, but all she could do was keep holding her hand. She was still stuck.

"Don't cry."

"You don't realise how much you mean to me, Caz. You really don't."

"I do. Just do one thing for me?"

Hannah lifted her head. "Anything. You know I'd do *anything* for you."

"Give me the benefit of the doubt next time. I can deal with most things but feeling like I'm being called a liar...I cannot. And it may not have been intended that way, but it was how I felt. After being with her for so long, always being told I was overreacting or that I *was* a liar, I don't want to go through that same feeling with you, Hannah. I don't ever want a relationship like that again."

Hannah nodded. "I am sorry. I really am."

"I know." Caroline shifted, the ache in her back subsiding. "Oh, thank God. I can move a bit."

"Where do you want to move to?" Hannah sat up on her knees, placing an arm around Caroline. "Did you want to sit up?"

"Yes. Please."

She groaned through the lingering pain, but she *was* moving a little easier. Once Caroline was sitting up, she exhaled a breath and let the tension fall from her shoulders. "You really don't have to get back home for Edie?"

"No. She's with Mum."

Caroline smiled. "Maybe you could go home and grab some things. Stay the night."

"I don't need to go home for anything. I have toiletries here, pjs, and a change of clothes."

"You don't have your work clothes, though. You'll need them."

"I'm not going to work the rest of the week. I've already spoken to Juliet. She said if you needed representation for the assault charge that she'd represent you."

"Firstly, you don't need to take time off work. Secondly, I really appreciate that, but I'm not pressing charges."

"You're...not?" Hannah lifted a brow. "Can I ask why?"

"Kirsty needs help, not a criminal record. And while I don't condone what she did, nor will I likely forgive her for it, that's all I wanted...help for her. I'm not sure she's very well, Hannah."

"Oh, I know."

"And now she's in the best place to be treated. *This*...I'll get over. Maybe with the right help, Kirsty can overcome what she's dealing with, too."

"You're a special person, Caroline Baker. And I can't believe that I get to call you mine."

"Will you stay with me tonight?"

Hannah leaned in, kissing Caroline for the first time since this morning. "I'd love to stay with you."

CHAPTER 30

"Hello?" Hannah whispered into her phone, mindful not to wake Caroline. She hadn't slept very well last night, unable to get comfortable, but she'd finally settled around 3 a.m.

"Mum, did you find Caz?"

Hannah smiled. "I did, love. I'm with her now."

"Kay." Edie fell silent. Hannah knew her daughter was worried she'd done something wrong, maybe caused Caroline's injury, but everything was going to be okay. Kirsty was getting the help she needed, and everyone was going to get on with their lives.

"Is Nanna going to drop you at school this morning?"

"I...don't want to go. She said I had to call you and ask if I could stay off today."

Hannah sighed. She really didn't want Edie missing school unless she absolutely had to. And she'd only recently gone back since being ill. "I'd rather you went in. Why do you need to stay off?"

"I wanted to come and see Caz. To say sorry."

"Edie, you have nothing to be sorry for." Edie sniffled down the line, Hannah's heart aching for her daughter. Kirsty really had left a mess behind. "Caz isn't feeling very good, but when she's awake, I'll see if she is feeling well enough to maybe come over and see you, okay?"

"She doesn't like me anymore," Edie sobbed, sending Hannah's concern for her daughter through the roof. "Can you tell her I didn't mean for her to get hurt, Mum? Please tell her I'm sorry."

Hannah slid from Caroline's bed, creeping out into the hallway. "Edie, Caz doesn't think you did anything wrong. She's okay, and she does still want us all to keep doing the things we've been doing together. Going out for dinner, girls' nights, you know."

"I've never been to Caz's house."

"I know. It's easier to be at our house because all your things are there. Your schoolwork and stuff." Hannah frowned. She had no idea where Edie was going with this conversation. "But I'm sure you'll come over one day."

"Nanna said I could borrow some money from her this morning. We went to the flower shop and got Caz some flowers. I...I wondered if I could bring them over with the get well soon card I got too."

Oh, Edie was the sweetest child. Hannah couldn't be any prouder.

"Do you think she would mind?"

"No, love. She wouldn't mind at all." Hannah peered through the crack in the door, smiling when Caroline's tired eyes stared back at her. "I'll call you in a little while, okay? Tell Nanna you can take the day off, but you're going back in tomorrow."

"Okay, Mum. I love you."

"I love you too, kiddo."

Hannah locked her phone and slipped back into the

bedroom, carefully making herself comfortable beneath the covers again. “Morning, gorgeous.”

“Mm. Morning. I don’t feel so gorgeous today.” Caroline shifted, wincing as pain jolted her. “Fuck.”

“Maybe I could make us some coffee while you wait for that body to wake up.”

Caroline took Hannah’s hand beneath the cover, pulling her closer. “Not yet. Stay here with me.”

Oh, that wasn’t a demand Caroline ever had to make. Hannah would spend forever lying here staring at this woman. Caroline had really gone above and beyond yesterday, and as Hannah lay here this morning, she’d only fallen further in love with her. “How are you feeling?”

“A little bit sore. Was that Edie calling?”

“It was, yes.”

Caroline stroked a thumb across the back of Hannah’s hand, her eyelids heavy. “And how is she?”

“She’s...a little anxious. I had a feeling she would be, but my mum will calm her down. She’s always been good with that.”

“Maybe you should go and be with her. I’m just going to take it easy today and rest. There’s really no point in you sitting around when you could be doing whatever needs doing at home.”

“Do you want me to leave?” Hannah asked, desperately hoping Caroline would say no. But Hannah had to consider that Caroline did want to be alone for a while. Yesterday had to have been a lot for her. And outside of work, too? She was probably feeling humiliated after what happened.

“It’s not that I want you to leave,” Caroline explained, squeezing Hannah’s hand. “But I’m used to dealing with things alone. So, you coming over last night and staying without complaining about not wanting to be here is a little odd for me. That’s all.”

"Why would I complain? If I didn't want to be here, I wouldn't have turned up."

"I couldn't even be sick without being criticised." Caroline's eyes flashed with that look she'd once had. Way back when they'd first met. As though she was a hindrance. "I ruined plans. I was being dramatic. There was nothing wrong with me."

"You won't find me doing that. If you want me to be here, then I'm going to be here. If you don't want to be alone, I won't leave you alone. But...if you do want some time to yourself, you only have to say the word, and I'll give you some space."

"I'd like you to stay a while, but you should probably see to Edie. She's your priority, Hannah. Not me."

"You're both my priority." Hannah leaned in, pressing a kiss to Caroline's nose. When Caroline nuzzled into Hannah, she wrapped an arm around Caroline, aware that she was in pain. "Would it be okay if Edie came over? It's absolutely fine if you don't want her here, but I thought there was no harm in asking."

"Why wouldn't I want her here?" Caroline's brows drew together. "Have I ever given you that impression?"

"God, no. And I wasn't implying that you ever had. I guess it's just never come up in conversation. But I think she'd like to see you if you're feeling up to it."

"Edie is welcome here whenever she wants to be here. The same goes for you."

Hannah feathered her fingertips across Caroline's cheek, a smile spreading on her mouth. She really hadn't expected to find herself in this position with Caroline back when they met, but she wouldn't change it for anything in the world.

"I'll go and call her. And while I'm there, I'll make myself useful and bring us coffee back up."

"I'd like that."

Caroline folded laundry, slowly shifting from side to side as she placed her clothes into the correct piles on the dining table. The more she moved, the less she hurt. Sitting wasn't doing anything for her back at all. She was only seizing up if she lounged around.

She took her cup of tea from the counter and moved towards the door. She'd done an hour of meaningless tasks, and now she was going to sit down for five minutes. Relax...or try to at least.

Caroline was concerned about Edie. The whole reason she'd sent her back into school yesterday was because she knew Kirsty could become violent. Edie wasn't supposed to see any of what happened. But she had, and now Hannah was left to pick up the pieces. Caroline too if Hannah would allow her that.

The doorbell rang as Caroline reached the living room. Hannah was upstairs showering, the soft hum of her voice as she did so making Caroline smile. She reached for the door, opening it slowly as she shifted back. What she was met with stole her heart once and for all.

"Edie. Hi."

"H-hi, Ms Baker." Caroline lifted a brow at that. "Caz. Sorry."

Caroline's eyes lowered, her heart almost bursting from her chest. Edie held a bunch of flowers in one arm, a card barely grasped by her fingertips, and a box of chocolates in the other hand. "These are for you. To say sorry for what happened yesterday. Mum said it would be okay to bring them over. But if it's not, I can go back home with Nanna."

Caroline looked behind Edie. An older woman was standing behind her. It had to be Hannah's mother; they all looked alike.

"Of course it's okay. Come in." Caroline opened the door

wider, winking when Edie sloped past her. Hannah's mum stopped at the doorway. "Hi, I'm Caz."

"Oh, I know who you are. My granddaughter doesn't stop talking about you. Ivy. Nice to meet you." Ivy held out a hand which Caroline took. "Seems my girls are smitten with you, Caz."

Caroline tried to fight back the blush, but it was useless. It was spreading faster than she would have liked. "Come in. Hannah is just finishing in the shower."

"Oh, I don't want to intrude."

Caz lifted a hand. "Absolutely not. It would be lovely to finally get to know you. I thought Hannah was keeping me a secret for a moment or two."

"Hannah? Oh, no chance." Ivy stepped inside, shedding her coat. "My daughter is very open about who she is and who she is dating. When she told me about you, her eyes lit up. Edie's too whenever she talks about you."

"Well, that's very good to hear. Can I get you some tea or coffee?"

"Hannah can take care of that. You should be resting." Ivy gave Caroline a knowing look, and then her lips spread into a smile. "This is lovely."

"It...is?" Caroline frowned. What exactly was lovely?

"Hannah is forever getting her heart broken. When she told me she'd met someone, I was waiting for it all to fall apart again. But I think she finally found someone worth the risk. A risk I'm happy she's taking."

Caroline wasn't used to this kind of praise. It felt odd, but it also felt comforting. She may have been forty-seven, and she may have had many years on Hannah in terms of life, but knowing someone trusted Caroline with their heart meant a lot. With Edie's heart too.

Ivy placed a gentle hand to Caroline's wrist, to the hand still holding her cup of tea. "I think Edie would really like a few minutes with you."

"Oh, right. Of course." Caroline moved into the living room, smiling at Edie where she sat. "What's all this? It's not my birthday."

Edie sat on the couch, her knee bouncing. "I needed to say sorry to you."

"For what, Edie?" Caroline slowly sat down beside her student, taking the flowers as they were thrust towards her.

"Yesterday. If I hadn't refused to go with Kirsty, she wouldn't have hurt you." Edie's voice broke, her bottom lip trembling as she stared at the coffee table. "I should have just let her pick me up from school."

"No, no. You did the right thing. Kirsty isn't authorised to collect you from school."

Edie lifted a shoulder. "But if I'd gone, you wouldn't have been hurt."

"She didn't hurt me because of you, Edie. She hurt me because she wasn't feeling very well and needed a little help. I just happened to be there and in the way. It could have been anyone."

That may not have been quite the whole truth, but Caroline saw the torment in Edie's eyes. She never wanted Hannah's daughter to feel that way about anything concerning Caroline.

"The main thing is that everyone is okay."

"D-do you still love Mum?" Edie asked, her brow furrowed. "Because she didn't do anything wrong."

Caroline grinned. "Of course I still love her. I love her more than I did before yesterday. What happened doesn't change anything."

"Kay." Edie wrung her hands in her lap. "And you're not angry that I came here?"

"No, sweetheart. Not at all." Caroline lowered the flowers to the coffee table, opening her arms. "Maybe a hug will make it all better."

"I...I'm allowed to hug you?"

Caroline almost burst out laughing at that but refrained from doing so. Edie was wary, but it only showed how thoughtful Hannah's daughter was. "Come here."

Edie wrapped her arms around Caroline, sniffling when Caroline held Edie against her. She felt that twinge in her back, the slight spasm that had been present since yesterday, but she pushed it away.

"Edie, I know you're a little worried about everything that happened, but I'm fine. And I hope you are, too."

"I am." Edie pulled out of Caroline's embrace, wiping a hand across her cheek. "I just didn't want you to be angry with me."

Caroline brought her hands to Edie's face, cupping her cheeks and wiping away her tears with the pads of her thumbs. "You did absolutely nothing wrong, okay?"

Edie turned her head suddenly, smiling in the direction of Caroline's living room door. "Hi, Mum."

Caroline followed Edie's line of sight, frowning when Hannah wiped tears from her cheeks. Why was she upset?

"Hi, love."

Edie got to her feet and rushed towards Hannah, holding her by the waist as she nuzzled into her chest. Caroline could only smile, along with Ivy who was standing just the slightest distance from 'her girls.' But then Caroline realised that they were her girls, too.

Her heart rate spiked at that, her palms clammy. Caroline had never been in this position before.

Oh, wow. This was incredibly fulfilling.

"Mum, can I stay at home with you tonight?"

Hannah eyed Caroline, silently asking for help. Caroline

knew Hannah wanted to be with her, but Edie needed home and a routine. She simply nodded and smiled.

"I...yes." Hannah held her daughter's face in her hands. "But I need to make sure Caz is okay before we go home, okay?"

"Yeah. I know."

"Okay, so maybe you could go back to Nanna's with her, and then I'll pick you up once I'm done here?"

Caroline suddenly didn't want Hannah or Edie to leave. She wanted them to be here with her, just lounging around and doing whatever they felt comfortable doing.

"I have an idea," Caroline said, getting to her feet. "Maybe Edie could go home and get her uniform for tomorrow and then come back here. We'll have a girls' night at mine instead."

Hannah grinned while Edie's eyes lit up like never before.

"I can stay here?" she asked.

Caroline lifted a shoulder, and then she winced. "Do you want to stay here?"

"Y-yes! Mum, can I?"

Hannah eyed Caroline again, a brow raised. "If that's really okay with Caz?"

"More than okay." Caroline moved towards Hannah and Edie, pulling them both into a hug. "I'd like to spend the rest of the day with you both. So, why don't we do that?"

Edie turned to Ivy. "Nanna, can you take me home for my uniform and homework?"

"Oh, Edie. I'd love to." She wrapped an arm around Edie's shoulder, guiding her towards the door. As Hannah and Caroline followed them, Ivy turned back and faced Caroline. "You've done well here. I look forward to getting to know you, Caz."

With an arm wrapped around Hannah's waist, Caroline simply offered a nod and pressed a kiss to Hannah's hair when she rested her head on Caroline's shoulder. "I look forward to it, too."

CHAPTER 31

"Edie! Ten minutes until dinner."

Caroline smiled when Edie came to the top of the stairs. "I'm just finishing my homework and then I'll set the table."

"The table is done, sweetheart. Just come down when you're ready."

Edie nodded and rushed back into her room, the door slamming shut.

To some, Edie could be considered a baby elephant, but Caroline preferred the noise around here. She'd spent so long sitting in her own silence, with her own thoughts... This was much better. There was life around here. And now that life was back to normal and Caroline had healed, she really felt this relationship progressing beautifully.

One month on since Hurricane Kirsty had crashed through, and Caroline was on cloud nine.

She walked back into the kitchen, folding the tea towel in her hand, and placed it on top of the counter. Hannah sat at the table reading through work documents, her reading glasses making her look even more intelligent than Caroline already knew she was.

"I wanted to let you know that Edie has won an award at school."

Hannah looked up, removing her glasses. "Pardon?"

"Edie. She'll find out at the end of the week in assembly. It's the compassion award."

"She has?" Hannah grinned as she got to her feet. "What does that mean?"

"Several students were nominated by school mentors, classroom assistants, that sort of thing. Edie's name came up a lot, Hannah. I can't say I'm surprised, but I'm so happy that she's won it. She deserves it."

Hannah's bottom lip trembled. "Did you put her forward for this?"

"No. It's nothing to do with me. I only know who won because I was in the staff room this morning when the votes were counted."

"So, what now? Does she get a certificate or something?"

Caroline pressed her index finger to Hannah's lips. "She can't know about it beforehand. I promised I wouldn't say anything. Please, keep your voice down."

"Okay, I'm sorry."

"But no, it's not just a certificate. She also receives a one hundred pound gift certificate for a bookstore in town, and a free meal at the new burger bar that's recently opened."

"Oh, wow. She's going to be thrilled."

Caroline lifted a hand when she heard movement upstairs. "I think she's coming down. Pretend you know nothing. I'll put dinner out."

Hannah followed Caroline to the other side of the kitchen, wrapping her arms around Caroline's waist from behind. "Let me help. You always make dinner."

"I...like making dinner." Caroline glanced over her shoulder, accepting a kiss from Hannah as she leaned in. "And anyway, you can sit there and tell me all about your call with Kirsty."

"Do I have to? I'd rather just watch you while you look all sexy with a spatula."

Caroline barked a laugh as she turned to Hannah, holding the spatula up between them. "You know, I can think of *other* uses for this."

"Oh, I bet you can." Hannah smiled into a kiss, and then she whispered, "But I think we're going to need something far more sturdy if you're planning to spank me, babe."

Caroline's blood rushed south, and she caught her bottom lip between her teeth. Hannah seemed to make it a habit to do this, turn her on at the most inappropriate times. When she should have been serving lasagne, Caroline was imagining Hannah whimpering for her.

"You're thinking about it, aren't you?"

"I think you may need to leave the kitchen until dinner is on the table. I can't work with you here."

"Put dinner out, babe. I'll go and make sure Edie has finished upstairs. She wants us to watch some new series thing with her after we've eaten."

"Hannah?"

Hannah turned back to Caroline, her brows drawn. "Yeah?"

"Kirsty. How did that go?"

"Okay. She's doing much better. She's taking meds, and they're moving her closer to home to continue her treatment. Her mum is palliative now."

"I'm sorry to hear that." Caroline may not like what Kirsty had done to her, but she understood that mental health and inevitable death didn't go well together. She'd already forgiven Kirsty. She just didn't need to see her ever again. "Is she going to be okay?"

"I think so, yes. She apologised and asked me to apologise to you, too. I think something had snapped within her, and we got the brunt of it. I am sorry that I ever put you in that situation with her."

"No need to apologise." Caroline pulled Hannah back in by the waist. "None of that was on you. I'm just glad I was there to stop it."

"I love you." Hannah tucked Caroline's hair behind her ear, smiling into a kiss. They swayed together, slow dancing to a song on the radio, Hannah's eyes beaming with love. "And I love nights like this together. It's cold outside but so warm in here. Because you're here with us."

God, Caroline couldn't deal with Hannah when she said things like that. It was too much for her heart. "I wouldn't want to be anywhere else."

Edie cleared her throat, leaning against the doorframe. "You two should get married!"

Hannah laughed as she pulled away. "And you need to sit down and eat before you get me into trouble, Edie Caffrey!"

Hannah stretched her body, grinning when Caroline slid in behind her on the couch and spooned her. Edie lay sprawled on the other couch, scrolling through her phone. Considering Edie wanted to watch some new show, she was doing nothing to make it happen.

"Love, if you want to watch TV, we should start. It's six already."

Edie locked her phone and turned her attention to Hannah and Caroline. "Could I…stay up later tonight?"

Oh. Hannah hadn't expected that. "Of course."

"I'll be okay, won't I?"

Hannah frowned. "Okay?"

Edie sat up. "If I go to bed later. You and Caz won't be going to bed the same time as me, will you?"

"No. we won't go to bed until you're snoring."

"Okay." Edie lay back down and returned to her phone.

As Hannah watched her, Caroline pressed a kiss below her ear and whispered, "That's a good sign."

It was. It was a *very* good sign.

Hannah settled her hand over the one resting on her stomach, entwining her fingers with Caroline's. "She feels safer having you here."

Hannah felt Caroline relax against her, a light sigh audible. "Good."

"So, what's this show you want to watch?"

"Oh, it's about lesbians," Edie said, not looking up from her phone. "We had another talk in school a few days ago. It's important that people from the LGBTQ+ community feel represented in TV and film, so I found something you and Caz might enjoy."

Hannah sat up on her elbow, clearing her throat when Caroline's hand 'accidentally' slid to her arse. "That's really lovely, but what is it?"

"Don't worry, it's educational too. Historical."

That instantly caught Caroline's attention. "Oh, that's great! Maybe you could speak to Mrs Hale about discussing it in your history class."

"Yeah." Edie put her phone down again, interested now that Caroline had struck up more conversation. "It's basically about a 19th-century landowner from Yorkshire. She had these really cool secret diaries. You know with like code in them?"

Hannah and Caroline looked to one another, grinning as they both said, "Anne Lister."

"You know who she is?"

"Um, yeah." Hannah snorted. "We all know who she is."

Caroline placed a hand to Hannah's hip, interjecting. "Edie, this show you want to watch...is it a documentary?"

"No. Her diaries have been turned into a period drama. It's called *Gentleman Jack*."

Caroline nodded slowly. "Your mum and I have actually watched it already. While I don't like to censor TV, it's...not really appropriate for you. But I'm sure we can find a documentary about Anne Lister. I'm certain I can."

Edie nodded slowly. "Okay."

Phew. That had been close. Going into that TV show without any knowledge of it, while watching it with a fourteen-year-old, wasn't a good idea. Not when there was a scene involving Suranne Jones with her head between another woman's legs. "But thank you for thinking of us."

"Caz, would you look for the documentary?"

Caroline climbed out from behind Hannah, reaching for the controller. "Of course."

"Kay, well, I'm going to shower first. I don't want to go to bed *too* late."

"You shower, and when you come back down, the TV will be ready for us." Caroline sat up on her knees, her elbows braced against the coffee table as she scrolled through the channels.

Edie left the living room, whistling as she ran up the stairs, the usual thud as the bathroom door closed startling Hannah. She didn't know why; it happened a million times a day.

"Thanks for taking the lead with that one. I wasn't quite sure how to let Edie down."

Caroline glanced over her shoulder, that gorgeous smile making Hannah weak at the knees. "No problem. It's the teacher in me. I find it much easier to be straight with kids."

"Imagine if we hadn't seen the show and we all sat down to watch it together."

Caroline laughed. "Don't. The thought fills me with dread."

She reached forward, her backside straining in her jeans as she took a different controller. Hannah sunk to her knees behind Caroline, palming her gorgeous arse as she pressed a kiss to the back of her neck. "Edie's going to be in the shower for a while."

"H-Hannah." Caroline moaned when Hannah slipped a hand around the front of her, popping the button on her jeans. "We shouldn't."

"We...definitely should. I've missed touching you this week. We haven't had a moment to ourselves."

Hannah lifted a hand and squeezed Caroline through her shirt. She felt her girlfriend's nipples become taut under her fingertips, a breathy moan telling Hannah exactly what Caroline wanted.

"But I can stop if you think it's a big mistake." Hannah lowered her hand down Caroline's stomach, cupping her through her jeans. "Your call."

Caroline rested her head back on Hannah's shoulder, her eyes closed as she barely managed to say no. When Hannah pressed the seam of Caroline's jeans to her lips, Caroline bucked her hips. "Fuck."

"Thought so." Hannah smirked against Caroline's neck, pushing her hand past the waistband of her jeans and underwear. Caroline's breath caught, her hips rolling, one hand gripping the edge of the coffee table.

"H-Hannah, you need to hurry."

The further she pushed, the more wetness she found. "Babe, have you needed me?"

"O-oh, I always need you." Caroline thrust her hips forward, encouraging Hannah to give her more. She pressed her finger between Caroline's lips, that delicious moan as she lightly touched Caroline's clit music to her ears. "Yes. Oh, God."

"I love you." Hannah took Caroline's earlobe between her teeth, slowly rolling her fingers over Caroline's swollen clit. "I love feeling you. I love how wet you are for me. I love watching you come undone, only for me."

Caroline bucked her hips faster, lifting one hand and wrapping it around the back of Hannah's neck. "Hannah, I'm close..."

Hannah lowered her hand, slipping two fingers inside Caroline, her palm pressed to her clit. "Then why don't you come for me so I can taste you, babe?"

Those words had Caroline shuddering against Hannah, her chest heaving as she came. "Oh, God. How do you do that?"

"Make you tremble?"

"Y-yes."

Hannah smiled when Caroline turned her head and captured her lips. It was hot, passionate, but filled with so much love. "Trust me, there's nothing I enjoy more than watching the woman I love come. Your pleasure is my pleasure. Always remember that."

"Oh, *you* are a fucking dream come true."

"Mm. I love it when you curse, Ms Baker."

Caroline grinned, slumping back in Hannah's lap. She stretched her legs out under the coffee table, palming Hannah's thighs. "If you keep doing that, I'll never want to go home again."

Well, that wasn't something Hannah cared about. Caroline was welcome to be here all day, every day. That would never change. "Then I'll definitely do it more often."

EPILOGUE

O*ne year later...*

Hannah watched Caroline as she came into the living room, her hair a mess and looking very flustered. A flustered Caroline was often her favourite Caroline, and today that was absolutely the case. Because as of this moment, Hannah, Caroline, and Edie lived together. As one happy family.

"All done?"

Caroline crossed the room and wrapped Hannah up in her arms. They sat around her waist, Caroline's green eyes sparkling today. "All done."

"I'm surprised Edie even agreed to go to Mum's today. I've never seen her so excited."

"Oh, I don't know. She was very excited when Dylan called to say Yvonne had gone into labour."

Hannah knew what Caroline was doing. She was trying to lessen the severity of this. But if it worked for Caroline—to dumb down how far they'd come to save herself from feeling overwhelmed—then Hannah was okay with that. Whatever worked for Caroline worked for her, too. "I can't believe it's actually happened."

They'd discussed moving in with one another around six months ago, but Caroline never seemed to be giving it too much thought. She was practically here all the time anyway, so Hannah had chosen to let it lie. Except, Caroline had been. Unbeknownst to Hannah and Edie. And then one day, Caroline arrived home from work to tell Hannah she'd put her own house on the market, and she hoped for a quick sale. Now, here they were three months on, ready to build a life and a home together.

"I can. I always knew it would deep down. I just didn't want to put too much pressure on it all. You know me. I like to go with the flow."

"And what *is* your flow?"

Caroline smiled into a kiss. "Oh, *you*. One hundred percent. You're definitely my flow."

"I like being your flow," Hannah said, her arms settling over Caroline's shoulders. "I *love* everything we've already built and everything else to come."

"It's been a whirlwind year, hasn't it?"

Hannah had to agree with that. Not only had Caroline sold her house and decided she wanted to be a family with Hannah and Edie, but she'd also applied for the headteacher position at work and gotten the job. To say Hannah was proud of her was an understatement.

"Sit with me a minute." Hannah guided Caroline to the couch, their hands entwined in Hannah's lap. "I just...I wanted to say a few things to you."

Caroline frowned as she turned her body to face Hannah more fully. "Is everything okay? I know this is what you wanted, what we all wanted, but if it feels too sudden—"

"*Don't* even think about finishing that sentence, babe. Having you here with us is *all* I want." Hannah squeezed Caroline's hand, stroking a thumb across her knuckles. "You've had a hectic year, and you've turned your life upside down for us. A life you were only just getting used to yourself. I just wanted to thank you, Caz."

"Thank me?"

"For giving me a chance. It's hard to imagine a time when we weren't together now, but when we first met, I didn't believe it could happen. It was all I wanted, all I knew I needed in my life, but you just always felt out of reach. To know that you gave me that chance to make you happy, trusted me with your heart when it was so fragile, I hope you know I'd never do anything to hurt you. You're my family. Edie's family. This is now *our* home, and if you hadn't taken that chance on me, we wouldn't be sitting here today."

Caroline brushed a hand across her own cheek as a tear fell. "I never expected any of this. When I left Naomi, I swore I'd never get involved again. It just felt too much like hard work for something that would likely only hurt me again in the long run."

Hannah offered a faint smile, bringing Caroline's hand to her lips.

"But you made it so easy. So effortless. When it comes to loving you, it seems I don't have to try very hard at all."

"Good. That's how it's supposed to be."

Caroline grinned. "Yes. I'm beginning to realise that."

"You're happy, right?"

Caroline cupped Hannah's face, feathering a thumb across her cheek. "You *know* I'm happy. I didn't know it was possible to feel this happy, and I know I pushed back for a little while, but happiness doesn't begin to describe how you make me feel,

Hannah. This is like nothing I ever imagined in my wildest dreams."

"I know how that feels. I always settled because I wanted Edie to be in some kind of routine. I always wanted to be seen to be doing the best for her. Now, right this second, I *know* I'm doing the best for her. If I had to choose one woman in this entire world to bring into my daughter's life...it's you. Ten times over."

"Thank you for loving me," Caroline whispered as she leaned into a slow, lingering kiss. "Thank you for trusting me with Edie's future."

"There *is* no future for Edie and me without you, Caz. If you're ever having those doubts you used to have, remember that."

Caroline seemed to be far more at ease as the months passed them by. Hesitancy wasn't commonplace in their relationship anymore. Okay, Hannah *did* notice if Caroline was having a reflective moment, usually brought on by something someone said or did, but it was fleeting.

"I haven't had those doubts in a long time."

"I know. But I want you to know that if you ever do have any doubts or you need a little reassurance, you can talk to me. We can talk it out together."

Caroline touched her forehead to Hannah's. "I haven't had a single doubt about us since this got really serious. If I did, I wouldn't be here with my life just unpacked from boxes. I wouldn't be ready to take my two girls out to the pumpkin patch. I...wouldn't be around."

"I love you." Hannah's voice broke. Caroline often referred to Hannah and Edie as 'her girls'. Her heart could barely take it each time it slid from her sensational lips. "The most stupid amount."

"Oh, I'm still not sure that's as much as I love you."

Hannah sighed, kissing Caroline one last time before they had to get ready to leave. "Okay, we have to stop. If we don't, Edie will be standing at my mum's door waiting a *long* time for us."

"I have to say, Caz. This is all very romance-novelly." Sharon nudged Caroline's shoulder, winking. "But Hannah is lovely. And we already know how great Edie is."

Caroline fought back the sigh she felt working its way to her lips. They really were both perfect. "Life is incredibly good."

"I know. I see it."

This had been a long time coming, going out with friends as a family. They'd considered it just being the three of them tonight, but Sharon had wanted to pick up a pumpkin for her new granddaughter, and Gail had insisted they come along so her daughter, Jenna, could spend some time with Edie. Since Hannah and Caroline had got together, Edie and Jenna had grown quite close. But that warmed Caroline. Hannah, too. It meant Edie was coming out of her shell a lot more.

"I was thinking of holding a dinner party in around a month or so. Can I count on you and Brenda to be there?"

Sharon's eyes lit up. "Oh, absolutely. We'd love to come along."

"Great. Now I just have to get Hannah on board. That should be fun."

"What should be fun?" Hannah's voice shocked Caroline, but that gentle arm around the waist quickly soothed her. "Are you plotting, babe?"

"I was thinking about having a dinner party."

"Oh my God, yes. That's a great idea."

Caroline smiled when Hannah squeezed her hip. Enthusiasm was a normal part of her day now. "Wait, you do realise you have to help me in the kitchen and not just sit around chatting, don't you?"

"I would *love* to help you in the kitchen. This is going to be epic!"

"Well then, that's settled." Sharon smiled as she threw a thumb over her shoulder. "I should find Gail. I believe we're having a competition with you, Hannah, and Edie. Something about who can collect the most unusual pumpkins."

Caroline laughed. "Yes, it's true. But we're obviously going to win so I wouldn't get too excited. Edie is brilliant at this kind of thing."

Sharon folded her arms across her chest, a brow quirked. "Listen, little miss perfect family. We're going to wipe the floor with you."

Hannah laughed too that time, resting her head on Caroline's shoulder. Really, it didn't matter who won. Caroline already had the greatest prize. She had love and a family.

"That's fighting talk, Sharon." Hannah piped up as she took her phone from her pocket. "Oh, bugger. Adele isn't going to make it to the pumpkin patch. She said to carry on without her and that she'll see us at the restaurant at the planned time."

"Okay. Then we should let the fun begin because I know Edie is already thinking about her steak later."

Hannah stopped Caroline as she turned to walk away, resting her arms over Caroline's shoulders. "I love you."

"I love you, too."

"Mummmmm." Edie groaned behind Caroline and Hannah. When they both separated and faced her, Edie pulled a face. "Stop kissing each other in the middle of a field."

"Excuse me, Edie Caffrey. I'll kiss Caz wherever I like."

"Fine. But we need to start looking for the best pumpkins

because I think Gail has something up her sleeve. She looks a bit shifty."

"You leave Gail to me. She's been my best friend since we were twelve, and if I tell her we need to win, we *will* win." Caroline strolled hand in hand with Hannah while Edie walked ahead of them with their wheelbarrow. She'd always wanted to go pumpkin picking in the autumn, and this evening, she'd successfully done so.

Wasn't that sad? Forty-eight and never picked a pumpkin. Huh, not anymore.

Hannah let go of Caroline's hand and slid an arm around her waist instead. She rested her head on Caroline's shoulder, the burgundy bobble hat she wore this evening quite cute.

"I love this," Hannah said, sighing as she squeezed Caroline's hip. "Having someone to hold while we pick pumpkins. Edie and I have been doing this since she was walking. But now? It feels like we're going to have a really cosy autumn and winter."

Caroline's heart skipped a beat at that. They'd spent a lot of time together last year once the dark nights rolled in, but she agreed. This year *would* be different. Even if she'd woken up with Hannah and Edie last Christmas, something about being an official part of their household made it all feel different. "I can't wait for those nights."

"And we've decided we're not calling it girls' night anymore."

Caroline's brows drew together as Hannah lifted her head. "Oh. Why?"

"We're calling it *family night* instead now."

Caroline's lips spread into a face-aching grin. God, she loved that far more than anything else she'd loved today. "Family nights." She nodded slowly, lifting Hannah's chin and drawing her into a kiss. "I can't wait for family nights."

"With your girls?" Hannah quirked a brow.

"With my girls."

"Mum?" Caroline and Hannah cast their gaze towards Edie as she stopped close to what could only be described as the biggest pumpkin in the field. "Mum!"

"Yes, love?" Hannah turned away reluctantly.

"Not *you*!"

Caroline's heart pounded. Edie...had just called her Mum?

"Edie, what are you talking about?"

Edie rolled her eyes, standing heavier on one leg, her scarf pulled up around her chin. "My *other* mum."

Caroline turned her face away, her eyes closing as she took her bottom lip between her teeth. She tried to force the emotion down, but the tears brimmed in her eyes regardless.

"You heard her," Hannah said, laughing as she nudged Caroline. "Edie seems to want her other mum."

Caroline puffed out her cheeks, turning back to face Edie. "Yes?"

"Do you think this one is perfect for carving out Hocus Pocus?"

Caroline strode towards Edie, inspecting the pumpkin. She crouched down, checking it in its entirety, then nodded. "I think it's absolutely perfect."

Edie leaned down and whispered, "I can't lift it. Can you help me?"

"You get the wheelbarrow, and I'll get the pumpkin." Caroline winked, standing upright. She glanced over her shoulder and watched Hannah, their interaction clearly stirring something inside her. "Are you just going to stand there watching?"

"Yes. I am." Hannah's voice trembled, those blue eyes tear-filled. "I definitely am."

Caroline turned back to the pumpkin, lifting it and then

dropping it into the wheelbarrow. Edie wrapped her arms around Caroline, squeezing her. "Thanks."

Why did this feel so natural? As though Caroline had always been a part of Edie's life? Should it feel that way, or was she allowing too much emotion to take over?

She wanted to question it in her own head, but Edie looked up at her and smiled. "Love you."

Oh, wow. Caroline hadn't known those words could bring so much emotion to the surface, but they did. God, they made her feel a way she'd never felt before.

"I do, Caz. And if it's okay with you, I'd like to call you Mum from now on. Because really, you are. You look after me, and keep me safe, and make sure I'm okay. That's the sort of thing a mum does."

Caroline sniffled, holding Edie close. She'd always known she wanted to be a mum, that was never a secret, but it hadn't seemed possible over the years. It wasn't even about carrying a child for her; it was about being a part of something special and meaningful. Someone that she would die for should it ever be required of her. Edie was that someone.

"Of course it's okay. But you have to speak to your mum and dad about it first. Yvonne, too."

Edie pulled back, shrugging. "I...want *you* to be my other mum. That doesn't mean Yvonne isn't like a mum to me, but she doesn't cook dinner for me almost every night through the week or make sure I have a freshly ironed school uniform each morning. But you do those things for me."

Caroline felt Hannah press a hand to her shoulder, reminding Caroline that she was close by if she needed her. "Well, if it's okay with them, it's okay with me."

"Mum, I can call Caz my mum, can't I?"

Hannah tried to bite back a sob but failed. "Y-yes."

"Why are you crying? Don't you want me to? I don't love you any less, I just...love Caz too."

"Oh, love. I know you love me. I'm just...happy. That's all. Happy tears."

Edie nodded, taking Caroline's hand, then Hannah's. "I feel like the luckiest girl in the world."

Edie really had to stop being so open and honest. Caroline would need a share in Kleenex otherwise.

"I think we have the pumpkins we need now. Can we go home?"

Hannah laughed. "Yes, ma'am. If you're done."

Edie lifted the wheelbarrow, struggling through the dried mud to get it moving. But Caroline remembered what Edie had told her a few minutes ago and smiled. "Hey, Edie?"

Edie dropped the wheelbarrow and turned. "Y-yeah?"

"I love you, too."

SIGN UP TO WIN

Sign up to my mailing list to be the first to hear about new releases, and to be in with a chance of winning books!

www.melissaterezeauthor.com

DID YOU ENJOY IT?

Thank you for purchasing Discovery.

I hope you enjoyed it. Please consider leaving a review on your preferred site. As an independent author, reviews help to promote our work. One line or two really does make the difference.

Thank you, truly.

Love,
Melissa x

About the Author

Oh, hi! It's nice to see you!

I'm Melissa Tereze, author of The Arrangement, Mrs Middleton, and other bestsellers. Born, raised, and living in Liverpool, UK, I spend my time writing angsty romance about complex, real-life, women who love women. My heart lies within the age-gap trope, but you'll also find a wide range of different characters and stories to sink your teeth into.

SOCIAL MEDIA

You can contact me through my social media or my website. I'm mostly active on Twitter.

Twitter: @MelissaTereze
Facebook: http://www.facebook.com/Author.MelissaTereze
Instagram: @melissatereze_author
Find out more at: www.melissaterezeauthor.com
Contact: info@melissaterezeauthor.com

Also by Melissa Tereze

Another Love Series

The Arrangement (Book One)

The Call (Book Two)

Before You Go (Book Three)

Mrs Middleton Novels

Mrs Middleton

Teach Me (Co-write with Jourdyn Kelly)

Vanessa

The Ashforth Series

Playing For Her Heart (Book One)

Holding Her Heart (Book Two)

Other Novels

The Stepmother

Behind Her Eyes

At First Glance

Always Allie

Breaking Routine

In Her Arms

Forever Yours

The Heat of Summer

Forget Me Not

More Than A Feeling

Where We Belong: Love Returns

Naked

Titles under L.M Croft (Erotica)

Pieces of Me

Manufactured by Amazon.ca
Acheson, AB